NORMANBY

BY

P G DIXON

Brindle Books Ltd

All of the characters in this book are fictitious, and any resemblance to actual persons, living or dead, is purely coincidental.

CONTENTS

CHAPTER ONE: A MEETING WITH A SPY

Shafiq Hussein was a spy. It was not a glamourous profession, he reflected as he stirred his tea and glanced idly around at the other customers in the small café; indeed, it could hardly be considered a profession at all. He was paid very little money for passing information to the Security Services, but he felt that it was his duty to protect civilised society from the people that he knew intended to harm it.

His involvement in the dark world of espionage had begun only six months before, but already he felt jaded, dirty and betrayed by the whole experience. He also felt very afraid, not only of the people that he spied on, but also of the authorities to whom he passed his intelligence. Some of this fear came from his first meeting with his controller, a man named Grant, and the ease with which Grant had found him.

Shafiq had made the first contact with M.I.5 soon after moving down to London, and now he was beginning to wish that he had not done so. He thought about how much of a relief it would be if he could simply walk away, leave the whole mess to the authorities to clear up, and just go back to Birmingham. However much he hated the place, he thought, and however much danger he faced in his own community, it was nothing compared to the threat that he faced here in London.

The whole affair had begun when he had decided to leave home and take a job in the capital. It was supposed to be his chance to escape from his parents and their culture which he found increasingly oppressive due to the awakenings that had been stirred within him.

He had been overjoyed on the morning that the job interview letter had arrived. The idea of being able to work for an advertising agency in London had thrilled him immensely. Looking back, he knew that much of the excitement stemmed, not just from that job and the money that it would bring, but from the liberation that would result from leaving home.

He had not, however, been prepared for the reaction of his parents although he should have been: His father, a quiet, reserved man who had been born and raised in Pakistan, had remained stoically quiet when Shafiq had announced at the breakfast table that he was going for a job in London. "It is really what you want?" the old man had eventually asked, without expression.

"Well, it's better than spending the rest of my life stuck in a carpet mill," Shafiq had replied, and then had immediately regretted saying it. His father had worked in the same carpet mill since arriving from Pakistan thirty years before. He had said nothing, but the look of hurt dignity on his face as he silently consumed his breakfast made Shafiq put his hand up to his mouth in remorse. The words had been said and he could not take them back.

His mother's reaction had been angrier and more direct. "How dare you?" she had exclaimed, slamming the oven door shut and turning to look at him over her husband's shoulder, her eyes burning with rage.

She was English and white. She had converted to Islam when she had first started courting her husband and like many converts, she had embraced the religion and its philosophy with greater zeal than many who had been born into it. "It's bad enough that you want to go into that sort of business," she said, "but to speak to your father that way, after all these years of working to keep us all. That's bloody disgusting!"

"I didn't mean it like that, you know I didn't!" Shafiq said defensively. He looked pleadingly at his father. "I'm not saying there's anything wrong with working at the mill," he continued reasonably, "but this is what I've studied for. It's my chance to make enough to pay you back for all those years, to be able to help you when you're old."

His mother had already taken a deep breath in order to continue her tirade. "Well, if you think you're going down there and consorting with whores and…"

She flinched as her husband snapped and stopped her with an uncharacteristic bark. "Bloody shut it woman!" he said harshly. "The boy has a chance to make good. Bloody carpet mill's a shit-hole anyway."

Shafiq had struggled to hide his smile as he caught a mischievous glint in his father's eye.

Not one to be silenced easily, his mother spoke again after a suitably cautious pause. "Well, if you're going down there, you can spend some time with your cousin Ali. At least he'll keep you out of trouble," she said.

Shafiq remembered the mixed emotions that he had felt at his mother's words. On the one hand he was annoyed at her attempts to keep him on a short leash by utilising his cousin, of whom she approved; On the other hand, he felt the slightest tinge of excitement at the thought of seeing Ali again. He remembered the glorious summer holiday that they had spent together as children.

Shafiq had gone to Pakistan one summer with Ali and his parents. It had been an amazing experience, partly because he was visiting the land of his forefathers, with landscapes and cultures that were so alien to anything that he had ever known. The other thing that had made it special had been the presence of Ali. He had not realised it at the time, but Shafiq suspected now that the strong affection and admiration that he had felt for the boy might have been his first crush. It was a suspicion that he would never dare to share with anyone, least of all his family, and the thought of having to keep his feelings a secret made him feel intensely sad whenever he let it.

He broke off from his reverie when he saw the familiar figure of his contact, Mr. Grant, on the pavement outside the café: Tom Grant was tall, athletic looking and traditionally handsome, though not really Shafiq's type for some reason that he could not quite fathom. He had short, neat brown hair and a tanned face with a heroic square jaw like an old-time matinee idol. He wore a tailor made dark grey suit with a crisp white shirt and a good quality knitted silk black tie. In the breast pocket of his jacket was a neatly folded handkerchief.

Shafiq gave a little snort of contempt. If the man was an M.I.5 operative, coming to meet an agent to covertly exchange information, then why on Earth was he dressed like somebody auditioning for the role of James Bond?

He took a sip of his tea and made an effort to ignore Grant as he entered the café and stepped up to the counter. Perhaps, thought Shafiq, it was the best disguise of all. After all, no-one in their right mind would actually expect intelligence operatives to dress that way in real life.

Grant ordered his cappuccino and took a seat at the table next to the one that Shafiq occupied. Both men studiously ignored each other for several minutes until the last two remaining customers, a pair of elderly ladies with bags of grocery shopping, got up and left the establishment.

"Are you waiting for a password or something Mr. Grant?" asked Shafiq impatiently.

Grant shot a quick, suspicious glance towards the bored looking girl behind the counter who sat perched on a stool, idly leafing through a copy of Hello magazine. It was obvious that she had no interest in the two men, he acknowledged to himself, but there were still protocols that should be followed. He gave the young Asian a cold, professional stare.

"I don't have time for games Mr. Grant," said Shafiq, "so let's cut the Secret Squirrel crap."

"Alright," said Grant, leaning a little closer and keeping his voice low. "You chose the meeting place; I'm just being careful. I could have just come to your house or your workplace."

"You're not coming anywhere near my house or my work," Shafiq replied with a warning glare. "The less you people know about me, the better."

It was Grant's turn to snort. "We already know everything about you Shafiq," he said with a mocking grin. "Just like when I was able to find you so easily after you sent us that very first online form."
It was true, Shafiq thought bleakly. He had first contacted the authorities with his suspicions about his cousin, Ali Hussein by using the contact form on the M.I.5 website. He had sent the form from a computer in the local library, and he had not even put his own email address on it. Less than a week later, however, he had been approached by Grant as he was shopping in Berwick Street market.

"People are easier to track than they've ever been Shafiq," Grant had told him at that first meeting. "When you booked onto that library computer with your library card number and sent that form from the library's I.P. address, you may as well have walked into the front door of M.I.5 and slapped your passport and driving licence on the reception desk."

"So, what do you need me for?" Shafiq had asked. "I've told you about Ali and the people he hangs out with. Why don't you just arrest him and keep me out of it?"

On that afternoon, months ago, Grant had patiently explained the limits of M.I.5's power to act without solid information. He had expertly played to the young man's sense of morality and had made him believe that there really was no alternative but to continue visiting Ali; to get closer and even become involved in his plans so that he could give the authorities enough information on which to act. In short, Grant had swiftly developed Shafiq Hussein as an agent.

How naïve he had been, Shafiq told himself as he deliberately took a noisy slurp of his tea and then banged the cup down into the saucer. He hoped that if he could attract the attention of the girl behind the counter, he might make Grant feel uncomfortable enough to cut their meeting short. He had plans for another meeting later that morning; one which he could not afford to let Grant find out about.

"Shafiq," said Grant patiently, his voice oozing with tones of empathy that Hussein dismissed automatically. "I know it's hard and I know it's scary, but we can't build a case without evidence. We can't act until we have something concrete that we can pull your cousin and the others in on. We *need* you Shafiq. We need your help."

Shafiq Hussein gave a long, resigned sigh. "Alright," he said, looking down. "There's another collection arranged for this weekend. I don't know where they collect from or how they get it into the country…"

"Can you find out?" asked Grant simply.

"Well, I'm not just going to ask them, am I?" Shafiq said irritably. "Hey Cousin Ali; I was just wondering where you get hold of massive supplies of pure Heroin? By the way, I'm a bit curious as to how you intend to strike at the heart of this kuffar nation and cause it the pain that it so richly deserves." As he said the words, he put on a bitterly comedic Pakistani accent, but the stress in his voice caused some of his natural Brummie twang to come through also.

Grant gave a small, warm smile. "Okay Shafiq," he said. "I don't want you to take any stupid risks. Just get what you can."

Hussein finally gave a smile of his own, tinged with resignation and sadness. "I'll do my best Mr. Grant," he said. "I don't really have any option, do I?"

Grant watched in silence as Shafiq got up from the table and walked out of the café without looking back. He had to admit that he admired the young man's courage and fortitude. After all, it couldn't be easy for him, having to keep going back and spending time with a group of fanatics like Ali Hussein and his gang; having to get closer and closer to them whilst knowing that they would happily kill him if they even suspected the truth.

He looked at his watch and felt his shoulders sag. Taking a sip of his cappuccino, he reflected grimly on the current strains on his own fortitude. He was disappointed with his current position and the secondment that had been forced upon him. He had not asked for the move, but had been told that it was simply a matter of operational requirements.

Becoming an operative in G-section of M.I.5 had been the pinnacle of Grants career to date. Indeed, it had been the culmination of a life-long dream for him. True, he acknowledged, the work was not filled with the kind of thrilling action that he had dreamt of throughout his childhood and teens, but it had been his goal for as long as he could remember. He had felt a little thrill every time that he walked up the steps in the archway to Thames House, the headquarters of M.I.5.

When Julie, his line-manager, had told him that he was being transferred on secondment to a department technically outside of M.I.5, he had been unable to hide his dismay. "I didn't apply for any secondment," he had said lamely.

"No," she had replied, "but the people down the street in the annexe have asked for you."

He had wondered how this other department had even heard of him. Perhaps he had made an impression with the quality of his work, he had pondered. As if sensing his thoughts, Julie had shot his dreams down in flames. "I think it's actually just your case-load that they're interested in," she had said. "You'll be taking some of your current assignments with you."

Grant suspected that Julie had simply wanted to get rid of him and had arranged the transfer herself. They had never really gelled, and she had often given indications that she thought him a foolish dreamer, not really cut out for the reality of Intelligence work.

It had happened that simply. He had gone from living the dream in the modern heart of the country's Security Service, to a battered desk in a drab office, in a somewhat dilapidated Victorian building that looked as though it belonged to some provincial town council. Gone were the high tech, modern equipment, the comfortable, stylish furniture, the carpets, the staff gym, and all of the other benefits that had made his job a joy to do, and in their place was a dull existence that made him feel, for most of the time, like a junior office clerk in a failing business.

He drank down the last of his cappuccino and stepped outside, mentally preparing himself for the dull atmosphere of the annexe. Even this he would be able to stand, he thought, if he at least had the banter and the camaraderie of his old G-section colleagues. That was the worst of it. The thing that really made Grant's days at the department drag so much was the company that he was forced to keep there.

CHAPTER TWO: NORMANBY

Normanby was busy. He was very carefully numbering the pages of a good quality, bound notebook. Around each of the small and neatly written numbers, he drew a near perfect circle. The tip of his tongue poked out slightly between his pale lips in concentration as he squinted through the spectacles perched near the end of his thin nose.

He liked to make sure that his notebook was numbered at least fifty pages ahead of his current page, and he liked it to be neat. Normanby liked everything to be neat. His short, mousey-brown hair, for instance, was neat and always combed back from his high forehead. The red and blue striped tie, which he had owned since school, (which was not Eton, as he was happy to confirm when asked), was always tied in a perfect Windsor knot, and *always* perfectly straight. His light blue cotton shirt was *always* immaculately ironed. The black suit jacket and black trousers, although far from fashionable, were *always* clean, pressed and smart, and the comfortable black boots that he wore to work were *always* polished to an immaculate sheen. Even the row of pens, in the breast pocket of his jacket, was *always* in perfect alignment.

Tom Grant's face creased in a look of disgust as he watched Normanby from across the office. The man was simply infuriating! Every single weekday in this office for the past month had been identical because of Normanby, and Grant was losing patience. In every other place that Grant had worked, he had managed to find at least some kind of rapport with his colleagues. The only conversation Normanby ever offered was, "Good morning, Mr. Grant," on arrival and, "Good evening, Mr. Grant," on leaving.

Grant had tried, in the first week, to start conversations with the man, but each one had quickly withered and died due to Normanby's apparent lack of interest in anything. Did Normanby see the match last night? "I don't really follow sport." Did Normanby see that brilliant show on TV? "I don't really watch television." Who did Normanby think would win the election? "I don't really follow politics."

At first Grant had thought that it was just him that Normanby didn't like, but as the weeks passed, he saw that the man was the same with everyone. He was simply not interested in socialising, and seemingly not interested in anything except the work on the desk in front of him. What Normanby's specific job was in the Department, Grant did not know and, as their work could broadly be defined as 'intelligence work', he knew better than to ask. All he knew was that, each morning, stacks of paperwork were put into the 'IN' tray on Normanby's immaculately neat desk and that he would quietly and diligently work his way through it, (sometimes without even referring to the somewhat dated PC on his desk). By the end of each working day, (sometimes even before lunchtime), the work was apparently completed and transferred to Normanby's 'OUT' tray. During the course of the day, Normanby would occasionally pause and make a note in the notebook which he kept in the inside pocket of his jacket. When his work was completed, he would sit and write in the spiral-bound reporter's pad which he kept in the top drawer of his desk.

The only other time that Normanby's attention was ever taken away from his work was during his (exactly) thirty-minute lunch break, when he would place his briefcase on his desk and open it to reveal that it contained a box of sandwiches, a packet of biscuits and a small thermos flask. He would consume his lunch slowly and thoughtfully whilst staring out of the window at the traffic, the people and the pigeons. As soon as the thirty minutes had passed, he would pack everything neatly away and go back to work in silence.

Grant looked down at the untidy stack of reports on his own desk and sighed. There was too much boring routine. When he had first joined the Security Service, he had hoped for at least some excitement. "It won't be like James Bond," they had told him on his first day, and he knew that. Still, he dreaded to think of himself being shackled to a desk for the rest of his career until he became a faceless worker ant...like Normanby.

He took a deep breath, stood up and fastened the middle button of his made to measure, grey suit jacket. He caught a glimpse of his own reflection in the glass that covered the portrait of the Queen on the office wall, and he scowled at it. He knew that he should be working somewhere more exciting than this dreary place, but for some reason, he had been sent here: 'The Department Of Lost Souls,' he thought to himself with a bitter snort. He was bored. "Whatever happened to that whole 'it's M.I.5, not nine to five' thing they used to say on telly?" he said, not really expecting a reply.

The little man turned in his seat and looked at Grant. "It's my understanding Mr. Grant," he said pompously, "that there is a flexi-time scheme in operation at the Security Service, very similar to the one that we operate in this department. I do believe that you're perfectly entitled to start work at any time between seven-thirty and ten-thirty, and can leave work anywhere between thirteen-thirty and nineteen hundred." He extended a finger and used it to push the spectacles up to the bridge of his nose. "Of course," he continued, "you're not allowed to be more than eight hours in credit or debit, and you can only pick your hours when there are no pressing operational constraints."

Grant stared down at him blankly. He spent a moment trying to work out whether Normanby was being serious or if he actually had a sense of humour. Did the man realise how ridiculous he sounded? Grant wondered. Watching the little man as he studiously returned to his work with a look of concentration, Grant decided that the answer must surely be a firm 'no'. He shook his head sadly. "I'm going to get some lunch," he said. "Do you want anything from the canteen, Normanby?"

Normanby looked at his wristwatch, and then glanced at Grant with an air of vague disapproval. "No, thank you," he said, returning his attention to his notebook.

'To Hell with Normanby and his accusing stares,' thought Grant as he stepped out of Room 131 and onto the wide corridor with its tatty Victorian mosaic floor and the distant echoes of footsteps that reminded him of his old school. He made his way glumly to the works canteen, which was a large, drab room with three large, battered tables surrounded by tatty, bent-wood chairs. There was a counter at the far end of the room, and behind it, a hatch that opened into a kitchen area. The place was hardly likely to ever get any Michelin stars, he reflected.

There was no-one else in the room, so Grant approached the counter and shouted through the hatch. "Hello! Is there anyone at home?"

"Just a minute," called a gruff female voice, impatiently from inside the kitchen. A dowdy looking middle aged woman in a stained smock appeared at the hatch. "If you want breakfast, we ain't got no eggs left," she announced with a challenging scowl.

*

Normanby got up from his desk and crept towards the door. He opened it slightly and then peered through the narrow crack. Satisfied, he closed the door carefully and prowled across to Grant's desk. Tutting at the untidy pile of paperwork, he picked up several folders in turn, discarding each disinterestedly until he found the one that he was looking for.

He shot a furtive look towards the door, tilting his head and listening for any sound of movement outside the room. When he was satisfied by the silence, he opened the file on Grant's desk, and leaning down so that he was very close to the pages, he began to read...

CHAPTER THREE: THE COLONEL

The Colonel took a last sip of his coffee and placed the cup back in the saucer. He folded the copy of the Daily Telegraph that he had been reading and placed it on the polished side table beside the tray, looking around the empty reading room of the Empire Club.

Although he enjoyed the excellent cooked breakfasts that the club served, he always felt a little sad and lonely when he got up to leave. Even after all these years he still missed the joy of starting the day in the company of Kate, his late wife.

He stood up and stretched, unselfconsciously. He was a big man, both tall and broad. In his younger days he had had an impressive physique but now, well into his sixties, he had to accept that he was getting a little thick around the middle. His hair was grey and thinning on top but was combed back neatly over his scalp, and his moustache was clipped to perfection with the ends drawn into small points. It was as close to Kitchener's style as one could get in this day and age without appearing ridiculous. His military bearing had never deserted him, and it would be obvious to anyone that met him, even before any introductions were made, that he was an old soldier.

"Watkins," he bellowed in the general direction of a nearby open door, "I'm ready to get off now."

Within seconds, Watkins stepped through the doorway. He also had a soldier's posture, smart and immaculately turned out in a butler's attire. He had close cropped steel grey hair and a severe, hawk like face. He held The Colonel's hat and umbrella in one hand and had his heavy wool overcoat draped over the other arm. "Very good sir," he said amiably. "Your timing's perfect, as always. Hopkirk has just pulled up out front."

He helped The Colonel on with his overcoat and then handed him the hat and umbrella with a formality that is nowadays seldom seen outside of a military parade ground.

"Thank you, Watkins," said The Colonel. "The breakfast was excellent as usual."

"Thank you, sir," acknowledged Watkins watching The Colonel march out of the room and grimacing slightly as he tapped the brass ferrule of the umbrella heavily onto the polished wooden floor with each step.

The Colonel stepped out of the Empire Club onto the damp pavement and looked around warily through force of habit. Hopkirk, his driver, was standing on the kerb beside his car, a shining black Jaguar XF. He opened the door formally and waited for The Colonel to get in and make himself comfortable before walking around to the driver's door and climbing in behind the wheel.

Only when he had started the engine and looked carefully around in every direction did he reach into the front of his jacket and remove a brown envelope which he handed back over his shoulder. "It's marked as 'blue priority' sir," he said as The Colonel reached forward and took the envelope.

"We'd better get to the office then Hopkirk," the old man said, tearing open the envelope and unfolding the sheet of thin paper from within it.

As the car swung out into the busy London traffic, The Colonel scowled at the sheet of paper before him. He glanced up and briefly caught Hopkirk's eye in the rear-view mirror.

"Anything serious sir?" asked the driver, noting the other man's bitter expression.

"Oh yes," said The Colonel. "It seems that we were right to bring this fellow Grant from up the road. There's been a development involving that contact of his; the one that both M.I.5 and the National Crime Agency thought was a fantasist and a waste of time. It would appear that he was neither."

"*Was*, sir?" asked Hopkirk.

"Yes; *was*," confirmed The Colonel. "I'd better go and have a word with our Mr. Grant."

*

Grant sighed as he turned the mouse-wheel and scrolled through the emails on his computer screen. "Why the Hell do I bother?" he muttered to himself.

Normanby turned in his chair, visibly irritated by the constant distractions from his colleague. "Are you having some kind of difficulty Mr. Grant?" he asked.

Grant scowled at him momentarily and then returned his attention to the screen. "Yes Normanby," he said. "I'm having difficulty getting anyone in this department to pay any attention to my reports. I've been moved from a modern, effective organisation to some kind of purgatory for lost souls, all of whom seem to have had personality bypass operations, and nobody is acting on the intelligence reports that I'm submitting. The place must be run by morons…" He stopped with a shocked expression on his face as he saw the imposing figure in the doorway glaring at him stonily.

The Colonel slowly looked Grant up and down with more than a hint of disapproval. He tapped his umbrella on the parquet floor several times, watching the ferrule make tiny dents into the woodwork.

"Did you have an agent by the name of Shafiq Hussein?" he asked, eyeing Grant with a withering stare.

"I do, sir," said Grant, "but I'm guessing that your use of the past tense means something's happened." He was already beginning to feel a flicker of dread. Hussein was one of Grant's most promising agents. He had taken months to develop, and had provided some useful information, though he had, admittedly been less forthcoming in recent weeks.

The Colonel's face hardened even further. "He's dead," he said flatly.

"How?" asked Grant, shocked, "and where?"

"Murder," The Colonel replied, "outside his house on Trilby Street. The Police are at the scene now. Go there. Investigate."

Grant gathered his thoughts. He opened his mouth to ask more questions but seeing the look on The Colonel's face, thought better of it. He took his overcoat from the coat stand in the corner of the room and started putting it on as he walked to the door.

A barked command from The Colonel halted Grant at the threshold of the room. "Grant," he ordered. "Take Normanby with you."

Grant turned and was about to protest. Once more, The Colonel's dead eyed stare silenced him.

Normanby was on his feet, silently fastening the buttons on a neat and very unfashionable black gabardine mac.

Grant sighed, looked from Normanby to The Colonel, and decided that any attempt to protest was futile.

"...An extra pair of eyes, Grant..." The Colonel said, in what Grant assumed was supposed to be a reassuring tone.

Grant watched Normanby finish buttoning his rain mac, barely able to hide his contempt for the dull little man. "Come on, Normanby," he said resignedly as he turned and left the room.

CHAPTER FOUR: HUSSEIN

Ali Hussein held the smoke in his lungs for as long as he could. When his diaphragm began to protest by throwing itself into a spasm, he coughed and released a thick plume of smoke that hung in the air. The grey cloud caught the light that streamed in through the living room window.

The heavily dilated pupils in Ali's bloodshot eyes slowly focussed on the rainbow-like patch of colour that cut into the cloud. He looked at the long, thin, roughly rolled joint between his fingers and then he slowly leaned forward to tap ash from the glowing ember at its tip into the ashtray on the floor between his feet.

He picked up the ashtray and leaned back into the comfort of the settee. A sense of dizzy euphoria engulfed him, and he smiled, turning his attention to the television across the room. "Shut up, you stupid white slag," he said, bursting into an uncontrollable fit of giggling as he watched a skinny young woman with bad teeth, on the screen, screaming abuse at an equally emaciated white male in an oversized check shirt and a baseball cap, worn the wrong way around. The male was trying to argue his point, but each time he opened his mouth to speak, the screeching harridan shut him down with another tirade of banal, unimaginative insults.

Ali shook his head in disgust. "Oh, the cradle of civilisation," he said scornfully, "the home of democracy." He put the joint to his mouth, his eyes still transfixed on the screen, and sucked in another lungful of smoke through the cardboard tube. He hated chavs, he reflected, watching the couple's ridiculous antics on the screen. He always had done, for as long as he could remember.

Even from his earliest memories of primary school it was always the white, English underclass scum that he detested the most. They were always the biggest trouble-causers. Most of the Asian kids in his class, even the non-Muslim ones, would just get on with life; the black kids would do the same. Even the Romanian and Polish kids were never a problem as long as everyone kept to their own part of the playground: The English kids though, they just didn't get it. They used to try and act like they owned the whole place. It wouldn't have been so bad, but all the English kids at his school were the really stupid ones. It was as if the white bastards had deliberately sent the stupidest, mouthiest, smelliest dregs of their own twisted society to the inner-city schools just to bring everybody else down.

Without taking his eyes off the screen, he reached out beside him and picked up the TV remote control. He pointed it at the face on the screen, as if sighting down the barrel of a handgun. "Bang," he said as he pressed the button to switch off the TV. He remained still for a moment, his arm still extended as he remembered, fondly, the first time that he had ever held a pistol:

It had been a beautiful summer in the year of Ali's awakening. He, his parents and his cousin Shafiq had travelled to see Uncle Majid and his family in Pakistan. Uncle Majid owned a large bungalow near Chaman in Balochistan Province. Upon their arrival, Uncle Majid had embraced his brother, Ali's father, and had looked down proudly at the boy. "You have a fine son," he had said, looking closely at young Ali before turning his attention to cousin Shafiq. "And this is my other nephew?" he had asked. "Where is his father?"

Ali's own father had explained that Shafiq's parents had been unable to afford the trip. Uncle Majid looked somewhat disappointedly down at Shafiq, almost as if it had been his fault. "My brother has no head for business," he had concluded sadly. "He will be working to make non-believers rich for the rest of his life."

The next day, Uncle Majid took Ali, his father and cousin Shafiq out for a drive in the country. They had gone to visit some old friends of Uncle's in a rambling old stone-built house in the hills at the edge of the Afghan border. That visit had changed Ali's life forever. The house was populated by a family of eight; two adults, four boys in their teens and two girls, roughly the same age as Ali and Shafiq.

The two girls had been brought into the sparsely furnished main room of the house and had been told to stand in the middle of the room. Ali and Shafiq had been made to stand facing them and had remained fearfully still whilst the adults spoke, bickered and haggled in a dialect that neither of the boys could follow. Ali had looked warily out of the corner of his eye at his father and had seen a worried glance thrown back in his direction in the midst of the conversation.

The girl facing him gave a nervous smile and looked at her own father briefly before hastily averting her eyes and staring fixedly down at the floor in front of her. Ali glanced back at his own father who seemed to be protesting until Uncle Majid put a hand on his shoulder and spoke to him in a conspirational whisper. He seemed to be convincing father of something, speaking slowly and in a patient, reasonable tone. Eventually, Ali's father sighed and nodded. There were smiles and nods amongst the adults, and some kind of deal had been made.

Uncle Majid walked into the centre of the room and stood in the space between the four children. He smiled down at Ali fondly. "Come with me child," he said, putting a gentle hand on Ali's shoulder and leading him to the door.

Outside the house, the shadows had been drawn long by the slowly setting sun and a cool wind blew in from the hills to the Northwest. Ali felt a slight shiver, but he refused to let it show as he walked with Uncle Majid away from the house. The old man looked down at him. "Do you like it here?" he asked suddenly.

Ali looked about him. "Yes Uncle," he answered, honestly.

His uncle nodded. "One day," he said, "you may have to defend this land from invaders."

"Invaders, Uncle?" Ali asked.

Uncle Majid nodded. "Yes," he confirmed. "They have already come to take the lands of our friends and neighbours," he said, gesturing idly towards the hills to the North. "They have done it before. They have been driven out before and we will drive them out again. We must fight to stop them coming back; to stop them coming this far!"

The old man reached inside his waistcoat and brought out a pistol. Ali's eyes widened; not from fear, but from excitement. "Do you like it?" asked Uncle Majid, weighing the weapon in his hand. The boy nodded enthusiastically, awestruck at the sight of a real gun.

"This," announced Uncle Majid proudly, "…is called a Beretta 92F. It is one of the weapons that the invaders use. They think that they are strong, but we are stronger. We will take many of their weapons from them and then use them to drive them from our lands!"

Ali was only half listening. His wide eyes were transfixed on the gun. Uncle Majid chuckled at the boy's enthusiasm. "Here," he said. "Do you want to try it?"

Ali gasped in excitement. "Yes Uncle," he said with a huge smile.

His uncle moved around behind him. He put the pistol grip into the boy's small hand and cupped his own around it, holding the weapon steady. "Now," he said gently. "Take your other hand and place it under the grip; yes, like that." He lowered himself to one knee so that he could sight over the boy's shoulder, selecting as a target an old, rusty bucket that stood atop a nearby wall. "Are you ready?" he asked quietly.

"Yes Uncle," nodded the boy.

"Then squeeze the trigger," he replied.

There was a sudden bang that made Ali start. He looked around the flat as if confused on being jolted from his reverie. He heard the bang again and then the rattling of keys in a lock.

"You need to ring the Council about this bloody door, Bro'," shouted Tariq Malik from out in the hallway.

Ali's hand slid slowly from beneath the seat cushion of the settee. It had automatically snaked there to grip the handle of the carving knife that nestled between the pages of a local area telephone directory when he had heard the door opening. He relaxed when he saw Tariq framed in the doorway of the room. "Did you get everything on the shopping list?" he asked.

"I think so," Tariq replied.

"You got the lightbulbs though, yeah?" Ali peered closely at Tariq as he asked the question.

Tariq Malik gave a slight twitch of the head. "Yeah, I got lightbulbs. Ten of them yeah?" he said.

Ali's bloodshot eyes fixed firmly on the trembling Tariq. He could see the tiny beads of perspiration on his forehead, below his knitted kufi prayer-cap, and on his top lip; the only part of his face that he shaved.

"Show me the lightbulbs," said Ali slowly.

Tariq bent and put the two carrier bags on the floor, his trembling hands fishing out a small cardboard box from one of them. "I made sure they were the fitting you asked for," he said quickly, "B.C.20, wasn't it?" He could already sense that he was in trouble for something by the way that he was being stared at, and his head gave a sudden, involuntary twitch to the left.

Ali gave a disgusted sigh and threw his head back to stare at the ceiling. "I can't fucking trust you to do anything, can I?" he said. "I told you I wanted *Osram* bulbs; the old-fashioned type!"

Malik looked down at the ground, fighting the urge to twitch his head. He lost the internal battle and his head automatically shot to the left a couple of times before he spoke. "They're the right fitting," he said defensively. "Sainsbury's didn't have them type; they're phasing them out. Anyway, these are energy saving bulbs. They're better for the environment."

Ali sighed again and shook his head. "I'm surrounded by fucking idiots," he muttered quietly. "Forget it, I'll do my own shopping in future," he said.

"Well, I did my best Bro'," whined Tariq picking up the bags and almost managing a defiant stare before his head twitched again.

Ali's face hardened as he returned the look. "Well, if that was your best it wasn't good enough, was it? Can you actually follow instructions?" he said harshly. "I'm beginning to wonder! Are you sure it wasn't you that blabbed about the shipments, because somebody did? *Somebody's* not been keeping their mouth shut: That's why we're getting taxed by gangsters on every shipment that comes in!"

Tariq's mouth fell open and his eyes became moist. "You know I'd never tell anybody, Ali!" he said, trembling. "I'm not a traitor! I'd die for our cause!" A tear rolled slowly from his eye and was flung off into the air as his head twitched.

Ali's face softened and he let out a long breath. "I know you would Bro'," he said. "I know you'd never betray us. I'm sorry."

Tariq gave a sniff and looked down at his sandals. "I'll put the shopping away," he muttered quietly, hefting the carrier bags and carrying them slowly into the kitchen.

Ali angrily stubbed out the joint in the ashtray, set it back on the floor and then sat back heavily on the settee. He closed his eyes and thought again about his childhood visits to Uncle Majid in Pakistan, and their frequent trips to the big house on the Afghan border. He thought about the girl who had stood and faced him in the middle of the room when they were children, the day that they had been betrothed to one another.

Her name was Shazia, and when it had first been explained to him that she would one day be his wife, he had experienced a feeling of dread at having no say in the matter. As time passed, however, his feelings changed. As each year passed and brought another visit to Pakistan, he saw that, little by little, the girl was gradually growing into a beautiful young woman. He also found that he was becoming ever closer to the girl's father and to Uncle Majid, who would sit up talking to young Ali well into the early hours of the morning.

The old man would tell him tales of the age-old struggle to free the region from the oppression of the invading infidels. Fire burned in his eyes when he spoke of the way the foreigners had tried to stop the people from following God's law; of the brutalities of the British, in the distant past, and then the Soviet invaders who had tried to conquer and tame Afghanistan, and of the men who had escaped torture and deprivation by seeking sanctuary with friends and brothers across the border in Pakistan.

The Godless Communists of the Soviet Union had been pushed back and beaten, Uncle Majid said, and for a time there was rejoicing amongst true believers. It did not last. It was only a matter of time before the West; The Americans, the British and the Europeans decided to take their turn. Even before they had invaded, he said, they were influencing the leaders in Pakistan, trying to crush the spirit of the people.

As a young man, Uncle Majid announced proudly, he had been a member of the *Tehreek-e-nafaz-e-shariat-e-Mohammadi*, The Movement for the Enforcement of Islamic Law. He had fought and campaigned, tried to make people see, that they should obey the simple truth of God's commands as relayed by The Prophet. He shook his head sadly whenever he mentioned instances of those who openly flouted these laws. He spat on the ground to his left when he mentioned the name of Musharraf.

Parvez Musharraf had been the President of Pakistan when, on January 12th, 2002, he had made membership of The Movement a crime. As Majid saw it, Musharraf had betrayed the people in an attempt to sell them into slavery under the infidels. Soon afterwards, the young Majid had joined with his brothers in the *Tehreek-e-Taliban Pakistan*, The Taliban Movement of Pakistan.

The Pakistani Taliban grew quickly, uniting many groups and factions who had previously been hostile to one another. Majid's wide social circle and his various business contacts had enabled him to broker many deals and treaties, and he had quickly escalated through the ranks of this new movement. This had, in turn, given him the opportunity to form stronger bonds with their Taliban brothers across the border in Afghanistan. Together, he affirmed, they would push back against the infidels. Soon, he had said through gritted teeth, the Taliban would not just be defending their own lands, they would strike back at the heart of the Western invaders just as Bin Laden had done before. One day, the old man had promised, Ali would be given the chance to make his mark and, *Insha'Allah*, he would become the head of an army of British Taliban fighters.

CHAPTER FIVE: TRILBY STREET

Trilby Street was a narrow, drab little dead-end street, populated by a long row of small, two up, two down, terraced houses on each side. The houses had been erected in the Victorian age to house the working-class families who worked in nearby factories. As Grant looked down the street, he was reminded of old documentary footage he had seen of some of the worse housing in West Belfast at the height of the Troubles, back in the '70's. He looked up at the grey sky and wondered whether yesterday's downpour would return this afternoon.

With Normanby in tow, Grant walked towards the line of police tape where a lone, female Police Community Support Officer guarded the various Police Officers, officials and white-paper-suit clad Scenes of Crime Operatives beyond. He glanced back at Normanby who was looking all around him, curiously. The little man probably felt uncomfortable in areas like this.

"Come on Normanby," said Grant. "There's nothing to be afraid of. I won't let the rough boys steal your glasses." Normanby looked at him blankly, used an index finger to delicately push his spectacles up to the bridge of his nose and then followed obediently.

Grant approached the pretty female PCSO at the police tape with hands in his overcoat pockets and a nonchalant smile on his face. She put up a hand in a gesture for him to stop. "I'm sorry, sir," she said. "There's no access this way. If you want to get to Marsh Road, you can go by…"

"That's okay," Grant interrupted. He brought his hand from his pocket and flashed some impressive looking credentials which the PCSO clearly did not recognise. She nervously thumbed her radio and, turning her head away, spoke into the microphone.

Grant took hold of the crime scene tape between thumb and forefinger, ready to lift it and step under. The PCSO repositioned herself in front of him, ready to bar access should he try to enter the crime scene without the proper authority. Her face held a look of defiance.

Normanby studied her with interest. She was in her mid-twenties, he guessed, and of medium build. Her blonde hair was tied back tightly under her hat, and the faint smattering of freckles across her nose made her look very young and innocent. Grant was smiling at her with some amusement. Normanby looked at her eyes, which were adorned with the tiniest amount of well-applied make-up. He felt that, if Grant were to try and push past, she would physically fight to stop him. She would doubtless lose, as Grant was a well-built man, in good physical shape, but she would fight, and carry on fighting.

It didn't come to that. A tall man with a bald head, an uneven brown moustache and a cheap, dark blue suit walked over from the group of police officials. He was thin, everywhere except around his stomach, which hung slightly over his tan belt.

Grant flashed the impressive looking credentials again and this time they worked.

"D.S. Doug Taylor," said the tall man; "Homicide and Major Enquiries Team."

"Grant," said Grant simply, lifting the tape and stepping under it before letting it spring back down, slightly stretched and a little looser. Normanby looked at the sagging tape sadly. It had been so pristine and neat just a moment before.

Grant and Taylor began walking to the crime scene. Normanby coughed loudly, and Grant glanced back over his shoulder. "Come on Normanby," he said, continuing to walk with Taylor.

The young PCSO lifted the tape and Normanby stepped under it.

"Normanby," he announced. "Thank you, officer."

She smiled at him, grateful that, even though the other gentleman had been arrogant and a little rude, at least his assistant seemed nice and polite.

Around the doorway of 19 Trilby Street, stretching the full width of the little house, past the next-door neighbour's front door and out past the pavement into the street was another cordon of crime scene tape. Inside the cordon was a mass of bloodstains, some of which had dribbled over the pavement edge and clouded into the small, shallow puddle in the roadside gutter left by the previous night's rain.

Normanby took out his notebook and began writing and sketching. The battered, off-white wooden door of number 19 had blood splatters and a particularly large blood stain which started thick, congealed and red at just below head height on the left side, as viewed from the outside. The stain grew paler and thinner the further down the frame it went. Normanby took his mobile phone from his pocket and snapped a picture…

Grant, whilst waiting for Taylor to return with one of the Scenes of Crime Operatives, watched Normanby and wondered what he was doing. "That bloody notebook," he thought. "I'd like to grab Normanby by the throat and ram that bloody notebook up his…"

"Mr. Grant." It was Taylor. "This is Simon DeVere, our top Crime Scene Investigator."

Grant nodded at a man in a white paper suit. He was still wearing latex gloves and did not offer to shake hands. He was young and serious-looking, with black, wavy hair, a neat little black beard and black-rimmed spectacles. The combination made him look as though he belonged in a 1960's jazz club.

"Cause and time of death?" asked Grant, simply.

"He was stabbed through the heart," said DeVere. "Exact time of death is uncertain, but within the last 12 hours. We'll probably find that out quicker through talking to the neighbours in the street than I can tell you at this stage."

Normanby had walked over and was poised, notebook and pen in hand. "What was the full extent of the deceased's injuries?" he asked. Grant glared at him.

DeVere adjusted his spectacles. "As far as we can ascertain so far; a very heavy blow to the left side of the head causing an open wound and a possible skull fracture, multiple stab wounds to the left side of the back – twelve in all. One of them appears to have ruptured the kidney, two more which pierced the heart; further cuts to the forearms, mainly the right arm. It's possible that these are defensive wounds. One stab wound to the top of the right shoulder."

He waited whilst Normanby made his notes, ready to repeat anything that he needed.

"Thank you, Mr DeVere," said Normanby after a moment.

"We'll want a full report as soon as possible," Grant said to Taylor, "and no press coverage for now. I don't want his name released."

Taylor shrugged. "I'll do what I can," he said.

Grant glanced over and saw that Normanby was facing the door again. He saw him glance over to the right and walk off that way, the opposite direction from which they had come.

The end of the street had a wall across it that reached up to Normanby's head height, with an opening onto a winding tarmac path that led down a hill, through a few patches of lack-lustre landscaped areas, to a high wooden fence. In the fence was another opening leading to a pelican crossing over a dual carriageway. This was Marsh Road, and just at the other side of it stood a bright, modern shopping complex.

Normanby guessed that the purpose of the high fence was to hide the slum-housing of Trilby Street and the area around it from customers to the complex, so as not to spoil their retail-consumer experience. At the end of the path, where it joined Marsh Road, there was more Police tape and another bored-looking female PCSO on guard. She glanced back and Normanby waved as he walked down towards the gap in the fence. She waved back and then turned and continued standing guard.

Normanby turned his attention to the surrounding area. The landscaped patches were beginning to look positively shabby and untidy. Amongst the clusters of shrubbery, the inevitable build up of discarded polystyrene fast food packaging was well underway, and here and there, he noticed crushed, empty cans of imported super-strength lager and the occasional squashed blue plastic bottle, formerly containing cheap white cider.

He looked out across Marsh Road and noticed that the road itself was more than adequately served by public space CCTV cameras. Glancing back, he realised that everything at the Trilby Street side of the fence would be a 'blind spot' for the cameras on Marsh Road.

Normanby started to walk back up the path. He paused once he was ten paces behind the fence, and looked around to see that this area was, indeed, out of view of the CCTV cameras.

As he approached the wall that marked the boundary of Trilby Street, he stopped and examined the ground. With a puzzled expression growing on his face, Normanby took out his mobile phone and began taking pictures of the ground to the sides of the gateway onto the street, and of the wall itself.

He took pictures of a bare muddy patch next to the gateway, the assorted footprints, some with little puddles of water in them and some without. There was one set of footprints which seemed larger than average, with a vaguely familiar pattern. He took more pictures of the pair of footprints that actually faced the wall from about a foot away, and of the wall itself. Next, he took a series of pictures of the various brown, mottled cigarette ends scattered around the floor and (without stepping off the path), close up pictures of four cigarette butts that were still white. Three of the cigarette butts had burned down to the filter and the other had at least an inch of cigarette left. He leaned over as far as he dare to get close up pictures of them, and then stood up with a satisfied smile on his face. He put his mobile phone in his pocket and marched back to the crime scene.

Grant was waiting impatiently with his hands thrust deep into his overcoat pockets and made no effort to respond when Normanby gave him an amiable wave from the end of Trilby Street.

"Where the Hell have you been, Normanby?" he asked, irritably, as Normanby approached.

"Investigating, Mr. Grant," Normanby replied with an icy glare. "I believe that was our brief when we were sent here."

"What's the point?" asked Grant. "We know what happened."

"Do we?" Normanby looked around, caught sight of Doug Taylor, and walked over to him.

Grant watched bitterly as Normanby stood with Taylor, pointing to the wall at the end of Trilby Street and gesturing. Taylor nodded and took a notebook from the inside pocket of his jacket, apparently jotting down instructions from Normanby.

Grant looked at his watch impatiently. When he saw Normanby returning, he began jangling his car keys in his hand, in a signal that he was eager to get going.

"You done now, Normanby?" he asked. "I want to get back to the office if that's okay with you. I've got an armed raid to organise…if it's not too late!"

"You're still convinced that Mr. Hussein was killed by the people he was meeting last night?" asked Normanby. Grant looked at him with disdain.

"Of course he was, Normanby, and he was my agent. I'm going to salvage what I can out of this mess."

On the drive back to the office, Normanby had spent most of the journey uncharacteristically engrossed in his mobile phone, and Grant wondered if the little man was checking his social media. He amused himself by trying to imagine what Normanby's Facebook page might look like, if he had one.

CHAPTER SIX: A LECTURE IN ROOM 131

The Colonel was waiting for them in Room 131 when they returned. Grant was glad of this. It would save time in getting Ali Hussein and his gang brought in.

"Well?" asked The Colonel.

"Yes, it was Shafiq, alright. Stabbed to death, and beaten! We have to move fast, sir, get Ali Hussein and the rest of them rounded up straight away, if they haven't already done a runner."

He noticed that The Colonel was looking straight past him, at Normanby. He glanced back at the little man, who had taken out his notebook, then back at The Colonel, finding it hard to hide his impatience.

"Sir, we have to act now!" he said.

The Colonel glared at him for a moment, and then turned his attention back to the other man. "Normanby?" he asked, raising an eyebrow.

Normanby pushed his spectacles up to the bridge of his nose, primly. "I believe we should waste no time in putting Ali Hussein and his associates under close and constant observation, sir," he said.

"Observation?!" spluttered Grant. "We need to get these bastards arrested or shot before they can do anything else!"

"Grant," barked The Colonel, "be quiet! Normanby; explain."

"Well, sir," said Normanby, pensively. "I'm not entirely convinced that Shafiq Hussein was killed by his cousin, Ali Hussein, or indeed, by any of his people."

"Oh, come on…" Grant began, fuming, but was immediately silenced by another glare from The Colonel.

"Go on, Normanby," The Colonel prompted, patiently.

"Well," began Normanby, "I feel that if Hussein and his people distrusted Shafiq enough to kill him, they would have done so at the meeting, or taken him somewhere quiet, rather than attacking him as he returned to his front door. I don't believe that Hussein and his people are stupid enough to do that. After all, Shafiq's death, outside his own house, alerted us very quickly. Why would Ali Hussein do that?"

"That's an interesting point," said The Colonel, "but perhaps Hussein and his people only became suspicious after the meeting. Is that a possibility?"

Grant sighed impatiently and, with an effort, managed to keep his voice even. "Sir," he said. "Can we afford to take chances and hang around?"

The Colonel half-turned and then reached back to pick up the phone from Grant's desk. He thumbed a button and spoke into the handset. "Betty?" he said. "Contact Major Green, immediately. I want his people watching Ali Hussein very closely, and I want it now. Tell him to report back in person if there's any movement at all."

Grant fought back his rage and disappointment. His agent was dead, The Colonel was ignoring his suggestions in favour of Normanby, and now, his project was being put into the hands of Major Green's team. He was shaking slightly in frustration and anger, and his jaw was beginning to ache from clenching his teeth. With an effort, he took a deep breath and tried to relax as he released it slowly under The Colonel's steady gaze.

The Colonel gave the slightest nod of approval before turning back to Normanby. "Go on," he said.

"In answer to your last question, sir," Normanby continued, "the answer is 'No'. I don't believe that Hussein's people followed Shafiq back from the meeting."

He stepped to his own desk, leaned down and switched on the computer, straightening up and continuing as the machine went through the start up process. "I am convinced that Shafiq was murdered by someone who had been waiting for him to return, someone who had been waiting for at least fifteen minutes at the opposite end of Trilby Street to Ali Hussein's flat. Whilst it is always dangerous to assume, I firmly believe that there is enough evidence to suspect that Shafiq's cover may not have been blown…at least, as far as Ali and his people are concerned."

Grant gazed, open-mouthed, from Normanby to The Colonel and back. Normanby leaned over his desk and opened up his email account on the computer, then clicked on the most recent message, which contained several photo attachments. He straightened up and glanced from Grant to The Colonel. Grant was still speechless, still doubting Normanby but unsure of how to break the spell that the little man seemed to have over the Old Man.

"Go on, Normanby," said The Colonel.

"Well," said Normanby, "when first informed that Shafiq Hussein was dead, murdered after a meeting with a group of suspected, or potential, terrorists, my first assumption was the same as yours, Mr. Grant. It seemed likely that his cover had been blown and that Ali Hussein's group had killed Shafiq to stop him passing any further information to you."

"What changed your mind?" asked Grant, dully. It was beginning to look as if, on top of everything else, Normanby had spotted things that Grant himself should have noticed.

"Well, the first thing that grabbed my attention," said Normanby, "was the blood-stain at head height on the right door frame, or left side as you face it."

"So?" said Grant.

"Well, if the attacker had come from Ali Hussein's flat, they would have come from that side. If that were the case, they would have had to pull Shafiq towards the doorframe with considerable force to bang his head there. Firstly, that seems like a very unlikely and impractical way to attack someone. Secondly, if someone were to grab me personally, my first reaction would be to turn my head towards them which would mean that I would not sustain the impact injury to the left side of my head."

Grant tried to find a hole in Normanby's theory.

"Maybe that wasn't the first move," he said. "Shafiq suffered multiple stab wounds."

"...which is what convinced me that the head injury was sustained first," replied Normanby. "The blood stain on the door frame is at head height. Very few people would continue to stand upright after such an attack, indeed the last injury that Shafiq Hussein received would probably have been the one to the shoulder as he doubled up in pain."

Grant felt his throat constricting at Normanby's matter-of-fact analysis of Shafiq's death. Normanby looked at him, then at The Colonel. On receiving an interested nod from the latter, he continued: "The supposition that someone had struck Shafiq from his right side led me to suspect that someone may have come at him from the other end of the street."

"Wait," said Grant. "Okay, it seems that he was attacked from his right, but that doesn't prove anything. Maybe Ali, or one of the others, went back from the meeting with him and stood to his right then killed him."

Normanby nodded and consulted his notebook. "That was also a possibility, Mr. Grant. However, the excellent dossier that you have compiled states that Ali Hussein, and his associates; Iqbal and Malik are all right-handed."

"Right-handed?" Grant struggled to see the relevance of the remark.

"Yes," said Normanby. "The majority of the stab wounds were sustained to the left side of the victim's back. I believe that Shafiq was struck a blow that forced his head into the door frame in a sort of 'setting up' strike, and then, before he could respond or recover his balance, he was subjected to a frenzied knife attack, with the knife held in the left hand."

He mimed the movement of striking with the heel of his right hand and stabbing with the left. Grant noticed a smooth agility in Normanby's movements that he had never before seen or even suspected.

"Of course," Normanby continued, "none of this was conclusive, but it was enough for me to look for other clues…"

"Other clues?" asked Grant, ruefully, "… and I suppose you found them?"

"I did indeed, Mr. Grant," Normanby replied, with a thin smile. "I did indeed."

He pulled out his chair and sat at his desk, touched the computer mouse so that the screen came to life and opened up the first photo attachment on the email. He placed his little black notebook on the desk, and then took a long moment to ensure that the spine of the book was precisely in line with the edge of the desk.

Grant raised an eyebrow and looked at The Colonel, who stared back with an expression that seemed to challenge him to comment. Both men remained silent and edged closer so that they could look over Normanby's shoulders at the screen.

"I e-mailed these pictures from my mobile telephone when we left the crime scene," announced Normanby, opening up the first image on his computer screen. It showed the blood stain on the edge of the doorframe. Grant looked at it and felt unhappy with himself. He had gone in with his mind made up about what had happened and Normanby had spotted the clues; clues which changed everything.

Even if he had gone in there with an open mind, he thought glumly, he probably wouldn't have spotted what Normanby had, or been able to make the same deductions.

Normanby brought up a picture of a patch of mud with various footprints in it.

"If you look closely at these footprints from the end of Trilby Street," said Normanby, "you will notice that almost all of them contain water. In fact, there is only one set which does not contain water, except where the print has been made over another footprint."

"So?" said Grant. The Colonel glanced at him, then back at Normanby with a questioning expression which seemed to indicate that he, too, required a further explanation.

"It rained yesterday, well into the evening," said Normanby. "The footprints containing water were made before the rain stopped at roughly 9pm last night. This other set..." He pointed with his pen at a large footprint with no water in it, "...were made sometime after that. They are dry because they were made after the rain had stopped, and they are the only dry set."

"Well, all that proves is that someone has been there after the rain," said Grant.

"It is a little thin, Normanby," agreed The Colonel.

"It would have been, sir," concurred Normanby, "were it not for this:"
He brought up a picture of a pair of dry footprints that matched the ones he had pointed out, this time facing the wall from less than a foot away.

"Somebody stopping for a pee?" asked Grant, scornfully.

"No, Mr. Grant," replied Normanby, "I don't think so. Firstly, the wall is relatively dry even after the rain, no doubt due to the direction of the wind, with no obvious signs that anyone might have relieved themselves there. Secondly, the footprints seem too close, unless the person was totally unconcerned with the urine that would undoubtedly splash back at that distance. Thirdly, there are the cigarette ends."

He tapped the screen to indicate the position of the four cigarette butts to the left of the footprints.

Grant and The Colonel looked at each other for a long moment, then back at Normanby. Normanby stared back at them to ensure that he had their full attention before turning back to the screen and continuing.

"The cigarette ends are relatively clean and white," he said. "They were dropped after the rain had stopped, and they were dropped by whoever made the footprints as they are the only footprints made after the rain. They were dropped to the left hand side of the footprints so, almost certainly by a left-handed person. There are four cigarette ends so whoever was there must have been waiting for at least, say, twenty minutes? One of the cigarettes has not been smoked all the way down and not burned away. I suspect it was discarded when Shafiq was spotted approaching his door."

"So, Normanby," said Grant. "We now know that Shafiq was killed by a left-handed smoker wearing Doc Martens."

"Doc Martens?" asked Normanby.

"Yeah," Grant said, with the slightest smile at having finally got something right. "Doc Marten boots; airwear soles; Quite distinctive. I've got a pair at home."

Normanby smiled happily for a moment. "Sir," he said, addressing The Colonel and suddenly becoming serious again. "I am convinced that Shafiq Hussein was not killed by Ali Hussein's people, but by a tall, left-handed smoker of Russian cigarettes, wearing Doctor Marten boots."

"Tall?" said Grant, growing more eager to join in. "Maybe he just had big feet?"

"No, Mr. Grant," said Normanby with a slight shake of the head. "His footprints faced the wall in the same spot whilst he smoked his cigarettes. He would have been looking over the top of the wall. To do so, he would have to be at least three or four inches taller than me."

"...And the Russian cigarettes?" Grant asked.

Normanby brought up a picture of the cigarette butts in close up. On one, Russian lettering could be seen where it had not been smoked down to the filter. Grant was squinting, trying to make sense of the lettering.

"It's pronounced 'Fest', Mr. Grant," said Normanby.

"Well done, Normanby," boomed The Colonel. "Grant; it seems that your agent wasn't blown after all. It's even possible that his murder may have been totally unrelated to his work. Do you know of anyone else, anyone at all, who might possibly have wanted him dead?"

"No sir," said Grant.

"Then it seems that your operation is still running," The Colonel replied, "even without your agent."

"My operation?" asked Grant, shocked. "But I thought that Major Green's team were watching Hussein and his gang now?"

"It's your operation, Grant," The Colonel said firmly. "I'll ensure that Green's people work under your supervision."

Grant stood for long moments in stunned silence. After the way that the morning had gone, he could not believe his luck at being allowed to continue. The Colonel surveyed him coolly, and then turned to Normanby, who had already opened the appropriate form on his computer to begin his report.

"Normanby: I want you to come at this from the other end," The Colonel ordered. "Whilst Grant continues to find out exactly what Ali Hussein and his people are up to, I want you to find out who killed his cousin Shafiq, and why. I don't like coincidences."

Normanby adjusted his spectacles, nervously. "Are you sure that's wise, sir?" he asked. "After all, the Police are already investigating the murder."

The Colonel glanced down at Normanby and for a moment, Grant thought he was actually going to shout. "Then you'd better hurry up and beat them to the correct conclusion, hadn't you?" he said, calmly.

CHAPTER SEVEN: SHAZIA

Ali Hussein smiled and placed the little Dremmel craft-drill on the kitchen table. He picked up the lightbulb that had been held in place on the table top by being pushed into a large dollop of Plasticine, and looked at it closely. He had stuck a strip of thick gaffer tape over the thin glass of the bulb, and he had carefully drilled a small hole through both the tape and the glass.

This had been his fourth attempt at drilling a hole into a lightbulb without causing the glass to shatter. The first two attempts had failed miserably, leaving tiny shards of fine glass on the kitchen table and on the floor around his chair.

He took a deep breath and very carefully peeled away the strip of tape, grimacing in the expectation of further disaster. The tape came away and the bulb remained intact. Ali let out a slow, satisfied exhalation and then peered closely at the hole in the surface of the lightbulb. He was almost sure that the hole would be big enough to half-fill the object with the amber liquid from the sealed flask that was locked away in his bedroom. It would have to be, he decided. He could not risk trying to drill a bigger hole into the fragile glass.

Carefully pressing the lightbulb back into the Plasticine on the table, he pushed his chair back and stood up, stretching his arms and rotating his neck to alleviate the stiffness caused by sitting in the same position for such a long period. He would take a break before continuing, he decided. If he could manage to drill two or three more bulbs tonight, he thought, that would be enough. Putting them in place at work would be an easy matter. The most worrying part of the job would be getting the liquid inside the bulbs and sealing up the holes. He prayed that his research had been thorough enough, and that the home made glove-box in his wardrobe would do the job.

He stepped out of the kitchen and peered around the doorframe into the living room of the flat where the sound of heavy gunfire was blaring from the television. He failed to suppress an amused smile as he watched Tariq, perched on the edge of the sofa, his eyes transfixed on the screen. Tariq's head twitched intermittently and in addition, he gave a series of tiny nods whenever there was enough carnage on the screen to meet his approval.

"What are you watching Tariq?" Ali asked, still smiling.

Tariq's eyes did not leave the screen, other than to give an excited twitch of the head. "Rambo," he said. "It's the third one, or the fourth, whichever way you look at it."

"No Chuck Norris tonight then Bro'?" asked Ali.

Tariq twitched again. "No, seen them all," he said. "I've got a Van Damme to watch after."

Ali shook his head in amused bewilderment. It seemed odd in the extreme that a young man so committed to the Jihad could be so obsessed with old American action films but, he reflected, Tarik Malik was an unusual young man by anybody's standards. "I'm having a cup of tea," said Ali. "Do you want one?"

Tariq gave a movement that could have either been a small twitch or a dismissive shake of the head. Ali placed a foot into the room and leaned forward to gain his attention.

"No, I'm alright Bro'" said Tariq without taking his attention from the screen.

Ali turned to step back into the kitchen and then stopped dead. He heard the rattle of a key in a lock and then the familiar bang of the front door being opened. He glanced back over his shoulder and saw that Tariq had slipped the cook's knife out from beneath the cushion of the settee, and was standing in the middle of the room holding it at the ready. His eyes were alert, and he was breathing quick, shallow breaths.

Mohammed Iqbal banged the door shut without locking it, and then stepped into the hallway.

"You forgot to lock the door Bro'," said Ali from the living room doorway. "We've got procedures..."

"Fuck procedures," said Iqbal breathlessly. "It's Shafiq. He's dead!" He continued walking forward and Ali took a step back to let him enter the room.

The three men stood in shocked silence for several seconds before Ali spoke. "How did he die?" he asked.

"He's been stabbed outside his front door," Iqbal replied flatly.

"Oh fuck, it's M.I.5., they're onto us," said Tariq, his head thrown into an uncontrollable series of twitches.

"Don't talk stupid you fucking retard!" spat Iqbal venomously.

"Don't you call me a retard," said Tariq, pointing the tip of the blade at Iqbal.

"Fucking shut up, both of you," ordered Ali. "Tariq; put the fucking knife away." He turned to Iqbal. "How do you know?" he asked.

Iqbal took a deep breath. "I was on my way to the shopping centre," he said. "The coppers have got the street cordoned off, so I asked that old woman at the end house and she told me. She said the coppers have been knocking on all the doors to see if anybody saw or heard anything!"

Tariq stamped his foot. "Bastards," he said. "I tell you boys; they're fucking onto us. We've got to be ready!"

Ali held up a hand to silence Iqbal before he could respond again, and then turned to face Tariq. "Listen Bro'," he said as calmly as he could manage, "stop panicking. M.I.5. don't stab people on their doorsteps, and even if they were going to do something like that, they'd have come for us, not Shafiq. He wasn't even involved with our business."

Tariq looked thoughtful for a moment until his head suddenly twitched a couple of times. "Well who's done it then?" he asked eventually.

Ali let out a breath that hissed between his gritted teeth. "I bet was some fucking smack head chav," he said, "trying to roll him for his wallet to pay for a fix."

"Dirty bastards," said Tariq, holding up the knife in front of him. "We need to find 'em and cut 'em up."

"No," said Ali sternly. "We need to stay calm and follow the plan. We'll get our revenge. You can cut up as many kuffar bastards as you want when we're done."

Tariq looked back at him, and then at the knife in his hand, still not convinced.

"Ali's right Tariq," said Iqbal quietly. "We've put too much in to mess things up now. We have to stay calm, so we don't attract any attention. We have to bide our time."

Tariq flopped down onto the settee, suddenly deflated. Ali rested a hand gently on his shoulder and sat down beside him. "Don't worry Bro'," he said quietly. "We'll get them. We'll slaughter them and we'll keep slaughtering them until there's none of them left."

Tariq nodded solemnly and then gave a sniff. "He was a good man was Shafiq," he said. "He was a friend. He never called me names."

"He was a good man Tariq," Ali confirmed, standing up slowly. He turned and walked out into the hallway. He did not want the others to see the tears welling up in his eyes. He knew that he had to show nothing but strength, to keep them focussed on their goal. "What the fuck am I going to say to Shafiq's family?" he thought to himself. In his mind, he saw an image of Shafiq's little brother, Sheraz. He was still at college and had wanted to do well, more to impress Shafiq than his own parents.

Ali went to his bedroom, closed the door heavily and then threw himself on the bed. He wanted to kill them all; all of the non-believers that had been attacking everything that he loved for almost as long as he could remember. He held his pillow tightly over his own face and sobbed.

In the darkness, he remembered the day that he had finally decided that he would carry out his uncle's wishes and give everything, even his own life, if necessary, for the cause:

He had been seventeen at the time and it had been the last time that Uncle Majid had taken him to the big house on the Afghan border. *His uncle had pointed out the plume of smoke ahead and had gunned the engine of the old Toyota pick-up truck. The dust from the road had engulfed them as the truck picked up speed, but Majid had ignored it.*

Ali coughed and spat out of the open passenger side window as the cloying dust cloud billowed in on the still, dry air. The dust and the screech of the protesting engine should have announced their arrival to the group of American soldiers who were stood at the front of the house, but they were too busy arguing amongst themselves to pay any attention.

"They told us the Intel was good," screamed the Sergeant.

"It was a fucking family," one of his men shouted back at him. Their faces were only inches apart, eyes wild; lips drawn back in furious snarls.

Another young soldier by the front door sank into a crouch, sobbing. His M4 rifle slipped from his grasp, and he angrily ripped off his helmet and threw it on the ground beside the weapon.

Ali stumbled forward in fear and confusion, a growing sense of dread descending upon him like the dust cloud that he had just left behind him. Uncle Majid shouted at him, but the voice seemed as if it was coming from miles away.

"Ali, no!" he commanded. "Come back Ali."

Ali ignored his uncle and stepped forward towards the open front door.

"You can't go in there sir," shouted the Sergeant. "Cooper, stop that man!"

The young soldier crouching by the door glanced briefly at Ali but did not move to stop him. Instead, he shook his head and gave a sob. "It wasn't us," he spluttered, his eyes fixed on the dry dusty ground. "It was a drone strike. Their Intel was wrong. We were supposed to find insurgents here."

Ali stopped and looked at the young man, unable to speak. He carried on walking and pushed the door wide open. Inside, the room was a smouldering ruin. Half of the roof was gone and there was a massive hole in the back wall. He squinted through the smoke from the still-smouldering pieces of furniture scattered around the room and he caught sight of Shazia's body, half-buried by rubble. He fell to his knees, suddenly feeling immensely weak as the shock caused his blood-pressure to drop.

In life, she had been beautiful and now she had been taken from him. Not knowing why, his mind in utter turmoil, he began to let out a long, low wail at the sight of the mangled mess that she had become.

CHAPTER EIGHT: RETURN TO THE SCENE OF THE CRIME

Normanby was happy, although anyone that didn't know him would not have realised this. Since no-one really knew Normanby, however, no-one knew that he was happy. The reason for his good spirits was that he had been pleasantly surprised by the police.

On returning to Trilby Street, Normanby had expected to be disappointed. He had left instructions earlier that the area behind the wall be investigated thoroughly, though he had expected nothing more than a perfunctory glance, and an assurance that there was nothing there worth noting. Instead, Normanby found that the police, under orders from Taylor, had been very thorough. They had not only taken photographs of the footprints and the cigarette ends, as he had asked, but had even 'bagged and tagged' the cigarette butts for analysis.

"Of course, they might not mean anything," Doug Taylor said, "but we won't leave any stone unturned."

"Very commendable, Mr. Taylor," Normanby replied. "However, I firmly believe that the footprints and the cigarette ends are of great significance. They have already eliminated our initial suspects from the investigation, at least for now. That means that you can continue to investigate the case as you normally would. Of course, due to the victim's connection with our department, I will need to be kept informed of any developments."

Taylor's face hardened slightly. "If you had suspects in the first place," he said, "I should be interested in knowing more about them."

"Unfortunately," replied Normanby, "I am not able to disclose that information, due to operational demands."

Taylor sighed, resignedly. "It's always the bloody same with you lot," he said, bitterly. "You don't tell us anything and yet we have to report our every move."

"Console yourself, Mr. Taylor, with the knowledge that your actions are assisting us in matters of national importance," replied Normanby, rather pompously.

Taylor wasn't sure if he liked the officious little Government man, but he was a realist. He had no option but to work with him, as best he could. "Well, we don't have much to go on," he said wearily. "We can analyse the cigarettes and the footprints, I suppose. Any idea how long I have I have to keep it all hush-hush? There'll be rumours flying around already, anyway. The neighbours can't all be sworn to secrecy."

"That's a very good point, Mr. Taylor," agreed Normanby. "There is no more need for secrecy on your part. From here on in, I would like you to conduct this case just as you would any other. Treat it as if you had not been approached by our department at all."

Taylor was pleasantly surprised. "That's more like it," he said happily. "We might actually get somewhere now. You'd be surprised how useful the press can be in cases like this, Mr. Normanby."

Normanby was genuinely interested. "Really, Mr. Taylor?" he asked. "I had always imagined that press appeals for information were one of those formalities that rarely yielded results."

"Are you kidding?" grinned Taylor. "Don't believe all that 'honour amongst thieves' crap that the scroats tell you. They can't wait to grass each other up whenever they get the chance."

Normanby still doubted that putting information out to the public would be worthwhile in this case, but if that was the usual procedure, he was happy for Taylor to go ahead.

At this point in time, he did not want Ali Hussein and his people having any suspicions about Shafiq's involvement with the Department. It was entirely possible that they would abandon whatever plans they had once they found out that Shafiq had been murdered, but there was a hope that they would still go ahead and reveal them. The only worry then was whether or not Grant and Major Green's team would be able to keep a close enough eye on them to stop them in time and bring them in.

From what Normanby had read and heard, Hussein and his people could well have information that could help bring down a much wider terrorist network than even they themselves realised. Like most Jihadists, they would, undoubtedly resist giving information but, Normanby reflected dryly, there were various ways of getting it.

Doug Taylor had been talking with the slowly dwindling group of crime-scene experts, and was now ambling towards Normanby, notebook in hand, a contented smile on his face.

Normanby could see that the man was happy, now that he had been given a free hand to investigate.

"I'm going back to the station, Mr. Normanby," he said. "Can I give you a lift anywhere?"

Normanby was looking at the gap in the wall at the end of the street with a thoughtful expression on his face.

"Is it far to the Local Council CCTV control room that watches this part of the city?" he asked, absently.

Taylor smiled proudly. "I'm ahead of you there, Mr. Normanby," he said. "I've already sent Lou to have a look at last night's footage."

"Lou?" asked Normanby.

"One of the PCSO's. She's been on this from the beginning," Taylor replied. He was ready for the look of surprise that appeared on Normanby's face.

"A PCSO?" Normanby asked, genuinely shocked. "Not a Police Officer?"

"Lou's good," said Taylor, somewhat defensively. "She knows the area and she knows the people 'round here. If the murderer's local, and if he's on camera at all, she stands more chance of spotting him than anyone else."

Normanby made an effort to produce a reassuring expression, despite himself. "That's good enough for me, Mr. Taylor," he said. "I'd like to go and liaise with her, if that's alright."

"I'll give her a ring and tell her to wait for you there," said Taylor, fishing a cheap mobile phone out of his pocket. "It's a bit out of my way for driving you there, but you'll be quicker on the tube anyway, if that's alright. I can give you directions. It's easy enough to find."

He thumbed two buttons and put the phone to his ear, then spoke almost immediately. "Lou," he said. "I've got a Mr. Normanby coming to meet you at CCTV, love...Yes...Can you make sure he's allowed in?...Yes, under my orders...Yeah, if you can liaise with him and let him know anything you find...I'm with him now...Yes, he is...Yes, you too."

He closed the phone and put it away before giving Normanby his full attention. "Directions," he said absently...

"...And a telephone number," said Normanby. "In case I need to contact you."

Taylor brought out his wallet and extracted a business card containing his name, position, mobile and office telephone numbers and an email address.

"Thank you, Mr. Taylor," Normanby acknowledged, as he brought out his notebook and carefully put the card into a pocket inside the back cover.

"Now...directions?" he asked.

CHAPTER NINE: BRAVE NEW WORLD

Grant pulled the mesh door closed, then heaved shut the inner gate of the ancient elevator. He pushed the button for the third floor, and the cage juddered and creaked into motion.

It would probably have been quicker to walk, Grant conceded to the nagging voice in the back of his head, but he had never used the lift before and his visit to room 331, exactly two stories above his usual place of work, seemed like the perfect opportunity to try it out.

When he finally stepped out of the ancient cage onto the third floor, Grant was somewhat surprised at how different it was from the floors below. The landing at the top of the stairs and elevator shaft looked just like the others, with a black and white tiled floor and polished, wood panelled walls. When Grant looked through an open wooden door and saw the corridor beyond, however, he was struck by the way it differed from the rest of the building.

The floor was covered in grey, shiny tiles. The walls were white on one side of the corridor, but on the other side, there was an expanse of glass and brushed steel, in between the white painted stone pillars of the original building.

Grant took a deep breath and stepped over the threshold into the gleaming, modern corridor. "Welcome to U.N.C.L.E., Mr. Solo," he muttered to himself with a satisfied grin.

Before he had taken three paces, a figure appeared from one of the glass-fronted offices further down the corridor and turned to face him.

The man was tall and slim, in an immaculate, light grey suit with a white pocket-square in the breast pocket. He wore a white shirt and a black silk tie. He was, perhaps, in his late forties, with close cropped, black hair. He seemed, to Grant, the epitome of what an Intelligence Officer should be.

"Mr. Grant?" said the man, with a friendly smile. "I'm Mike Green. Welcome to the third floor."

Grant glanced into the first glass-fronted office, which was unoccupied. Inside, there were two large, modern desks facing each other. The chairs accompanying them looked plush and comfortable; the kind usually reserved for managers and executives.

"Nice place you've got here, Major Green," he said, walking forward.

"Yeah, it's not bad," Green replied, "and 'Mike' is fine. I know the Old Man likes to refer to people by rank if they have one, but we're a bit less formal up here."

Grant smiled warmly and held out his hand. "Tom," he said simply. They shook hands, and Grant silently noted the Major's firm, dry handshake with a slight nod of approval.

"Well, you'd better come in and have a look around," said Green, stepping into the large, modern office that was Room 331.

Grant followed him inside, and then stood for a moment, savouring the air of modernity around him. It seemed a million miles away from the stuffy, old-fashioned atmosphere of Room 131.

"A bit different from downstairs," said Grant.

"Just a little," Green agreed. "Come and have a look at this, Tom," he said, tapping the surface of the huge, glass-topped table that dominated the room. Suddenly, the surface of the table came to life with light and colour: The whole tabletop was a giant, touch-sensitive screen.

"That is one Hell of a tablet," said Grant.

He noticed that the screen was divided into separate sections. In one section was a photograph of Ali Hussein with his name printed beneath it.

Green tapped the right hand side of the picture and a virtual page was flipped, revealing the first page of Grant's own dossier on Hussein.

"Amazing," said Grant, impressed. "So, my reports don't just gather dust after all."

"No," smiled Green, "they're scanned and put into the system." He tapped the left side of the document and the photograph re-appeared.

"It's surprisingly easy to use," Green continued. He swiped the picture to one side and Iqbal's picture appeared.

"You can scroll through, move, open and close documents, anything that you can do with paper, in fact…except pick them up and walk out with a stack of secret files under your arm." Green said, continuing to toy with various sections of the table. "This is the future, Tom!"

Grant nodded slightly, still watching in awe. "It's bloody magnificent," he said, simply.

"From what you've put together so far," said Green, "I'm surprised you didn't just pull Hussein and his people straight in as soon as Shafiq was killed."

"I would have," Grant replied, "but the Old Man said he wanted your people watching them…thanks to Normanby."

"Normanby?" There was a hint of mockery in Green's tone at the use of the name. "What's he got to do with it?"

"Oh, he came to the crime scene with me, on the Old Man's orders," Grant replied. "He snooped around and did his Sherlock Holmes bit, and figured out that Shafiq was probably killed by someone else."

Green looked doubtfully at Grant, as if he was trying to make a decision. Eventually, he made up his mind and spoke. "I'm not sure that was the right choice," he said. "It's probably not my place to say…" Green spoke slowly, treading carefully and watching Grant's reaction. "…I'm just…I'm not sure about Normanby," he concluded. Grant gave a short, mirthful chuckle and Green's apprehension vanished.

"You and me both," said Grant. "He's certainly a weirdo. I mean, his deductions seem to make sense, and his attention to detail's amazing. It really was like watching Sherlock Holmes or Hercule Poirot…unbelievable!" There was a pause and Grant felt a growing sense of unease as Green stared in silence.

"Unbelievable," Green echoed at last.

"Your people are watching Hussein right now, aren't they?" asked Grant, concerned.

Green nodded. "I've got Toby Hughes watching his flat. The rest of his gang are apparently there too, at the moment. It'll be hard to keep an eye on them all once they split up though."

"That's a good point," said Grant. "I don't suppose we've got the manpower available at short notice to watch them all if they split up?"

Green shook his head. "It's not just the number of people," he said sadly, "it's the logistics, not to mention the authorisations. It would have been much easier just to bring them in and question them, or shoot them."

"Damn Normanby," Grant said through gritted teeth. "If it weren't for him we'd have done just that…Bring them in, I mean."

"It would certainly be safer than letting them wander around free," said Green. "There must be some way around it."

Grant shook his head. "No," he said glumly. "The Old Man wants it played the way Normanby suggested, just because he thinks Hussein and his crew didn't kill Shafiq."

"…Even though he could very well be wrong." Green finished the sentence for him. "Can't you convince the Old Man? After all, it's your operation. Normanby's just butted in on it."

"I think that The Colonel's totally convinced by Normanby's detective work," Grant replied with a little shake of the head. "I certainly can't change his mind, at least until I've had a chance to go through the Police Forensic reports."

Green took a deep breath. "Well, let's get a hold of them now," he said. "With luck, we might be able to find something to convince the Old Man to let us bring these bastards in, dead or alive, before they disappear into the woodwork. I don't know how long Toby will be able to keep an eye on them without being spotted, not without using tech, anyway."

"Tech?" asked Grant.

"Well, an electronic tracker would make things a lot easier," replied Green with a shrug.

"A tracker," mused Grant. "Let's get one then!"

Green looked ruefully at Grant. "You haven't been with The Department long, have you?" he asked. "These things need the proper authorisation. You'd get a right bollocking off the Old Man if you signed a tracker out and anything went wrong."

Grant thought for a moment. "I think I can stand a bollocking," he said. "How would I get a tracker?"

"Well, you just sign one out from the Quartermaster down in B1," said Green, "but you'll have to make sure you bring it back in one piece."

CHAPTER TEN: WATCH WITH LOU

Normanby was waiting patiently at the bottom of a wide staircase in the Municipal Building that housed the Local Council's CCTV department.

He had announced himself at the intercom on the wall, just inside the impressive dark-wood double doors from the street and a set of toughened glass inner doors had automatically unlocked for him, allowing him to step into the newly decorated foyer. The white paint on the walls still smelled fresh and the glass covering the poster-sized black and white prints on the walls was pristine and unmarked.

He liked the cleanliness and order of the building, but something was troubling him. One of the prints; a black and white portrait shot of Alan Turing, with a few lines of type below, explaining his contribution to both the nation and to computing, was hung at a slight angle.

Normanby looked away and hoped that someone would come down and meet him soon. He looked at his watch, then back at the picture on the wall. He turned his attention to the plush seating, with the low modern coffee table, strewn with leaflets and magazines. Finally, his eyes rested on a moulded plastic chair in a room just off the foyer through the gap where the door had been left slightly ajar.

*

Lou Fowler finished writing up her notes and drained her mug of coffee. She looked around for someone who could tell her what to do with the cup but, as the four CCTV operators in the room looked busy, she left in on the desk and headed for the door, taking a last look around as she reached it. Stepping out into the corridor, she blinked as her eyes adjusted to the glare of the strip-lights after the dimness of the CCTV Control Room. She poked her head around the door of the office next to the Control Room entrance.

"Thanks Michelle," she said brightly to the woman inside. "I'm getting off now."

Michelle looked up with a pleasant smile. She was a tall woman, in her fifties, though she looked younger. She flicked back a few strands of her blonde mane. "Okay Love," she said. "Isn't that chap coming over from the station to meet you though?"

"He's down in the hallway," said Lou, "but I don't think there's much for him to see. I've watched the footage twice and made notes," she continued, waving her notebook, "but his man doesn't appear on the cameras."

"Oh well," said Michelle, "it was worth a try."

Lou smiled and walked down the corridor. When she reached the doors that led to the landing, she pressed the door release button and pushed through, savouring the golden, late afternoon sunshine through the skylights as she stood for a moment at the head of the staircase. She reached the turn of the stairs and peered around, down at the foyer. Puzzled, she watched the little man who she had met on Trilby Street.

He carried a moulded plastic chair to a room off the foyer and carefully placed it inside, before coming out and closing the door. He sat down in the comfortable seating area and glanced at his watch, before gazing happily at the row of perfectly aligned black and white prints in the wall. He drummed his fingers on his knee in apparent boredom, then picked up a magazine from one of the immaculately neat stacks on the low coffee table and began to leaf through it.

She set off down the stairs again and unconsciously cleared her throat, announcing her presence.

Normanby glanced up at her then closed the magazine and placed it carefully and neatly back on the pile. He stood up and faced her, almost standing to attention.

"Good afternoon Officer," he said.

"Good afternoon, Mr. Normanby," she replied with a smile. "I've had a look at the camera footage from last night, but there's nothing of use, I'm afraid." She shrugged slightly.

"Nothing?" asked Normanby. "Are you sure?"

Her face hardened slightly. "Yes, Mr. Normanby, I'm sure. I've noted everyone that appeared on camera with the times that they appeared. There's no-one there that fits the description of the suspect; no tall men wearing anything that look remotely like 'Doc Martens.' "

His expression did not change, so she took out her notebook and opened it. "There are times and descriptions for everyone that appeared on camera…"
Normanby glanced at the open notebook in her hand.

"There are even some names," he noted; "Excellent work, Officer!"

She smiled. It was nice to be appreciated, even though he had at first seemed to doubt her competence. Her face dropped when he spoke again, however.

"I'd still like to see the footage myself," he said, "just for my own peace of mind."

She held her breath for a moment, controlling her irritation with great effort. "If you insist, Mr. Normanby," she said. "Bear with me a moment."

She took a few steps towards the door, turned her back to him and took out a cheap, flip-front mobile phone. She opened it deftly with one hand and dialled with the thumb of the same hand, pressing two keys in what Normanby realised must be a pre-set speed-dial for a stored number.

"Hi, it's me," she said. "…No, nothing. I just might be a bit late. Yeah, I'm at CCTV…yeah…going through some footage…Well, I'm going through it again…He wants to see it for himself…Look, I'll call you later." She turned and glanced at Normanby, giving a small smile that did not reach her eyes, and lasted no more than a second. "…I know…I'll tell you later. Bye."

She closed the phone and put it away, heaving a resigned sigh. "Sorry about that, Mr. Normanby," she said. "Just letting my other half know I'm going to be late for tea."

"My apologies Officer," Normanby offered with a slight bow of the head. "I'll try to be as quick as I can." He made a gesture with an outstretched arm towards the stairs to indicate that she should go first and he would follow.

Lou rang the bell at the door on the landing. She tried to hide her annoyance as she glanced at Normanby.

Michelle came along the corridor and pressed the door release button on the inside.

"You forgotten something, love?" she asked, as Lou pulled the door open.

"No," Lou replied, "…well, sort of. Okay to come back in?"

"'Course you can, love," said Michelle. She gave Normanby a smile, which he returned with a polite bow of the head.

In the Control Room, Lou pulled another chair up to the CCTV monitoring station at which she had been working previously and gestured for Normanby to sit. She took out her notebook, opened it and put it on the desk beside the keyboard.

Normanby moved close so that he could see both the screen and the notebook.

She brought up an image of Marsh Road on one of the two screens on the desk. The camera was located on the far side of the road from where Normanby had looked out when he visited the crime scene. It was positioned near the shopping complex, and faced across the road towards the wooden fence, giving a good view of the gap in the fence and the first few yards of the path which led towards Trilby Street.

Lou consulted her notebook and hit buttons on the computer keyboard, putting in a start date and time. The picture changed. The image became a little darker and grainier, and it showed the glow of a streetlight in the top right corner of the screen.

"This is where I watched it from," she said. "This camera's a P.T.Z., which means it can move…"

"Pan, Tilt and Zoom," replied Normanby with a smile. "I'm familiar with closed circuit television operations, Officer."

She clenched her teeth. 'Pompous little dick,' she thought, irritably. "Fortunately, the camera's resting position has been set to cover the path because of the amount of Scroats that use it to get back to the estate when they've been nicking from the shopping centre, and nobody had a reason to move it last night," she said.

"That is, indeed fortunate," Normanby agreed. "When is the first sign of any movement?"

Lou pressed and held a button, and the clock numbers at the bottom of the screen speeded up. When she lifted her finger from the keyboard, the seconds clicked by at the normal rate. She tapped the right hand edge of the screen with a fingernail.

Two young women appeared at the edge of the screen. They were inappropriately dressed for the cool of the evening, and tottering drunkenly on impractical high-heels as they turned and walked up the path towards Trilby Street.

Normanby looked down at Lou's notebook and noted with satisfaction that her timings and description of the two women were accurate and complete. He took out his own notebook and began to make notes.

"I see that you have a name for the next person that appears," he said, glancing at her notebook.

"Yeah," she acknowledged. "It's Mr. Crookes. He usually walks his dog about that time."

"Do you know a lot of people in the area?" asked Normanby.

"Yes," she replied. "It's part of my beat. It's my job to get to know the people around there." She turned her attention back to the keyboard and speeded up the playback until a man in a flat cap, a yellow high visibility work coat and brown rigger boots appeared on the screen, with a dog. The dog appeared to be a Staffordshire bull terrier, as far as Normanby could tell, and Lou's accurate and complete notes confirmed this. The man and dog carried on, along Marsh Road and off camera.

Although he did not show it, Normanby was very impressed with Lou Fowler's efficiency. He silently continued making his own notes.

After watching more of the CCTV footage, and seeing various individuals walking past the camera, exactly as described in Lou Fowler's notebook, Normanby was beginning to think that she might have been right. Maybe there was 'nothing to see'.

Lou sighed and turned another page in her notebook. "Nearly there," she said, with some relief.

Normanby nodded solemnly, and then glanced down at her notebook. "I see you have more passers-by with names next," he said.

She wound the footage forward a little. "And here they are," she said, absently pointing to two figures as they appeared on the right hand edge of the screen. "John Meadows and Danielle Church. What a charming couple."

Normanby watched them as they staggered up Marsh Road. Meadows was tall and thin. His hair was grey, but Normanby could not make a reasonable guess as to his age. He wore a filthy grey hoodie and faded blue jogging bottoms with two white stripes down the seam. On his feet was a pair of trainers that had probably once been white. Lovingly cradled in the crook of his arm was a large, blue plastic bottle, like the ones that Normanby had seen dumped in the landscaped area. Staggering a respectful five paces behind Meadows was one of the most disturbing examples of womanhood that Normanby had ever seen.

Danielle was short and fat with a gait not unlike that of a gorilla walking on its hind legs. Her huge head was shaved nearly to the bone in an absurd contrast to the pink floral dress that she wore. On her feet was a pair of massive lace up boots which she stamped heavily down on the pavement in pursuit of her partner. Her head lolled about absurdly as she walked, in a way that suggested some kind of mental handicap, and she carried an identical blue bottle to her partner's.

"Real beauties, aren't they?" smiled Lou as she glanced back at Normanby's raised eyebrows.

"Friends of yours?" asked Normanby.

"Oh yeah," she replied. "I move them on out of there quite regularly. They sit for hours in there sometimes, drinking that shit."

"She's wearing very large boots," observed Normanby.

"I know," Lou replied, "but hers aren't Doc Martens. Besides, they didn't stay long enough to kill anyone last night."

Normanby watched in shocked fascination as Meadows bent and picked something up from the pavement, repeated the movement a few feet further on, and then put the items into the pocket of his scruffy jogging bottoms.

"Tab ends," said Lou absently, on catching Normanby's eye. "They pick them off the streets and roll them into new ciggies."

Normanby nodded without taking his eyes off the screen.

The strange couple marched up the path, through the gap in the fence towards Trilby Street. Seconds later they re-appeared and hurriedly went back the way they had initially come, back down Marsh Road and off camera to the right.

The screen showed an empty pavement with nothing but the occasional glow of headlights from passing cars.

"Well, I know you have to be thorough, Mr. Normanby, but I told you there was nothing worth seeing." Lou tried to keep the accusatory tone out of her voice, and more or less succeeded.

Normanby seemed not to have heard her. He was deep in thought, staring into space with a vague expression. Gradually, his brow furrowed and then, all of a sudden, his eyes became alert and he stared straight at her. "You said that Meadows and Church usually spend some time in the area behind the fence," he said.

"Yes," she confirmed. "It's out of the way, so they hang about there to drink."

"So, why didn't they do so last night?" he asked. "What made them turn back straight away with their bottles still full?"

The realisation dawned on her, even before he continued.

"I think something made them change their minds officer," he said. "Something, or someone."

"They've seen the killer," she said simply, feeling numb. "We need to find them!"

CHAPTER ELEVEN: A STATEMENT

Grant finished reading and put the documents back into the buff card folder. "Well," he said, "it looks like your forensics people agree with Normanby's theories about how Shafiq Hussein was attacked. Any more leads on the footprints and the cigarette ends?"

Doug Taylor shook his head. "Not yet, Mr. Grant," he said glumly. "It could be days before we get anything back from the lab. All that sort of work's been outsourced to the private sector now. All we have to go on is that the boots were Doc Martens, and the fag ends are apparently of a Russian brand."

"Russian?" said Mike Green. He had been standing a little way back and observing the conversation between Grant and Taylor.

Both men turned to look at him. "Is that significant?" asked Grant.

Green shrugged. "Maybe not," he said, "but you never know with those bastards lately, do you?"

Grant eyed him speculatively for a moment. He wondered if there might be something more to Green's remark but decided that now was not the time to ask. He turned back to Taylor. "If you get anything else, Doug, let me know. I'm okay to keep the file, yeah?" Without waiting for an answer, he tucked the file under his arm.

"Well, we'll be checking any local dodgy tobacco dealers we can think of, and a few of the local shops that sell smuggled cigs under the counter, but I don't think we'll find much," said Taylor. "To be honest, we stand a lot more chance with the press appeal."

"With the what?" Grant's voice was harsh. "I thought I told you to keep it under wraps for now!"

Taylor's face reddened. "Your Mr. Normanby told me I could investigate as normal from now on," he said defensively. "If you've got a problem, you take it up with him!"

"Oh, I will," replied Grant. He was seething.

"Well, it's too late now," said Taylor. "It's already in The Standard."

"Marvellous!" spat Grant.

"Well, don't blame me," blustered Taylor, beginning to get irate himself. "If you people don't communicate with each other, it's not my fault."

Grant gave a resigned sigh. "I know," he said, more calmly. "You weren't to know. It's bloody Normanby, getting in the way again. Just let us know if you hear anything Doug. I'm sorry I flew off the handle."

Taylor relaxed visibly. "Okay, Mr. Grant," he said. "I take it I should contact you first and not Mr. Normanby?"

Grant gave a slight smile. "Yeah, if you would, Doug," he said. He fished a pen and a used envelope out of his pocket, jotted down his number, and handed it to Taylor.

"I'll put it in my phone," Taylor assured him.

Grant nodded his thanks and headed for the door. Green fell into step beside him as they walked down the corridor.

"Sounds like Normanby's being a pain in the arse," said Green.

"That's putting it mildly," Grant replied, as lightly as he could manage. "If Hussein and his people panic and run, we're knackered!"

Green nodded thoughtfully. "What are you going to do?" he asked.

Tom Grant took a deep breath and let it out slowly. He had made up his mind what to do. It may cause problems later, but he was prepared to take the consequences. "I'm going to 'Q' branch," he said with a smile.

"Going where?" asked Green.

Grant shook his head and gave a small chuckle. "Doesn't anyone in the Service ever watch movies?" he asked. "I'm going to the Quartermaster and I'm signing out three trackers. No matter what happens, or where they go, I'm having Hussein and his little gang. Nobody is going to stop me; not The Colonel, and certainly not bloody Normanby!"

Mike Green looked impressed with Grant's resolve. "Well, if you're sure," he said, "but the Old Man won't be happy."

"Damn the Old Man," said Grant as they stepped out of the front doors into the cool, early evening air. He felt good about himself. He had a plan and he was sticking to it. That's how things got done, he told himself. It was all about making your mind up and acting on it, not pottering about playing silly bloody detective games like Normanby.

"You ought to cover your back," said Major Green, tentatively. "If the Old Man pulls you for taking out the trackers, you'll need to have a round in the chamber, so to speak."

"How do you mean?" asked Grant.

Green lowered his voice conspirationally, as if there could be someone to overhear.
"I think you need to put in a statement against Normanby, just in case," he said.

"A statement?" asked Grant.

Major Green nodded. "Yes," he said. "This is still your operation, Tom. Normanby shouldn't be ignoring your instructions like that. You need to have it on record that you signed out those trackers because Normanby's actions may well spook Hussein and his people into running."

Grant thought for a moment. "Well, you're right, of course," he said. "I don't like doing it, mind."

"Well, it's up to you mate," replied Green, "but you need to cover your back."

"Yeah," said Grant. "I suppose I'd better do it really."

Grant suddenly felt a little deflated. He didn't like Normanby particularly, but he wasn't happy about putting in a statement against a colleague. Still, as Green had said, he would be as well to cover his back. "Let's get back to the office and sign those trackers out before the Quartermaster goes home, then I can do a quick statement," he said.

"It's for the best," confirmed Green. "In fact, if you do it in 331, we can put it straight into the system for you. That way, it doesn't have to pass the Old Man's desk, and if it turns out you don't need it, we can just delete it from the system."

"I hadn't thought of that," said Grant. He felt a little happier. If the shit didn't hit the fan over his use of the trackers, the statement against Normanby would vanish into the ether and all would be well. He was beginning to feel extremely grateful for the technology at Green's disposal.

"Thanks, Mike," he said earnestly.

Green gave a little shrug. "It's a pleasure, mate," he said. "Listen, if we crack on now, we might have time to get a drink afterwards."

"Sounds good to me," said Grant. "I've got no plans."

CHAPTER TWELVE: CAT AND MOUSE

Normanby made a careful inspection of the card that Lou handed him before delicately placing it into the pocket in the back of his notebook.

"Thank you for all your help, Officer Fowler," he said.

She was in a much better mood than she had been half an hour ago. Her plans for the evening had been scuppered, but at least they had another lead to work on. The more she thought about it, the more she was convinced that Normanby's theory was correct. Meadows and Church had intended to go to their usual drinking haunt but had either been frightened off, or convinced to leave by the killer himself.

"I should be thanking you, Mr. Normanby," she said. "We're one step closer to finding our killer thanks to you."

Normanby inclined his head in a courteous movement that wasn't quite a bow. "The question is, Officer," he said. "Can we find Meadows and Church, and can they identify whomever they saw?"

"We'll find them, Mr. Normanby," she asserted, firmly. "I'll give D..Detective Sergeant Taylor a call and let him know, and Michelle's going to get her CCTV staff to put a message out on the Shop Watch Radios. Meadows and Church are pretty well known amongst the retailers and security around here, so someone's bound to spot them. On top of that, we'll have every Copper, PCSO and Environmental Enforcement Officer on this side of the city looking for them."

"That's excellent news, Officer," said Normanby. "Please contact me immediately if there are any developments, irrespective of the time."

She smiled at his archaic turn of phrase and wondered if he really spoke that way all the time, or if it was just an act. "We will," she said, flipping open the cheap mobile phone and tapping the two buttons that would ring Doug Taylor.

Normanby gave a wave of the hand and turned on his heel. He took a deep breath of the early evening traffic fumes and began walking towards the tube station.

The first streetlamps had begun to come on and some of the shops had turned on their interior lights, even though dusk was still an hour away.

The traffic was heavy as the evening 'rush-hour' was underway and doubtless had been for longer than an hour, Normanby realised, without a hint of amusement.

The first spots of rain landed as Normanby walked carefully down the concrete steps to the tube station. Soon, he was engulfed in the mass of commuters making their way home from their mundane jobs.

Two armed Police Officers watched the sea of bodies surging past, Heckler and Koch machine pistols slung across their chests, fingers resting gently on their trigger guards.

Normanby stopped at a vending machine and purchased a bar of chocolate. He surveyed the reflections of the commuters in the glass front of the machine as he waited for the chocolate bar to be dispensed. He noted, not for the first time, how many people walked around staring at mobile phones, oblivious to their surroundings. It was because of this that the man who was motionless and staring at a London Underground map stood out. It was somehow reassuring to see someone who actually still used paper.

Normanby retrieved his chocolate bar from the tray at the bottom of the machine and headed for the escalator down to the platforms.

The platform was alive with the echoes of conversations and trains in the distance. The familiar smells and sounds of the Underground during the rush hour assaulted Normanby's senses. He disliked the smell of stale sweat and it was everywhere down here. There were people who had been working in overly warm offices and shops, and those who simply did not bathe often enough.

Normanby made his way along the platform until he found an area that was not so crowded and stood with his back against the wall.

The constant stream of new commuters onto the platform brought the seething mass of humanity ever closer and Normanby felt the usual uneasiness of the journey through the bowels of the city.

He turned up the collar of his overcoat and eyed the people about him, a collection of disinterested cattle. Half of them stared ahead with lifeless eyes; the other half gazed hypnotically at mobile devices. Surely, he thought, there is no telephone signal down here. Are they all so intent on shutting themselves off that they will stare at any kind of application on their devices?

He saw the man with the Tube map again. The map was now neatly folded, and it protruded from his overcoat pocket. He looked around him, an interested, searching expression on his chubby features. The man was obviously not a Londoner, Normanby decided. If he stayed, though, he would eventually end up like the rest of them.

The singing of the tracks and the usual cacophony of bangs and rattles announced the coming of the train. Normanby pushed himself back as if trying to become one with the wall behind him. He waited until the train had stopped before he broke contact with the wall and started moving forward. The commuters were already forming a series of disorderly scrums before the doors opened on the train. They broke, here and there, some even letting passengers disembark before forcing their way into the cars and filling them like some kind of infection.

Normanby's heart was racing. He looked at his watch, then at the crowds in the tube train. He would wait for the next train, he decided. Having made the decision, he relaxed slightly and took a breath.

Suddenly, he noticed something that caught his attention and set his nerves on edge. The map man got back off the train and looked around with a confused expression. He did not even pause to look at Normanby, the only other person left on the platform.

The doors closed and the train pulled away with its grotesque ascending wail and attendant clattering.

The man pulled out his tube map, opened it out and began studying it as he ambled slowly towards the wall thirty yards along the platform from where Normanby stood. Beads of perspiration broke out on Normanby's forehead. When he lifted his hand he noticed, with some annoyance, that it was shaking slightly.

It was patently obvious that the man was following him, and Normanby began to convince himself that it was somehow connected to Shafiq's murder. Perhaps it was the killer himself, he thought, and he felt the flutter of adrenaline in his belly. He slowed his breathing and glanced sideways at the man, who was making a show of being confused by the Tube map.

The man was tall enough to be the killer, thought Normanby, but at the moment he was making no hostile moves, thankfully. Normanby still wished that some more commuters would hurry up and arrive on the platform.

He tried to remain calm and to go through the situation rationally. Whether or not the man was the killer, he was not showing any danger signals. There was, of course, a possibility that he might be following Normanby for some other reason, totally unconnected with the Hussein case. Normanby doubted this, however. His work was usually office based and he seldom came into contact with other agencies, let alone enemy agents, terrorists or hired killers. He was still absolutely convinced, however, that the man was following him.

He let out an almost audible sigh of relief when the first groups of passengers started to appear on the platform for the next train. Within the space of a few minutes the small, isolated groups of commuters had grown into another seething mass.

This time, Normanby decided, he would board the train, no matter how much he disliked crowds of people.

The train announced its impending arrival with its disturbing call of bangs, rattles and squeals from the darkness of the tunnel. Normanby stepped forward to lose himself in the mass of sweaty, ignorant, soulless bodies preparing to board. He risked a glance up the platform and caught his pursuer watching him. In that split second, Normanby could see that the man had realised that he had been spotted.

Normanby's anxieties began to return. It was clear now to both of them that the game was up. There was no more pretence, no feigned innocence. With this knowledge, a new game had begun; one which could turn out to be much more dangerous.

Normanby craned his neck to try and see whether the man had got on the train. Of course he would have…He weighed up his options. Should he try to disembark as the doors were closing, leaving his pursuer stuck on board? Whilst tempting, Normanby thought about the dangers. If his pursuer also managed to disembark, they would be alone on the platform. There may only be a few minutes before the next passengers arrived, but Normanby still didn't like the possibility. He was unarmed and relatively unskilled in any kind of fighting art that would be of use. The man was much bigger than Normanby and might well be carrying weapons.

The doors closed, along with the option of escape. Normanby stood on his tiptoes and anxiously scanned the car for any sign of the man. He stood there for long moments, drawing amused glances from one or two passengers. He looked like some kind of suited and bespectacled meerkat, scanning the horizon for predators.

Normanby felt another rush of fear induced adrenaline as he saw the man again. He was in the next car, shouldering his way through the commuters, slowly coming closer.

Normanby's breathing grew rapid. He began to wonder how much protection the crowd of people on the train would actually give him. He was reminded of many assassinations that he had read of. Back in the late '70's, Soviet Defector Georgei Markov had been jabbed in the leg with the ferrule of an innocent looking umbrella whilst standing on the steps of the British Museum. The umbrella had silently fired a tiny metal ball bearing laced with deadly poison. On crowded streets of the townships of South Africa, assassinations had been carried out using nothing more complex than a sharpened bicycle spoke concealed inside a rolled-up newspaper. One casual thrust could drive the spoke through a victim's heart…and of course, more recently, with the use of Plutonium and Novichock, there were countless ways to deal death silently, even in crowded places.

Normanby felt panic clawing at his reason. These things were real. These things actually happened. Despite his current role being primarily office based, his was a dirty, dangerous job…

The man had stopped at the end of the next car and was staring through the window at Normanby. There was no pretence at innocence now. Normanby's pursuer simply held him in his belligerent glare.

So that was how it would be, he thought. The man was not going to make his move here, in public, but the expression on his face made it clear that he meant to do Normanby no good.

Suddenly, looking back at the stony face through the glass, Normanby's mood was transformed. He was still afraid, his nerves were still shredded, but he felt the first flicker of anger. Who was this man that dared to terrorise him so? He gritted his teeth and stared back. They stood for a long moment; their eyes locked on each other. The man's eyes widened slightly, in surprise. Normanby maintained his cold, dead expression. He would not show his fear, however much he felt it.

The train clattered to a halt at the next station. Normanby's pursuer glanced at the doors as they opened. He wondered whether his target would make a run for it and try to give him the slip.

Normanby shook his head slowly and his thin lips drew back in an icy, hateful smile. As his resolve grew firmer, he noticed the other man blink several times. This heartened Normanby, who continued to stare. In his mind, he counted slowly, the voice in his head hissing the numbers in a spiteful tone. He had found that, by using this technique, concentrating on the numbers and locking his expression, he could stare down those who relied on confidence or bluster alone. Each number that Normanby counted out in his head beat back the fear and panic that had threatened to engulf his will. It had cleared a part of Normanby's mind where the seed of an idea had taken root and begun to grow.

As the train set off again, the other man's eyes flickered and broke contact with his own death-stare. Normanby nonchalantly removed his spectacles and cleaned them with a handkerchief from his trouser pocket. Not once did he take his eyes from his opponent throughout the whole process. In his mind, he carried on counting: "ninety-three, ninety-four," the rhythm of the numbers and the concentration keeping his thoughts from drifting. In a vacant space of his consciousness, where the fear had been beaten back, his plan was growing and developing, as if by itself.

Normanby put his glasses back on and pushed them with an index finger up to the bridge of his nose. The man was staring again, trying to re-establish eye contact. It was obvious that he felt a need to 'win' and regain his psychological dominance over his target.

Instead, Normanby contemptuously dismissed him and deliberately turned his back, whilst looking up at the line map on the wall of the car above the door. He would not play the game and he would not be a victim…

…At station after station, Normanby played his own game. He had become almost oblivious to the irritation of the people around him. At some stations, he would glance at his pursuer and make a slight move towards the doors. At one station, he actually disembarked and then, just as the man also got off the train, he leapt back on. He kept the doors jammed open so that his pursuer would have the chance to re-enter his own car. At each glimpse, he could see that the man was getting angrier and more frustrated by his antics.

At King's Cross, Normanby gave a little nod to the man and disembarked. He glanced around to see his pursuer warily eyeing him, whilst staying close enough to the doors to jump back on if needed. Suddenly, Normanby set off walking, rudely elbowing his way through the hordes of indignant, startled commuters. He stepped through the archway to the next platform. He did the same thing several times, moving from one platform to the other. He glanced back every once in a while, to check that he was still being followed.

When he was sure that his pursuer was still intent on catching up, he went to the escalators and headed for the surface. He glanced back to reassure himself that he had not been lost amongst the throng of people, and relaxed when he was sure that he was still being followed.

For the first time in many years, Normanby found himself enjoying the ambience of his journey through the city's underbelly. He actually paid attention to the posters on the walls as he sailed elegantly up the escalator. His gaze hung on an advertisement for one of the latest Movie releases. Perhaps, he thought, when this was all over, he might actually go to a cinema and watch it. How long had it been since he had entered a cinema? He recoiled from the thought: Too many painful memories.

The entrance to the Tube station announced itself with a gust of cold air. Whilst not actually fresh, the breeze was different from the lifeless combination of gasses below in the tube.

He breathed in, filling his lungs with the cold and damp. Despite the fumes and the filth that the city had spewed into the air, Normanby felt the cold breeze was like a bracing walk in the countryside. It was almost as if he tasted it for the first time.

He passed through the main entrance out into the open. A few steps took him up to street level. He looked up at the sky, now almost fully dark. The odd spot of rain fell, and he felt a strange joy in the thin drizzle.

Normanby felt that he was in the throes of an epiphany. Something was changing. Something real was happening. His fear had gone. He pulled the collar of his coat closed against the cold and walked slowly and deliberately down the street.

It was only when he came to a pedestrian crossing that he remembered to look around and make sure that he was still being followed. Assured that his pursuer was still behind him, he made his way to a small stationer's shop that he knew quite well.

The last two customers were at the tills being served and the shop assistant looked at him with disapproval as he entered.

"We're closing now sir," she said firmly.

Normanby fixed her with a determined stare. "That's alright," he said. "I know exactly what I want."

He went to a display of pencils by the counter and ran his fingers along the little pigeonholes until he found the section marked 'drafting pencils'. He selected two 8H pencils, the hardest that the shop had in stock, along with a pencil sharpener from a nearby display.

The other customers had been served and Normanby fished out the exact change to pay for his purchase. The shop assistant followed him to the door as he left and turned the sign that hung there to the 'closed' position.

Normanby stepped out onto the pavement and looked around. He saw his opponent across the street, half-heartedly pretending to look in an estate agent's window. It was as if he was no longer sure how the game should be played now that Normanby not only knew that he was being followed, but was actively encouraging it.

After waiting a moment to ensure that he had been seen, Normanby set off slowly back towards the Tube station. The streets had gradually become quieter as the main flow of commuters had already made their way out of the city.

Normanby momentarily felt a renewed flutter of anxiety when he found himself alone with his pursuer on a quiet side street. He glanced back and saw the man's right hand move into the front of his overcoat. He stopped and held his breath for a moment. The hand came out empty and Normanby looked around to see that a group of students had appeared around a nearby corner. He hurried on, back to the main road and the relative safety of the dwindling crowds.

He breathed a sigh of relief as he neared the station and saw that it was still quite busy. He knew that he did not have to look back and check any more. The man would still be following. He hurried down to the platform for the Victoria line and boarded the train that had just pulled in.

Just as before, the man boarded the next car and kept his eyes fixed on Normanby. Normanby turned his back on him and found an empty seat near the door. He took the pencils and the sharpener from his pocket and began honing the points until they were sharp as pins. He looked up at the line map above the door of the car: Kings Cross, Euston, Warren Street, Oxford Circus, Green Park, Victoria then Pimlico.

With eyes closed in concentration, he pictured the streets around Pimlico tube station. He would have limited time to get to the little side-street that he wanted. If any of the streets around it were deserted, his pursuer may indeed have a chance to act. He put the thought out of his mind and concentrated on the mental image of the alleyway in the forefront of his mind; of the big commercial waste skips and the constant coming and going of the staff of the restaurant that backed onto the far end of the alley.

When the train eventually stopped at Pimlico, Normanby moved fast. His pursuer was taken by surprise, and it took him a moment to realise that Normanby was making his way down the platform. Both men hurriedly shouldered their way through the smattering of commuters. Normanby elicited an obscene oath from one man as he barged past. He ignored it and pressed on, up the steps and onto the street. His nerves were jangling with a strange mixture of fear and excitement. The game was almost done, one way or another.

Normanby's hasty backward glance revealed that the man was picking up the pace. As he reached a street corner, Normanby turned and ran, full pelt, towards the alleyway.

The man jogged up to the corner where Normanby had turned off and saw him running down the street. He began to run after him, furious that after all of his games, the little man was now trying to escape. When he caught him, he decided angrily, he would make the little worm pay.

Normanby steamed into the alleyway and carried on running for a few paces before turning back a little and ducking behind the commercial waste bins that lined the side of the alley.

He was just in time, for a second later, the man turned the corner. He stopped, gasping from the exertion, and surveyed the alleyway and the bins. His hand went to the front of his coat and he stood motionless for a second.

There was a sudden bang as a door slammed at the other end of the alley. His prey must be escaping that way, he thought, and set off running again.
He had only made three or four paces when he saw a flash of movement to his right and slightly behind him. Before he had managed to turn his head, he felt a bolt of agonising pain at the top of his left leg, near the groin.

Normanby had stepped out behind him as he passed and rammed a sharpened pencil, with all his might, upwards between the man's legs and into the inside of his thigh.

The man went down in shock and pain, and curled up, gingerly feeling where the embedded pencil protruded from his inner thigh. He was making a muffled, whimpering sound through gritted teeth. He saw Normanby looming over him, another pencil grasped firmly in his left hand.

Fearing another attack, the man reached into his coat, struggling to reach the pistol nestling under his arm. Normanby's hand flashed down, ramming the sharp point of the second pencil into the exposed area above his thick overcoat where his neck met his shoulder. The man screamed as Normanby kept hold of the pencil and took a step back.

"Don't try it!" spat Normanby. "If you want to live, I suggest that you apply pressure with both thumbs just above the pencil in your leg. I have punctured your femoral artery and you will bleed to death very quickly unless you do exactly as I say."

His eyes wild with fear, the man gripped his leg and pressed hard with both thumbs, despite the pain. His hands and leg were bathed in thick, sticky blood.

Normanby waved the pencil in his hand menacingly in front of the man's face. His fear-stricken eyes followed the movement minutely. With his free hand, Normanby reached carefully inside the man's jacket and slipped the handgun from the shoulder-holster there. He stepped back two long paces, eyed the gun briefly and then slipped it into his own pocket. Without taking his eyes from his victim, he brought out his mobile phone and dialled a number from memory.

He held the phone slightly away from his ear and waited. There were loud tuneless pips followed by a recorded message. "The number you have dialled has not been recognised. Please hang up and try again," said the slightly plummy, yet authoritative voice. Normanby listened patiently as the message was repeated four times. His victim began to stir, as if he might attempt to get up.

"Sit still!" Normanby snapped, harshly, and the man capitulated under his icy stare.

There was a long bleep on the phone and Normanby spoke when it ended:

"This is Normanby," he said. "Code seven. Assistance required." He gave a brief description of his location and then hung up, before returning the phone to his trouser pocket...

CHAPTER THIRTEEN: THE RUSSIAN

Grant was getting bored with paperwork. So far, he had filled in three very complex forms to enable him to take out three small tracking devices.

Lieutenant Philips, the Quartermaster, pushed another form across the countertop towards Grant. "This is the last one, sir," he said.

Grant heaved a sigh of relief and peered down at the document. He ticked the boxes that needed ticking, signed the dotted lines that needed signing, and slid the completed form back to Philips, who eyed it carefully.

"That all seems to be in order, sir," the Quartermaster confirmed. "I suppose you'd like your trackers then."

"That would be nice," Grant replied, dryly. He looked at Mike Green with a tired expression as Lieutenant Philips disappeared through a doorway behind his counter.

"Just think how much paperwork you'd have to fill in to get an Aston Martin," said Grant with a wry grin.

The Quartermaster reappeared presently, carrying three small, brown cardboard boxes, each roughly the size of a cigarette packet. He placed them on the counter in front of Grant.

"Here we are sir," he said. "They're quite simple to operate…"

"That's fine Lieutenant Philips," said Mike Green. "I can give Mr. Grant all the training he needs in their operation."

Philips looked disappointed. "Very good sir," he said, glumly.

Grant picked up the boxes and thrust them into the pocket of his overcoat. "Thank you, Lieutenant Philips," he said with a smile.

"Let's go out and get that drink, Tom," said Green.
They walked together towards the doors, their footsteps on the concrete floor echoing through the dark basement. Grant pulled open the heavy metal door and indicated to Green to go first. He did so. Grant stepped out after him and let the door slam shut with a heavy bang.

"We can go to the King's Head if you fancy," said Green. "It's not far away and it serves a decent pint. I can give Toby Hughes a ring once he's been relieved and tell him to join us. We can see about how best to deploy those trackers with him."

Grant nodded. "Sounds good to me," he said. For the first time since his transfer to the Department, he was actually enjoying himself.

As the two men stepped out of the elevator on the ground floor, Grant's mobile phone rang. He looked at the number and gave a resigned sigh. "It's The Colonel," he said, and Green raised an inquisitive eyebrow.

Grant thumbed the 'answer' button. "Grant here," he said dully.

"You're not at your desk," said The Colonel. "Where are you?"

Grants teeth clenched in annoyance. "I'm on the Ground Floor, sir," he answered. "I was just leaving."

"Wait in the foyer," ordered The Colonel. "Normanby's just called in with a Code Seven on the emergency line. He's two minutes away from the office. You can come with me."

Grant was about to speak, but The Colonel hung up without another word. Green looked at him questioningly, and he gave a shake of the head in reply.

"It's Normanby," said Grant. "He's called in a Code Seven and he's nearby. The Colonel wants me to meet him in the foyer."

"A Code Seven?" said Green with a startled look. "That is serious!"

"Yeah," replied Grant. "You want to come for the ride?"
Green gave a little shake of the head. "I'd best not," he said.
"The Old Man won't want me poking my nose in. Let me know
how you get on."

He set off for the doors, leaving Grant standing, vaguely
disappointed, in the corridor.

"I'll see you up at the King's Head," Grant called, hopefully. He
was annoyed. Just when things had started looking up, bloody
Normanby had messed things up for him again. He looked
bitterly towards the foyer and saw The Colonel staring at him
and impatiently tapping his umbrella on the tiled floor. With a
sigh, Grant walked out to meet him.

"Come on Grant," said The Colonel. "My car's out front.
Normanby's location is just a couple of minutes' drive away."

The Colonel's driver, Hopkirk, had pulled the big black Jaguar
XF up to the kerb outside on double yellow lines. He revved the
throbbing engine impatiently when he saw Grant and The
Colonel approach. They got into the back of the car.

"You have the location, Hopkirk?" asked The Colonel.

"Yes sir," Hopkirk replied, easing the big car out into the sparse
evening traffic. "'Be there in two ticks."

"Do we know who Normanby's got sir, or why?" asked Grant.

"Not a clue," replied the Colonel, "but I thought it wise to take
precautions."

He leaned away slightly so that he could extricate a small
revolver from his overcoat pocket. Grant looked at it and felt a
pang of unease. "I'm surprised you could get one of those things
at such short notice, sir," he said.

The Colonel eyed him coldly. "It's amazing the things that one
can pick up from the Quartermaster," he said.

There was an uneasy silence in the car until Hopkirk pulled over on the roadside, a few yards from a deserted alleyway.

"It's down there sir," he said.

Grant got out and held the door open for The Colonel.

"Wait here, Hopkirk," The Colonel said into the open front window. He turned to face Grant and gestured with his umbrella towards to the alleyway. "After you, Grant," he said.

Grant nodded and both men set off towards the alley at a steady pace. The Colonel carried on for a couple of paces past the opening as if he were going to pass it completely. He gave a glance into it and then wheeled, almost theatrically along the cobbles, swinging his umbrella and tapping the ferrule on the floor with each step that he took. Grant followed a couple of paces behind him.

"'Evening Normanby," boomed the Colonel.

"Good evening, sir," Normanby replied, without looking around.

Grant saw the big man sitting on the floor, clutching his leg. Normanby was standing away in the shadows watching the man intently. In his left hand, he held a pencil, in his right, a pistol.

Grant leaned forward and peered at the gun. "Walther PPK?" he asked with interest.

The Colonel also leaned closer to have a look at the weapon. "Makarov," he said nonchalantly. "It's the Russian equivalent."

"Interesting," said Grant.

"Well, Normanby," inquired The Colonel, "aren't you going to introduce us to your friend?"

"I would sir," replied Normanby, "but he's not being very communicative."

The Colonel eyed the man with an expression like that of an old-time policeman confronting a young street urchin. "Well," he said. "Do you want to tell me why you've been following my operative?"

The man was sweating, in pain and fear. "*Ya ne ponimayu*," he hissed through gritted teeth. He gave a grunt of pain as he adjusted the grip on his leg.

Grant noticed something protruding from the man's inner thigh, just below his bloodstained hands. "What's that in his leg?" he asked.

Normanby did not take his eyes from his captive. "A pencil," he said mildly.

Grant glanced down at the other sharp pencil in Normanby's left hand. "You bloodthirsty little bastard, Normanby," he said in shocked amusement.

The Colonel tapped his umbrella on the ground impatiently. "Answer the question," he said patiently.

"*Ya ne ponimayu*," the man hissed again.

"He's foreign," said Grant.

The Colonel slowly turned his gaze on Grant and raised an eyebrow. "Brilliant, Grant!" he said.

Grant flushed slightly. "I mean, we need to know what language he's speaking," he said.

"He's speaking Russian, Grant," said The Colonel. "He's saying that he doesn't understand."

"Oh," said Grant.

"He's lying," said Normanby.

The Colonel turned his glare on Normanby and waited for an explanation. Normanby looked back at him levelly. "I told him to grip his leg above the pencil because his femoral artery was punctured and he did exactly as I told him," he said.

"Jesus, Normanby!" said Grant. "You punctured his femoral artery?"
"I've absolutely no idea, Mr. Grant," the little man replied. "I'm not a surgeon."

The three of them stood in silence for a long moment, looking at the agonised man on the floor. Eventually, The Colonel spoke. "Grant," he said. "Go and wiggle the pencil in his leg. Let's see if it loosens his tongue."

The man's eyes widened in fear.

"What?" said Grant. "Wiggle the pencil? Why me? Can't Normanby wiggle it? He's the bloodthirsty little bastard that put it there!"

The Colonel glared and looked as though he was about to shout.

Normanby gave an impatient sigh. He carefully tucked the pistol into his waistband and slipped his remaining pencil into the breast pocket of his jacket. He took a moment to ensure it was in perfect alignment with the three pens that nestled in the pocket, and then he stepped forward.

The man on the floor recoiled automatically and gave a yelp as the movement caused his leg to straighten. "No!" he hissed. "This is torture!"

"He speaks English then," observed Grant, dryly.

The Colonel glanced back at him impatiently. "Grant, go and tell Hopkirk to bring the car down here. Tell him we've got a guest staying the night," he said.

Grant turned and walked back to the main road.

The Colonel took a deep breath and returned his attention to the man on the floor. "We're going to get someone to look at your leg," he said in a loud, slow voice, as if he was talking to a simpleton.

The man on the floor sneered at him. "You cannot take me anywhere," he said in a thick Russian accent. "You must release me. I have diplomatic immunity!"
The Colonel stared at Normanby with a comedic expression of puzzlement. Normanby stared back blankly, and then used a forefinger to push his spectacles up to the bridge of his nose.

"I'm terribly sorry," boomed The Colonel, turning his attention back to Normanby's victim. "I don't understand your Russian language. We'll try to find you an interpreter once we've looked at your leg."

The alleyway was suddenly illuminated by bright headlights, and it was only then that Normanby noticed how dark the night had become. The lights dimmed and the front of the big Jaguar XF became visible. Grant and Hopkirk got out and came around to the front of the car.

"Put a blanket on the back seat Hopkirk," The Colonel ordered. "We're taking this man back and I don't want the upholstery ruined. Normanby and Grant, you can ride in the back with him."

Hopkirk went to the boot of the car. He brought out a plastic-backed, tartan picnic blanket and spread it out on the back seat.

The Colonel glanced from Normanby to Grant expectantly. "Well, get him in," he ordered impatiently. "We haven't got all night!"

Normanby and Grant looked at each other with resigned expressions, and then walked towards the man on the floor. As they approached him, he began to protest. "This is not allowed," he squealed, his voice rising in panic. "I am Sergei Illyitch Kurylenko," he babbled. "I work at the Russian Embassy! I have Diplomatic Immunity!" He gave an agonised screech as the two men each grabbed an arm and hoisted him to his feet, dragging his hands away from his leg.

"Don't worry Old Chap," said The Colonel, blithely ignoring his protestations. "We'll soon get that leg fixed up."

Normanby and Grant bundled the gasping, whimpering Kurylenko into the back of the Jaguar, and then positioned themselves on either side of him. The Colonel climbed into the front passenger seat and twisted around to look at him.

Kurylenko was trembling in a combination of pain and abject terror. He felt the barrel of the Makarov pistol jabbing into his ribs as Normanby and Grant glared at him and made it clear that there was no escape.

"If you wish to remain alive," said The Colonel slowly and menacingly, "you will remain silent until you are asked to speak."

Kurylenko's flabby chin quivered as if he were about to cry. With a gargantuan effort, he maintained his composure and managed a slight nod of acquiescence.

Hopkirk had started the engine. "The back doors, I assume sir?" he said.

The Colonel nodded. "Yes," he replied, "and I suppose we'd better have a reception group waiting for us."

Hopkirk set the car in motion and edged it towards the end of the alleyway. "Already arranged sir," he said, as they turned out into the road.

There were four stern looking men waiting for the big Jaguar as it pulled into the underground car park. Only when the electronic shutters had closed did The Colonel get out of the car and speak to them. "This one needs some medical attention," he said. "Make sure it's provided on site, and then put him in room twelve. Two guards outside at all times, and no-one speaks to him without my say so."

The four men nodded silently and in unison.

Normanby and Grant climbed out of the car as the men approached. Kurylenko gave a little yelp as the men manhandled him out of the car, but he offered no resistance. His spirit was entirely broken, and his face was a drained mask of total despair. The Colonel stepped over to Normanby and Grant as Kurylenko was led away in silence. "I'll need a full report on my desk tomorrow morning, Normanby," he said.
"Yes sir," replied Normanby, gingerly handing him the pistol.

"Can I go now sir?" asked Grant. "I have things to do."

The Colonel eyed him sternly. "Not yet," he said. "You can take Normanby home in your car first. He's had a busy night."

Grant opened his mouth to protest, but seeing the look on The Colonel's face, he decided not to bother. "Yes sir," he answered flatly. He set off walking towards his own car, trying to hide the look of bitterness on his face. "Come on Normanby," he said.

The Colonel watched the little man follow Grant to his car and shook his head sadly.

In the car, Grant glanced across at Normanby who sat in the passenger seat and stared straight ahead. "What the Hell was all that about, Normanby?" he asked.

Normanby took long seconds to answer, and Grant noticed that the little man was shaking with some kind of delayed shock. "Kurylenko was following me, Mr. Grant," he said. "He was following me, and he was armed!"

"This is getting bloody serious," Grant mused. He reached into his overcoat pocket and brought out the three plain card boxes containing the trackers. Normanby glanced at them, and then looked questioningly at Grant.

Grant stared back sternly. "It's none of your business what they are, Normanby," he said, before Normanby even had the chance to ask. He reached across and put them in the glove compartment in front of the little man.

"I've got to stop off for a moment before I take you home, Normanby," said Grant. "What's the best way to the King's Head from here?"

Normanby shrugged. "I don't really go out drinking, Mr. Grant," he said lamely.

"Of course you don't," sighed Grant, starting the engine.

*

The King's Head was a lively and well decorated public house, filled with a well-to-do clientele. Grant pushed through the door and looked around. Most of the customers seemed to be smartly dressed office workers from the city, meeting up for a few drinks after a hard day of extreme wealth creation.

He scanned the crowd and saw Mike Green sitting at a table, chatting amiably with two other men, one of whom Grant had seen once or twice in the corridors at work.

"Hi Mike," Grant said cheerfully.

"Tom, you made it!" smiled Green. "What are you drinking?"

"Well, nothing just yet," replied Grant. "I've been instructed to give Normanby a lift home."
"Normanby?" said Green. There was the usual hint of contempt in his voice as he said the name.

Grant gave a little shrug. "Yeah, I've left him in the car," he said, smiling. "He doesn't really go drinking." He pulled a face as he said it.

Green and his comrades gave assorted chuckles and guffaws at the remark, and Grant guessed that they too must know Normanby. "As soon as I've dropped him off, I'll come back here if you're still going to be here," he said hopefully.

Green looked at his companions questioningly and waited for their nods of assent. "Yeah, we'll hang about," he said, "as long as you're not going to take too long. How comes you're driving him about anyway?"

Grant held an expression as if he were about to give a whistle. "Oh, he's been having fun and games," he said. "I'll tell you all about it when I get back."

When Grant got back to the car, Normanby was sitting silently and staring straight ahead. He was still trembling slightly, and his face looked very pale.

"Are you alright Normanby?" asked Grant. Normanby gave a little nod and remained silent.

"Alright Normanby," Grant sighed. "Let's get you home. You'll feel much better once you're tucked up at home in bed with a cup of cocoa." He started the car and pulled out into the street, wondering how quickly he could get Normanby home and then return to the King's Head.

CHAPTER FOURTEEN: MEADOWS AND CHURCH

Lou Fowler looked at the text message on the cheap little mobile phone and scowled. "*You stood me up for Normanby???* □" it said. She gave a little snort and carefully thumbed the keys to send a message back: "*Sorry. Make it up 2 U 2morrow. Cud B worth it,*" she typed. She wished that she could use her smart phone and type freely, rather than having to scroll through the letters to send a text, but she knew it would not be safe to do so.

Eventually satisfied with the message, she hit the button to send the text and put the phone in her pocket. She knew it could be hours before the message was even read, let alone responded to.

Mr. Normanby was a strange little man, she thought. He seemed so weak and ineffectual, and he had such odd little habits and quirks. When he had first come to the CCTV suite, she had disliked him, had thought him pompous and arrogant. After watching through the footage with him, however, she had found that her opinion had changed. She wondered how many other people would have drawn the conclusions that he had done, and so quickly. She herself had already seen the CCTV footage and had thought nothing of Meadows and Church walking up the path towards Trilby Street and then returning immediately. Normanby had seen it though, and when he had explained his conclusion, it had made perfect sense.

She thrust her hands into the front of her yellow tactical vest for protection from the cool evening breeze and set off walking. It would be worth spending an hour or two to track down Meadows and Church. She might well get some very useful information from them with the right approach. She thumbed her radio and reminded the staff at CCTV that she was still looking for them as she walked slowly back towards Trilby Street.

She had been walking for twenty minutes when the call came through on the radio from a security guard at a local mini mart. Meadows and Church had been in to buy white cider and they were walking towards Marsh Road.

She felt a flicker of excitement and quickened her pace. "Let me know as soon as you pick them up on camera please, CCTV," she said. "I want a word with those two."

She considered asking if there were any regular police in the area, then decided against it. She wanted to be the one to speak to them. If she could find out who the killer was, it would be a huge feather in her cap.

Lou broke into a jog when the message came through that Meadows and Church had been picked up on camera near the roundabout at the bottom end of Marsh Road. She could make it in just a couple of minutes if she got a move on, and neither Meadows nor Church were known to be particularly fast. Indeed, their lack of speed was one of the reasons that they were so well known to the Police. They couldn't even outrun the average supermarket security guard, and got themselves caught with laughable regularity whenever desperation led them to attempt a shop-lifting spree.

As Lou neared the bottom end of Marsh Road, she caught sight of them and slowed to walking pace. She consciously steadied her breathing after the exertion of jogging. They were sitting on a low wall, deep in animated conversation as she approached.

"'Evening you two," said Lou happily as she walked over to them.

Meadows looked up and gave an exaggerated sigh at the sight of her. "Aw, what now?" he whined in his thin, nasal voice. "We're not doin' anythin'."

Church spat on the ground and bared what few teeth she had. "Yeah," she concurred, "not doin' anythin'."

"I didn't say you were, did I?" said Lou lightly. "I've just come to see how you are."

Church nursed the big blue bottle of cider to her breast. "We're just restin'," she said. "Ain't even opened this, so we're not drinkin' or nothin'."

"That's alright Danielle," said Lou. "How comes you're not up at the fence tonight?"

Danielle didn't answer, and instead stared at the ground. It was Meadows who finally spoke. "You know why," he whined. "It's full of coppers up there innit? It's 'cause that Paki got stabbed!"

Lou hid her distaste at his turn of phrase and tried to remain casual. "Oh, word's got around about the murder then?" she asked.

"Yeah, a Paki got stabbed," chuckled Church, exposing the massive gaps between her sparse, blackened, rotten teeth.

"Does it really make a difference whether he was Asian or White?" asked Lou.

Meadows laughed; a harsh burst of high-pitched cackling. "Does it matter?" he echoed. "Of course it matters! It's one less of 'em, innit?"

This time, Lou failed to hide the contempt in her voice when she spoke. "What's the matter John?" she said. "Steal your job, did he?"

He looked absently back at her for a long second as the implication of her words sank in. "Hey!" he said, "I've done my bit. I was in the army! You've got people who've done it and people who 'aven't." He made a gesture with his hands, palms up, as if weighing the two alternatives.

Lou suddenly had an idea. "Yeah, I wanted to speak to you about that," she said. "The homicide detectives have been wondering about the way in which Mr. Hussein was murdered. They seem to think it might have been someone with military training."

She waited for his slow, alcohol addled thought processes to catch up. As soon as she saw him comprehend the implication that he might be a suspect, she continued. "You were up that way last night, weren't you?"

She saw shock and fear dawning in his eyes. His mouth opened and he shook his head. "Don't deny it John," said Lou. "I've just come back from the CCTV offices up town. You two were seen going towards Trilby Street just before Mr. Hussein was murdered."

"That don't mean nothing!" Meadows whined. "Just 'cause somebody goes near…"

"John," Lou interrupted. "A man is murdered and a known offender with previous military service is seen going to the murder scene at the time of the murder. Of course, C.I.D. will want to talk to you!" She sounded so matter of fact that she almost believed the lie herself. No doubt that belief would make it all the more convincing, she reflected.

Meadows was visibly shaking with fear. Church was looking at him dully. The seriousness of the situation had not yet dawned on her.

"John," Lou said softly and reasonably. "The police are looking for somebody to lock up in order to avoid a race war, and you fit the bill perfectly. Now, I'm trying to be straight with you. Whenever I've had to speak with you, you've always been alright with me…Look, *I* don't think it's you, but let's face it, it looks bad the way they're seeing it. I'm trying to help you out here, mate, because you've always been straight with me. There's coppers all over town looking for you. I'll help you if I can, John, but I just need something to work with."

Meadows' lips moved slightly, as if he was reciting a silent prayer, but no sound was forthcoming. It was Church who broke the pregnant silence. "It weren't him," she said. "I know it weren't him."

"Shut it Danielle," snapped Meadows, his eyes wild with fear and confusion.

Lou looked defiantly at him. "No Danielle," she said, still staring into Meadows eyes. "Tell me, because if I don't find out the truth, John's probably going to end up locked in Bellmarsh Prison along with all those Islamic Extremists for a very long time."

Church's dull expression barely changed. "It weren't him," she said again. "It were that Polish Skinhead."

"Danielle," hissed Meadows through gritted teeth, "he'll kill us! Shut it!"

Lou held her resolve. "Shut up, John," she said firmly. "Tell me everything you know Danielle."

Danielle stared back at her blankly, her mouth was moving as she worked her way through the words that she was about to say. "It were that new Polish bloke," she said at last. "'E's a right 'ard bastard. 'E were stood at end of street. When we went up, 'E pulled this big knife out an' told us to get out." She stopped and looked at Meadows for a moment then directed her gaze to the ground.

Lou looked at Meadows and his gaze also fell to the ground. "Is that right John?" she asked. There was no response. "Is that right?" she asked again, more firmly. He nodded silently.

"So, who is this new Polish bloke?" she asked.

CHAPTER FIFTEEN: THE TRACKERS

Normanby got out of the car and closed the door carefully. He turned his head and looked back as the window opened and Grant leaned across the passenger seat. "Just get an early night, Normanby," said Grant. "You'll be fine in the morning."

"Yes, I'm sure I will," Normanby replied without conviction. "Thank you for the lift, Mr. Grant."

Grant gave a small wave, and then set off without waiting for Normanby to return the gesture, which he didn't. Normanby watched the car shrink into the distance with a vague feeling of sadness. He always had that feeling when being dropped off from a car. He knew why, and he tried to forget it.

When Grant's car had totally disappeared from view, he turned away from the road and faced the row of imposing Victorian terraced houses before him.

He pushed open the large, iron gate and stepped into a small but immaculate garden. Pausing for a moment, he took a deep breath and relished the scent of the roses that grew in the borders of the garden. His keys were in his hand with one big key extended and ready as he mounted the three steps leading to the huge panelled front door.

Once inside, he scanned the big bare hallway with a darting glance, and then closed the front door and locked it. There was a strong smell of boiling vegetables coming from the flat to his right. Mrs. Turner, the owner of the building would be making stew, he thought.

Normanby went to the door of his own flat to the left and checked it for signs of entry, as he always did. Satisfied that everything was as he had left it that morning, he unlocked the door. Once inside his flat, he carefully locked the door behind him.

The living room of the flat was large. It was cheaply furnished, but immaculately clean and tidy. Along the back wall, by the door through which he had come, was a long sideboard with a table lamp at one end and an old stereo music centre at the other. Normanby clicked the lamp on and looked about him. Under the big bay window, was a small drop leaf table with an old dining chair at each side. Covering most of the scrubbed floorboards was a large carpet square.

In the centre of the room, facing the big open fireplace stood two rather tatty armchairs of matching plain brown fabric design, with a small side table between them. In one alcove next to the fire, on the same side as the window, was a large office desk with a desk top computer connected to an old CRT monitor, and two shelves running the full length of the alcove. The shelves carried a small, neatly arranged collection of books, small boxes and stationery supplies in labelled jars. The other alcove was taken up by floor to ceiling cupboards which were an original feature of the building. Next to the cupboards, against a side wall was a portable television on a small table. The television's position to the side of the room bore witness to how little it was used. Beside the television set was a door which led out to the small kitchen, bedroom and bathroom at the back of the flat.

Normanby held out his hand, fingers outstretched, and noticed the visible tremor. The events of the evening had disturbed him greatly. He felt weak and drained. Taking a deep breath, he went to the big, built-in cupboards. He took out a bottle of Haig Club single grain whisky, and a glass, then set them on the table between the armchairs. He poured himself a two-finger measure and looked at the bottle before carefully placing it back in the cupboard. He sat down in one of the armchairs, loosened his tie and unfastened his shirt collar.

He took a small sip of the whisky and rolled it around his mouth before swallowing it. His nose wrinkled at the taste of it. After taking a moment to compose himself, he reached into the inside pocket of his jacket and noticed that his hand was trembling again.

He took two identical small items from his pocket, arranged them neatly on the side table and stared at them worriedly. He felt another involuntary shudder as he looked at them. He had that sickening feeling that he may have done something very foolish in taking them, something that may have terrible repercussions which now could not be undone.

The items were small gunmetal grey blocks, each slightly smaller than a matchbox, with a tiny switch and a dial that could only be moved with the use of a screwdriver. They were trackers, and he had taken them from the glove compartment of Grant's car whilst Grant had been inside the King's Head.

Normanby was well aware that Grant had begun acting outside of the orders of The Colonel, and that he had formed some kind of association with Major Green. He had his own reasons for disliking and distrusting Green, but he could not help feeling disappointed about Grant. He had, in the few short weeks that he had known him, begun to feel that the man had the makings of a good operative, despite his annoying manners and his over-familiar attitude.

CHAPTER SIXTEEN: A NIGHT ON THE TOWN

The King's Head was busy, and Grant was enjoying the jovial banter of the company all around him. He swerved to avoid a rotund, red-faced gent who stepped back to give a bellowing laugh at some amusing remark made by one of his own party.

Grant happily congratulated himself on not spilling a drop from any of the three pints of Guinness that he held, and continued weaving back to his own party.

"Nice manoeuvring!" said Mike Green as Grant proudly placed the three complete pints on the table.

"I have a particular set of skills," replied Grant with a smile. For the first time since his transfer to the department, Grant was happy. Perhaps, he thought, there was a future for him here after all. He pushed one of the pints across to Mike Green, and the other to Toby Hughes, who had joined them shortly after Green's other two friends had left. Grant had learned that they were also part of Green's team; Jacko Goodman and Andy Burnett. They had gone to relieve Toby in the task of watching Ali Hussein's flat, and he had come to report back, before accepting Grant's kind offer of a pint.

Grant liked Toby, he decided. He was an affable and good-natured young Cockney in his mid-twenties. He was thin and wiry, with blonde hair, cut very short to disguise the fact that, despite his youth, his hair was going very thin on top.

"I was just telling Toby," said Green, "that we might be able to free up some man-hours watching Hussein's gang now we've got the trackers."

Grant gave a nod. "As long as we can deploy them," he said.

"Don't worry about that," Green replied, clapping a hand on Toby's shoulder. "If anybody can find a way to deploy them, Toby can."

"No worries Guv," smiled Toby, proudly. "I'll 'ave a good look tomorra'. Just let me 'ave the trackers when yer can."

"You can have them whenever you need them Toby," said Green before turning his attention back to Grant. "So, what about this Russian that was following Normanby?" he asked, eagerly.

"I dunno," said Grant. "Normanby seems to think that he followed him from the CCTV offices. I mean, he didn't really look like a brutal killer to me, but maybe there's something in Normanby's theories, what with the Russian cigarettes that he found at the scene of Shafiq Hussein's murder."

"I can't see it myself," said Green. "I still think Ali Hussein's people did Shafiq in. His cover must have been blown."

"Well," said Grant. "I'm going to have a word with the Old Man tomorrow to see if we can get anything out of this Kurylenko bloke."

Toby finished off his pint in one long, thirsty draught. "Well," he said. "I'll leave you gentlemen to oil your thumbscrews. I've got a busy day tomorra', findin' an openin' to get at these bleeders. Drop them trackers off when you get chance, Guv. I'll 'ave somethin' worked out."

He got up and gave Grant the kind of firm, dry handshake which, for some reason, always impressed him. "Nice meetin' yer, Mr. Grant. See ya' tomorra' Guv."

Grant and Green murmured their farewells and watched him weave through the crowd to the door. "Seems like a good guy," said Grant.

"Yeah, he's useful to have around," nodded Green. "Once he's been freed up from watching Hussein, you could put him on keeping an eye on Normanby."

"Normanby?" said Grant, failing to hide his astonishment. "Why?"

"Well," said Green, "you know yourself that he's not exactly a team player. I think you ought to know exactly what he's up to. After all, he does seem to be doing his own thing and not keeping you in the loop."

*

"You're sure that's where he's staying?" said Lou Fowler, looking up at the grimy window.

"Yeah. There!" said Danielle. She and Meadows were shuffling their feet uncomfortably, and looking around, their nerves in shreds.

"Right," said Meadows. "We've shown you where he lives. We're not doin' any more. We're off!" He set off walking and, after a moment, Danielle went plodding along behind him.

Lou glanced at them, thought about calling them back, and then decided not to bother. They wouldn't be too hard to catch up with if this turned out to be a dead end. She just wanted to ensure that the man was at home, then she would call for back up to bring him in. "Don't leave town," she called to Church and Meadows, "I might want to speak to you later."

She stood for a moment in the overgrown patch of wasteland and looked up again at the window in the back of the run-down terraced house. This could be big, she thought. If Church and Meadows were telling the truth, she had found where the number one suspect in Shafiq Hussein's murder lived. She thumbed her radio, and then thought better of it. She didn't even know the address for the place, she realised.

She set off through the chest-high weeds, towards the end of the block. Her heart was pounding with excitement. At last, she thought, she would prove herself to them all at the station. No-one would be able to say that it had been handed to her. She had done this herself...

She drew level with the back gate of the property, which led into a back yard with a couple of dilapidated out-buildings. She walked past, heading for the end of the block, just metres away. Once she had the street name and house number, she would call it in and wait for back up to arrive.

Suddenly she heard a sound behind her, but before she could turn, she felt an arm about her neck. She tried to bend her knees, lower her centre of gravity to perform the *seoi-nage,* shoulder throw that she had learned in Judo class...She was too late. She felt a huge hand press against the back of her head, high up, forcing her neck against the tightening arm. She brought her hands up and grabbed the arm, but her strength suddenly drained from her. Her vision became blurred, and then darkness grew rapidly around her. She felt the world drawing away from her. Then there was nothing...

*

"Well," said Grant, looking forlornly at the last inch of Guinness in his glass, "I suppose I'd better make tracks."

Mike Green looked at him with a hint of disappointment. "Oh, you're going already? The night's still young!"

Grant looked around him and noticed that the customers in the King's Head had begun to thin out. "Well, it can't be far off closing time," he said.

"Oh, there's bags of time yet," said Green. "I was going to invite you to my club if you're up for it."

"Your club?" said Grant. "Well, I guess I could give you a lift there, but I'm pretty close to the limit." He held up his almost empty glass in explanation.

"Don't worry about that, old man," said Green. "You get me to my club, and I'll make sure you get home safe and sound."

Grant wasn't sure. "Well," he responded. "I'll take you to your club and drop you off…"

"Stop worrying," said Green. "You're not just one of the Colonel's pen-pushers anymore. You're a Secret Agent now." He chuckled at the sight of a proud smile on Grant's face. "Look," he continued. "Jacko and Andy will be finishing at Hussein's in a few hours. They'll drop by at the club to report to me. If you give them your keys, we can get Toby to take car home for you when he's done his last stint, and we can stay on at the club."

"But I have to be in work tomorrow," protested Grant.

Green waved a hand, as if swatting a fly. "Oh, you only need to show your face," he said. "You're heading up the operation. We can be out in the field taking it easy tomorrow."

Grant wasn't entirely convinced, though Green was making a strong case. Obviously that's the way things were done in Green's team. "Well, go on then," he said. "At least, we'll see when I get to the club."

Green clapped his hands happily. "Good man!" he exclaimed. "I knew you had the balls to do things in style!"

Grant drank down the remains of his Guinness with some trepidation. "Well," he said. "In for a penny, in for a pound."

They left their empty glasses at the bar, said their good nights to the bar staff and went out into the car park. Grant got into the driver's seat and waited whilst Green stood beside the car and made a call on his mobile phone.

"Hello Jacko?" he heard him say.

Whilst waiting, Grant reached across to the glove compartment and opened it to reassure himself that the trackers were still there. He lifted one of the boxes out and was surprised at its weight. He didn't remember them being so heavy. He was about to open the box and look inside when the passenger door opened and Green got in. Grant handed him the box automatically.

"Ah, the trackers," said Green, slipping the box back into the open glove compartment and shutting the door. "We're all set. Jacko and Andy will meet us at the club and Toby will take your car back."

Grant started the engine. "Well," he said. "You'd best direct me to this club of yours."

*

Gorszky had to act fast. He made a mental effort to slow his breathing, which had become rapid due to both the exertion and the excitement. He looked down at the unconscious woman at his feet and then checked around the pouches on her belt and the pockets of her tactical vest. There were no handcuffs anywhere. What was this country coming to when Police did not even carry handcuffs?

His hand went to the big knife on the back of his belt as he frantically looked around for something with which to secure her. Just as he was becoming resigned to the idea that his only option would be to silence her permanently with the knife, he noticed the washing line in the next yard. He breathed a sigh of relief. With luck, he could secure her and still have time to catch the two who had brought her here.

He took two steps towards the yard with the washing line, then, cursing himself, he returned to the unconscious woman. Frantically, he yanked the various pieces of equipment from her person: Two walkie-talkies, a body worn camera, a small P.D.A., and two mobile phones. How disorganised these people were, he thought, to need all this equipment and yet send Police out with no handcuffs or weapons. He stuffed the various gadgets into the pockets of his combat trousers and darted off to cut down the washing line. He needed to get her secure and silent very quickly and catch up with the other two before they could interfere any further…

CHAPTER SEVENTEEN: THE NAPOLEON SOLO
SMILE

She was beautiful. Her dark, slumberous eyes half closed as her full lips parted in a smile. Noticing that she had his attention, her eyes widened and her thick, dark eyelashes fluttered slightly. Her lips began to pout into the shape of an 'o'. She turned her head this way and that, as if surveying everyone present, but her eyes stayed on one man at the table and the coy smile played about her lips again as their eyes met. "Place your bets please, ladies and gentlemen," she said.

Grant tried to pull his gaze from her in order to see where Green was, but he couldn't. Her beauty was captivating in the extreme and every time he thought of looking away, her eyes sought his.

A small sound to his left broke the spell for a moment and he glanced down to see the cocktail glass which had been placed next to his left elbow.

"Vodka Martini," said Mike Green. "What else?"

"Did they mix it the way I asked?" asked Grant.

Mike Green gave a silent sigh. "Two measures of Vodka, one of Vermouth, a half measure of Limoncello and a dash of Angostura bitters, shaken over ice until it's very cold, and with a slice of lemon," he recited.

Grant smiled, lifted the glass by its long stem, and took a sip. "Then it's not just a Martini," he said. "It's my masterpiece. I present to you, 'The Dame Judi'."

His eyes went back to the woman, and he saw the mischievous smile. He looked straight back at her, his own eyes dancing with laughter. He kept his lips set in a neutral, almost thoughtful pose, then let the smile grow slowly across his face. This was what he called his 'Napoleon Solo smile'. He had practised it many times since first watching his childhood hero, Robert Vaughn, on TV many years ago. It was one of his secret weapons in the art of seduction, and it worked for him more often than not. Her own smile grew in return, along with one challenging, provocative raised eyebrow.

"Thank you, Napoleon," he muttered, almost silently. He picked up three chips from the pile in front of him and placed them squarely on the red thirteen square on the green baize.

The little silver ball jumped and danced in the whirling carousel of the roulette wheel. It tantalised the players like a free-spirited temptress, briefly offering a promise to one, before darting away to tease the next.

Grant did not notice where the ball landed, so captivated was he with the woman; her face, her figure, her slender brown arm reaching down to clutch the edge of the table in front of her.

"Red thirteen," she announced, her eyes gazing into his.

"Good lad!" said Mike Green. "You're doing well at this."

Grant gave a shrug. "Well, it's a game of luck really," he said.

"Then you're a lucky man," replied Green. "Napoleon would approve!"

"Napoleon?" asked Grant, startled.

"Yes," replied Green. "He always thought it was important for his Generals to be lucky."

Grant smiled. "Oh, *that* Napoleon," he said.

Grant stared back into the woman's eyes. "I think I am lucky, Mike," he said. "I think I am."

"I want you to come and meet someone," said Green.

Grant shot him an annoyed glance. "Now?" he asked.

Green's gaze slowly tracked to the woman, then back to Grant. He smiled. "Don't worry, old chap," he said. "She'll still be here when you get back."

The woman had already pushed Grant's chips across the table with her croupier's rake and he gathered them up. He thought for a second, then selected one of the higher denomination chips and slid it back across the table towards her with a wink. She gave an almost imperceptible nod and a coy smile in return.

Grant scooped his impressive pile of chips into his jacket pocket and turned to Mike Green. "Okay," he said, with a touch of impatience. "Lead the way."

They went out of the small casino area of the club and into a large, oak panelled hallway. To one side was an open doorway to a quiet, but spacious bar area, and further along an opening barred by an ornate rope barrier and a sign indicating that staff only were allowed beyond that point. To the other side was a large, imposing oak door with a brass plaque screwed to it. The lettering on the plaque read: 'members only'. Green pushed through the door and with a jerk of the head indicated that Grant should follow.

The oak panelled theme was carried on beyond the door which opened into a large, opulent reading room. One long wall was lined with floor to ceiling bookcases, filled with immaculately arranged bound leather volumes. There were four leather Chesterfield sofas at right angles to the wall, facing each other in pairs, with large, solid coffee tables between each pair. The opposite side of the room was dominated by massive windows hung with heavy red drapes. In front of the windows stood pairs of leather club chairs, with side tables between them. Each table was stacked with newspapers.

At the far end of the room stood a huge and ornate open fireplace, which had logs crackling satisfyingly in the grate. At each side of the fireplace, half facing the hearth was a high-backed chair, each with its own side table. In one of the alcoves beside the fireplace there was another door marked 'Private'.

There were four other men in the room. Two of them were sat, talking quietly on one of the Chesterfield sofas. The other two were sitting quietly in the fireside armchairs.

"I half expected to see the Old Man here," muttered Green.

"He's a member?" asked Grant, worriedly.

"Oh yes," Green replied. "It's a bit late for him though. He's more of a Sunday morning man from what I gather."

"Well, what am *I* doing here?" asked Grant, feeling very much out of his depth.

"Seeing what's open to you," Major Green replied. "Your ship's come in, mate. You don't have to spend your life as a little pen-pusher like Normanby any more. This is your future, if you want it. I can get you recommended and signed up now if you like."

Grant sighed loudly, eliciting a contemptuous glare from the slightly built, bespectacled man in one of the armchairs by the fire. He averted his eyes. "Oops," he whispered, smiling at Green. "I don't think he likes me."

Green glanced at the man and gave a slight shrug. "Who cares?" he said. "That's Dominic Moore. He's been a member here for years. He's a banker." There was contempt in his voice. "Tom," he continued. "We defend this country from all sorts of threats. If anybody has a right to a slice of the good life, it's us."

Grant had to concede that the man had a point. "Well, yes," he said, "but how much are the membership fees here? I mean, I'm not exactly the best paid man in the Department."

"You'd be surprised," said Green. "The casino and the bar bring quite a bit in, so the fees are quite low. They're more concerned with the quality of the members than large fees."

"Well, I suppose it's a nice place." Grant mused.

Green stared at him then suddenly broke into a quiet chuckle. "It's more than that, Tom," he said. "This club is a clearing house for information in our business."

Grant didn't quite follow, and his face made that fact clear.

"Look," said Green. "There's Dominic Moore. When I said that he's a banker, I didn't mean a manager at your local high street branch. Sat across from him is his old friend, Jason Steele. Steele's the Managing Director of one of this country's most exclusive Private Security Companies. They offer high level close protection and personal security to the great and the good, along with services to industry like industrial espionage investigations, insurance investigations, hostage rescue, you name it."

"Sounds like they get more excitement than us," said Grant.

"They probably do," Green agreed. "What I'm saying is that the people who come to this club are World Class players, Tom. This place can be a very important source of information, and a very good source for useful contacts."

Grant looked again at the two men who leaned close to each other, deep in whispered conversation. He wondered how many deals and decisions that affect the nation might be made here.

"...And, here on the sofa," Green continued, "we have Sammy Parsons." As he said the name, one of the two men on the sofa looked briefly towards him with a slight smile. "Sammy is an import and export mogul. He's already worth about twenty million and that's probably going to double within the next year. He's also a very useful contact for people in our business."

Grant looked at Sammy Parsons and thought about how much he stank of money. He was a well-built man, with a physique honed through hard work and dedication in the gym. This was apparent even through the immaculately tailored blue pin stripe suit that he wore. He was tanned, with perfect white teeth. His hair was short, well groomed, and blonde. His beard, of the same shade as his hair, was little more than a perfectly honed thin strip that followed the line of his jaw. As he sat forward on the sofa with his elbows on his knees, his sleeves were drawn back to reveal expensive, diamond studded gold cufflinks. He wore a gold Rolex watch on one wrist and a gold bracelet on the other.

Parsons was in quiet, but good-natured conversation with a plain looking, overweight man of middle-eastern appearance. The man looked to be in his fifties with a bald patch and a somewhat unkempt moustache. He wore a cheap and ill-fitting light grey suit which looked creased and unkempt, in total contrast to Parsons' sartorial perfection.

"Once Sammy's finished talking to his guest," said Green, "I'll introduce you. In the meantime, let's take a seat."

Within a minute of them sitting down in the nearest of the remarkably comfortable club chairs, they were approached by a tall, thin man with close cropped grey hair and a long, hawk-like nose. He was dressed in traditional butler's attire, replete with white gloves. He stood with a military air, almost to attention as he greeted them. "Good evening gentlemen," he said quietly. "Can I get you anything?"

Green gave him an automatic nod of greeting. "'Evening, Watkins," he said coolly. "I'll have a Scotch, thank you."

"Any particular preference, sir?" asked Watkins.

"Oh, the good stuff," said Green, dismissively.

Watkins turned his attention to Grant, and raised an eyebrow inquiringly.

"Do you have a Laphroaig?" asked Grant.

"Of course, sir," replied Watkins with an approving nod of the head.

"Yeah, that's what I'll have too Watkins," chipped in Mike Green, "with ice and soda."

Watkins glared at him for a second, his nostrils flaring with suppressed indignation. With an effort, he relaxed his features and looked back at Grant who shook his head slightly. This seemed to be enough to calm the man down. He gave the slightest of bows directly to Grant, threw a sharp glance in Green's direction, and then disappeared through the door towards the bar.

"Snob," muttered Green when the man was out of sight.

Grant suppressed a smile. "Do you know him?" he asked, innocently.

Green nodded. "He's been here about a year," he said. "Got the job because he's ex-Royal Artillery, from what I can gather. Still, if all he managed to come out of service with is a bit of parade ground bull, I suppose that waiting's as good a job as any for him." There was bitterness in his voice, and Grant decided not to pursue the line of conversation further.

Watkins returned with the drinks balanced on a silver tray. He placed one glass, with a generous measure of whisky on the side table at Grant's elbow. "Your whisky, sir," he said pleasantly.

He placed the other glass on the table close to Green without a word, and then followed it with a small bottle of soda water. He held the tray to his chest like a shield and gave a slight bow. "Enjoy your drinks, gentlemen," he said, before taking his leave.

Grant saw movement out of the corner of his eye. He glanced across and saw that Parsons and his companion had stood up. They hugged briefly, and then shook hands. Both men were smiling. The other man said something into Parsons' ear and they both grinned. The man seemed almost to bow before he finally turned and stepped away. Before he had even reached the door, Watkins was there to wish him good evening and to ensure that everything had been to his satisfaction.

Grant looked back towards Parsons and saw that he was standing, hands on hips like some kind of pantomime pirate, a huge happy smile on his face. He shot a look at Mike Green and saw that he was smiling too.

Green stood, picked up his drink and walked across to where Parsons was standing, giving Grant a gesture with his head to follow. Grant took a moment before he got up so that he could hang back and observe.

Green and Parsons faced each other for long seconds, their faces impassive. Suddenly, they both broke into huge smiles and threw their arms out to the sides in some kind of personal gesture, Green spilling a little of his drink as he did so. "You old dog!" said Parsons, happily.

The two men in the high-backed armchairs stirred. One gave an impatient sigh, and then they both got up to leave the room, each of them giving Grant a contemptuous glare as they passed him on the way to the door.

He turned his attention back to Green and Parsons and saw the smiling and back-slapping of two old friends. "Tom, come over here and meet Sammy," said Green.

"I didn't realise that you two were old friends," said Grant, stepping forward with a bemused smile.

"Friends and comrades," said Sammy Parsons in a distinctive gravelly Essex accent. "I worked with Mikey back in the day. Bloody hero he was an' all. He saved my life more than once, and most of the lads' too!"

That figured, thought Grant. In fact, it explained a lot about Green's persona and his methods: The relaxed and amiable way that his team responded to him, his disregard for the pen-pushing and the slow methodical work of the rest of the Section. Yes, thought Grant, Green certainly fitted the profile of a war hero, of a man of action rather than words.

Grant noticed that Parsons' hand was extended towards him, and he responded, smiling. He was rewarded with a bone-crushing but hearty handshake, and Parsons' smiling eyes looked into his own, assessing him. It was as if Parsons was reading him in that split second. He hoped that the appraisal was positive.

Parsons gave a sudden laugh and let go of his hand as if he had read Grant's mind. "Yeah! He's alright, this lad, Mikey," he said. "He could do with firming up a bit in the gym, but he's got potential."

Grant was pleased at even the conditional approval, and both he and Sammy looked at Green.

"He wouldn't be here if he didn't have," Green said with a smile. "Sit down fella's," he continued, "and we'll get down to business. Tom:" He turned to Grant, who was seated to his right on the Chesterfield. "I do believe that I have a little gift for you...or rather, Sammy has."

Grant was baffled. He looked at Green, then past him, to Parsons who was sitting to Green's left.

Parsons reached into the inside pocket of his immaculate suit and withdrew a bulging, brown, DL sized envelope. He chuckled at Grant's confusion. "Mr. Grant," he said happily, "I believe you'll find this very 'andy in your ongoing investigation."

"What is it?" asked Grant, taking the envelope.

"You tell 'im, Mikey," said Parsons, and both men looked at Green.

"Ali Hussein," Green began, "is a terrorist, and an evil little bastard. We know this much from the reports that your agent, Shafiq, sent to you. We know that he and his team are planning something big, something that will make every other terrorist attack in this country seem like nothing more than a slapped arse. Something that big needs finance, lots of finance. Shafiq had already mentioned in some of his reports that Ali Hussein was dealing in drugs. The natural assumption, indeed the assumption that you made in your own reports, Tom, is that Hussein was just making a bit here and there as a small part of a supply chain somewhere."

Grant was literally on the edge of his seat. He looked at the envelope, then back at Green. "Well," he said. "Shafiq told me he always has plenty of cash knocking about, but just the kind you have to live a decent lifestyle and have a better flat than someone in his job normally would have. I take it you're saying he was much bigger than that."

"Oh yes," said Green. "Much, much bigger. Hussein's been checked out quite thoroughly in terms of incomings and outgoings. He lives quite well, very well, in fact for a cleaner in a shopping centre, but there's been no proof of where the money's coming from, until now. He hasn't been getting funding directly from Islamic State or any other terror group. If he had been, our partner agencies would have found it by now. I figured that the money must be coming from somewhere, so I looked a bit closer at Shafiq's reports about drug deals. I started it think, 'what if these deals are bigger than we suspected?' That's when I got in touch with Sammy."

At this point, Grant glanced across at Sammy Parsons questioningly. "No, Tom," Parsons said with a chuckle, "I'm not dodgy. Well, I'm not *that* dodgy, but I do know the import and export business. I move products around the world. I have a lot of fingers in a lot of pies. I get offers and requests from a lot of people who really *are* bloody dodgy! Normally, when I get that kind of interest, I politely refuse to 'ave any part of it, then forget it ever 'appened. When Mikey told me it might be financin' terrorism though, I did a bit of diggin'."

"In short," continued Green, "what Sammy's obtained is credible intelligence of huge shipments of Heroin being delivered to the UK, linked to Hussein. The Heroin is coming from Afghanistan via Pakistan. In short, the smack-heads on our streets are directly funding the same Taliban bastards that have spent years trying to kill our troops. If we pick him and his gang up on that, we take him out of circulation. More importantly, we can stop his plot before it even gets off the ground."

"Jesus!" Grant exclaimed softly. He looked at Parsons with awe. "That's bloody marvellous work, mate."

Parsons chuckled. "It's for Queen and Country," he said, "and the standard agent's fee, of course."

Green threw his head back and gave a short laugh. "You tight bastard!" he said jovially, and then brought out an envelope of his own, this time in white. He then produced a printed sheet of A5 paper from his pocket. He handed both items to Parsons who pocketed the envelope and carefully read the printed sheet. He plucked a gold Parker pen from his pocket, signed the sheet and handed it back to Green.

Green checked that the signature was correct and carefully folded the piece of paper before putting it away. Both men looked back at Grant, who was staring at them, open mouthed.

"It's all above board here, Tom," said Green. "Sammy is my agent. Despite the fact that he's a multi-millionaire, he's paid the agreed agent's fee for the information that he provides."

"I could charge a lot more for that," said Parsons, nodding to the envelope in Grant's hand, "but I won't. All the money I get for working as an agent gets donated to Help for Heroes. Not all the lads that come back get all the breaks that I did."

Grant was dumbfounded and he sat in silence for several seconds, to the obvious amusement of the other two men. "That's bloody marvellous," he said at last. He raised his glass. "Regnum Defende!" he said earnestly, before swallowing down his drink.

CHAPTER EIGHTEEN: GORSZKY

"Slow the fuck down, Danielle," gasped Meadows, jogging through the long grass and wincing as he stubbed his toe on a stone in the undergrowth. "Just wait for me a minute!"

Danielle stopped dead, her breath coming out in a consumptive pant. She hugged the blue plastic bottle close to her, upright between her large sagging breasts and leaned forward, breathing heavily. "'Am not stayin' there," she announced with all the authority that she could muster. "If 'E finds us, 'E'll kill us!"

Meadows finally caught up in a tired, lumbering trot, and bent forward beside her, gratefully sucking in air. "'E's not gonna find us, is 'E?" he gasped. "Lou's gonna get 'im! There'll be armed coppers waitin' for 'im. They'll shoot the Polak bastard an' that'll be the end of it!"

Danielle looked unconvinced. "'E's an 'ard bastard," she said.

Meadows chuckled. "Not 'ard enough to stop an MP5 or a Glock," he said knowingly. "Them armed coppers is tooled up to fuck! They'll get 'im. We're alright. Trust me, I know 'ow they work."

Danielle looked at him and smiled, baring the few brown teeth that she had. "Are you sure Johnny?" she asked. She was uncertain, but strangely more lucid than she had been in years.

"Yeah, I'm sure," he said, and he was smiling too. "We'll be alright as long as we're clever. We always manage, don't we?"

They set off walking again, through the long grass. "We just got to stay out of the way for a bit, that's all. Keep off the roads and lie low. The coppers'll get 'im and they'll not bother us..." Meadows was saying.

Suddenly, Danielle stopped walking and turned to look back. The look on her face changed from puzzlement, to shock, and then despair. It was only then that Meadows heard the rustling of the grass behind him. He turned and the look on his face mirrored that on Danielle's.

"Do not run," said Stanislav Gorszky. "I want to ask you some questions."

Meadows and Church stood as if rooted to the spot, dumbstruck and terrified.

"What did you tell the Police lady?" barked Gorszky.

Danielle was the first to speak. "Didn't tell 'er nothin'," she stammered, and her voice cracked on the last word.

"You are lying to me," said Gorszky, slowly and patiently. "I saw you bring her here." He stepped up to Meadows and stared down into his eyes.

Meadows was shaking, and his knees felt very weak. "I didn't tell her anything," he said, swallowing several times before continuing. "I swear it!" His eyes flicked to Danielle in desperation. "It was 'er!" he said.

Gorszky's eyebrows raised, and his head turned to look back at Danielle.

"Lyin' bastard," she spat. "It weren't me!"

"Oh dear," said Gorszky with great amusement. "Somebody is lying to me." His massive arm suddenly tensed and shot forward, throwing his big, clenched fist into Meadows' body with the force of a cannonball. The blow struck directly into Meadows' solar plexus, knocking him backwards and down. He lay on the floor with his knees drawn up, and made a whooping sound as he fought to breathe against the agony and the uncontrollable spasms of his diaphragm.

Gorszky looked down at him and spat to show his utter contempt for the weakling. He turned to look at Danielle. She was rocking backwards and forwards on the balls of her feet, trying to decide whether or not to run.

Gorszky pulled the big knife from the sheath at the back of his belt. "Yes," he said. "Run!"

Her chin quivered and tears welled up in her eyes. She knew that it was hopeless, knew that she had no chance of outrunning the big man. She ran anyway, dropping the plastic bottle at her feet and lumbering off into the long grass.

Gorszky satisfied himself that she was heading across the wasteland and that she would remain visible in the moonlight for some time. He glanced down at Meadows, still curled up, gasping on the ground.

An idea came into Gorszky's head, and he quickly put the knife away before dragging Meadows up to his feet and casually turning him around. He put an arm around Meadows' neck from behind, forcing the windpipe into the crook of his own elbow. He brought his other arm up to complete the hold, and squeezed.

Meadows had been too terrified to put up any kind of struggle. He made a quiet, guttural sound and then his body went limp.

Danielle could run no more. She fell to her knees and retched before desperately dragging in another lungful of air. He hadn't caught up yet, she thought. Maybe she had lost him. Maybe Johnny had kept him busy.

A flicker of hope started to grow in her mind. It was immediately snuffed out as she felt the vibrations of his heavy footsteps through the ground at her hands and knees. She began shaking as a strong hand gripped the back of her dress and dragged her back to her feet. The stitching at the seams ripped slightly under her weight as she allowed herself to be pulled upright and held there. She wasn't sure if her legs would support her, they felt so weak.

"I'll do anythin' you want me to," she said desperately. "You can do anythin'." She heard a harsh, contemptuous laugh over her shoulder.

"All I want to do," said Gorszky, "is this!"

Danielle felt a sudden, agonising pain in her back as the knife was plunged into her. She gave a groan through gritted teeth as her legs buckled, and she sank back down to her knees. Gorszky let her fall to her right and she lay, mouth quivering as the pain began to wash away with the last panic-stricken vestiges of consciousness. He leaned forward and thrust again with the knife. As he yanked the blade free, he felt the blood spatters hit his face. He thrust again, and again, and again…

CHAPTER NINETEEN: THE DIRTY GAME

Normanby put down the six-page paper copy of the report that he had been checking. He ensured that the bottom edge of the report was perfectly aligned with the edge of the desk. When he was finally satisfied with the arrangement before him, he opened the top drawer of the desk and then glared at it angrily. Amongst the carefully arranged contents of the drawer, he noticed that the two boxes of staples were not stacked together. One of them had, instead, been stacked on top of the box of paper clips.

There could only be one answer, he surmised. Somebody had been in his desk drawer. He glanced accusingly at Grant's empty desk, and then sat back in his chair, thoughtfully. He would report the matter to The Colonel upon his arrival, he decided.

He toyed absently with the three pens, the pencil and the small electricians' screwdriver in his breast pocket, finally selecting a pen. He took out the notebook from his inside pocket and opened it to the page already marked with the day and date. Checking the time with the clock on the office wall, he made a neat entry in the notebook.

At 0845, Normanby was surprised to hear The Colonel's footsteps, interspersed as usual with the click from the ferrule of his umbrella on the tiled floor of the corridor outside room 131. The Colonel's walk was always a business-like march, but today the footsteps had an added degree of urgency.

The door burst open, and The Colonel stepped in. He stood ramrod straight and looked around the room. His gaze rested for a second on Grant's empty desk, then moved slowly to Normanby. "Good morning, Normanby," he boomed.

"Good morning sir," said Normanby. "You're early."

"Things to do, Normanby. Things to do!" The Colonel replied. "Where's Grant?"

"Grant usually starts at nine o'clock sir," said Normanby, "or at least, claims to do so on his timesheets. In actual fact, he usually turns up at around ten past." He took off his spectacles and wiped them with a handkerchief from his trouser pocket. When he replaced them on his head, he noticed that The Colonel was still watching him with raised eyebrows. Normanby looked quizzically back.

"I'm sensing an absence of domestic bliss between you and your colleague," said The Colonel. "Now would be a convenient time for you to spit it out."

Normanby thought for a moment. "I'm beginning to have some reservations about Mr. Grant," he said. "Since he began working with Major Green, he seems to be bypassing protocols. I also have reason to believe that he may have been searching my desk."

"Really?" said The Colonel.

"Yes sir. Someone has been in the top drawer of my desk," Normanby announced, "and until Lancer and Cole return from their current assignment, Mr. Grant and I are the only persons currently occupying this office."

"And what do you keep in your top drawer, Normanby?" asked the Colonel.

"Well, stationery, sir," said Normanby.

The Colonel's jaw hardened. "Stationery?" he said. "Are you complaining to me because Grant might have stolen a couple of your paper clips?" He turned angrily towards the door. He was about to reach for the handle when Normanby's voice stopped him.

"He's withdrawn trackers from the stores, sir," said the little man. "Did you authorise that requisition?"

The Colonel turned his head slowly back to Normanby. "No," he said thoughtfully, "I didn't. Did Grant tell you himself that he'd taken out the trackers?"

"I saw them sir, when he drove me home," Normanby replied. "He put them in the glove box of his car before stopping off to visit Major Green at a public house."

"I see," said The Colonel. "Why do you think he has them?"

"Well, my first thought," said Normanby, "was that he wanted to keep an eye on Ali Hussein and his people. I can't see why though, as Major Greens' team have them under surveillance."

The Colonel walked towards Normanby and looked at him very closely. Suddenly, his face broke into a smile, and he slowly reached out and withdrew the electricians' screwdriver from Normanby's breast pocket. He held it up and examined it closely before replacing it. Normanby remained perfectly still.

"Of course, if Grant were to, ah, *misplace* the trackers it would be his problem, wouldn't it?" said The Colonel.

Normanby allowed himself a small, shy smile. "I suppose it would sir," he said. "Of course, if Mr. Grant and Major Green are operating outside of Operational instructions, it may be useful to have an idea of where they are at any given time."

"And would we have such an idea?" asked The Colonel.

"We might know where Mr. Grant is," Normanby replied non-committally, "if, for instance, one of his trackers had got lost in his car and suddenly become activated."

"That is an interesting possibility," said The Colonel, with a smile. "I'll sign a chit for you to get a receiver from the Quartermaster, just on the off chance that something like that should happen." He took a deep breath. "First, however, we have other business to attend to. I believe that a chat with our guest in Room twelve is long overdue."

CHAPTER TWENTY: KURYLENKO

Sergei Illyitch Kurylenko was afraid. He sat in the sparsely furnished room, little more than a prison cell, and looked at the untouched breakfast on the table in front of him.

Since he had been brought here, no-one had spoken a word to him. He had been put on a stretcher and carried here from the car park by two large, silent men dressed in black. They had ignored all his questions and protestations, and had transferred him to the plain but surprisingly comfortable bed in the corner.

They had left the room silently and locked the large metal door behind them, leaving him alone and terrified in the harsh light of the single bright 150-watt bulb in the ceiling. A few minutes later they had returned and stood at each side of the door whilst two white coated men with a simple trolley full of medical equipment had entered.

Kurylenko's nerves had been shredded at that moment, expecting some terrible torture. Instead, the two white coated men had expertly and gently treated the wounds in his leg and his neck. Once again, all of his protestations and questions had been completely and stoically ignored.

After a short while, Kurylenko himself had decided to remain silent. There seemed to be no point in speaking, and furthermore, he was beginning to feel that the one-sided conversation was putting him at a huge disadvantage.

After treating him, the men had left the room, along with the two guards. They had left behind a pair of clean, neatly folded pyjama bottoms to replace the bloodied trousers which they had cut away to the top of his leg so that they could treat the wound in his thigh.

He had lain on the bed for perhaps an hour, wondering about his fate before the light had gone off, engulfing him in total darkness. He was not sure how long he had lain in the dark with panic gnawing away at his mind before sleep had finally taken him.

When he had awakened, drowsy and thick-headed, the light in the ceiling was on and the two black clad men were back in the room. The only furniture in the bare, white walled room, other than the bed, was a small table, about three feet square, and two plain wooden chairs. One of the two guards had a tray in his hands, which he placed on the table before he and his colleague left and locked the door.

Kurylenko had carefully got up from the bed, gingerly testing his leg by standing slowly. He had been surprised to find it virtually painless, though the muscle felt very stiff. He ignored the pyjama bottoms, instead choosing to remain in his own shredded and bloody clothes, and he sat down on one of the hard wooden chairs facing the door.

He looked at the contents of the tray in front of him. It contained a plastic bowl of cornflakes, a smaller, plastic bowl of sugar, a plastic jug of milk, a Styrofoam cup of black coffee and two plastic spoons. He wondered if the food and drink had been contaminated with drugs. It seemed likely that they wanted information from him, and he was sure that the use of truth drugs was not beyond them. From what he had been told about the British, he didn't doubt that their experts would have created truth drugs far more efficient and subtle than the sodium pentathol injections of the cold war years.

He had some things to be thankful for, he told himself. After all, if they had wanted to kill him, he would be dead by now. They had already shown that they were not above murder, he thought bitterly. If they didn't want information, he surmised, he would have ended up just like Shafiq Hussein.

Kurylenko gave a start as he heard a key in the lock of the door. He quickly wiped a bead of sweat from his forehead and took a deep breath, trying to steady his nerves for whatever ordeal was to come.

The door swung slowly open and Kurylenko's breathing quickened. There, in the doorway stood the little bastard who had stabbed him. He looked like nothing more than a nervous little clerk, yet Kurylenko knew that the man must be some kind of psychopath. One of their top assassins, no doubt.

The little man stared at him, then lifted a finger and pushed his spectacles up onto the bridge of his nose. He stepped into the room and stood by the open door. Another man entered; the leader who had turned up with the one called Grant after the little man had attacked him.

The older man stepped into the room. "Close the door, Normanby," he boomed. As Normanby obeyed, The Colonel pulled out the other chair and sat down facing Kurylenko. "Good morning, Mr. Kurylenko," he said mildly. "How's the leg feeling today?"

Kurylenko stared back sullenly.

"Still having trouble with your English?" asked The Colonel. The Russian gave no answer.

Normanby folded his arms and sighed impatiently. Kurylenko's hateful gaze fell upon him, and a slight smile played on The Colonel's lips. "Why were you following Normanby last night, Mr. Kurylenko?" he continued, "and why did you kill Shafiq Hussein?"

Kurylenko's face registered surprise for a moment, then he let out a short, harsh chuckle. "You are playing games," he spat. "You killed Shafiq! It was your Mr. Grant, or….him!" His spiteful gaze was directed to Normanby on the last word.

The Colonel's eyebrows had raised slightly at the use of Grant's name. Obviously, Kurylenko had heard the name last night in the alley, but the accusation seemed totally absurd. "Why on Earth," The Colonel asked, "would either Grant or Normanby want to kill Mr. Hussein?"

"You know why," replied Kurylenko. "Why would you ask me such stupid questions? It was your people who killed him! I am only here because it is your country's policy to blame Russia for everything!"

The Colonel glanced over his shoulder at Normanby and saw an expression of puzzlement that mirrored his own. He turned his attention back to Kurylenko and continued. "Enlighten me," he said. "What makes you think that they, or indeed, we had anything to do with Shafiq Hussein's death?"

"Do not play games with me," Kurylenko hissed.

"Sir," said Normanby, as if Kurylenko was not present, "if Mr. Kurylenko really does believe that either myself, or Mr. Grant killed Shafiq Hussein, it does raise an interesting possibility."

"Oh really, Normanby?" said The Colonel, sarcastically without taking his eyes from the Russian.

"Mr. Kurylenko, what is your interest in Mr. Hussein, and why did you follow me last night armed with a pistol?" asked Normanby.

"You know why, you murdering bastard!" spat Kurylenko with savage hatred.

"Well," interjected The Colonel reasonably, "if we already know, then you won't be giving away any secrets by telling us, will you?"

Kurylenko remained silent, but a flicker of confusion showed through the hatred on his face.

Normanby gave a sharp intake of breath as a sudden realisation hit him. "Shafiq Hussein was your agent too, wasn't he?" he said.

"You know he was," replied Kurylenko, icily, "and that is why you killed him!"

"I assure you, Mr. Kurylenko," Normanby replied, "that I did not kill Mr. Hussein. I am also quite certain that you didn't kill him either."

The Colonel turned slowly in his chair until his baffled stare fell upon Normanby. "Explain," he said, simply.

"I believe that Mr. Kurylenko is telling us the truth sir," said Normanby. "I can think of no other reason for a Russian spy to be interested in the murder of Mr. Hussein, unless he knew that Mr. Hussein was an agent. I think it is safe to assume that Mr. Kurylenko followed me, armed with a pistol because he believed that we had killed Mr. Hussein. He no doubt intended to interrogate me at gunpoint to find out how much we had learned about his own involvement. It isn't the only possibility, I admit, but from Mr. Kurylenko's reaction to our questions, it does seem by far the most likely one."

Both men looked at Kurylenko questioningly. He stared back, open mouthed and in utter confusion.

"If you're telling us the truth, Mr. Kurylenko," said The Colonel, we may have a 'mole' in our department. If you value your life and your freedom, you need to convince me that our 'mole' is not working as your agent."

"You think I would help you?" sneered the Russian.

"I think that you would like to know who really killed your agent Shafiq Hussein," said Normanby. "I think that you would also like to see that person brought to justice. I very much doubt that you would be able to extract retribution personally. If you were a professional G.R.U. assassin, I think that you would have been armed with a more up to date weapon than the pistol that you carried, if indeed you would have been relying on a firearm at all. That particular Makarov is quite an old one, as far as I can ascertain from its markings and condition. It would have been issued back in the days of the KGB. It's a Cold War relic. I suspect that it has been lying around in a safe at the Russian embassy for years. Furthermore, if you really were a professional killer, or indeed any kind of killer, I doubt that I could have incapacitated you and disarmed you with a pencil." Kurylenko's face turned red with embarrassment and anger at the final blow to his pride.

"Believe it or not," said The Colonel, staring straight into Kurylenko's eyes, "we want the same thing, you and I. I do not want any sensitive or confidential information that Mr. Hussein may have given you. I simply want to know who killed him. You have my word that if you help us find his killer, you will be released without charge and allowed to go free."

Kurylenko blinked back tears of fear and confusion. Normanby was right, he admitted to himself. He was no professional killer. He was little more than an office clerk who had been offered an important task, one that he had taken to impress his colleagues at the embassy, especially Yuri, the young idealist who looked up to him with admiration. Most of all, he was now, way out of his depth, due to the way things had developed with Shafiq. How much dare he tell them, he wondered. Where was the line between helping the British to achieve a common goal, and giving information to an enemy state? After a long moment, he made up his mind. "It is Mr. Grant," he said. "He is your 'mole'!"

The Colonel looked shocked. He glanced at Normanby and saw that the little man's expression was neutral. "What makes you say that?" asked The Colonel.

Kurylenko spoke slowly, careful not to give any more information than he had to. "Shafiq first came to me because he no longer trusted Grant," he said. "He gave us very important information about a serious threat which he had already given to Grant. He also gave Grant information about drug deals that were being used to finance a terrorist plot. When he gave that information to Grant, the deal was, how do you say, 'thwarted'. This was not done by the Police. It was done by a gang who stole a percentage of the drugs. He became suspicious of Grant, and then he was murdered. When I saw Grant and Normanby at the murder scene, I thought they must be working together. Then I saw Normanby go to the Closed Circuit Television office. I thought, maybe he is covering his tracks and destroying evidence…"

Normanby and the Colonel looked at each other with shocked expressions. "Grant!" hissed the Colonel. "If this is true, I'll have his balls!"

CHAPTER TWENTY ONE: THE MORNING AFTER

Tom Grant gradually became aware that he was awake when he felt the room lurching and spinning. He was warm under the duvet, laid on his back with a weight pressing down on his chest that he could not immediately identify. He breathed in and caught the mesmerising mixture of scents that brought flashes of memory from the previous night, cascading into his mind.

He slowly opened his eyes and saw her head resting on his chest, her beautiful raven hair unkempt and tangled. The feeling of her warm flesh against him brought back images in his mind of the night before. He felt a thrill of adrenaline rush through him as he was stirred by the thoughts.

She stirred, slowly opening her eyes, and she lifted her head to look at him. For a long moment they stared into each other's eyes. A small smile grew at the corners of his mouth. It was infectious. Her full lips widened into a smile of their own. "Good morning," she said quietly. "What time is it?"

He glanced at the clock on the bedside table, and then did a double take. It took a second or so for the information to sink in. "Jesus Christ!" he exclaimed, struggling to raise himself from beneath her. "The Colonel will have my balls! It's a quarter to ten!"

She moved aside with an amused chuckle. "You're late for work?" she asked. "Was it worth it?"

He stopped moving for a moment, sat on the edge of the bed. He looked back over his shoulder at her and smiled. The tension and worry seemed to drain from him. "Yes," he said. "It was."

"That's alright then," she said lightly. "Will you get into a lot of trouble for being late?"

He thought for a moment. "Not too much," he said. "I'm sure I'll be able to wing it." He reached out and ran a finger softly down her cheek, stopping just next to her mouth. She grabbed the finger and kissed it, holding on for several seconds before releasing it. "You'd better get to work," she said.

He scanned the room until he saw a pile of clothing that contained his trousers. He picked them up, fumbled through the pockets and found his mobile phone….Six missed calls… "Balls," he muttered. "Left the bloody thing on 'silent'." He ignored the messages and dialled a number from memory.

"The number you have called has not been recognised," said the plummy, recorded voice. "Please hang up and try again."

Grant gritted his teeth and sighed through them. 'Damn The Colonel and his stupid bloody games,' he thought. He waited and listened to the message until it was repeated again and again. Eventually, the voice stopped and there was a long beep.

Grant took a deep breath before speaking, keeping his tone light. "Good morning," he said. "This is Tom Grant. I'm going to be late in this morning, but I'm on my way. My Aunt Edna is fine now, by the way."

The last part of the message was delivered self-consciously. Grant did not have an Aunt Edna. That part of the call was a code phrase, designed to let his employers know that the message was genuine and that he was not under duress. Had he phoned in late and not mentioned the fictitious woman, the office would have known that there was some more sinister reason for his late arrival.

He turned again to face the beautiful young woman on the bed as she sat up and let the duvet fall forward to expose her magnificent body. A deep hunger grew within him and with an effort, he quenched it.

She smiled mischievously at the effort of will that was so clearly expressed on his face. "I have to go," he said sadly. "You can stay as long as you like, though. Just drop the latch if you have to leave. Will I see you again?"

"You might," she smiled. "You know where to find me."

He nodded silently, and then bent forward to pick up his clothes from the floor. As he did so, his head was spinning, and he nearly lost his balance. He realised that he was still a little drunk, and he felt as though he might be sick. He gathered up the clothes and hurried away towards the bathroom.

*

Normanby used an index finger to push the spectacles up to the bridge of his nose. The Colonel glanced across at him and struggled to hide his annoyance at the little man's ticks and habits.

"Well, Normanby?" he asked, raising an eyebrow.

"Well, what sir?" asked Normanby.

The Colonel threw a long, hard stare at Kurylenko before turning his attention back to his operative. "Do you think that this man is telling the truth?"

Normanby took his turn at staring at the Russian. His gaze rested on the quivering, sweating Kurylenko for several, unblinking seconds before he spoke. "Yes," he said flatly. "I think he is."

Kurylenko let out a long sigh of relief.

"Mr. Kurylenko," said The Colonel formally. "It is our belief that you are telling the truth. We'll find you some new trousers and return you to your embassy."

Kurylenko managed to muster an indignant look. "Is that all?" he asked. "After I have been tortured by your agent and then held here against my will?" He put as much righteous anger into the question as he could muster, but his expression quickly shrank back into one of cowed subservience under The Colonel's wrathful glare.

"Mr. Kurylenko," barked The Colonel. "I am doing you a very great favour in not having you immediately interred for threatening my *operative* with an illegal firearm which it would appear was issued to you by the Russian Intelligence Services. Be grateful that you are not to be held as a bargaining chip to be swapped for one of ours!"

Kurylenko's gaze dropped to the floor. "You talk as though there was still Cold War," he muttered, sullenly.

"You mean it's over?" asked The Colonel in mock surprise. He glanced at Normanby and gave him a theatrical wink. "See to it that our guest is returned home safely, Normanby," he said, rising from his seat. "Good day, Mr. Kurylenko. I trust that we will not have reason to meet again."

The Russian looked up and watched The Colonel leave the room before turning his attention to Normanby. The previous hatred had gone from his eyes, though it was obvious that he was still suspicious and wary. "So when can I go?" he asked.

"As soon as we can find you some new trousers, I'll arrange for your belongings to be returned to you," said Normanby thoughtfully, "and we'll get you a ride back to the Russian embassy."

"And my pistol?" asked Kurylenko.

Normanby shook his head slowly. "I don't think so, Mr. Kurylenko," he said sadly. "I don't think so."

An idea was beginning to form in Normanby's mind; one which might prove useful in getting to the bottom of this whole messy business. As he got up to leave the room, Normanby struggled with the decision of whether or not to tell The Colonel his plans and risk having them overruled, or to simply go ahead with them anyway.

As he left the room, Normanby turned to the guards outside the door. "See to it that our guest is made as comfortable as possible whilst he waits," he said, "and have the box containing his personal belongings sent to Room 131 as soon as possible, along with the paperwork. I'll sign his things back to him."

The guard nodded silently, and then turned to face his colleague. "You heard the man," he ordered, passing the book with the air of a seasoned military veteran.

*

Grant looked along the street, praying that Toby Hughes had kept his promise of the previous night and brought his car back. He breathed a huge sigh of relief when he saw it parked in a 'residents only' spot a few doors down. As he approached it, he looked up and down the street to make sure that no-one was watching before reaching into the front, nearside wheel arch and feeling around for the magnetic hook that had been stuck there.

"Good lad, Toby," he muttered, unhooking the key that had been left there. At least the morning wasn't a total disaster. With any luck, he wouldn't get stopped and breathalysed on the way to work and he'd be able to wing it through whatever bollocking The Colonel might give him. The day might still turn out rosy.

He got into the car. It felt surprisingly warm and comfortable, despite the cold and damp of the morning air outside. He started the engine and pulled away from the kerb.

*

Normanby looked down into the shoebox sized plastic container on his desk and scowled. He extracted a pen from the neat array in his breast pocket and poked around amongst the box's contents. After a moment, he fished out a mobile phone. He pressed the activation button and saw that the phone required a PIN code to unlock it. He gave a slight, perplexed frown and then pried the back off the phone. He took out the battery and laid it down on his desk in neat alignment with the back of the phone. He reached into his inside breast pocket for his notebook with a slight, satisfied smile. Using the code numbers from the phone and the SIM card, it would be possible to track Kurylenko's position wherever he went, as long as the phone was with him.

Normanby re-assembled the phone and returned it to the box, and then picked up the handset of his desk phone and dialled The Colonel's extension number.

"What is it, Normanby?" asked The Colonel.

"I have Kurylenko's personal effects, sir," Normanby replied. "I've taken the details of his mobile telephone. I think it might be wise to put a trace on it sir."

There was a pause before The Colonel spoke. "That would be Major Green's team's job, wouldn't it?" he asked.

"Normally, sir," answered Normanby. "Normally."

CHAPTER TWENTY TWO: TOMORROW, THE WORLD

Major Green was scowling. His lips were pursed and his hands, which had been resting on the big glass table in front of him were clenched tight, making the knuckles white. His grey eyes had taken on a lifeless quality, and he appeared to be staring through the wall of the office at something in the distance.

Toby had seen the Major like this before and he didn't like it. He looked down at the floor and kept his attention there, in the hope that Green would not be drawn to speak to him. The hope was forlorn, and Toby felt as though his blood had turned to ice water when the Major turned his cold, deathly stare upon him.

"So, there were no trackers in Grant's car?" Major Green asked.

Toby shook his head, still avoiding eye contact. "None at all, Guv," he said. "There were just the empty boxes. Well, there was a two quid coin in each box to make them feel the right weight."

To Toby's immense relief, some animation returned to the Major's face, and his gaze seemed to come into focus. "Just what the Hell is Grant playing at?" Green asked.

Toby shrugged. "'Beats me, Guv'," he replied. "He seemed like an okay sort of bloke an' all."

Green wrinkled his nose briefly. "Well," he said. "You never know what kind of bastards people are going to turn out to be. Did you take his car home for him as you were asked?"

"Of course, Guv," said Toby. "Nice little motor an' all."

"I'm sure," replied Green. "Did you also go and watch Hussein's flat in Mr. Grant's car as I asked you to?"

Toby nodded. "You know me, Guv," he smiled.

"Yes," said Green, suddenly dry. "That's why I'm asking. Did you?"

Toby looked a little crestfallen at Green's implication. "Yeah, of course Guv," he said.

"And you parked *exactly* where I told you?" Green asked pointedly.

Toby swallowed, feeling that he was being put on the spot. "Yes Guv," he said patiently. "I parked exactly where you said."

Green suddenly beamed, and there was no tension in his face at all. "Good lad, Toby," he said. "That parking space is within the view from the resting position of two separate CCTV cameras, so I hope you stayed in the car!"

"Of course I stayed in the car, Guv," Toby chuckled. "I'm a professional!"

Green activated the built-in screen on the desk's surface and rifled through folders of virtual papers. He gave a grunt of satisfaction and then smiled archly at Toby. "This'll show him not to mess with the best," he said. "It's Grant's statement against Normanby. Oh yes, we'd better make sure that the Colonel gets a hard copy in his in tray too."

"That'll throw a spanner in the works," chuckled Toby.

"Hopefully," replied Green. "I've suspected for some time now that someone downstairs has been watching us when it should have been the other way around. What an amazing stroke of look that it appears to be Grant."

"Luck?" said Toby, looking puzzled.

"Well, it sort of kills two birds with one stone," said Green. "We get our clean slate, and get rid of our spy, all at once. I'll have to deal with our other asset a bit sooner than I planned, but it all still fits together, as long as she's done as she's told."

Green leaned back in his chair, a contented smile growing across his face. "It's only a matter of time now before The Colonel and all of the dinosaurs of his era have had their day. Intelligence gathering is a modern art, Toby, but those idiots downstairs are still living in the age of microfilm and invisible ink. This is where it's at, mate!" Green tapped a finger lightly on the glass table so that the whole surface lit up. "When you watch The Colonel's team at work, it's like watching Neanderthal's foraging on the plains, and knowing that you can swoop in and take it all away from them."

Toby chuckled. "You don't 'alf have a way of puttin' things, Guv," he said.

Green looked at Toby Hughes for several seconds. Toby shuffled uncomfortably and then broke eye contact, glancing down at the floor. Green smiled in satisfaction. "Toby, my boy," he said. "I'm going to be Director General one day, and then we'll *really* start to turn a profit!"

Toby's eyes widened and he looked up at Green again. "Even more than now Guv?" he asked.

"Oh yes," said Major Mike Green. "Much, much more than now."

CHAPTER TWENTY THREE: THE PISTOL

The Colonel took a long draught of milky tea and then let out a long sigh in an attempt to relax before turning his attention to the little man waiting patiently across the desk. "I take it that Mr. Kurylenko has been released and given a ride home, Normanby?" he asked.

"Yes sir," replied Normanby, making a neat mark beside an entry in his pocket notebook.

"And his mobile telephone details have been passed to GCHQ so that he can be tracked, with all the paperwork thoroughly filled in, and only *this* department is allowed access?" asked The Colonel.

Again, Normanby made a mark in his notebook. "Yes sir," he said. He waited, with his pen poised, to see if The Colonel would guess the third item on the list.

The Colonel thought for a moment, and then smiled. "You've found some pretext under which you could draw a receiver from the Quartermaster, despite the fact that you don't have any trackers booked out in your name," he said triumphantly. His amusement grew as he saw the disappointed look on Normanby's face.

Normanby pursed his lips and sullenly made another neat mark in his notebook. He hadn't expected The Colonel to guess that he had found an excuse to procure a receiver device, and he had hoped to surprise him.

"Never mind, Normanby," The Colonel chuckled, as if reading his operative's mind. "You can still surprise me by telling me how you can get the receiver unit from the Quartermaster without any difficult questions," he said.

Normanby's mood immediately perked up at the remark. "Well sir," he said, pushing his spectacles up his nose. "I told Lieutenant Philips that you had a... well, a 'bee in your bonnet' about waste within the service. You are worried about the number of trackers left going to waste and you have set me the task of finding and retrieving any operational trackers that are still out there unnecessarily. For this reason, you want me to have the best receiver, capable of picking up signals from all our trackers without having to first pair with specific devices." Normanby stood almost to attention and the expression on his face was bordering closely on a smile.

"Really, Normanby?" bellowed The Colonel, playfully raising his eyebrows. "Well, if I've got that much of a bee in my bonnet, I'd better start producing some snotty memos about it, hadn't I?"

"Yes sir," confirmed Normanby.

The Colonel signed the chitty which had been waiting on his desk, and which would allow Normanby to draw the receiver from the Quartermasters store. "Oh, when you go down there, Normanby," he said, pushing back his chair and pulling open the top drawer of his desk, "could you sign this back in for me?" He lifted out the revolver that he had taken with him when Normanby had reported detaining Kurylenko the night before. He put it down carefully on the desk, and then reached back into the drawer and placed a box of cartridges beside it.

Normanby picked up the revolver. He pointed the barrel down towards the ground and, holding the weapon in both hands, he carefully thumbed forward the catch which allowed the revolver's cylinder to swing out to the side. One by one, he checked each of the six chambers to ensure that they were all empty, and then clicked the cylinder back into place. He then pulled back the hammer so that the cylinder turned a notch, before squeezing the trigger whilst applying enough pressure on the hammer with his thumb to let it down gently. He nodded slightly, satisfied that the weapon was both safe, and functioning.

The Colonel watched the almost ritualistic checking process closely. For those few seconds, he thought, Normanby appeared to be a totally different person from the one he usually portrayed. There was no sign of the nervous little ticks and habits that he was wont to display in his day-to-day life. In those few brief moments that he was following his training, he appeared as efficient and deadly as any operative that he had ever met.

The Colonel probably knew more about Normanby's life and history than any other man alive. He reflected, a little sadly, that had it not been for a certain event, years before, Normanby's career within the Intelligence Services could have taken a very different path.

"It's quite a frightening prospect when operatives in our department face the kind of threat that requires them to go armed, even a mere couple of streets away from this very building," The Colonel announced. "I think, Normanby that we're going to see more danger before this current business is dealt with. It's beginning to look as though we may have enemies within the Intelligence Service itself, and if that's true, then nowhere's safe."

Normanby nodded, and then stared for a long moment at the gun in his hands. He took a deep breath and looked up, as if a spell had been broken. He picked up the box of shells and slipped them into his jacket pocket. "I'll get these back to the Quartermaster, sir," he said.

"Just a minute, Normanby," said The Colonel. "There's also the matter of this." He reached into the drawer again and brought out the Makarov pistol that Normanby had taken from Kurylenko. He thumbed the release catch to slide out the magazine, which he placed on the desk, before working the pistol's slide and checking that the breech was empty.

He extended his arm and sighted down the barrel. His aim swept across the paintings on his office wall. He immediately lowered his aim as he passed the classic portrait of the Queen, couldn't bring himself to pull the trigger on Horatio Nelson, and sighted briefly on Winston Churchill, before finally aiming at a hat stand. "Where's Harold Wilson when you need him?" he growled, squeezing the trigger. There was the slightest of clicks as the firing pin fell in the empty breech.

He re-inserted the magazine, thumbed the safety catch, and then weighed the weapon in his hand, before leaning forward and handing it to Normanby. "Of course," he continued, "it doesn't actually belong to us, so I don't know if the Quartermaster can accept it. We could hardly let Kurylenko have it back, could we? After all, Normanby, I'm not even sure if it is indeed technically Russian property, bearing in mind that it has Soviet era markings, and the USSR no longer exists."

"What should I do with it then sir?" asked Normanby, seriously.

"Do whatever you think is best, Normanby. Just don't play with it around here," said The Colonel.

"Without the proper authorisation, sir," said Normanby, "I'd never get this thing out of the front doors of the building."

The Colonel thought for a moment and sighed. He looked at his watch. "Well, if you hurry up and sign the revolver in," he said, "we can go out and grab some lunch. We can go in my car. How does that sound?"

*

Tom Grant marched slowly down the corridor towards room 131. Each step that he took caused his sense of foreboding to grow stronger and darker. He stopped outside the door, popped an extra strong mint into his mouth and took a deep breath.

"Brass it out, Tommy," he muttered to himself before flinging the door open as brazenly as he dare and stepping into the room. He stopped dead. The room was empty. He sighed, partly he had to admit, from relief. He had been expecting to walk into a hostile reception committee in Room 131, and he was pleasantly surprised that even Normanby wasn't in. Perhaps The Colonel had sent him on some errand.

Grant sat down at his desk, switched on his computer, and then set about his working day. He worked in silence, very much like Normanby, he reflected. The thought disturbed him somewhat. He had joined the Security Services because he had wanted a job with interest and excitement. The thought that he might end up like Normanby worried him. How could the man spend day after day chained to a desk?

After his umpteenth mistake, Grant closed the document that he was working on and took a deep breath. He was tired and he needed some fresh air. He stood up and paced the room, hands in pockets, head down. His mind kept wandering back to the previous night, and the girl from the club's Casino. He felt a deep longing to hold her, to feel her warm, lithe body pressed against his. He marvelled at what a stroke of luck it had been to bump into her, to find someone with whom he shared an immediate and mutual attraction.

He wondered briefly whether Green would have any hard feelings about the girl. He had noticed Green trying to catch her eye as soon as they had entered the Casino, but she had showed him little or no interest. She had preferred instead to flirt exclusively with Grant. "…and who could blame her?" he thought with a slight smile. He allowed himself to relax. He was sure that Mike Green wasn't the kind of man to sulk over a thing like that.

CHAPTER TWENTY FOUR: GORSZKY'S GUESTS

John Meadows' eyes rolled upwards and half closed. Drool ran down his chin and his head lolled back, tipping his balance. He fell back into the stained cushions of the settee and lost consciousness.

Stanislav Gorszky looked at Meadows' wretched figure with utter contempt and snorted before giving a little chuckle. "You like the spice, my friend?" he asked, knowing that Meadows was incapable of answering. "Plenty more for you, later. Maybe you even get to have new girlfriend too, before you die." He threw his head back and laughed briefly, glancing across the room at the unconscious female lying on a pile of damp, dirty cushions. Her hands and feet were bound with plastic tie-wraps, and she had been stripped down to her vest and pants before being tied up. The sight of her firm young body stirred a desire in Gorszky. He tried to put it out of his mind.

Lou Fowler's clothes, boots and tactical vest lay in a pile at the side of the settee where Gorszky sat. Her personal belongings, which he had extracted from the various pockets, resided on the coffee table on front of him in neat piles. Also scattered about the coffee table was a small collection of drugs paraphernalia. This collection included cigarette papers, a lighter, a bag of 'spice', some of which Gorszky had forced Meadows to smoke. Beside the bag of Spice was a saucer containing a stub of candle, a blackened and bent dessert spoon, a hypodermic needle, and a small polythene bag of heroin. It was this combination that Gorszky had used to keep Lou Fowler docile.

He poked around amongst her belongings on the coffee table and picked up the item that intrigued him most of all; the cheap little mobile phone that had flashed and buzzed several times in the night. He looked at it with a puzzled expression, and then flipped it open and pressed the 'on' button. As he looked at the little L.E.D. screen he tutted in mock admonishment towards the unconscious young woman on the floor. "Really, young lady," he said, smiling. "You should install password on your device. Just because you are Police Officer does not mean I will not steal it!"

He chuckled to himself and continued his examination of the phone. It took him only a few moments to work out the controls of the simple little device. He smiled at the realisation that there was only one number in the contacts list. The smile slowly grew wider as he read the text messages, all of which were from the same number. "What is this?" he muttered to himself. "It is *secret phone*!"

His eyes widened as he read the messages. Suddenly, he guffawed, unable to stop the laughter escaping. He could not believe his luck. It seemed that the 'secret phone' was used to communicate covertly with a high-ranking Police Detective. Whilst the text messages had no sexual content, and Gorszky did not understand all of the abbreviations and colloquialisms used, he could see that the messages were between people who were very fond of one another and on first name terms. They were also passing secret messages on a phone that was not used to contact anyone else. It seemed obvious to Gorszky that the woman must be having an affair with one of her bosses.

He switched the phone off and then thought about how he might use this new-found knowledge. He nodded to himself absently as a plan began to form in his mind. The Big Man would be pleased with him, he thought happily. He had already been promised that his criminal records back home in Russia would be eradicated when this operation was complete. Who knows? he thought. Perhaps they would even give him a permanent job in the G.R.U. when he returned home.

Gorszky smiled, slowly looking from Lou Fowler to John Meadows. How strange that such worthless people could be so useful, he thought. These two, along with the repulsive shaven headed female that he had got rid of last night would actually prove incredibly useful in diverting the attention of the British authorities from the truth. He sat back with a satisfied smile and then used his teeth to extract a cigarette from a 'Fest' packet, then lit it. 'Yes,' he thought, 'The Big Man will be very happy.'

He started to chuckle again as the plan in his mind took shape. He looked down at the phone and thought about the wording that he would use to lure the Policewoman's boyfriend here. He had created in his mind a spectacular scenario that would cause more scandal and embarrassment for the British authorities. This would be good, he thought. They would give him a medal when he returned home to Russia.

It would not be long now, he thought, before someone found the body and things started happening. He went into the back bedroom and looked out of the window. In the distance, he could see the overgrown patch of wasteland where he had stabbed the ugly woman to death the night before. His breathing grew faster, and beads of sweat broke out on his forehead as he remembered the thrill, the excitement, the sheer *joy* of killing. He prowled back across the landing into the big front bedroom that served as the lounge and looked down at the two unconscious figures. The smile grew slowly wider on his lips. There would be more killing soon: The excitement; the joy; the power!

CHAPTER TWENTY FIVE: RUTH

"So, what do *you* think Grant's playing at, Normanby?" asked The Colonel after a long silence.

Normanby took a sip of his tea and took a moment to compose his thoughts before he answered. "I'm not sure sir," he said. "It does appear that Mr. Grant is not exactly being a 'team player', and I'm not entirely sure of his motives, but I find Kurylenko's accusation hard to believe. I'm sure, though, that Mr. Kurylenko believes it. I don't think that he was trying to deceive us. Perhaps Mr. Grant has trust issues due to the fact that he has only recently moved to the department…" he let the sentence trail off.

The Colonel raised an eyebrow and looked candidly at Normanby. "You don't trust him though, do you Normanby? Do you think that there's another reason for his behaviour?" he asked.

Normanby re-adjusted the position of his spectacles with an extended forefinger. "I think that Grant may well be working against the interests of the Department," he said after a long pause. "Furthermore, I believe that Grant may well be the least of our worries. I have suspected for some time that Major Green has hostile intentions towards our department that go beyond good-natured competition, and I think that Mr. Grant may well be working with him."

The Colonel put his own teacup slowly back on its saucer, and then looked around the tearoom to check that there were no customers in earshot. "Normanby," he said with tired patience. "I know that you don't trust Major Green, and I understand your reasons, but we've been through this before. You know, as well as I do that Green's team get results. The Director General thinks the world of them, and with the current political climate, we can hardly afford an inter-departmental war." He waited patiently and did not rush to elicit a reply. Instead, he slowly stirred his tea and took a sip, trying not to look at the other man.

Normanby was shaking, and for long moments his eyes were unfocussed behind the lenses of his spectacles as his mind drifted back...

....The bright sunshine beat down with its usual oppressive heat. He put the palm of his hand on the roof of the car and then immediately pulled it away with a start and rubbed his scorched hand, grinning.

She threw her head back and laughed, exposing a perfect row of white teeth. "Was it a bit hot, darling?" she chuckled.

"A bit," he confessed, smiling. He leaned forward and put his head through the open driver's side window. She depressed the clutch, took the car out of gear, and applied the hand brake, leaning out to him. Their lips met in the softest of kisses. They stayed there, motionless until her arms went about his neck and pulled him deeper into the car. He reached in and put his own arms around her.

"I love you, Corporal Normanby," she said in between a succession of warm, gentle, soft kisses.

"Yuk!" announced the ten-year-old girl sat in the back seat of the car.

"Wait until you get a boyfriend!" said Normanby, glancing over at her before returning his attention to his wife, Ruth, and her warm, soft lips. He ran a hand up the back of her neck and weaved his fingers into her short black hair.

"I love you, darling," he whispered, kissing her once more before gently pulling away and standing upright beside the car. He reached back in and rested a hand gently on her arm. "I'll see you tonight," he whispered, before directing his attention to the little girl in the back seat. "Good luck today, Charlie," he said. "I love you too."

"Thank you, Dad, love you!" she said.

Ruth blew him an arch kiss and then put the car back in gear. "See you tonight Darling," she said. "I love you."

"Be careful Darling," he said, with a wave. He stood for long moments as the car pulled away down the lane towards the gatehouse and the barrier of the compound, a quarter of a mile away. He watched until it became little more than a black dot in the distance, in contrast against the distant white blur of the gatehouse itself, then he turned towards the front door of the bungalow. He reached out to the door handle, and then suddenly stopped...

There was a dull, muffled bang from somewhere in the distance, somewhere near the gatehouse. He turned and looked back in that direction with a growing sense of dread. Something was happening; something bad. He squinted into the distance and thought that he could see a plume of smoke near the gatehouse. His heart sank and the awful feeling grew into a sense of terror as he heard the distant, repeated cracks of automatic gunfire from the same direction.

His legs felt weak and rubbery as he stepped back onto the lane and started walking in the direction of the commotion. Barely aware of his own movements, he quickened his pace in strange, awkward steps. At the sound of the next rattle of automatic fire, he found himself running towards it, his mind numbed with panic and terror for his family.

As he drew closer, he could see mayhem engulfing the gatehouse area. There were people running in confusion in all directions. There seemed to be an ongoing firefight between two groups of Police officers and several of the American Military Contractors that guarded the compound.

Normanby stopped and felt his heart skip a beat at the sight of Ruth's burned and blackened car. The front of the vehicle was smashed and smouldering, just outside the broken barrier by the gatehouse. He stumbled forward towards it in a daze, oblivious to the gunfire around him. There was a loud crack and a terrifying loud buzz like the sound of a giant insect, as a bullet sailed within an inch of his head, but he did not care. He continued stumbling, like some kind of mindless zombie, towards the smoking wreck of the car.

He approached the open driver's door, peering in through the smoke, and his heart leapt for joy. His wife and daughter were not inside. They must have managed to get out somehow! He heard shouting in English. The Americans were telling him to get away from the car. He ignored them. His only concern was to find Ruth and Charlie and to keep them safe.

A bullet smashed into the bodywork of the car, scant inches from him. He ignored it and stumbled around to the other side of the vehicle. He looked down, two feet in front of him and then stopped dead, falling to his knees with his arms reaching out. What he saw left him shattered: The two lifeless bodies, their tattered clothes soaked with fresh blood. Ruth had little Charlie wrapped in her arms, lying almost on top of her to offer what protection she could. It had not been enough. The bullets had torn through her body into the child's.

Normanby let out an inarticulate wail of agony and threw himself forward onto them, holding the two bloodied, shattered bodies in his arms. He continued to wail and gasp, crushed by an overwhelming and total despair that left him unable to do or say anything except to pray silently that death would come to him too, so that he could be with them. Then, there was another almighty bang, and everything went black...

..."Normanby," said The Colonel. "Normanby, are you alright?"

Normanby looked up slowly, still shaking. The Colonel could see that his eyes were moist behind his spectacles. "Yes sir," he said quietly. "I know that you don't believe me about Major Green sir," he said, "but I will prove it, somehow."

The Colonel looked at him in sympathy. He could not think of anything to say to the man. Mercifully, Normanby's mobile phone rang, and he fished it out of his pocket. The Colonel gave a quiet sigh of relief as Normanby took the call. "Normanby," he said. "Yes…yes…oh dear! You're sure?.. Where?…Is he there now?…"

He took out his notebook and pen, and then began to quickly make notes. "Can you repeat the street name and postcode?" he asked. He wrote it down quickly. "Thank you," he said. "I'm on my way right now." He hung up and put the phone away, and then checked his notebook briefly before putting it away also.

The Colonel was watching him expectantly. He drew in a breath to ask what was happening, but Normanby spoke first. "There's been another murder sir," he said lightly, "and it would appear that Shafiq Hussein's killer is responsible."

"Are you sure it's the same killer?" asked The Colonel.

"It's an identical murder weapon sir," replied the little man, "and the same modus operandi. The location is close to the last one, and the victim is a possible witness to the first murder."

"Ah," said The Colonel, simply.

"Could I trouble you for a lift to the crime scene sir?" asked Normanby.

The Colonel chuckled, happy that the news of another murder had brightened Normanby's mood. "I'm not a bloody taxi service," he growled. His smile suddenly grew broad at the momentarily indignant look from the other man. "Go on then Normanby," he said, "seeing that you've asked nicely." He drank down rest of his tea and then picked up his coat.

CHAPTER TWENTY SIX: CLUES AND TRACKS

Almost as soon as Normanby and The Colonel stepped out onto the pavement outside the Tea Rooms, the sleek Jaguar XF pulled up at the kerb. Hopkirk got out of the driver's seat, walked around to the nearside and then pulled open the back door, giving The Colonel a brief salute as he did so.

"Thank you Hopkirk," said The Colonel, getting in and shuffling across the back seat. Normanby followed suit in silence. Hopkirk closed the door behind him and then returned to the driver's seat. "Where to sir?" he asked, looking at The Colonel in the rear-view mirror.

"Normanby?" inquired The Colonel. Normanby consulted his notebook and gave Hopkirk the address and post code.

"Very good sir," said Hopkirk, setting off immediately. He had no need of the car's built in Satnav system. Hopkirk's knowledge of London's streets was excellent, equal, at least to the best London cabbie.

Normanby sat in silence for a while, leafing carefully through the pages of his notebook. The Colonel watched him for a moment and then turned his attention to the view out of the window as London sped by outside. He noticed the gradual change from opulence to squalor in both the surroundings and the appearance of the pedestrians as the car made its way towards the scene of the latest murder.

The streets outside grew narrower, with rows of small Victorian terraced houses lining them. Here and there, there were open patches of land where the factories that the houses had been built to service had once stood. In the distance, The Colonel could make out a larger patch of wasteland ahead, with crowds beginning to gather at its fringes.

"Pull over here please Hopkirk," he said before turning to Normanby. "You can put your report in tomorrow morning," he continued.

"Yes sir," said Normanby, getting out of the car. He set off walking along the pavement.

"And Normanby," called The Colonel, poking his head through the still opening window.

Normanby stopped and turned back towards the car. "Yes sir?" he asked.

The Colonel sat in silence for a moment. "Be careful," he said, before giving Hopkirk the nod to set off.

A fine drizzling rain began to fall. Normanby watched The Colonel's Jaguar turn in the road and drive away. He waited with a familiar melancholy feeling, until the car had shrunk to a black dot and disappeared the way it had come.

Taking a deep breath of the cool, damp air, Normanby made his way towards the small crowd of rubberneckers assembled on the pavement beside the patch of open wasteland. As he approached, he saw that the area was cordoned off with crime scene tape. Amongst the milling crowds, he saw the yellow jackets of Police Officers, keeping the public back. As he approached, Normanby presented the credentials that would give him access. The Police Officer studied them for a moment and then lifted the tape for him to duck under.

"Is Detective Sergeant Taylor here yet?" asked Normanby.

"He's somewhere about sir," said the Constable. "That's his car." He nodded in the direction of an old, blue Rover 75, parked nearby.

Normanby looked at it, then back at the Officer. "I rather suppose that he might be at the centre of things," he said, looking towards a large, white tented area.

The Constable nodded. "I imagine so sir," he said.

Normanby began to walk carefully down the path towards the forensics tent, wondering how thoroughly the vicinity had been examined. At least the public were being kept well back, he reflected. He looked around the scrubby wasteland and along the rough path towards the tent. A few yards ahead, he saw a line of trampled down long grass where someone had cut through, rather than using one of the more established paths. He squinted along the line of trampled grass and saw that it joined a wider path up to several rows of derelict looking houses. He stopped and drew out his notebook and pen, making careful notes and sketches before continuing down the path towards the forensics tent.

As he neared the front of the tent, Normanby saw the familiar figure of Doug Taylor, his unfashionable suit hidden beneath a white paper forensics overall. He was impatiently studying the cheap mobile phone in his hand, and he did not see Normanby approach.

Normanby watched Taylor for long moments and saw something akin to desperation in his expression as he frantically typed on the phone.

"Good afternoon, Detective Sergeant," said Normanby, habitually checking his watch to make sure that was indeed, afternoon.

Taylor looked up irritably. He took a moment to compose himself. "Mr. Normanby," he acknowledged, "there's been another." He shook his head, realising that he was stating the obvious. "Danielle Church; I believe that you were eager to speak to her from what L..PCSO Fowler told me."

"Yes indeed," said Normanby. "I believe that this young woman may have been killed because she would have been able to identify Mr. Hussein's killer. Would it be possible to speak to Officer Fowler?"

Taylor gave a start, and even more of the colour drained from his face. "Unfortunately not," he said quickly. "She hasn't reported in this morning. She was on the lookout for Church and her boyfriend last night and she hasn't been heard from since." "I see," said Normanby. He was about to speak again when he was interrupted by the ringing of a mobile phone.

Doug Taylor reached into his pocket and fished out a large, modern smartphone. "Taylor," he said curtly. "Yes…yes…still nothing?…Keep trying." He hung up and put the phone away, scowling. He looked closely at the other phone in his hand before putting this away also.

Normanby narrowed his eyes as the full realisation of the situation dawned on him.

"Listen Mr. Normanby," Taylor was saying, "I really need to be getting back to the station."

"Oh, I'll walk with you," said Normanby quickly, falling into step beside Taylor.

Taylor looked irritated. "I really am in quite a hurry Mr. Normanby," he said sharply. "Simon DeVere's on site, so I'm sure he'll be able to help with any questions that you may have."

"Oh, I won't keep you, Detective," said Normanby, rushing to keep up with Taylor as he took long strides back towards the edge of the site. "So, did you say that Officer Fowler hasn't reported in?" he continued. "Do you think she's alright? I mean, could it be connected to this?" He gestured back over his shoulder, towards the crime scene tent.

Taylor took a deep breath and tried to hide his anger and frustration. "I don't know Mr. Normanby," he said through gritted teeth. He quickened his pace further, eager to get away from Normanby and his questions.

They reached the Police Crime Scene tapes at the edge of the site and Taylor ducked underneath and stepped out onto the pavement. Normanby tenaciously followed suit. As Taylor fumbled furiously through his suit pockets under the paper overalls to find his car keys, Normanby caught him up.

Upon finding the keys, Taylor got into the driving seat of the Rover, doing his best to ignore the pompous, annoying little man. He was about to pull the door shut, then sighed irritably when he found Normanby in the way.

"Detective Taylor," said Normanby slowly, reaching a hand out to the back of the driver's seat in a comforting gesture. "Please let me know if you hear anything from Officer Fowler. I'll make sure to pass on anything I find here."

Taylor looked back at him for long seconds, and Normanby saw the fear and desperation etched on the man's face. "Thank you, Mr. Normanby," he said, pulling the car door shut as the little man stepped back. He started the engine and Normanby watched the car pull away and drive off into the distance.

Normanby took out his mobile phone and dialled a number. He waited patiently as the plummy, recorded voice told him repeatedly that the number that he had dialled had not been recognised. When he heard the bleep, he spoke. "It's Normanby," he said. "I need to speak to the Colonel as soon as possible."

Before he had chance to hang up, he heard a click and then the voice of Betty, the Colonel's secretary. "Mr. Normanby?" she said. "Hold the line please. He wants to speak with you." There was another pause, then another click.

"Normanby?" said the Colonel.

"Yes sir," said Normanby. "I've activated tracker number two."

"Really?" asked the Colonel. "And where has it been deployed?"

"I've placed it in the car of Detective Sergeant Taylor of the Homicide and Major Enquiries Team," said Normanby. He was almost sure that he heard a sharp intake of breath from the other end of the line.

"Are you telling me you're tracking the movements of a serving Police Officer?" the Colonel asked.

"Yes sir," Normanby replied in a matter-of-fact tone. "I believe he may have, or may obtain, information about a missing Police Community Support Officer who is involved in my investigation."

"The plot thickens," said the Colonel, dryly.

"Yes sir," replied Normanby. "It's essential that I'm kept up to date with Detective Sergeant Taylor's movements. If my suspicions are correct, he may well try to act without my knowledge. Tell me sir," he continued, "did we get any interesting results from Tracker number one?"

"Yes," said the Colonel very slowly. "It appears that Grant spent over an hour last night parked outside Hussein's flat."

"That's interesting sir," Normanby mused.

"Yes," said the Colonel, "it is. Keep me informed of any developments and I'll ensure that you're kept up to date with the tracker locations. Hopefully you should get to the bottom of this whole business soon."

"Hopefully sir," replied Normanby. He hung up and put his phone away, and then stood for long moments looking out over the wasteland, down towards the big white crime scene tent. He ducked under the Police tape unchallenged and made his way back down the path to the tent and the centre of Crime Scene activity.

As he walked, Normanby wondered about the relationship between Doug Taylor and Lou Fowler. It had become obvious to him quite soon after he had seen the identical cheap mobile phones, separate from their own high quality smart phones and their Police issue equipment.

Of course, these sort of relationships did form now and again, he supposed; the experienced Police Officer and the promising and attractive young PCSO. He had probably impressed her with his stories and of course, the power that his position brought. Power was, after all, as strong an aphrodisiac as wealth. He was still mildly surprised he confessed to himself, that someone like Officer Fowler would have been so easily impressed, however.

Normanby put these thoughts out of his mind as he approached the Crime Scene tent. He saw Simon DeVere, the Crime Scene Investigator, step out and pull back the hood of his paper overalls and then remove the specially designed hairnet that covered his beard.

"Good afternoon, Mr. DeVere," called Normanby as he approached.

DeVere looked up, a little startled. "Good afternoon," he said. "Mr. Normanby, isn't it?"

Normanby nodded. "I understand that the victim is," he consulted his notebook, "Miss Danielle Church," he concluded.

"So I'm told," said DeVere, reaching inside the paper boiler suit that he wore. He found a packet of cigarettes. "Do you mind if we take a walk Mr. Normanby?" he asked. "I need a cigarette after that." He indicated towards the tent with a movement of his head.

Normanby took a deep breath. "Can we go that way?" He pointed down the path in the opposite direction from which he had come. He hoped to be able to get to the other path which had been linked to the one they were on by the line of trampled grass.

DeVere shrugged. "I suppose so," he said, "as long as we get outside the cordon." Normanby nodded happily and they set off walking to the other end of the patch of wasteland.

As they approached the strip of Police Crime Scene tape at the perimeter, a bored looking Police Constable gave them a nod and prepared to lift the tape. DeVere waved a hand at him in thanks and stopped to remove the plastic covers from his shoes before stepping out onto the pavement. He looked up with distaste as a fine mist of rain blew over him.

"So," said Normanby, "I take it that this Church woman was murdered by the same person that killed Hussein."

DeVere nodded, toying idly with his cigarette. "I'd say so," he confirmed. "He really loves his work too." He lit the cigarette and drew in the first lungful of smoke greedily. He held it in for a few seconds and then blew it up into the air in a long, thin stream.

"Both the weapon and the modus operandi are the same?" Normanby asked.

"Yeah," said DeVere. "This one wasn't as strong as Hussein and went down quicker. He carried on, though. Forty-three separate insertions. He wasn't just making sure she was dead. I'd say he was in a frenzy."

"It doesn't sound like the work of a cold, efficient assassin, does it?" mused Normanby. "That is, assuming that such people really exist."

DeVere looked puzzled at the remark for a moment and then shrugged. "I'd say he was pretty efficient," he said. "Both of his victims are well and truly dead."

"A good point," Normanby conceded. He took out his notebook and made careful notes.

"What makes you think that he's an assassin, Mr. Normanby?" asked DeVere. "I had that first murder down as a racist attack. You know; lots of rage and fury. I'm not sure about this one though. I suppose the female's got a skinhead haircut and big boots. The most likely guess would be that she was an accomplice, or at least an associate of the racist killer and there's been some kind of falling out between them. That could be drink-related, judging by the amount of alcohol in her system and the stink of white cider."

"I take it that that is the official Police take on the matter," said Normanby.

"Of course," DeVere replied. "It's the only theory that fits all the facts."

"Good," said Normanby with a smile.

DeVere took a last long pull on his cigarette and then crushed the filter between his fingers until the last glowing embers fell to the pavement. He looked about him for somewhere to deposit the cigarette end and, seeing no alternative, he pitched it expertly into a gulley grate at the side of the road.

Normanby looked shocked. He turned and looked at the bored Policeman standing by the tape barrier and elicited nothing but a slightly puzzled look from the man. He looked back at DeVere. "You do realise that's an offence?" he asked.

DeVere gave a baffled expression. "What is?" he asked.

"Your cigarette," said Normanby.

"I put it down the drain," replied DeVere, a little defensively.

"Mr. DeVere," said Normanby seriously. "Littering a watercourse is still an offence under section eighty-seven of the Environmental Protection Act of nineteen ninety."

DeVere looked at the strange little man with an expression of total bewilderment. Unsure whether or not Normanby was actually serious, he turned and lifted the band of yellow tape. Normanby ducked under it and they both stepped back onto the patch of wasteland.

"Can we just have a look over there for a moment?" asked Normanby, pointing down towards the other well-worn path that led up towards tatty rows of terraced houses.

DeVere, still nonplussed by Normanby's behaviour, shrugged. "Why not?" he said mildly.

"Has this path been examined for clues?" Normanby asked, eagerly marching ahead.

"Erm, I'm not sure," panted DeVere, hurrying to keep up. "I mean, I haven't had a look yet, but it's a big area. We'll get to it, if no one else has."

Normanby halted and pointed to the longer grass where a trampled line joined this path to the one that they had been on earlier.

"And?" said DeVere, a hint of sarcasm in his voice.

"Someone passed through the long grass between this path and the other," said Normanby.

"Yes, people do that sometimes," DeVere replied, dryly.

Normanby glanced at him coldly before returning his attention to the long grass. "Someone passed from *this* path to the one on which the body was found. Look at which way the grass is leaning."

DeVere looked at the grass doubtfully for long moments. "Well, most of it is," he said, "but there's a bit there leaning the other way." He looked again, scanning the trampled grass. "...and there, look!" he said.

Normanby squinted and examined the area in detail. "So there is!" he said with a satisfied smile. "So, the grass was trampled in *that* direction," he made a gesture with both hands, "and then somebody came back along the exact same route! Those few bits of grass that hadn't been trampled down fully in that direction were caught and bent this way on the return journey!" There was something close to sheer joy in the expression on Normanby's face.

DeVere still looked doubtful. "As a theory," he said, "it still seems a bit thin."

Something had caught Normanby's attention at the edge of the path: A blue, shiny object, partially obscured by the grass. "Mr. DeVere," he said with a satisfied smile, "I do believe that my theory is about to receive enough nourishment for it to put on some weight."

He leaned down towards the object. "A plastic bottle," he announced, "of the type in which cheap white cider is sold!" He put his hands on the ground and with surprising agility, assumed a push up position, so that he could look closely at the bottle without having to put his knees on the damp ground. He bent his arms to bring himself closer to the bottle and held the position with no sign of strain.

"There's quite a bit left in here," he said. "I would suggest a very thorough analysis of the bottle and this part of the path." He got up and dusted the palms of his hands by rubbing them together, before taking out his mobile phone and using it to take pictures of the bottle and the trampled grass. He turned around and photographed where the path led in both directions.

Simon DeVere watched him for a moment, angry with himself. It did seem as if Normanby had again spotted clues which neither he nor his trained colleagues had seen.

Normanby put away his mobile phone and took out his notebook. He was totally engrossed in his work, making neat notes and sketches.

DeVere watched him work for several minutes before taking out his own phone and calling one of his colleagues. "Winston," he said, "come out of the tent and then look straight forward across the long grass. You'll see me and another man. Bring a roll of Crime Scene tape and four stakes to where I am. Make sure you come the long way 'round and not through the long grass. We think we've found something." He put his phone away and then turned his attention back to Normanby who was standing, notebook in hand, looking along the path towards the shabby terraced houses nearby.

"Lovely area, isn't it?" said DeVere, stepping up beside Normanby. "It will be one day, at any rate. This whole area's due for demolition and redevelopment soon."

"It's rather sad, isn't it?" said Normanby, still staring out at the grimy blocks of houses.

"What? This lot coming down?" asked DeVere. "I don't see what's sad about slum clearance and replacing it with modern social housing and shops."

Normanby thought about some of the other modern social housing developments that he had seen and was about to voice his doubts to DeVere, but he held his tongue. After all, he admitted, this area was run down. But was it the buildings themselves that were the problem? Could they not be modernised? He thought about his own rooms in Mrs. Turner's large Victorian Terraced house, and about how fond of them he was.

"Are there actual plans and blueprints for the redevelopment of this area?" he asked, absently.

"Of course," DeVere replied. "Don't you read the papers? Since phase one of the Marshside Redevelopment has done so well, phase two's going to extend it to cover all this side of Marsh Road, right down to the roundabout at the bottom."

"Oh yes," said Normanby, remembering his visit to the first crime scene on Trilby Street. "There's some kind of shopping complex over there, isn't there?" He pointed in its general direction.

DeVere chuckled. "You really don't read the papers, do you?" he said. "The Marshgate Centre's the biggest success story in years around here. It's even getting a Royal Visit this week!"

"Really?" said Normanby, genuinely interested. "Then I suppose it must have its positives."

Both men looked around to see a tall young black man in paper overalls struggling up the path with two heavy kit bags on his shoulders. His forehead, under short dreadlocks was beaded with sweat.

"Ah, Winston," said DeVere. "It looks like you've brought the whole shop."

"I thought I'd better," Winston replied. "I didn't know how big an area you wanted cordoning off."

DeVere let out a breath and made an expansive gesture with his hands to cover the area of long grass. "Well, all of this," he said.

Winston looked over the area and gave a nod. "It'll take a while for them to look this over," he said gravely. "They've barely covered the centre of scene."

"I know," said DeVere, resignedly, "but it could be important. I'll give you a hand."

Winston put down the kit bags and opened them before going through the contents to make sure that they had everything they needed to seal off this part of the crime scene.

DeVere turned to Normanby. "Well, Mr. Normanby," he said. "We're going to be rather busy for a while. Do you need anything else before we get started?"

"No, Mr. DeVere," Normanby replied, "and thank you. You've been most helpful." He turned his attention back to the rows of terraced houses. He thought it very likely, in light of the evidence, that both victim and killer had come from that direction. Giving DeVere and Winston a final nod, he set off walking towards the houses, his eyes scanning the path for signs or clues, anything that might help him build a more detailed picture of the previous night's events.

Normanby stopped dead. He had been trying to imagine the murderer's actions and something had occurred to him. The man had committed a frenzied knife attack. He would have been covered in blood. He would surely not go far through the streets in that state, even at night. He must have stopped somewhere nearby, at the very least to clean up or change his clothes. Normanby felt a chill of excitement and fear as he quickened his pace towards the houses. He would check every door, every outhouse in the area until he found any traces of blood. Even if the killer had cleaned himself up and moved on, there would be traces left somewhere, he was sure of it.

As he neared the houses, his eyes wandered over every visible window looking for signs of movement. The clues that he had seen in the trampled grass had indicated that the killer had come back in this direction after stabbing Danielle Church to death. He felt a cold shiver at the possibility that the murderer might be hiding in one of the houses; might have simply returned to his lair and be waiting for his next target.

Normanby scanned the houses that backed onto the wasteland, again checking the windows for any signs of him being watched from within. There was a row of twelve houses in the nearest terrace, some of which were occupied. Most of them, however, had their downstairs windows boarded up.

The first house that he came to appeared to be occupied. There was the sound of a radio playing, coming from inside. The tattered blind in the grimy kitchen window was pulled down so he could not see inside. There was an upturned plastic paddling pool in the back yard, and next to the back door stood a push chair with a tatty, but more or less intact polythene rain canopy. The push chair itself was filthy. There was a sagging clothes line across the yard with several items of baby clothes pegged onto it.

Normanby dismissed this first house. He thought it unlikely that the murderer would have a family of any sort, and other than the filth and grime that seemed to cover everything, he could see no stains that might be blood. There could be some around the front of the house, he supposed, but he doubted it. He moved quietly along towards the next house.

At first glance, this one seemed a little more promising. The first thing that Normanby noticed as he approached was the stench. He reached to the open gateway to the back yard and looked in. The plastic dustbins by the gateway were crammed full, and additional black bin bags had been piled against them. The bags had been torn open by cats, dogs or rodents, and their rotting contents had spilled out onto the floor. Normanby looked closer and saw the remains of a charred fish head, a portion of which had been eaten away by something. Just next to it he saw that what he had at first assumed to be maggots were actually grains of rice with a couple of squashed peas amongst them.

He peered into the ripped open bags and saw the packaging for several new mobile phones. Looking across the yard at the back of the house, Normanby saw a length of shiny new chain with a brass padlock fastened around a cast iron drainpipe on the wall. He gave a slight, disappointed shake of the head. Whoever lived here, it would seem, travelled by bicycle. He thought about it and decided that it was unlikely that the murderer lived here.

The next house was empty, with the ground floor doors and windows boarded up. The boards were recent with no damage or graffiti, and the nails holding them in place were shiny and new.

Normanby took only a matter of seconds to dismiss the next house. The acrid stench of cat urine, the badly and unevenly fitted cat flap in the back door, and the three pairs of oversized and ancient ladies knickers on the washing line were enough for him to write off this house as the lair of a murderer.

He made his way along the first two blocks of terraced houses that boarded this side of the wasteland, checking each house in the same way. He jumped as he felt the vibration of his mobile phone ringing in his pocket, and he quickly answered it. "Normanby," he said simply.

"Ah, Normanby," boomed the Colonel. "Your friend Taylor is on the move again."

"Interesting," said Normanby. "Is he heading back towards the crime scene?"

There was a pause whilst the Colonel checked. "Yes," he said, "it would seem so."

"Thank you sir," Normanby replied. "I'll be in touch shortly." He put away his phone and turned his attention to the third block of houses that bordered the wasteland at this end.

At the first house of the third block, Normanby felt a strange sensation. It was as if he instantly knew that this was the house that he had been looking for. His heart raced and he felt a cold sweat break out all over his body. The feeling was most disconcerting. He glanced at each window in turn, looking for signs of movement, and ducked back behind the outhouse at the bottom of the yard.

He held a hand out in front of him and saw that it was shaking. When he took a deep breath to try and calm himself, the exhalation that followed came out in a staccato rattle. Why had he suddenly become so nervous here, he wondered. He could not put a finger on what had caused it, but as soon as he had looked at the house, he had known that this was the murderer's home.

Normanby took another deep breath and willed himself to relax, struggling to push the demons in his mind back into their box. He did not believe in the supernatural, nor in any kind of sixth sense. His nervous reaction must therefore, he concluded, be due to information that his five senses had picked up without his conscious mind realising their significance.

He took off his spectacles and cleaned the mist of condensed sweat from their lenses. The slow, methodical movements that he made, along with the steady, deep breaths, relaxed him slightly. He slid a hand into his coat and ran his fingertips over the reassuring bulge of the Makarov pistol in the waistband of his trousers. He sighed. It was time to take a look at the house and see exactly what had caused his strange reaction. He stepped into the open and his eyes darted across the windows at the back of the house, anxiously searching for any signs of movement. He saw none, and moved forward into the yard.

He felt his senses heightened by the adrenaline coursing through his blood, and he took in all the information that he could gather. The downstairs windows had been cleaned, which struck him as odd, and the yard was tidy. Around the kitchen window frame, he noticed that there were holes. The windows and doors had been boarded up, but the boards had been carefully removed. The house must have been cleared in preparation for the redevelopment in the area, but it appeared that someone had decided to re-open it and 'squat' there.

As he looked at the back door, Normanby's heart raced. The lock and handle of the door were new, and whilst the brown surface of the door showed nothing, flecks of what appeared to be brown dried blood were visible on the gleaming handle. Normanby stepped closer, adjusted his spectacles, and peered at it closely.

Suddenly, he gave a start. The sound of a footstep inside the house, at the other side of the door, set his nerves jangling in something close to blind panic. He edged slowly backwards down the yard; his eyes fixed on the door. He jumped again at the sudden sound of a bolt being drawn on the side of the door. His trembling hand found the butt of the pistol in his waistband as the sound was repeated and another bolt was drawn. He brought out the gun and clumsily de-activated the safety catch before turning and stumbling towards the outhouse at the end of the yard. His legs felt as though they had turned to soft rubber beneath him. Once inside the outhouse, he pushed the door closed as quietly as he could, leaving a gap through which to peer.

For long seconds he stood trembling, his shallow, rapid breathing hardly providing the oxygen that his body needed. He forced himself to take a slow, deep breath and was disappointed to find that it did nothing to assuage the panic that he felt.

He tried to calm his racing mind and to think about the situation logically. Someone at the other side of the door had unlocked it and drawn back the bolts. They had not come out to confront him and they had made no other move. It was possible, he decided, that they were hoping to lure him inside, knowing that he was here investigating.

Well, he thought, he wasn't going to fall for that. He would call The Colonel and then wait here with his pistol for protection until back up arrived. He hoped that whoever was inside would not escape through the front of the house before then, and he cursed himself silently for not checking the situation at the front first. It couldn't be helped now, he concluded. He would not risk stepping out into the open again until it was safe to do so. He took out his phone and carefully thumbed the keypad.

CHAPTER TWENTY SEVEN: THE TRAP

Doug Taylor's hands were shaking when he stopped the car and put on the handbrake. He looked at the white plastic carrier bag on the passenger seat next to him and he felt nauseous. His career was over, he thought bleakly. He did not know what would happen to him after this was over, but he was convinced that he had made the only choice open to him.

The text message that he had received from Lou's phone had been clear and straightforward. She was being held hostage by a madman who had already killed at least two people. If Taylor did not come to the house alone, and carrying a specified quantity of Heroin, the kidnapper would kill her: If the kidnapper suspected that there were other policemen on their way, he would kill her.

Taylor had had no choice. He had returned to the Station and signed out drugs from the evidence locker, claiming that they were needed for a sting operation. He knew that as soon as his story was checked out, it would be patently obvious that there was no such operation in progress, and that he did not have the authority to remove the drugs. That would be it; whatever reasons he may have had, it would mean the end of his police career, possibly even a custodial sentence. It was worth it, he decided, if it would save Lou from this madman. He couldn't risk telling anyone. He'd seen how badly those sorts of operations could go too many times, and he had no doubts that this lunatic would kill Lou at the first sign of trouble.

He flexed his legs to get ready to exit the car, but he could not bring himself to move just yet. He took out a packet of cigarettes and lit one with trembling hands, hating himself for his cowardly procrastination.

The cigarette would calm him, he told himself. It would give him a chance to prepare mentally for what lay ahead. The first inhalation made him retch. He opened the door and flung the cigarette onto the wasteland at the side of the road, then grabbed the carrier bag and got out. He closed the door quietly and looked about him, making sure that his car could not be seen from the site of the crime scene down the hill.

The cheap mobile phone was in his hand. He looked at it again for the address that had been sent to him before slipping it back into his pocket and setting off walking.

His pulse was racing when he got to the address on Brighton Street. He could see no sign of movement, but he wasn't surprised. The front door and downstairs window were boarded up. Looking up, he thought he saw a flicker of movement in the curtain of the front bedroom window.

He walked around the block to the back of the house as he had been instructed in the text messages. When he drew level with the opening to the back yard, he stopped and took a deep breath to steady his nerves. Then, moving quickly in case his courage left him entirely, he walked straight up to the back door, pushed it open and stepped inside.

The kitchen was surprisingly clean and tidy. There was no cooker or fridge, but the worktops and kitchen sink had been scrubbed. A pan, an enamel plate and a spoon lay, clean on the draining board. Taylor's pulse was racing as he peered through the doorway, past the hall, into the living room. It was dark in there due to the boards that had been left covering the living room window. As far as he could tell, the room was empty.

He shifted the carrier bag into his left hand and thrust his right down the front of his trousers. Fastened in place with gaffer tape, next to his groin, he felt the lock knife. He prayed that he would be able to extract it and deploy it quickly enough if it were needed. He stepped into the dimly lit hallway from the kitchen and looked up the steep bare staircase.

Suddenly, from somewhere upstairs, he heard a sound that chilled his blood. It was a low, inarticulate wail of a female voice. It had to be her, he realised, and without another thought, he bolted heavily upstairs and stamped open the door of the room from which the sound had come.

He took in the scene in an instant. The large front bedroom of the house had been turned into a living room with two cheap, battered settees at right angles to each other and a small, square side table placed at the right angle between them. Along the third wall, by the door, there stood an old sideboard with no doors. In the fourth wall, the fireplace had been crudely re-opened with a salvaged paving slab serving as a hearth and a plain dog grate pushed into the old opening.

Taylor's eyes were fixed for a long, gut-wrenching second on the scene that was being played out on the settee under the window: Half on the settee, on her knees and bent forward over it, was Lou Fowler. She had been stripped down to her bra and pants, and her hands had been tied behind her back with a plastic tie-wrap. Her head lolled from side to side as she was unable to keep it straight in her state of semi-conscious delirium. Her breathing was noisy and laboured. Kneeling behind her was John Meadows. He wore nothing but a pair of filthy stained boxer shorts. His clothes had been thrown carelessly on the floor beside Lou's. He looked about him with vacant eyes, barely able to focus on his task as he tried to grip the waistline of Lou's pants to pull them down.

Doug Taylor was consumed with a sickened rage. He flung the carrier bag aside and surged forward. Coming up behind Meadows, he reached around and gripped him by the windpipe, lifting him bodily off the ground and slamming him back down onto the other settee. Taylor dropped his knee hard into Meadows' midriff, pinning him down with his own body weight. He tightened the grip on Meadows' throat with his right hand and brought his left fist back.

Meadows was struggling feebly to wrench the hand from his throat, but he lacked the strength to do so. His attempts to protest or beg for mercy came out as absurd, gurgling sounds like a drowning duck. Taylor looked down into the desperate, pleading eyes with hatred and contempt. "You filthy little bastard!" he spat, bringing his left fist down hard into Meadows' face. He was disappointed with the result of the blow. Some of the impact was being absorbed by the soft surface of the settee beneath Meadows' head.

Taylor squeezed as hard as he could on the throat in his right hand, and then angled his subsequent blows with his left so that they struck Meadows from the side, hitting him in the temple, the right cheek, and the side of his jaw. That was better, Taylor decided. He took a deep breath and struck again, and again, and again.

He lost count of how many times he had hit Meadows, whose feeble struggles had totally subsided as consciousness was beaten from him. Taylor's bloodied hand slipped and lost its grip on the wretch's throat, but his left continued to swing. Although his fatigued arm was delivering ever weaker blows, there was still a strange satisfaction to be had from the loud smacking sound and the splatters of blood that seemed to reach further and further up the back of the settee with each blow.

Something made Taylor stop his attack. At the edge of his consciousness, he registered the absurd sound, given the situation, of someone politely clearing his throat. He froze. For a long moment, his only movement was that of his heaving, exhausted breaths. Slowly, he raised his head to look at the source of the sound, and his heart sank. The big muscular man with the large gleaming knife was smiling. He gave a small chuckle that grew and transformed into something like a giggle as he failed to hide his amusement at the scene before him.

A voice in the back of Taylor's mind screamed with fury at his own stupidity. He had walked straight into a trap. He had complied with the ransom demand, foolishly believing that it was the best chance of getting Lou back alive and well, and he had been lured in here with such blind urgency that he had failed to check the other bedroom before rushing in. He had that sickening feeling that one gets with the stark realisation that disaster has struck, and time cannot be changed or rewritten.

His overwhelming sensation, however, was one of despair. Even on equal terms, he doubted that he would stand much chance against the big man. Now, kneeling on the settee on top of Meadows, and as exhausted as he was, he knew that there was no hope. Even the weapon that he had brought was too hopelessly out of reach to be of any use. Tears of frustration welled up in his eyes and the mocking expression on the other man's face added shame onto Taylor's misery. The big man raised the knife above his head and Taylor, shaking, screwed up his face and closed his eyes as tightly as he could...

The bang was loud and almost physically sharp as it reverberated against the bare floorboards and walls of the room. Taylor jumped with the shock and now, confused, he opened his eyes in time to see the big man lose his grip on the knife in his hand. He let it fall to the ground and immediately grabbed at the top of his right thigh, near the groin. He crumpled to the floor with a tortured wail.

Behind him and slightly to one side, just on the threshold of the room, stood Normanby. The smoking pistol in his hand was still levelled at the man writhing on the floor. "Remain exactly where you are please Detective," said Normanby, calmly. "My colleagues will be here very shortly."

Taylor ignored him and went over to Lou. Her eyes were rolling up into her head and her mouth hung open. "Lou," he shouted, shaking her by the shoulders. "Lou, speak to me." Her skin felt clammy, and her body was limp as he heaved her around and lifted her into a sitting position on the edge of the couch. "Lou, for God's sake, talk to me. What have they given you? What have they done?"

Within seconds, Taylor heard the squeal of multiple sets of tyres on the road outside as cars pulled up to the kerb. There was the sound of car doors slamming, and then the crash of the house doors being kicked in. Without taking either his cold stare or his aim from the gasping man on the floor, Normanby shouted to the men downstairs. "Front bedroom," he called. "Code seven!"

The Colonel's voice boomed above the banging of heavy boots marching up the stairs. "Code seven?!" he exclaimed. "Another one? Oh, for Christ's sake Normanby!"

Two black clad, hard looking men entered the room and took positions by the door. Each of the men was armed with a Heckler and Koch MP5 machine pistol and, taking their cue from Normanby, they took aim on the man on the floor. Normanby lowered his pistol, carefully applied the safety catch, and then slipped the weapon into the waistband of his trousers.

The Colonel appeared in the doorway and stepped forward so that he was standing behind Normanby's left shoulder. "You've been at it again have you Normanby?" he asked with mild surprise and a hint of reproach.

Grant stood out on the stairs landing, raising up onto the balls of his feet to try and peer over The Colonel's shoulder. He struggled to keep his balance, and put his feet flat on the floor. He felt sick, dizzy, and tired. The excesses of the night had caught up with him.

"Who's this one then?" asked The Colonel loudly.

"This one," said Normanby coldly, "is, I am sure, the murderer of both Shafiq Hussein and Danielle Church. He has also kidnapped the young lady over there, who is a serving Police Community Support Officer." He pointed towards Lou. "I think that the young lady requires urgent medical attention."

"It looks as though your victim does too," said The Colonel. "The man looks as though he could bleed out any minute."

"She's the priority," said Normanby, so firmly that The Colonel glared at him for a second. He let out a breath and then nodded to one of the men in black, who immediately slung his machine pistol and stepped over to Lou.

"And the others?" The Colonel asked.

Without taking his angry, hateful glare away from Gorszky, Normanby gestured towards the battered, barely conscious form of Meadows. "This is John Meadows, a possible witness to both murders."

The Colonel looked at Taylor. "And who's this?" he asked.

Taylor's face nearly crumpled as he felt himself once more engulfed by a feeling of despair. His career was about to be ended by his own stupidity. Normanby obviously knew that he had come here against all standard procedures. He probably even knew that he had been blackmailed by the kidnapper into stealing drugs from the evidence locker and bringing them here in order to try and negotiate Lou's release. He would be lucky to avoid a prison sentence. When Normanby answered The Colonel, Taylor's mouth fell open in shock.

"This is Detective Sergeant Taylor of the Homicide and Major Enquiries Team," said Normanby. "Between us, we managed to formulate a plan to rescue the hostages and catch the murderer."

The Colonel gave Normanby a quizzical look, but made no remark. Normanby did not see it, or the expression of amazement on Taylor's face. He was still staring into Gorszky's eyes with a venomous and vengeful fury. Gorszky tried to tighten the grip on the gushing wound in his thigh. Was the psychopathic little man going to let him bleed to death?

For the first time in many years, Gorszky felt the sensation of fear. He had prided himself for a long time on his ability to get inside his opponent's minds, to crush their will and turn them into victims before the first blow had even been struck. He had gradually destroyed many hard men over the years by finding the slightest weakness, the tiniest crack in their confidence, and then capitalising on it. The strange little man staring at him now was something new. There was no overbearing bluster in this man. Looking back through those silly little spectacles and at the eyes behind them, Gorszky could see no confidence, and therefore no hidden fear of losing that confidence. He could see nothing, not even life…

The black clad man who was examining Lou addressed The Colonel. "It looks like a heroin overdose sir," he said. "She needs urgent attention."

The Colonel nodded. "Get her back to base immediately," he said. "Tell Hopkirk to call the medics to have them waiting." He looked at Gorszky, whose head was beginning to sway. "Tell him we also need one of our ambulances here for this one as soon as possible, before he bleeds to death."

The man lifted Lou as though she was weightless, and carried her out. Grant stepped into the room to give him space to carry her downstairs. He stood, swaying slightly and then looked around. Finally seeing Gorszky, clutching his leg and panting with short shallow breaths, he gave an amused start. "Oh, you're definitely a 'leg man' Normanby," he said: "First Kurylenko and now this one." He fell silent under The Colonel's angry, withering glare.

Normanby, however, did not notice the silent rebuttal. He had seen something far more interesting. At the mention of Kurylenko's name, Gorszky had broken eye contact with Normanby, and stared at Grant. It had taken a full second for him to turn his glazed eyes back to the little man.

Normanby's thin lips widened into a cruel smile. "Ah, Kurylenko," he said slowly.

The Colonel turned his gaze on Normanby. "What?" he said.
"Kurylenko sir," replied Normanby. "When Mr. Grant used his
name, our friend here definitely reacted."

"So," said The Colonel, eyeing Gorszky. "You're one of
Kurylenko's lot, are you?"

Gorszky sneered back glassily, his agonised breathing hissing in
short bursts through clenched teeth. "*Ya Ne Ponimayu*," he spat.

The Colonel gave a look of amused astonishment, and let out a
bitter, bellowing laugh.
"Definitely one of Kurylenko's," said Grant with a smile. "Have
you got any more pencils to wiggle, Normanby?"

Normanby paid no attention to the comments. His eyes were
locked on Gorszky with an expression of cold hatred. Gorszky
himself could not hold the stare. He looked down at the floor,
unable to face the little man. He knew that Normanby would
happily kill him with the slightest excuse, and he was afraid. His
spirit had finally been broken.

Suddenly, there was a commotion outside. The screeching of
tyres was followed by the sound of car doors slamming and then
urgent shouting. The Colonel sighed, wearily. "It sounds as
though the Police have arrived," he said. "Normanby, take the
Detective Sergeant with you and diffuse matters before anyone
else gets shot."

Normanby pulled his gaze away from Gorszky and checked that
he was still being covered by the remaining guard with the MP5.
Gorszky's head was beginning to sway and his eyes were
unfocussed, but one could never be too careful. It could be a
bluff, he thought. "Would you come with me, please Detective,"
he said to Doug Taylor.

Taylor nodded dumbly and followed Normanby out of the room
on legs that felt that they might fold at any moment. As they
made their way slowly down the stairs, Taylor reached forward
and gently touched Normanby on the shoulder. "Thank you, Mr.
Normanby," he said.

"That's quite alright, Detective," Normanby replied absently. "Although I had already found this location, your intervention did make it easier to incapacitate our friend. Without you to keep him busy, I doubt that I would have been able to take him by surprise."

"Oh," said Taylor in confusion, "so you didn't follow me here?"

"No, but I knew you were coming," the little man replied. "Officer Fowler is obviously more than just a colleague to you." Normanby stopped at the bottom of the stairs and turned to see Taylor's face flush.

"I don't know what you're trying to imply," The detective stammered.

"Detective Taylor," said Normanby, patiently, "I am making no judgements, I am simply stating fact. You have matching mobile telephones which you use to contact only each other; you are prepared to risk your career and put your life in danger, ignoring protocols to save her. I notice that you wear a wedding ring and that she doesn't, so the obvious conclusion is that of an illicit affair."

Taylor's mouth began to move, but he was speechless. Normanby stepped through the downstairs front room which was no longer in pitch darkness as the board that had covered the front door had been ripped away by the Colonel's men, and the front door hung open. In the street at the front of the house there was something of a stand-off going on: Two more of the black clad guards stood on the pavement with fingers resting lightly on the triggers of their MP5's. They were watching a colleague who was in a heated conversation with two uniformed Police Armed Response Officers, each also armed with an MP5.

Normanby walked confidently into the middle of the altercation. "Good morning gentlemen," he said breezily.

The Policemen scowled at him. "Who are you?" asked the nearest one.

"Normanby," he replied, holding up his credentials for inspection.

"Are you in charge here?" said the Policeman, looking down at him with a sneer.

"Along with my colleague," Normanby replied coldly, "or should I say, *your* colleague." He turned and glanced back at Taylor, who produced his warrant card and held it contemptuously close to the Officer's nose.

"D.S. Taylor, HMET," he announced. "What are you two doing here?"

The Armed Response Officer looked uncertainly at his colleague. "There was a report of a gunshot sir," he said, defensively. "We came to investigate and came across these lot." He gestured with a nod towards the armed guards. "We haven't been informed of any operations going on and we've got back-up on their way."

"Stand them down," said Taylor. "Tell them I said so."

The officer tried to stand his ground and follow protocol. "Well, we haven't had…"

"Stand them down!" Taylor said again, his face inches from the other man's.

The Armed Response Officer took a step back, his face reddening.

"This is a joint Metropolitan Police and M.I.5. operation. It is classified! Now, go away!" barked the Detective Sergeant, as if dressing down a rookie Constable.

The two Armed Response Officers looked at each other. The one who had spoken nodded to his colleague, who activated his radio and spoke into it. They reluctantly turned back to their vehicle. "I'll be putting in a detailed report about this, Sergeant," said the one that Taylor had spoken to, as he opened the car door.

"You do that, sunshine," Taylor called back belligerently before turning back to Normanby. "I'm going to be in the shit for this," he muttered.

"Oh, I doubt it Detective," said Normanby confidently. "The Colonel has the power to pull strings for those who help our department."

Taylor hoped that Normanby was telling the truth. "Mr. Normanby," he said. "About my relationship with PCSO Fowler…"

"It doesn't matter," said Normanby, dismissively. He turned and set off walking back to the house before Taylor could continue.

They both turned as a black van came screeching around the corner and halted near the house. Taylor shot a worried glance at Normanby, who gave a slight shake of the head. "Private ambulance," he confirmed simply. He looked up to the window of the room that they had left. The Colonel stood framed in the window. He looked back at Normanby with a sad, bitter expression on his face and shook his own head, slowly.

Normanby took off his spectacles and rubbed his eyes. He felt drained and weary, and oddly empty inside. It was a sensation that he had not felt in many years, and one that he had hoped never to feel again. There was a sense of impotence at not being able to undo an action once it had been taken. He felt self-contempt for the stupid, childish wish that life could have some kind of reset button that would wash away the stain that had been left on his soul.

The Colonel looked down coldly into Gorszky's lifeless eyes which stared back, unblinking. He had bled to death from the gunshot wound inflicted by Normanby. He felt no sorrow at the man's death. His only concern in the matter was how Normanby would cope with the situation.

The two paramedics who had arrived in the private ambulance entered the room. One began to examine Gorszky's body for any signs of life. The other set about trying to revive the battered and bloody form of John Meadows.

The Colonel tapped the guard on the shoulder and gestured towards the two busy paramedics. "Give them any help they need," he said. He received a curt nod in response. "Grant," he continued, "let's leave them to it."

Grant nodded silently. He shot one last glance at the body on the floor and then followed The Colonel out of the room and down the stairs.

On the pavement at the front of the house, Doug Taylor was smoking a cigarette. He drew the smoke deep into his lungs in a long draught and then held it there for long seconds before exhaling it high into the air. He took another deep pull, straight away.

The Colonel looked at him closely and saw that the man was close to breaking point. His face was drained of colour and his hands were trembling. The glowing end of the cigarette was long and pointed. It had not been given time to turn into grey ash between inhalations.

Taylor looked back at the Colonel and kept his face set hard. "He's dead then?" he asked sharply. The Colonel nodded.

"Can't say I'm sorry," The Detective continued bitterly. "Have you heard any news about…about my PCSO?"

"Not yet," The Colonel replied, "but she's in good hands. Where's Normanby?"

Taylor gestured vaguely with a wave of the hand. "He went around the back," he said. "I think he needed a moment."

"I imagine he did," said The Colonel. "Grant, wait with the Detective Sergeant," he continued. "Ring Betty and see if you can get any news on how the young lady is doing." Without waiting for a reply, he set off to look for Normanby in the direction that Taylor had indicated.

Normanby was standing perfectly still and was looking out over the stretch of wasteland down towards to crime scene tent and the Police tape. The clouds had cleared, and the bright sunshine and the slight breeze turned the overgrown grass into a dancing sheet of gold, hemmed by the Crime Scene Tape. He felt the warmth of the sun on his face as he closed his eyes and drew in a deep breath. As he slowly exhaled, his mind raced back through the years…

…He was breathing out slowly and making an effort to relax, the way he had been taught. He could feel the sweat beneath his right eyebrow where it had come into contact with the eyepiece of the telescopic sight and cooled slightly into a droplet.

The crosshairs of the sight were lined up on the back of a man's head. He resisted the urge to squeeze the trigger until he was absolutely sure of the target's identity. The head turned to one side, giving Normanby a profile view of the man's face. There was an ugly scar reaching from the top of the man's bedraggled, greying beard to the corner of the left eye. The distinctive, hooked nose was visible, and Normanby tensed slightly. The hand that brought the half-smoked cigarette up to the cruel mouth became visible in the sights. The man was holding the cigarette between his middle and ring fingers. The index finger on the hand was no more than a short stump protruding from the main knuckle.

Normanby had the positive identification that he needed. He adjusted the position of the weapon minutely so that the crosshairs in the sights lined up with the side of the target's head, just behind the temple. Keeping his body relaxed, he squeezed the trigger in a smooth movement. The weapon bucked slightly in his relaxed grip. There was a small sound, like an absurdly polite cough, from the sound-moderated barrel of the rifle.

Normanby watched as a small hole appeared exactly where the crosshairs had been trained on the side of the man's head. The target vanished from the image through the lens as he fell, dead, on the dusty ground.

There was a moment of absolute silence, and then all Hell broke loose. The group of men, scattered between the two Toyota pick-up trucks began shouting and waving the AK47 Assault Rifles that they carried. The angry shouts quickly became curses and accusations, and suddenly the group seemed to split into two factions.

Normanby remained absolutely still, trusting his camouflage, even though some of the men seemed to be looking straight at him. When they saw no visible sign of an attacker from outside, the curses and accusations rose to fever pitch. It didn't take long before the first shot was fired, and almost instantly, another rang out. Within seconds the sporadic gunfire had developed into a fully-fledged firefight between the two factions. Agonised screams rang out among the rattle of the guns as men lay writhing in agony on the dusty ground.

As Normanby watched silently, his face creased in a thin, cruel smile...

...The Colonel stood and watched the little man for several seconds before quietly stepping up beside him. He poked the ferrule of his umbrella absently into the muddy path whilst he tried to think of something to say.

It was Normanby who spoke first. "There'll be an enquiry, I suppose," he said simply.

The Colonel nodded. "Yes," he said, when he noticed that his operative wasn't looking at him. "Don't worry about the gun Normanby, we'll sort that out."

It was Normanby's turn to nod. He looked down at the floor. "I suppose I'll be on suspension," he mumbled.

The Colonel sighed. "Obviously," he said patiently, "until the enquiry's complete. The Director General will demand it."

Normanby gave a snort of contempt. "There'll be politicians screaming for my head."

"Oh, I don't doubt it," The Colonel replied. "I dare say half of The House will be more interested in our friends 'human rights' than the fact that you stopped him killing three people, to add to the at least two that he's already killed. Don't worry about it, Normanby. I won't let them feed you to the wolves. You're much too useful to be wasted like that."

Normanby gave the slightest of wry smiles at the remark. "Shall I hand the gun in now sir?" he asked.

"Good God, no," replied The Colonel with a shocked expression.

"But, my suspension..?" said Normanby, feeling confused.

"The Director General hasn't ordered it yet," The Colonel said lightly. "Go and bring me Kurylenko. I want a word with him." Normanby looked back at the older man, and his mouth fell open in a stunned expression.

"Well don't just stand there man," The Colonel barked. "Bring him in! I'll get GCHQ to send you his location if he's still carrying that phone that you examined."

With a visible effort, Normanby shook off his stunned surprise. He turned and began walking back towards the house.

"Take Grant with you," called The Colonel over his shoulder.

Normanby stopped and turned. "Grant sir?" he asked. "Are you sure?"

The Old Man scowled back sternly. "It was Kurylenko who told us that Grant was bent," he said. "If Kurylenko is also sending out psychopathic hitmen and lying to us about it, his word is hardly to be trusted, is it? That puts Grant in the clear."

Normanby shrugged. "If you say so sir," he said. He turned and continued walking to the house.

CHAPTER TWENTY EIGHT: THE GAME

Normanby's mobile phone was ringing, and he struggled against the constraints of the seatbelt to fish the device out of his pocket. He answered it and spoke to Willoughby, whom Normanby knew vaguely as a colleague from GCHQ.

"Mr. Willoughby?" asked Normanby. "Do you have the location of Kurylenko's telephone?"

Grant pulled the car up to the kerb and parked illegally across the road from the large, white Georgian mansion near the Bayswater Road end of Kensington Palace Gardens. He reached over and clicked on the car's hazard warning lights. It wouldn't be long, he thought, before they attracted the attention of the Police for hanging around across the road from the Russian Embassy.

He saw movement inside the black metal gates that were framed between white stone pillars. Squinting to see through the bars, he could see that they were already being watched from within the grounds. A large, thuggish looking, shaven headed man in a black suit and tie was peering suspiciously out at the new arrivals.

The man had an earpiece in his left ear, and the wire from it ran down into the back of his shirt. One hand reached casually up to his tie, as if he was about to adjust it, and Grant knew that he would be activating the press-to-talk button on his microphone, and alerting someone inside to their presence.

"So, what do we do now, Normanby?" asked Grant. "Shall we knock and ask to see Kurylenko, or jump the fence and get him, like Bond in 'Casino Royale'?"

Normanby shot him an irritated glance and then shushed him
with a sound like an angry cat. He pressed the phone closer to
his ear and concentrated on the directions that he was hearing.
"We shall do neither at the moment Mr. Grant," he said, sharply.
"Kurylenko is no longer here. He's on the move. Head East on
Bayswater Road…that way," he pointed.
Grant sighed impatiently and started the engine. In his wing
mirror, he saw a short, stocky black man in a peak cap staring,
challengingly at the car. It took Grant a moment to recognise the
man's uniform as that of a Traffic Warden.

"Hey, you!" the Warden shouted sternly, walking briskly
towards them. His hand was reaching behind him to the pouch
on the back of his belt and tugging out the ticket book that
protruded from it.

"Not bloody likely," growled Grant, and he gunned the engine as
the Traffic Warden broke into a run. He let out the clutch and
pulled away from the kerb and into the traffic, eliciting a furious
beep of the horn from a black cab that had been forced to brake
sharply by his manoeuvre. He glanced in his wing mirror and
chuckled at the sight of the wild-eyed Traffic Warden, still
running along the pavement in a vain pursuit. "Next time
Mistah!" he shouted as his energy ran out and his legs ground to
a halt.

The car lurched as Grant swung it wildly out onto Bayswater
Road and stepped heavily on the throttle, before having to brake
sharply for the traffic ahead. Normanby fixed him with a
disapproving glare and then pressed the phone back to his ear to
listen for further directions from Willoughby.

As he drove on, Grant could see the grand structure of the
Marble Arch in the distance. "Where do I need to be going next
Normanby?" he asked. "Well?" he said impatiently, after
waiting a few moments for the little man to reply.

Normanby was deep in thought, the phone still pressed to his
ear. "Bear right onto Park Lane," he said.

Grant braked hard and swerved, just in time to be able to follow the instruction. "A little forewarning would be nice," he muttered tersely.

Normanby ignored the remark. "You can slow down a little Mr. Grant," he said calmly. "Apparently, we're gaining on him."

Grant slowed a little, but he was still eager to catch up with Kurylenko. He was curious to know why the Russian had had Shafiq killed, but more than anything, he was angry. A tiny part of him hoped that Normanby might shoot Kurylenko. 'God knows', he thought, 'he's capable of it.'

Normanby gave a small, deflated sigh at the next set of directions from Willoughby. "Turn left onto Piccadilly Mr. Grant," he said.

"Oh, the bloody Toll Zone," Grant hissed bitterly.

"At least it's open today," replied Normanby mildly.

"Oh, where the bloody Hell is he going?" Grant asked irritably when Normanby directed him right onto Coventry Street and right again onto Haymarket.

"He's stopped on Orange Street," said Normanby. "Next left."

Grant took the turn and slowed the car to a crawl, to the annoyance of the driver of the car behind. In his rear-view mirror, Grant could see the man gesturing irritably for him to speed up. He ignored him and continued at a speed not much faster than walking pace. His eyes scanned the pavement at each side of the road for any sign of Kurylenko. The man in the car behind, a red Ford Fiesta, finally lost his patience and overtook, bellowing a colourful oath at Grant as he passed.

"He stopped somewhere very near here," said Normanby, "and then moved very slowly onto St. Martin's Street. I think he may be walking."

"Marvellous," muttered Grant. "Now I suppose I should find somewhere to park."

"Stop here," said Normanby, opening the car door. "I'll see if I can spot him on St. Martin's Street." He got out and set off walking, the mobile phone still pressed to his ear.

Grant sighed heavily and set off to look for a parking space. He wondered gloomily if he had enough change in his pocket to feed a parking meter. An empty parking space came into view, and he pulled into it sharply, drawing an angry glare from an elderly lady in a Fiat Panda who had been waiting for a gap in the traffic so that she could take the space herself. He got out of the car and stepped to the Parking Meter, digging deep into his pockets for whatever change he could find.

Normanby was standing on St. Martin's Street with his arms folded in front of him. As Grant approached, he wondered why the little man was no longer taking directions on his mobile phone. "Well?" he asked worriedly.

"The last signal from his telephone came from here, or within a hundred yards of here," Normanby replied. "It has since been switched off."

Grant's fists clenched in anger. "Bollocks!" he spat. "The bastard must have known we were onto him."

Normanby's head turned slowly, as he surveyed the area, and then he suddenly stopped. His gaze was fixed on the large, white fronted gothic building on the corner, a little way up the street. "Not necessarily Mr. Grant," he said. "Many people of a certain age simply have the good manners to switch off their telephones when they enter a library."

Grant slowly followed the direction of Normanby's eyes, and he stared for a long moment at The Westminster Reference Library. He raised his eyebrows and looked at the little man with a slight smile. "Shall we go and check?" he asked. Normanby nodded and together they walked to the front entrance of the library.

The air was cooler inside the main doors and the smell of the old building reminded Grant of his schooldays. Normanby peered through the glass of the inner doors to a large, almost deserted reading room. Around the walls of the room were banks of solid wooden bookshelves filled with fine volumes. These surrounded two long rows of tables. On one row, a line of desk top computers sat, currently unused. The other row consisted of bare tables surrounded by plastic chairs.

The room was overlooked on three sides by a mezzanine level, itself filled with bookcases, which was accessed by two staircases reaching down to each side of the doors. At one end of the row of empty tables a man sat with his back to the door. Another man stood facing him, his back against the bookshelves at the far wall. He was large and well-muscled, with a shaved head and a hard, cruel face. He was wearing a cheap black suit that was a little too small for him. The material of the jacket was stretched taut around his huge chest and shoulders.

Normanby wanted to be sure that the man sitting with his back to him was actually Kurylenko before he moved in, but he knew that the menacing looking man would see him as soon as he entered the door.

Grant was standing a little behind Normanby, and he shuffled his feet impatiently. "Well, is he in there?" he asked.

Normanby kept his attention on the two men inside. "Possibly Mr. Grant," he said absently, "but I want to be sure…aha!"

The big man inside the library nodded respectfully to his seated companion and moved away to one side, disappearing between banks of bookshelves.

Normanby saw his chance. He glanced back at Grant, beckoned him to follow, and then quickly put a finger to his lips for silence. The big door opened quietly with surprisingly little effort and Normanby stepped inside. He moved to the staircase on the right of the door and crept up the steps. Grant followed him, deciding to let the little man play it the way he wanted, even though he would have preferred a more direct approach.

They walked quietly along the mezzanine floor, glancing carefully over the carved wooden railings and down into the reading room. Normanby gave a satisfied grunt when it became apparent that the seated man was indeed Kurylenko.

"So, what now?" whispered Grant. "Do we leap down and grab him, or are you going to shoot his pet gorilla?"

Normanby looked reproachfully over his spectacles at his colleague, and then pushed them up into position with an extended forefinger. "What we do now Mr. Grant," he said, "is watch and wait. The Colonel will have a team tracking our location, so all we need to do is let headquarters know if Kurylenko moves."

Grant gave an impatient snort. He craned his neck so that he could look down at Kurylenko without exposing his own presence. The stocky Russian struggled out of his overcoat and twisted awkwardly to hang it on the back of his chair without getting up. He then reached down and lifted a large briefcase from the floor beside him, up onto the table.

Grant leaned forward for a better view as Kurylenko carefully opened the briefcase. He extracted a plastic lunch box, a small thermos flask and a black and white chequered box of roughly A5 size. After carefully arranging the items on the table, he closed the case and returned it to its resting place on the floor beside his chair.

Watching Kurylenko's slow and fussily precise movements, Grant could not help being reminded of Normanby's own lunch-time ritual. "Will you be sending him a Valentine's Card this year, Normanby?" he whispered.

Normanby ignored him and continued to watch in apparent fascination as Kurylenko opened the box and scooped out a handful of objects from it. He pushed the lid back fully open and turned it over so that the chequered exterior became a chess board. Slowly and delicately, he set the little chess pieces on the board in their starting position. His companion returned from the shelves with two hardback books which he carefully placed on the table before resuming his position facing the door.

Kurylenko unscrewed the Thermos flask and poured himself a cup of tea. He savoured the drink for a moment and then dragged one of the books across the table towards him and started leafing through it, apparently searching for something in particular. He paused, pushed the book wide open on the table, with obvious disregard for its binding, and then moved a white pawn on the chessboard.
Normanby edged forward and crouched down so that he could peer through the gap in the railings without being seen from the library floor. He squinted, straining his eyes to see the layout of the board as Kurylenko consulted the book again before moving a black piece.

Grant let out a long breath and then looked at his watch. He hoped that The Colonel's men would get there soon to take Kurylenko in. He was looking forward to the interrogation, to finding out what link the Russian had with Shafiq and why he had had him killed. He looked across at Normanby. The little man was still watching Kurylenko who, it appeared, was following the moves of a chess game from a book.

Normanby shot Grant a quick glance over his shoulder before returning his attention to the scene below. "I know this game," he whispered, almost to himself.

"Yes Normanby," Grant replied. "It's called 'chess'. My school had a club where all the boys who couldn't get girlfriends used to go and play it."

Normanby ignored him. "Karpov and Kasparov," he muttered, closing his eyes in thought.

Grant's head snapped around and he looked, urgently down into the library. "Who? He's brought back-up?" he asked.

Normanby looked at him and then shook his head with an expression halfway between surprise and pity. He stood up slowly and walked quietly to the top of the staircase that led down to the ground floor.

Grant's mouth fell open in surprise. Did Normanby know something he didn't? he wondered. Why was the little man giving away his position? He got up and warily began to follow Normanby, trying to stay in the shadows cast by the bookcases and to avoid being seen. He waited, unsure of his own next move, as Normanby trotted lightly down the stairs and out onto the ground floor.

The big man in the black suit shifted his position and took a threatening half-pace forward as Normanby stepped out onto the polished surface of the library floor. Kurylenko's head snapped around. His startled expression softened slightly, and his chubby features broke into a slight grin at the sight of Normanby. He glanced back at his big companion and gave a slight, placating wave of the hand. "*Nyet, Vladimir,*" he uttered, shaking his head in a dismissive gesture.

Normanby walked around the table and stood with his back to Vladimir, facing Kurylenko. The Russian looked up at him, his hands resting casually on the table at either side of his chess board.

"Mr. Normanby," he said jovially. "To what do I owe the pleasure?"

Normanby seemed to be rudely ignoring him and instead looked down intently at the chess board. "Karpov versus Kasparov," he said absently. "Moscow: October the fifteenth, 1985. Game sixteen."

Kurylenko's eyebrows raised in astonishment. He looked down at the board and then back at the little man.

Normanby pushed his spectacles up to the bridge of his thin nose, his face a mask of concentration. "Move fifteen," he said. He reached down and moved the white Queen one space forward.

Kurylenko consulted the open book on the table beside the board. He nodded, genuinely impressed. He slid a black pawn two squares forwards. "You must be quite an enthusiast, Mr. Normanby," he said, "to have memorised the game. You have, however, chosen to be the loser in this game."

Normanby moved a white rook along the back row. He stood in total silence and stared coldly at his opponent.

Kurylenko glanced at the book again and moved a black knight, placing it down before the white Queen. "I take it that the sound of mouth-breathing coming from the stairs is your friend Mr. Grant," he said loudly.

Grant sighed and cursed under his breath. He clomped loudly down to the bottom of the stairs and leaned nonchalantly on the bannister, watching Vladimir, warily. The big, mean-looking Russian sneered back and flexed the bulging muscles beneath his tight jacket, menacingly.

"Would you care for some tea Mr. Grant?" asked Kurylenko over his shoulder, in a mocking tone.

"No thanks," drawled Grant, icily. "Novichok gives me indigestion."

Kurylenko chuckled drily. "Your friend is…" He thought for a moment, "The new Oscar Wilde," he concluded, winking conspirationally at Normanby.

The little man moved a knight back to offer protection to the white Queen and the Russian checked the book, knowing that it would be the correct move from the original game.

"Mr. Grant has a point," said Normanby. "It seems that we can't trust you after all, Mr. Kurylenko."

The expression on Kurylenko's round face darkened slightly. "You are always prepared to think the worst of us," he said. He moved a pawn one space forwards.

"We are now," Normanby replied flatly, "since you lied about your involvement in Mr. Hussein's murder." He picked up a white Bishop and moved it back towards his own lines, banging it down emphatically on the board.

Kurylenko moved a black pawn forward, placing a white Knight in danger. "I don't know what you mean," he protested, studying the book for the nineteenth move of the game.

Normanby automatically moved the Knight to safety, then placed his hands, palms down, on the table and leaned forward to get the Russian's full attention. "I happen to have bumped into Shafiq Hussein's murderer, and he seemed to know exactly who you are Mr. Kurylenko," he said.

Kurylenko's gaze rose slowly from the page to Normanby. He did not flinch under the little man's angry glare. "Shafiq was my agent," he hissed harshly. "He came to me because he no longer trusted your Mr. Grant. I have proof of this! I have proof that, once again, the British Intelligence organisations are trying to blame Russia for their own crimes!" He moved a Bishop out of immediate danger and banged it angrily down on the board.

Normanby forced himself to relax a little. "Do you really believe that," he asked, "or is that just what your President wants you to think?"

Kurylenko too seemed to relax slightly, echoing the little man's body language. "I am a good soldier," he said lightly. "What the President wants me to believe always happens to be what I *do* believe."

"Ah," said Normanby simply as he reached down and moved a white pawn forward.

Barely looking down, Kurylenko reached out to make the next move and then suddenly glanced up. There was a strange, thin smile on the little man's face, and he was staring intently at the board. Kurylenko followed Normanby's gaze and as he took in the position of the chess pieces, his eyes narrowed. "Mr. Normanby," he said. "You seem to have taken a wrong move. Your last move should have been the Bishop, back to square G3."

"Only if I'm prepared to play someone else's game," said Normanby, icily. "I sometimes prefer to think for myself, whatever my leaders may tell me."

The Russian stared down at the board for several seconds. So, the little fool wanted to play for real, did he? "Very well Mr. Normanby," he said. He slowly slid his Queen along the back row into a position from which she could protect the pawn that Normanby's move had endangered.

Normanby took the pawn anyway with his own, leaving his piece exposed to attack from both Kurylenko's Queen and one of his Knights.

"Pawns were made to be sacrificed," smiled the Russian, moving one of his Knights forward in an attempt to dominate the centre of the board whilst keeping pressure on Normanby's court pieces.

Normanby moved a pawn forward to threaten the Knight, and Kurylenko saw his chance to rack up the pressure even further. He moved a Bishop across to a square guarded by his Knight, diagonally one square from Normanby's King. "Check!" he said triumphantly, staring intently at the little man.

Normanby moved his king into the only safe square available to him, in the corner of the board.

Feeling confident that he had Normanby cornered, Kurylenko moved his other Bishop forward to tighten his grip on the corner that Normanby was defending.

The little man did something unexpected: He pulled back his own Bishop to threaten Kurylenko's. Surely he would not try to take the piece, thought the Russian. The square was guarded by Kurylenko's Knight.

Kurylenko decided to press on with his aggressive strategy. He moved his Queen forwards and took one of Normanby's pawns. The move left both Queens in a diagonal line, ready for conflict, though both were guarded by their own supporting pieces.

His face devoid of any expression, Normanby extended a finger and pushed up his spectacles. Kurylenko smiled, feeling that he was gaining the advantage. His mouth fell open in surprise, however, when the little man made his next move. Normanby took Kurylenko's Queen with his own.

"That was not very nice Mr. Normanby, and a little foolish," Kurylenko said, and he reached across to take Normanby's own Queen with his Knight. "Now where did it get you?"

Normanby's expression did not waver. "It got the big, easy-to-use weapons out of the way," he said. "There may yet be a need for subtle strategy." As if in contrast with his own words, he moved a Bishop and took Kurylenko's Knight.

A cold sweat broke out on the Russian's forehead. A moment ago it had been going so well. He moved his Rook along the back row in an effort to regroup.

Normanby took the Bishop that had been threatening his King, and Kurylenko cursed himself for letting his concentration slip. He scowled at the little man and began to grow increasingly annoyed by his calm, methodical manner. He knew that his anger would only make things worse, but with each passing move he found himself becoming more and more frustrated. He watched with growing despair as his pieces were coldly picked off, one by one, like disorganised troops in the sights of an expert sniper.

By the fifty-second move of the game Kurylenko was left with only his King on the board. He suspected that Normanby could probably have put him in Check Mate some time ago, but had instead chosen to cruelly decimate his forces.

Normanby slowly adjusted his spectacles and stared coldly, waiting for his opponent to give up and acknowledge defeat.

Kurylenko looked down at the board for long moments. He was shaking with frustration and fury. With a very great effort, he breathed slowly and relaxed his tense muscles a little. "If only real life were so simple, Mr. Normanby," he blustered, forcing an icy smile. "You see, your bodyguard is really no match for my bodyguard. Vladimir is easily capable of killing both of you, even before you can shoot me with my own Makarova."

Normanby held his angry glare without blinking. "Oh, you don't have to worry about me shooting you, Mr. Kurylenko," he said, lightly. "We have plenty of other people for that sort of task."

It was then that Kurylenko caught a glimpse of movement out of the corner of his eye. He sat up straight in his chair and craned his neck to look past Normanby, at Vladimir. The big bodyguard was nervously panting and staring down worriedly at three red dots, which danced like angry bees around the centre of his chest.

'Laser sights,' thought Kurylenko bitterly. Normanby's chess game had been nothing more than a distraction to allow their people to get into position.

"I would advise everyone present to keep their hands in view," The Colonel's voice boomed happily from the doorway of the library.

CHAPTER TWENTY NINE: HARD TALK

Kurylenko sat at the little table in Room 12 in despair. The tall, balding Police Detective with the badly trimmed moustache and the ill-fitting suit had simply told him that he was under arrest for the possession of an unlicensed firearm, assault, conspiracy to murder, conspiracy to pervert the course of justice and espionage against the Crown and the government of the United Kingdom. When Kurylenko had opened his mouth to protest, the Policeman had simply held up a hand for silence, and then read him the short caution, before leaving the room. The door had banged shut and then had been securely locked behind the departing officer.

Kurylenko had not moved since then. He looked glumly at the three straight-backed wooden chairs across the table from him. It was obvious that he would be interrogated in the near future. 'Who knows?' he thought. 'They may even torture me.'

He placed his elbows on the edge of the table and let his head fall into his hands. If only he could work out what kind of game the British were playing, he might be able to work out how much it would be safe to tell them.

*

The Colonel slapped his hand down on the thick card folder on the desk. "Well Grant," he said. "Do we have any clue as to the identity of Normanby's victim?"

Grant gave a slight shrug and shook his head sadly. "I've put a request through to my contacts in Europol sir, but nothing's come back yet."

The Colonel gave a snort of contempt.

"Sir," said Grant, immediately defensive. "I've always found Europol to be helpful and co-operative. If this man hasn't committed crimes anywhere in the E.U., there's no way that they could have a record of him..." His voice trailed off as he heard a sharp tap on the door.

"Come," boomed The Colonel.

The door opened a few inches and Normanby's head poked timidly through the gap. Scanning the room, he pushed it open a little more and squeezed through the gap. He stood for a moment just inside the room, holding a thin, card folder proudly against his chest.

The Colonel raised his eyebrows. "You have something Normanby?" he asked.

"Yes sir," said the little man, pushing his spectacles into position with an extended forefinger. He stepped forward and placed the folder on The Colonel's desk. "Stanislav Gorszky," he announced. "He is, or was, wanted in three different countries of what we tend to regard as the Eastern Bloc, for various crimes, mainly violent assaults."

The Colonel glanced at Grant and gave an amused grunt at the man's crestfallen expression. "And where did you get this information?" he asked, indicating with a finger for Normanby to sit in one of the worn leather club chairs that faced his desk.

"From Interpol sir," replied Normanby, perching delicately on the edge of the seat. "Obviously the Russians would not normally share that information with us, but they had already circulated Gorszky's details to Interpol. They've been after him for some time sir."

"And not all of the friends of our enemies are our enemies," smiled The Colonel, as if finishing Normanby's sentence. He opened the folder and quickly scanned the first two or three sheets of paper inside. "It looks as though he was quite a nasty piece of work," he said.

"Indeed," concurred Normanby. "Having learned of his criminal history, I confess that I don't feel quite so bad about…about what happened to him."

Grant remembered the last moments of Gorszky's life: bleeding to death on the floor in the squalid, damp squat. He remembered how, when the man finally slumped, flat on the ground, the last vestige of life draining from him, no-one had gone to his aid. He swallowed hard, but he still felt sick at the images in his mind.

"Grant," said The Colonel sharply, causing him to start, "we still have work to do. Concentrate!"

Grant looked across at the older man and he was surprised to see a look of empathy in his eyes. "So, this Gorszky was wanted by the Russian authorities," Grant said slowly. "Doesn't that make him an unlikely choice as their agent?"

"Not at all," said Normanby. "If he was useful to them, they would use him quite happily. They may even have promised him a pardon in his home country for a job well done."

The Colonel nodded. "The Intelligence business does tend to attract some very unscrupulous people," he said dryly. He turned, then leaned down and lifted a cardboard box from the floor, onto his desk.

"What's that?" asked Grant.

"This," The Colonel replied, "is all of Gorszky's personal effects."

*

Kurylenko raised his head at the sound of the door being unlocked. He let his hands fall to the table and then watched in sullen silence as the three men filed into the room.

The Colonel stood with his arms folded, behind the middle chair of the three that faced Kurylenko. Grant, to The Colonel's left, placed a large cardboard box on one side of the table. Normanby, to his right, placed two files on the other side, and then took a moment to ensure that they were neatly aligned and perfectly parallel with the table's edge.

The Colonel looked at him with a bemused expression. "All in order Normanby?" he asked.

Normanby lowered his gaze as if mildly embarrassed. "Yes sir," he confirmed quietly.

The Russian watched silently as the three men took their seats in unison. They looked like some kind of comically choreographed vaudeville act, and Kurylenko hated them.

There was a long pause as he looked at the three British Intelligence men in turn. As none of them made any sound, he decided to break the silence himself. "I am being held here illegally," he said officiously. "I demand that you release both myself and my colleague from the embassy at once."

"Shut up!" barked The Colonel suddenly, and with such venom that Kurylenko sat back in his chair in shock. "You have been implicated in the murders of two British nationals, one of whom was an agent for the Security Services. You were also caught with an unlicensed and illegal firearm following one of my operatives with the intention of shooting him."

He glanced at Normanby who opened one of the files and drew out an 8"x10" photograph, which he held up for a second in front of Kurylenko's nose before slamming it down on the table in front of him.

The Russian looked down at the photograph with obvious distaste for the image. It showed the head and shoulders of a heavy boned, shaven headed male. The male's face was distorted as if in shock or pain, and the eyes stared out of the picture, glassy and unfocussed, not quite looking at the camera. Kurylenko felt the acid taste of bile in his throat as he realised that the man in the photograph was dead.

"Stanislav Gorszky," said Normanby; "Your agent, or should I say, your hired killer?"

Kurylenko looked across the table at his accuser in bewilderment. "I have never seen this man before," he whined. He turned his pleading gaze to each of the three men facing him and received only cold, hard stares.

Normanby selected another photograph and slammed it down on top of the first. "Danielle Church," he said; "Gorszky's most recent victim."

Kurylenko's mouth moved as he tried to form some protestation. Again, his gaze moved between the three men in desperation.

"Look at the picture!" yelled The Colonel furiously.

The Russian looked down at the hideous photograph. The face of the woman that it showed was contorted hideously. The mouth was wide open, and the lips were drawn back in a grimace of agony that revealed almost toothless gums, stained black with dried blood. "This is nothing to do with me," he said, barely moving his lips.

Another photograph was slapped down heavily over the last, and this time Kurylenko's hand shot up and covered his mouth in shock and anguish. He let out a sob and his faced creased. Tears came to his eyes, and he closed them tightly.

"Open your eyes," ordered The Colonel, coldly. "Open your eyes and look!" he shouted.

Kurylenko did as he was told, and a tear dropped from his eye onto the photograph. With his free hand, he gently wiped it away and gazed sadly down at the image of Shafiq Hussein. Even in death, the young man was handsome, he thought. Mercifully, the photograph that they had chosen to show him was from the morgue. Shafiq's eyes were closed and the wound on his head had been cleaned. Even his shining black hair had been combed back neatly. He almost looked as though he might just be sleeping. Another tear fell onto the glossy surface of the photograph, and then another. Kurylenko gave a low moan, and then broke into a series of uncontrollable sobs.

Grant stared at the pathetic wretch before him with utter contempt. This bastard had had his agent murdered, and now that he had been found out, he was sobbing like a baby. He wanted to punch the Russian's fat face into a pulp. It took a supreme effort of will to unclench his fists and relax the tensed muscles in his arms. "That man was my agent," he spat through gritted teeth.

Kurylenko stared back at him with red, watery eyes. Despite his sobbing and his tears, when he spoke, his voice held an edge of defiance. "Your agent?" he snarled furiously. "He did not trust you! He came to me! He was my agent! He was more than that." As he finished his sentence, another wave of sobs convulsed him, and he put both hands over his face. "He was my lover," he said in a quiet voice, muffled by his hands. He became quiet, but his body shook with silent sobs.

Grant's mouth fell open in surprise. He took a deep breath and slowly leaned forward to reach into the cardboard box on the table. The Colonel and Normanby watched him quizzically as he brought out a packet of 'Fest' cigarettes and opened it, carelessly discarding the cellophane wrapper on the table. He extracted a cigarette and lit it with a disposable lighter from his pocket. Whilst inhaling a deep breath of the harsh, menthol-tinged smoke, he expertly extended another cigarette halfway out of the box with his thumb.

Normanby coughed and wrinkled his nose at the unpleasant stench of the cigarette, but Grant ignored him. He took another pull and then tapped Kurylenko lightly on the arm. "Here," he said gently. "Have a smoke and tell me about him."

Kurylenko brought his hands down from his face. He was no longer crying but he looked drained and in the depths of despair. "Thank you," he said, "but I do not smoke."

Grant held the cigarette packet out for several seconds as if to tempt the other man. "Okay," he said quietly. "Are these the ones you gave to Gorszky?" He placed the packet on the table.

Kurylenko sighed. "I promise you," he replied, "that I do not know this Gorszky. Are you sure that he is the one who killed Shafiq?"

"Yes," said Grant flatly.

"And how did he die?" asked the Russian.

Normanby shuffled uncomfortably in his seat. "I shot him," he said.

Kurylenko turned his bloodshot and swelled eyes on him slowly and then gave a small, sad smile. "Thank you Mr. Normanby," he said solemnly.

"Mr. Kurylenko, we need you to tell us everything you know," the little man replied softly.

"Why not?" Kurylenko sighed. "I have nothing more to lose. If your people do not kill me, my own people probably will." He paused for a moment, hoping for some kind of reassurance. He received none and decided to carry on anyway, feeling a strange kind of relief at being able to set the record straight with someone.

"I am not a spy," he began. "I have an administrative position at the Russian Embassy in London. The breakdown in diplomatic relations between our countries has led, as you know, to a great many Russian Diplomats being expelled from your country. I do not know if any of these people were ever involved in any kind of espionage operations here in the United Kingdom. What I do know is that several months ago I was contacted by a representative of the Russian government and instructed to obtain certain information. I do not know if this person is involved with our intelligence services. I have always assumed that his department was something like your own Foreign Office. The information that he asked me to obtain was not anything that concerned the government of the United Kingdom. I hope that you remember that fact before you decide to hang me or shoot me."

He glanced at Normanby. "I was told that operatives of the Russian security services were trying to locate certain stolen weapons which they believed had been transported from Syria to Afghanistan, weapons which may have fallen into the hands of the Afghan Taliban. Intelligence had suggested that some of these weapons may also have been passed on to Taliban fighters in Pakistan."

The Colonel sat forward. "What kind of weapons?" he asked.

Kurylenko gave a noncommittal shrug, hoping that it would be enough. It wasn't.

"What kind of weapons?" The Colonel repeated firmly.

"Just a crate of small arms," replied the Russian, casually. "I think it was just a matter of national pride that they had gone missing."

The Colonel wasn't convinced. "Specify what kind of small arms, man," he boomed impatiently.

Kurylenko shrank back slightly under the Old Man's angry glare. "They are sniper rifles," he said solemnly. "Orsis T-5000 sniper rifles."

"So, the Taliban have their hands on Russian sniper rifles," The Colonel said, before adding sarcastically: "I wonder how that happened?"

Kurylenko averted his eyes. "I do not know," he said. "They are probably from the days of our occupation of Afghanistan, before your invasion."

Normanby adjusted his spectacles. "Unfortunately, we can discard that theory," he interjected. "That particular weapon did not come into use until after the Soviets…ah…retreated from Afghanistan. Certain sections of the American Intelligence community have maintained that Russia may currently be giving aid to the Taliban in order to destabilise the region further, of course."

"Destabilise?" said Kurylenko, in a mocking tone. "Of course, the region was so incredibly 'stable' under Western control!"

Grant put a hand to his mouth to hide his smirk at the nationalistic sparring between Normanby and Kurylenko. "Can we hurry this up guys?" he asked lightly. "You boys can play chess with the world another time."

The Colonel threw him a dark look, which he was not surprised to receive. "Put that bloody cigarette out, man!" he barked. "And you, Kurylenko: Your people are concerned about missing sniper rifles, which may have been passed from Afghanistan to Pakistan. Hardly a big enough issue to involve civilian Embassy staff in espionage work and risk a major international incident, wouldn't you say?"

Before the Russian could raise his shoulders in a shrug, The Colonel pressed on harshly. "You're lying, Kurylenko. There's more to this than the Russians arming the Taliban with sniper rifles to stir up trouble. What are your people really looking for?!"

Kurylenko began to fold his arms. Maybe he had said too much already, he thought.

Normanby leaned forward and tapped the photograph on the table with his index finger. "What did Shafiq Hussein die for Mr. Kurylenko?" he asked, softly.

Kurylenko glanced again at the young man's picture and his chin trembled slightly. With a great effort, he maintained his composure. "The operatives that spoke to me," he said, very carefully, "claimed to have received information from official Syrian Government sources that the same group, connected to the Taliban, may have also obtained a substantial quantity of Sarin nerve-agent."

"My God!" sighed The Colonel. "How did they get it? How does the Syrian regime even know about it unless it was theirs? More to the point, Kurylenko, why did your people come to you about something that's happening in Afghanistan and Pakistan?"

Kurylenko was uncomfortable. "I am sure that they would have checked with Embassies throughout the world," he said.

 "Or perhaps they already knew that someone in this Taliban faction had contacts in England," The Colonel suggested bitterly. "You wouldn't be able to tell me how they might know that, would you?"

Kurylenko averted his eyes. "I could not tell you," he muttered.

"You're not being very co-operative all of a sudden," said the Old Man suspiciously.

"I am not a traitor, Colonel," said Kurylenko defiantly. "I will help you in your investigation, but I will not sell out my country's agents so that you can treat them the way that you are treating me!" He took a deep breath before continuing. "Yes, we had information from a source that I cannot disclose; a Russian businessman whose work brings him to your country. This information was little more than a very short list of people in London who had links with the Taliban. I am sure that your own lists are much more detailed."

"Perhaps," said The Colonel, blithely. "Go on."

Kurylenko held out his hands, palms showing. "But I have told you everything," he said.

"How did you recruit Shafiq?" asked Grant, pointedly.

The Russian let out a long sigh, shaking slightly as he did so. "We started to watch the people on the list," he said slowly. "It took time because we do not have the resources to carry out surveillance work. With Ali Hussein's people it was a little easier as there were three names from the list that stayed together a lot. When Shafiq was observed visiting his cousin, Ali Hussein at his flat regularly, he was photographed. I decided to take a turn at watching him, also." His gaze became slightly distant as he recalled fond memories.

"You chose to watch Shafiq because you were attracted to him?" asked Grant.
Kurylenko gave a shrug. "Russian society is not like British society," he said candidly. "A man with my tastes cannot be as open as he can in the West."

"Yes," said Grant. "We decadent Westerners tend to be a little more open-minded about that sort of thing, don't we?"

Kurylenko ignored him and continued, re-living the memory with a sad smile. "I would be a useless spy because Shafiq spotted me the very first time I followed him," he said. "I thought that I was being clever, but he managed to…how do you say? 'Shake my tail'"

Grant quickly put a hand to his mouth and, with an effort, managed to stifle a guffaw at the unintended innuendo. In doing so, he elicited a furious glare from The Colonel and a raised eyebrow from Normanby.

Kurylenko seemed not to notice. "I was disappointed," he continued. "I lost him in the crowd near a little marketplace in Soho. I knew that there would be no chance of me being able to follow him again. I was feeling sad, so perhaps I was not concentrating as I returned to the Embassy. This would explain why Shafiq was able to follow me there. It was not hard for him to work out who I was."

There was a long pause. The three Englishmen stared intently at the Russian, who had lapsed into a silent reverie. "So, how did you make contact with him," asked The Colonel, after a long pause.

Kurylenko gave a start, as if suddenly awakened from a dream. "I did not have to," he said. "It was Shafiq who came to me, two weeks later."

"What?" said Grant, his eyes wide with incredulity. "He came to you?"

"Yes," the Russian replied, staring pointedly back at him. "He came to me because he could no longer trust you."

"Bullshit!" snapped Grant angrily.
"Shut up Grant!" The Colonel's barked order brought the room to silence and drew all eyes to him. He waited for several seconds and then broke the spell by speaking again. "Continue, Mr. Kurylenko."

Kurylenko's accusing stare swung back to Grant. "Shafiq told me that he no longer trusted Mr. Grant," he said. "He told me that he had passed on information about how Ali Hussein was financing his plot by smuggling heroin into the United Kingdom. He said that he had given Mr. Grant details of a large shipment that was coming in. He expected Ali Hussein's people to be arrested for it, and the gang to be broken up before they could do harm, but this did not happen!"

Grant shuffled uncomfortably in his seat. He could feel his face flushing with fury. "It's all in my reports," he started to say, but The Colonel silenced him with another angry stare.

"Go on, Mr. Kurylenko," the Old Man said quietly.

"The shipment came through," Kurylenko continued. "But there was something else. There was a message in the shipment explaining that the shipping company could ensure that there would be no interference from the British authorities in exchange for thirty percent of the goods. As the gang were picking up their shipment, a group of armed *British* men came and collected their thirty percent"

"Weren't Hussein's people suspicious?" asked The Colonel.

"Of course they were," affirmed Kurylenko, "but they were convinced that it would be worth continuing if they could be guaranteed a safe route into the country for whatever they wanted to bring in."

"He seems to have confided in you in detail," said The Colonel.

"We were very close," the Russian replied sadly. "In a very short time we realised that we had feelings for each other. I advised him to continue meeting Mr. Grant and to keep giving him just enough information to stop him being suspicious. In this way, we could wait until Ali Hussein was ready to act. If he was going to bring in any of the weapons that we were looking for, then our own people could deal with it." He gave a shaking sigh and he put a hand to his mouth. "It seems that we were not careful enough. We had spent a night away together and Shafiq had rushed to meet Mr. Grant the next morning. He had told me that the meeting had not gone well. A week later, he was murdered." He broke down on the last word and buried his face in his hands, weeping openly.

CHAPTER THIRTY: THE DIRECTOR GENERAL

The Colonel sat back heavily in his chair and rubbed his eyes wearily. This whole messy business was making him feel very tired indeed. There were too many loose ends and too many unanswered questions. To make matters worse, he had to accept the possibility that there may be a mole in the Department.

He looked at the two men that were facing him across his desk. "Grant," he said. "Before you go home tonight, I want you to dig out all your reports from your meetings with Shafiq Hussein. Leave them on your desk and I'll collect them shortly."

Grant's face reddened slightly. "Surely you don't believe Kurylenko's accusations sir," he said.

"Just get me files out man," The Colonel snapped. "It doesn't matter what I believe." He looked at the other man, seated beside Grant. "Normanby," he said sadly. "The Director General has been trying to contact me. I don't doubt for a moment that he will order me to put you on immediate suspension, pending an inquiry into Gorszky's death."

The little man swallowed and then nervously adjusted his spectacles.

"Now, don't worry about it," The Colonel continued. "It's a formality, and I'm sure you'll be back at your desk very soon. I will ensure that you will be on full pay for the duration of your suspension."

There was a sharp rap on the door, which opened slightly before The Colonel could give either an acknowledgement or an invitation. Betty, The Colonel's secretary, leaned into the room. "It's the Director General again sir," she said, looking exasperated. "I've told him that you're in a meeting, but he says that it's urgent and he won't be ignored anymore."

The Colonel sighed. "Very well Betty," he said. "Just tell him I'll be there in half an hour."

Her expression made it clear that the reply was less than she had hoped for, and that she had been hoping that The Colonel would have taken the call himself. She nodded sullenly and then pulled back out of the room and closed the door gently behind her.

The Colonel looked at his watch. "Get those files Grant, and then take Normanby home," he ordered.

"But I had plans for after work," Grant said tersely. He caught the Old Man's stare and gave a resigned sigh. "Very well sir," he said, defeated. "Come on Normanby." The two men got up and left the room without another word.

The Colonel waited for several seconds after they had gone. He turned his gaze on the portrait of Winston Churchill, who stared out defiantly from the wood panelled wall. "We're going through Hell, Winnie," he muttered. He took a deep breath and then blew it out sharply, having already concluded that the only option was to keep going. He reached for the telephone on his desk, then pressed a button to un-mute the device, before dialling an extension number. "Major Green?" he asked when the call was answered.

"Ah, Colonel," said Green jovially. "How are you sir?"

"Never mind the pleasantries Major," The Colonel replied. "I want you to bring up everything you have on the Hussein investigation, and send it all to the D.G.'s desktop for a meeting."

There seemed to be a hint of mockery in Green's voice when he replied. "Of course sir," he said. "Is there some kind of investigation going on?"

The Colonel was seething with anger, but with effort he managed to hold it in. "Just send the files Major," he said coldly.

*

The Director General polished the lenses of his spectacles and put them back on to gaze out of the big window at the dimming sky over the Thames. He caught a glimpse of his own reflection in the glass, and he straightened his hand-knitted blue silk tie. His short, dark-brown hair was immaculately styled, and the blue suit that he wore was a perfect, tailored fit. Ever since Stella Rimmington had brought the Director General position out of the shadows and become a public figure herself, image was important for all of her successors in that post.

He turned when he heard the light knock on the door, and he seated himself behind his huge, glass-topped desk. "Come in," he said.

The door opened silently, and The Colonel stepped into the room. He was carrying a bundle of bulging, A4 folders under one arm. He stopped, facing the Director General across the desk, and waited, almost standing to attention.

The Director General made a point of ignoring The Colonel for several seconds, instead putting all his attention into reading from the screen of his desk-top computer. He shook his head sadly and tutted several times.

Eventually, he looked up. "Sit down Colonel," he said sternly. "I think it's about time we had a little talk, don't you?"

The Colonel placed the pile of folders on the edge of the desk and sat down heavily in one of the plush leather and chrome chairs that faced the man across the big desk. "Yes sir," he said with an edge of defiance in his voice. "What would you like to talk about?"

"Oh, we have plenty to talk about Colonel," The Director General replied coldly, "and you won't like what you're going to hear!"

The Colonel's eyes narrowed. "Go on," he said.

The Director General struggled to control his temper. He was already furious and the insubordinate tone in The Colonel's voice threatened to push him over the edge. "Good God man! What have you and your little gang been playing at lately?" he fumed. "I've been looking at these reports and it reads like a biography of the bloody Kray twins!" He made a sharp gesture to the screen on his desk and turned it so that the Colonel could see what he had been reading. "You've got your little cowboy outfit shooting people dead, carrying out unauthorised surveillance, kidnapping foreign diplomats and covering up God knows what other criminal acts," he continued angrily. "I've got a damned good idea what the Home Secretary's going to say about it all. Have you?"

The Colonel sighed wearily. He was well aware that certain Home Secretaries, on learning of the existence of his department, had often made their disapproval quite clear, but none had ever acted on those feelings. His feeling was that Home Secretaries came and went, and he had been allowed to continue because during their often short periods in office, there had always been someone to point out the necessity the Department. "I can only imagine sir," he said lightly.

"Christ Almighty!" The Director General shouted. "Do you think this is some sort of game? You're not above the law Colonel, and this time you've gone too far. Your department is dirty. In fact, it's worse; it's a cancer that's affecting my organisation, and I intend to remove it! It's the only way to minimise the damage that's been done!"

"The damage, sir?" asked The Colonel mildly.

"Yes, damn it, the damage!" raged the Director. "Your man Normanby shot dead a suspect in a murder investigation!"

"Thereby saving the life of a serving Police Detective," interjected The Colonel, "along with the lives of a kidnapped Police Community Support Officer and a witness. Normanby acted properly in the matter, and he has been suspended, pending my enquiry, as protocols demand."

"*Your* inquiry?" fumed the Director. "Oh no Colonel, you're not just sweeping this under the carpet! This is the same operative who, only days ago, stabbed a foreign diplomat in the leg!" He held up a hand to silence The Colonel's response before continuing. "The diplomat was then taken to your department's offices, denied proper hospital treatment and then interrogated without any Police involvement!"

"Would you have preferred the publicity that would have come with that sir?" asked The Colonel tartly. "Is the Home Secretary up to a muscle-flexing competition with the Russian President?"

The Director General's mouth fell open in shock at The Colonel's insubordination. "You really don't get it do you?" he shouted, turning back to the screen. "And what about this other man of yours, Thomas Grant? When I authorised his transfer to your department, I thought it might do some good. I thought an injection of new blood into your team might help bring you into the twenty-first century, but no. You've dragged him down with you. You've got him taking out surveillance equipment without the proper authorisation and failing to report large-scale drug smuggling by the people that he's supposed to be watching."

"What?" said The Colonel, suddenly shocked. "Grant's reports have been thorough and inclusive of all of the facts." He banged a hand down onto the folders on the desk. "I have all the transcripts right here!"

"And I have them here, Colonel!" shouted The Director, jabbing a finger at the screen.

"Now, that is interesting," The Colonel said slowly, raising an eyebrow.

"Oh, it's more than interesting Colonel," the other man replied. "It's damning! As is the statement that Grant has submitted about your man Normanby!"

"A statement?" asked The Colonel. "It's the first I've heard about a statement." He leaned forward to look at the screen and he began to feel sick at the realisation that his men had turned on each other.

CHAPTER THIRTY ONE: NAMING OF PARTS

Grant drove in silence. He glanced across at Normanby who was staring, un-moving, out of the passenger side window at the view of London's evening streets flashing by.
The little man was obviously deep in thought.

"He's probably trying to figure me out," thought Grant. "He obviously believes Kurylenko, and so does The Colonel." Another thought suddenly occurred to him. "What if Normanby himself is the mole?" The more that Grant thought about it, the less absurd it seemed. After all, Normanby's powers of deduction at the first murder scene had seemed a little too good to be true. And, how easily had he tracked Gorszky and then conveniently shot him before he could be properly interrogated?

Grant pulled up to the kerb outside the dark, imposing terraced row where Normanby lived. "There you go Normanby," he said, before adding sarcastically; "don't worry about the tip."

Normanby got out. "Thank you, Mr. Grant," he said flatly, and then he closed the door.

As Grant pulled away into the street, he glanced in his rear-view mirror, expecting to see Normanby standing on the kerb edge watching, but the little man had gone straight inside the house.

Normanby had made all the usual checks before going into his flat. Once inside, he locked the door behind him and looked around. The realisation that he was currently suspended from duty and that he had a lot of time on his hands made him feel listless and instantly bored.

He took the Makarov from the waistband of his trousers, checked the safety catch was on, and then carefully placed the weapon on the side table in between the two armchairs.

Striding over to the cupboard by the fireplace he took out a glass and the bottle of Haig Club and held them both in one hand. With the other hand, he reached down into the bottom cupboard and fished around in an old wooden box of small tools and DIY materials. He gave a small, satisfied grunt as he found some soft, clean rags and a small tin of superfine machine oil.

Returning to one of the armchairs, he placed the items that he carried on the little table, next to the pistol and then poured himself a generous measure of scotch. He took a sip of the golden liquid and rolled it around in his mouth, then put down the glass and picked up the little pistol. He removed the magazine and pulled back the slide to clear the round that was in the breech, standing the bullet on its base on the table. He pulled down on the spring-loaded trigger guard and deftly began stripping the gun down to its component parts for cleaning.

As he worked, a snippet of an old poem drifted into his mind: Henry Reed's 'Naming of Parts'. "Today we have naming of parts," he muttered to himself absently. "Yesterday, we had daily cleaning. And tomorrow morning…"

The task that he performed, automatically and without conscious thought, seemed to clear his mind. The rhythm of the words acted like some kind of mantra, and he slipped into a state of meditative stillness that he had not experienced in many years.

*

Grant opened the door to his flat and stepped inside. After the presence of the girl there last night, the place now seemed so empty and lonely. He prowled from room to room and wondered how those few hours of her company could have made such a difference.

She had tidied the flat and made the bed before she had left, he noticed. His heart sank a little as he looked around and noticed that there was no sign of her having been there.

Feeling a little dejected, he stepped over to the kitchen area, off the main room of the flat and went to the refrigerator. Although he did not feel hungry despite having eaten nothing all day, he supposed that he would feel better if he had something in his stomach. A shower and a change of clothes would help too, he thought.

When he opened the refrigerator door, a smile spread across his face. There was a full protein shaker and a plastic sandwich box with a note taped to it on the middle shelf. The note read; "Keep your strength up. You're going to need it! XXX"

"Well, that's a promising sign," he said to himself, smiling. It helped to lift the dull and melancholy mood that had been growing on him all afternoon, to know that she wanted to see him again.

He took the box and the shaker out of the fridge and sat down with them at the dining table. The box contained a ham salad sandwich, which he bit into and struggled to chew through. He simply did not feel hungry, and he couldn't understand why. He took a sip of the vanilla flavoured protein shake from the shaker bottle to help wash down the mouthful of sandwich. He took another bite, determined to finish the food and drink. To do so was, he was sure, the best way to clear his delayed hangover and to make himself feel better.

After he had consumed the sandwich and the drink, he felt a little better, though he was still thirsty and dehydrated. He went to the bathroom and stripped off his clothes. It was only then that he realised how clammy and sweaty he had been feeling. He turned on the electric shower and waited for a moment for the water to get hot, glancing at his reflection in the mirrored wall. He looked down at his naked body and gave a wry smile. "My, my, we're a bit shrivelled old son," he muttered. "I must be even more dehydrated than I thought."

He stepped under the shower and stood for a moment relishing the feeling of the pinpricks of hot water on the back of his neck. He worked each of his joints in turn, feeling his muscles starting to relax. "Ah, that's better," he said to himself, reaching for the tube of hair and body wash on the shelf beside him and squeezing a large dollop of it into his palm.

Twenty minutes later, he felt like a new man. He had brushed his teeth twice and rinsed and gargled with mouth wash. After this, he had shaved, brushed his teeth again and then drunk several handfuls of water from the bathroom tap. Finally, he had dressed in fresh clothes and placed the suit that he had taken off on a hanger, ready to be taken to the dry cleaners.

He thought about going to the club to see the girl again, and when he did so he felt his heart begin to pound, and the tickle of adrenaline like butterflies in his stomach. Yes, he decided, he would go to the club later. First, however, he thought that he had better catch up with Mike Green and discuss the day's events with him. With the responses that he had received from Normanby and The Colonel regarding Kurylenko's accusations, it was beginning to look as though Major Green was the only one that he could trust.

He brought out his phone, dialled Green's number and waited, listening patiently to the dialling tone. He looked at his watch, wondering if the Major might still be at work. There must be something important going on, he thought, for Green not to answer. He hung up and decided that he would ring back in ten minutes, and then began pacing around the flat, fidgeting impatiently.

*

Major Mike Green picked up the vibrating mobile phone from the big glass-topped table in front of him. He looked at the device, scowling irritably at the name on the screen, and then put it back down.

"So, are we clear on everything gentlemen?" he asked, scanning the faces of the other three man seated around the table in room 331. The men facing him; Andy Burnett, Jacko Goodman, and Toby Hughes, all nodded soberly.

"Remember guys," Green continued. "This is the big one! We need to shut them down for good this time. Take all but ten percent of their shipment and make sure that you don't leave any of them alive. Be as messy as you want. We want it to look like it was rival dealers."

Again, the other men nodded and murmured sounds of assent. Toby Hughes, however, looked deep in thought and Green noticed. "What is it, Toby?" he asked.

Toby gave a little shrug. "Nothin' really Guv'," he said. "I was just thinkin' 'ow much easier it'd be if we 'ad them trackers."

"Well, we don't have them Toby," said Green coldly. "It looks as though Grant got cold feet about letting us have them. You'll just have to manage with the skills you've got, won't you?"

Toby lowered his eyes in subservience and gave a nod. "Yes Guv'," he acquiesced quietly.

Jacko took the pressure off Toby with a question to Green: "Do you think Grant knows or suspects anything sir?" he asked in his deep Scottish burr.

Green fixed him with a stare. "I doubt it," he replied. "Don't worry about Grant anyway. His reputation's already being flushed down the pan and very soon he'll be in no position to cause us any problems. In fact, he's going to be very useful in diverting attention away from us."

Jacko smiled. "That's good enough for me sir," he said confidently. "You've always got us through before." The congratulatory tone and the show of faith in the Leader lightened the mood of the whole room.

"Have faith lads," boomed Major Green, enthusiastically. "We're coming to the end of this campaign, but there'll be plenty more ahead."

"Here's to more of 'em," said Toby Hughes with a smile that grew even wider at the nod of approval from the Major.

Green slapped his hand on the table, lightly. "Go on lads," he said. "Get out there and make us all rich. When you get back, I'll be a step closer to being Director General."

With smiles, chuckles and guffaws, Andy, Jacko, and Toby left the room, each glancing back at the threshold to acknowledge the Major. They were a good set of lads, he reflected. The way that they had all pulled together since he had brought them back from the war was a matter of great pride to him. He had taken a small group of men who had been broken by their experiences and he had given them a new sense of purpose, a sense of hope and a belief in themselves that life had threatened to beat out of them.

The mobile phone on the table vibrated again with a buzz like that of a trapped and angry insect. He looked down at it, knowing that the call would be from Grant. He took a second to decide how to play his next move with regard to finding out why Grant had changed his mind about the trackers. In the long run, it didn't matter, he thought lightly. The damage had already been done. Grant had booked them out without the proper authorisation, and the act had contributed to The Colonel's fall from grace within the Security Service.

Green picked up the phone and answered it, smiling. "Hi Tom," he said happily. "How's it going?"

"Not bad," replied Grant, a little breathlessly. "How are you? Are you busy? I've tried calling a couple of times, but there was no answer."

"Yes," chuckled Green. "I've just been finishing a few things up at work. Listen, I'm about done now though, if you fancy a couple of drinks."

"Yeah, that'd be good," replied Grant, eagerly. "Where shall we meet?"

A thin smile played on Major Green's lips as he answered. "Oh, I'll pick you up at your flat," he said. "That way, we don't have to worry about dropping cars off and things. What's your address?"

Grant gave his address absently whilst fumbling through his pockets. "You'll be more than ten minutes, won't you?" he said. "I've just got to nip to the shop at the end of the street for a couple of things."

"That's fine," said Mike Green. "If you're not back when I get there, I'll wait. See you soon Tom." He hung up and stared at the phone in his hand. The smile on his face widened and he gave a slight chuckle. It was clear from talking to Grant that everything was going to plan.

Grant looked at his phone for long seconds before putting it away. His mouth felt dry, so he filled a glass of water from the kitchen tap and drank it down greedily. He wiped his mouth with a shaking hand and then fumbled for his door key as he walked to the front door of his flat.

Out on the street, he took a deep breath of the cool evening air and it felt good. He strolled quickly and confidently to the Mini-Mart at the end of the street. Once inside, he went to the refrigerated shelves, selected two bottles of lightly flavoured still water, and then joined the queue at the checkouts. He stood fidgeting for a moment, drumming out a rhythm with his fingers on the two plastic bottles of water.

The pretty brunette in front of him in the queue glanced back over her shoulder and he smiled at her, holding eye contact until she turned her attention back to the checkout with a stern expression that showed she was not impressed. He tilted his head to one side and watched as she took a step towards the till. She was athletic and statuesque, wearing a white blouse and a reasonably tight, light blue skirt that showed the curves of her body. Here bare legs were bronzed with a natural tan, and she wore blue pumps on her feet.

Grant's eyes wandered up and down her splendid physique and then followed her as she paid at the checkout, collected her purchases and walked out of the door. She was beautiful, he thought, as he watched her step out onto the pavement with a deep longing.

"Next please!" said the Checkout Girl loudly and impatiently.

With a start, Grant realised that he was next in line, and he stepped forward, placing the bottles on the counter. The plain looking and rather plump Checkout Girl glared at him, but oblivious to her disapproval, he smiled back at her and then asked her for cigarettes and chewing gum. He had been trying to give up smoking for over a month and had been doing very well, but he felt a sudden craving now.

His polite small talk, smiles, and eye-contact seemed to win the Checkout Girl over a little. He wished her good evening, with a dazzling and charming smile, and told her that he looked forward to seeing her again, and then gave the slightest hint of a wink as he left the counter. She even gave a slight, blushing smile at his obvious flirting as she watched him leave the store.

As soon as he was outside on the pavement, Grant opened the packet of cigarettes, took one out and then lit it. He devoured the smoke hungrily, suddenly aware of how much he had missed smoking. It must have been the cigarette that he had lit up during Kurylenko's interrogation that had caused this relapse, he thought, but he was glad of it. He drew another lungful of smoke and savoured it as he strolled happily back down the street towards his flat.

By the time Major Green's car finally pulled up at the kerb, Grant had consumed both bottles of water and was in the process of stubbing out his third cigarette on a parking meter. He yanked open the passenger door and climbed in, nodding amiably at Major Green, and then sat chewing enthusiastically on a piece of gum

"Sorry it took a while Tom," said Green, smiling. "I was a bit unlucky with the traffic."

"No worries," Grant replied. "Where are we off?"

"I dunno," said Green. "Fancy somewhere a bit livelier than the King's Head?"

Grant nodded enthusiastically. "Yeah, that sounds good to me," he said. "It'll be nice to let off a bit of steam after the day I've had. You wouldn't believe it Mike. That bloody Kurylenko's got Normanby and the Old Man wrapped around his little finger. He's accused me of being crooked and I think they believe him, you know. He's been saying that Shafiq went to him and became his agent because he couldn't trust me! The thing is…The thing is; I think they actually believe him!" The words gushed out in a torrent of dismay, the pitch of his voice raising as he went on.

Green hid his amusement as well as he could. "Alright, old son," he said. "Calm down. Don't worry about Normanby or the Old Man, or Kurylenko."

"That's alright for you to say," Grant went on hurriedly. "You're not the one who's being accused of being crooked! I can't believe it, I really can't. They actually believe that bloody Russian rather than me!"

"Relax Tom," said Green, a little impatiently. "I've got it all sorted out for you."

Grant's wide, staring eyes swung onto him, his pupils heavily dilated. "Sorted out?" he asked in surprise: "How?"

Green smiled broadly. "I've been speaking to the Director General," he said. "The Old Man and Normanby aren't in his good books. My department's taking over the Hussein investigation, so you've got nothing to worry about."

Grant's open mouth slowly broadened into a smile. "Bloody Hell, Mike," he said. "You're an absolute bloody marvel!"

Green nodded. "I know," he said before adding a little coldly: "You see, you should have trusted me with those trackers after all."

Grant looked at him with a baffled expression. "What are you on about?" he asked.

Mike Green gave a tired sigh and then shook his head sadly. "Oh, come on Tom," he said wearily. "You don't have to play games. If you'd changed your mind about letting us use the trackers, you could've just said so."

"What the bloody Hell are you talking about?" Grant snapped irritably. "I left the trackers in the glove box like we arranged."

Green reached into his inside pocket and drew out a small cardboard box which he tossed into Grant's lap. Grant picked it up and shook it, feeling the something solid inside moving around. He opened the box and tipped the object from it, into his hand. In the centre of his palm lay a £2 coin. He looked at it, totally bewildered. "Eh?" was all he managed to say.

"Yeah, that's what we thought too Tom," said Green sharply.

"But I left the trackers in the boxes," Grant insisted.

"Well, maybe it's a new model," said Major Green sarcastically. "Looks just like a forty-bob coin! Isn't that clever?"

Grant was becoming ever more exasperated and irate. "I swear to God," he said emphatically, "that the trackers were in the box when I put them in the glove compartment."

Green's face hardened. "Toby Hughes brought me these boxes with £2 coins in them," he said. "I've known Toby for a long time. I served with him in the army. I seriously hope that you're not trying to accuse him of being dishonest with me."

Grant was quiet at the hint of a threat in the other man's tone. "Well, no-one else even saw the bloody things in my car…" he paused and drew in a sharp breath. "…Nobody except Normanby," he finished slowly.

"Normanby?" said Green, with a hint of surprise in his voice.

Tom Grant slapped a palm to his own forehead. "Normanby," he said. "I should have bloody known it! He's the mole!"

Green looked startled. "The mole?" he asked, bewildered.

"Yes, God damn it!" said Grant. "Kurylenko was telling the truth, he must have been! He just got the wrong man and thought it was me."

Green looked sharply at him, but Grant did not notice. Instead, he carried on, frantically chewing on his gum as he spoke. "Don't you see Mike? Kurylenko said that we had a mole. Somebody arranged to have Shafiq killed because he didn't trust us anymore. Suddenly Normanby turns up at the crime scene like Sherlock bloody Holmes, instantly 'solving' the crime and then, guess what? He just *happens* to be the one who *catches* the murderer and shoots him dead so that we can't bring him in. Oh, the crafty little bastard! I'll kill him when I get my hands on him!" He was breathing heavily, and every muscle in his body was tensed with anger and frustration.

Mike Green glanced across at him and raised his eyebrows. Secretly, he could barely believe his luck. Although he had no idea why Normanby had chosen to interfere by stealing the trackers, he was immensely glad of it. The stupid little twerp had played straight into his hands without Green having to do any extra work. Serendipity, he decided, was a wonderful thing. "Relax Tom," he smiled. "Don't worry about Normanby. We'll get him, I guarantee it!"

*

Normanby took another sip of the Haig Club whisky and placed the glass down carefully on the side table next to him. He gave the reassembled Makarov pistol one last, loving wipe with the soft cloth and then placed it beside the whisky glass. He sat for long moments with his chin resting on his hands, looking at the row of seven 9mm rounds that stood like toy soldiers in a line on the table. The pistol's magazine had been fully loaded with eight rounds when he had obtained it.

He doubted that Kurylenko had ever fired the weapon, and he wondered how long it had been left unused. The markings on the gun, as he had noted earlier, were from the Soviet era. In many ways, he reflected, it was surprising that the weapon had worked at all. He had noticed when he first disassembled it, how difficult it had initially been to break the weapon down to its fifteen component parts for cleaning. It had obviously not been field-stripped for many years.

He had to admit that the Soviets had always produced effective and rugged weaponry. Even after all this time, the Makarov was still a reliable weapon. It was simple and sturdy. At 26 ounces, there were doubtless many lighter small pistols around, but it had worked when needed, delivering its load at 1,030 feet per second into the body of the repulsive animal, Gorszky…

…An image of the man's face kept coming back to Normanby. He had been right to fire, he told himself. Gorszky had been the epitome of evil. He had brutally murdered at least two people, and planned to kill more. Normanby had aimed low and had shot him in the leg in an attempt to stop him without killing him. That, in itself, had been a foolish move. He had been taught, many years before, that only a fool shoots to maim. The only sure way to stop an enemy was to shoot to kill. Gorszky had died anyway, a slow and painful death.

Normanby blinked slowly and the man's image was there again in the darkness behind his eyelids, waiting for him. The fear that he had shown in his eyes when he had looked into Normanby's own was visible in the detail of the image. It was as if the man had seen something there that no-one else could, something that Normanby thought he had extinguished within himself years ago.

He felt a shiver move up his spine, and the hairs on the back of his neck felt as though they were sticking out. He looked slowly around with the old half-buried feeling that he knew so well, the ridiculous fear that he might see the ghosts of those that he had killed out of the corner of his eye. He reached for the whisky glass and his hand was shaking violently.

He jumped so hard when the telephone rang that he spilled some of the whisky from the glass onto his hand and his shirt cuff. He stared with anger at the instrument that had caused him to act so foolishly and after a pause he decided to answer it.

"Normanby?" It was The Colonel.

"Yes sir," he replied with a growing sense of disquiet. The Colonel would not call at this time unless it was important, and the way that things were going any news was likely to be bad, he reflected. He was right.

"It's not good I'm afraid," said The Colonel. "I've spoken with the D.G. this evening and he's not happy. He's taken us off the Hussein investigation and handed it all to Major Green's team."

"I see," said Normanby, flatly.

"There's more I'm afraid, Normanby," The Colonel continued. "He's not letting me conduct the investigation into your handling of Gorszky. I'm sorry."

"So am I sir," the little man replied. "They'll crucify me."

The Colonel tried to think of something positive to say, and failed. "Yes," he said. "They'll certainly try. I'll do what I can Normanby, but that might not be much."

"What about Grant sir?" Normanby asked. "After all, he's working closely with Major Green."

"It looks as though Grant's in quite a bit of trouble himself," The Colonel replied. "It seems that his paper reports don't match up with the official electronic copies that Green sent down to the D.G. It's beginning to look as though Kurylenko might have been right about him."

"Yes, it's beginning to look that way sir," Normanby said dully. "Did you get the tracker report that showed him going to Hussein's flat?"

There was a long pause. "I did," The Colonel replied thoughtfully, "but I have a contact who says that he was at my club at that time, and that he left with a young lady who works as a croupier in the Casino lounge."

Normanby's brow furrowed. "That's very odd sir," he said thoughtfully.

"Well, it's out of our hands now Normanby," The Colonel sighed. "Our problem is what to do about that gun you used on Gorszky. We're not above the law anymore I'm afraid, and it's bound to come up in the investigation. Your best bet is probably to go and hide out for a little while. Hopefully, when they bring Grant in, it may take some of the heat off you."

Normanby pushed his spectacles up to the bridge of his nose. "Yes sir," he said absently. "Thank you for the warning, sir." He hung up and sat for a moment staring at the pistol on the table. He reached out for the whisky glass with a steady hand and then drained the remainder of the drink in one swallow.

His mind suddenly racing, he scooped up the seven shells and pushed them into the clean, freshly oiled magazine and then slotted it into the butt of the pistol. He deftly pulled back the slide to feed a round into the breech and clicked on the safety catch before tucking the weapon into the waistband of his trousers. Picking up his jacket and rain mac from one of the straight-backed dining chairs, he slipped them on as he headed for the door.

CHAPTER THIRTY TWO: THE HIT

Toby Hughes gently closed the car door and peered over the vehicle's roof at the two men in the distance. He glanced back at his two companions and peered at them in the dim light. "Let's get 'em lads," he said with an excited smile. Clumsily, he brought the Glock 19 pistol from his overcoat pocket and then casually slipped the weapon into the front of his coat to conceal it. His companions, Jacko Goodman and Andy Burnett, made similar movements with identical pistols.

They walked on quietly, their rubber soled shoes making no sound on the crumbling pavement. Each man's eyes were focussed on the two figures ahead.

"I wonder where the other one is," muttered Jacko quietly.

"Don't worry," said Toby. "We'll find 'im. 'E might even be waitin' for 'em."

"Well, it would be terribly nice if we could get them all together," Andy Burnett whispered lightly. "It would make things an awful lot neater."

Two hundred yards ahead, the two men that they were following came to the big, metal gates of the compound. "Just check it brother," said Mohammed Iqbal in a loud hoarse whisper. "It should be unlocked. That's the way I left it." He patted the pockets of his black nylon Security Uniform jacket and found the packet of cigarettes in his pocket. He extracted one and lit it from a clipper lighter.

His companion, Tariq Malik, stared at him in shock. "What you doing, brother?" he whispered urgently. "If they're following, they'll see your cig glowing!"

Iqbal glared back contemptuously and then let out an impatient sigh. The idiot was wearing a traditional white kameez tunic and a white prayer cap, and he was worried about Iqbal's cigarette. "Brother," he replied as patiently as he could, "they're meant to follow us. I'm just making sure they don't lose us. Now, check the gate!"

Tariq smiled as realisation dawned on him. He gave an involuntary jerk of the head and let out a snort. "I didn't think of that brother," he said, turning his attention to the gate.

Iqbal shook his head in dismay as Tariq fumbled with the open padlock that was hung onto the chains holding the big gates together. Eventually, he freed it and pushed the gates apart a couple of feet. "We're in brother!" he announced as if he had completed some elaborate magic trick.

They slipped through the gate and left it open as they walked out into the moonlit yard lined by rows and rows of metal freight containers. Some of the rows were stacked three containers high, and cast impenetrable black shadows in the white moonlight, giving the impression of a ghost town of eerily darkened streets.

Outside the compound, their pursuers were crouched in the shadows. Toby Hughes peered from one side of the gates, squinting into the shadows for signs of his prey. At the other side, Jacko and Andy waited patiently for his signal.

It was just like the old days, thought Andy Burnett excitedly. They had been lucky to have a boss like Major Green, he reflected. Without the Major, they would have all ended up going their separate ways on civvy street, all suffering the same fate as so many of their comrades who had come back damaged and broken by the things that they had seen and done. He wondered how many had come back unable to cope with the terrible burden that they carried, with no-one to talk to who would understand their pain. The Major had spared them that suffering. He had kept them together as if they were a family, and in a way they were. They were brothers, he reflected, joined together by bonds that the ordinary man in the street could never understand.

Toby gave a quick signal that drew the attention of the other two. "I've got visual," he hissed in a loud stage whisper. "I'm going in!" The Glock pistols were brought out from the cover of their overcoats and held in professional two-hand grips as the three men slipped silently into the compound.

Ali Hussein squinted down into the shadows from his hiding place at the top of the freight container. He quickly wiped a bead of sweat from his eyebrow and then looked into the unearthly glow of the infra-red weapon scope at the three figures moving side by side below him.

*

The air in the dimly lit nightclub was humid. 'It's like a bloody jungle,' thought Grant as he chewed intently on the spent and tasteless wad of gum in his mouth. He squinted out onto the dancefloor at the cavorting bodies in the flickering strobe lights, and fixed his gaze on the lithe-bodied girl dancing near the edge of the floor. The sweat glistened on her toned thighs beneath the hem of the tight black mini-dress that she wore. As she writhed wildly in time with the beat of the music, her mane of blonde hair swung high, like waves in a storm. Strands of hair stayed plastered to her face with perspiration. She ran her tongue around her mouth to lick the sweat from her top lip, and Grant let out a sigh. He was aroused, both by the sexuality of her movements and by the almost orgasmic abandon in the expression on her face.

Mike Green picked up his champagne glass and leaned back into the plush, soft leather seating of the VIP booth beside Grant and gave a satisfied smile. Grant really didn't have a clue what was happening to him, Green noted happily. The man was a naïve fool, and a perfect pawn for his plan. Very soon, that plan would come to fruition, he thought. Poor Grant would never get to know just how useful he had been. "Not bad is she Tom?" he shouted cheerfully, noticing the intensity of the other man's gaze as he watched the dancing girl.

Grant's head whipped around; his eyes so wide that the whites were visible all around his irises. He gave a grotesque grimace that was supposed to be a smile, and his head bobbed in rhythm to the music. "Not bad at all," he confirmed quickly. "I could certainly have a bit of fun there, Mikey!" He turned his lascivious and intense attention back to the girl.

Mike Green hid the smirk on his face by taking a long sip from his champagne. He reached forward and took the bottle from the ice bucket on the low table. After pretending to pour some into his own glass, he leaned forward and filled Grant's glass to the top. "There you go, old son," he said, raising his voice to be heard above the thumping music. Grant glanced at him with an idiotic expression and raised both thumbs before returning his attention to the girl.

Green peered into the gloom of the dancefloor and beyond, and then checked his watch. He told himself to stop fretting. Everything was going to plan, and by tomorrow the whole operation would be wrapped up. He breathed a sigh of relief when he saw the big man shoving his way through the crowd towards the VIP booths.

Tom Grant glanced up and followed Green's gaze, his face suddenly lighting up. "It's Sammy Parsons!" he announced, smiling, and giving a wave when he saw the big man was coming towards them.

"So it is," concurred Green with mock surprise. "Hello Sammy."

Sammy stood at the edge of the dancefloor, facing the two men and nodded his greetings with a big, confident smile. "Good evening fellas," he said.

"Good evening Sammy," said Green. Grant smiled and nodded enthusiastically as he chewed rapidly on his stale chewing gum. "You joining us, Sammy?" he asked.

"Maybe later mate," Sammy replied. "I just need a quick word with Mike, somewhere quieter than this." He gestured towards the loudspeakers suspended high on the walls.

Grant began to get up from the soft seating but was restrained by Green's hand on his shoulder. "Tom, stay and keep an eye on the drinks mate," Green said, leaning close so that he could be heard above the music. "We won't be long."

Grant looked a little crestfallen at being excluded and Green noticed. "Keep an eye on that bird on the dancefloor too mate," he said. "I think she fancies you."

Grant looked back at the girl and noticed her glance in his direction. 'Yes,' he thought, 'it's worth keeping an eye on her.' He nodded and smiled at the two other men. Sammy gave him a big smile and a conspirational wink. Returning the gesture, Grant took a long sip of his champagne and sat back to watch the dancing girl as the two other men made their way back across the dancefloor.

Mike Green was relieved to be out of the stuffy, humid atmosphere of the club as he stepped out and took in the cool night air on the rooftop smoking terrace. He followed his companion to a quiet corner and then gazed out for a moment at the lights of the city, picking out the faint outlines of the landmarks on the banks of the Thames below. "Well, Grant's well and truly primed," he said. "Are you all set for tonight Samuil?"

The man who Grant knew as Sammy Parsons ran a hand thoughtfully along the line of his immaculately groomed beard. When he spoke, it was not with the Essex accent that he used to create that persona. Instead, there was the faintest trace in the rolled 'R's and guttural hard consonants of an Eastern European accent. "I'm all set Mike," he said, "if you are sure that's how you want it."

Major Green's eyes were cold as he watched Samuil reach into his perfectly tailored jacket and bring out a gold cigarette case. "It's exactly how I want it," he confirmed flatly.

"You were close to her for a long time," the big man pointed out, lighting his cigarette with a heavy gold lighter.

247

Green's expression did not change. "She's outlived her usefulness," he said. "Kill her as we arranged. I'll contact you as soon as my boys have the rifle and the Sarin. You should get a good reward for them."

Samuil gave a small chuckle and blew out a plume of acrid, menthol-infused smoke. "It'll be reward enough to see them realise that they should have hired me in the first place instead of expecting that fool Kurylenko to be able to sort it out for them." He took another pull on the cigarette and then flicked it out over the parapet. It glowed brightly as it arced through the night sky before descending to the street below.

Green raised an eyebrow and nodded, smiling to his companion when he saw one of the club bouncers walking towards them. "I don't think you're supposed to throw your cigarettes over the edge," he said with a throaty chuckle. "The bouncer's coming to have a word with you."

Samuil turned slowly to face the approaching bouncer. He flexed the muscles in his massive chest and gave the man a contemptuous, hard stare.

The bouncer slowed his pace at the imposing sight of Samuil and gradually changed his direction so that he would bypass the two men. "'Evening fellas," he said, nodding shyly as he passed them and carried on walking.

Before the bouncer was even out of sight, Green and Samuil could contain themselves no longer. Simultaneously, they lost control and burst into childish giggles.

"Did you see how his face changed when you stared at him?" Green said breathlessly, holding back another wave of laughter.

"Ah, the heroic Door Supervisor," chuckled Samuil. "He'll take some drunk girl home from here tonight and spend hours telling her about all the big guys that he's knocked out!"

Green fought to set a more serious expression on his face. "That reminds me," he said. "I'd better get back to Grant before he finds himself a new girlfriend."

"Okay," Samuil replied. "Everything will be ready for you when you get to Sofia's place."

"Good," said Green, "and remember Samuil, it needs to be exactly as we planned."

"It will be," the big man confirmed, reassuringly. "I'm a professional too Mike."

Green nodded his approval and then made his way back into the club. He felt the sticky, oppressive heat generated by the mass of sweating bodies as soon as he stepped back out onto the dancefloor to make his way back to the VIP booth.

*

Normanby stepped off the bus and glanced up at the black sky as the first spots of rain fell. It was a light drizzle, and he did not bother to button up his raincoat. He walked quickly and with purpose to the large, Victorian building that housed the Empire Club. The big doors were open, and he sprang lightly up the short flight of stone steps and into the spacious and opulent foyer.

Although he was not a member of the club, Normanby knew that he would have no trouble gaining access. He had been there on many occasions to meet The Colonel on business and whenever he had been early for such meetings, Watkins, the redoubtable doorman had simply invited him in to wait until The Colonel arrived.

He sidestepped a group of four well-dressed, elderly gentlemen who were gradually making their way to the door amid their final wave of cheery goodbyes, and looked around. Watkins was standing, ramrod-straight and to attention behind his lectern, the Visitors Book open on the polished surface in front of him.

"Good evening, Mr Watkins," said Normanby uncomfortably. "I'm supposed to be delivering a message for The Colonel but I'm afraid I'm a little early…"

Watkins smiled politely and his answer caused Normanby's mouth to fall open in shock. "Oh, not at all Mr. Normanby," he said lightly. "The Colonel said you'd be along. He's waiting for you in the Reading Room upstairs."

Normanby was momentarily speechless. He took off his spectacles and cleaned the lenses with a pocket handkerchief to give himself time to think. "Oh," he muttered. "I didn't think he'd be here yet."

Watkins eyed him for a long moment. "Would you like me to take you to him Sir?" he asked.

"No, that's alright," replied the baffled little man. "I know the way." As he walked slowly through the foyer towards the wide staircase, he wondered how on Earth The Colonel could have known that he would come here. He mounted the stairs with a growing sense of apprehension and made an effort to prepare himself for whatever further shocks might present themselves.

Normanby entered the large oak-panelled reading room and saw that The Colonel was the only other occupant. He was sitting quietly in one of the big leather armchairs by the fireplace, staring into the flickering flames of the fire and slowly swirling the contents of a large brandy glass with a slight movement of his hand.

"Come in Normanby," The Colonel said without taking his gaze from the fire.

"How did you know I was coming here sir?" Normanby asked as he walked the length of the room. He halted beside the other armchair, facing The Colonel.

The Old Man turned his gaze upon him, still swilling the brandy in its glass. "I know how your mind works Normanby," he said. "I wouldn't be in the job that I currently hold if I didn't have a thorough understanding of how my operatives function. I knew that you would feel compelled to check out Grant's alibi, and since you're currently suspended, coming to the club to find the girl would be your first line of enquiry. I know how bloody-minded you are. I also know how stupidly conceited you can be, in that you assume that no-one else would be clever enough to check also. Well, I did Normanby: I checked, and I found that Grant did leave here with her. It wasn't him that was hanging around outside Hussein's flat, whatever the tracker log may indicate. When he left here with the girl, they took a taxi back to Grant's flat. It seems that someone is trying to set him up, Normanby, and bearing in mind that he put in a statement against you, you will be the prime suspect."

"Surely sir," Normanby stammered, somewhat shocked, "you don't believe…"

The Colonel cut him short. "It doesn't matter what I believe Normanby," he said coldly. "I won't be in charge of the investigation. Don't you see that snooping around here like some sort of amateur detective is only making you look more suspect? Stop being such a conceited little bastard. Let the experts investigate. Go home and don't involve yourself any further until you're summoned to a hearing!"

There was a long pause and Normanby could feel his cheeks reddening as a result of the slap that his pride had received from The Colonel's words. "Have you spoken to the girl herself sir?" he asked tersely.

The Colonel glared at him, his own face colouring with anger. "Did you hear a damn word that I said?" he bellowed. "I will speak to the girl when she turns up for her shift! Now stay out of it!"

The little man opened his mouth to speak and then thought better of it. He gave a sigh like a sulking teenager, turned on his heel and then prowled silently from the room.

The Colonel twisted in his chair to watch Normanby's petulant exit with eyebrows raised. As he watched the heavy door close behind the little man, he leaned back in his armchair and allowed himself a slight smile. He took a small sip of the brandy and held it there in his mouth, savouring it. Yes, he decided. He had played Normanby just right. His words had stung the man's pride just enough to stir him into action.

Normanby pulled the door closed behind him and let out a deep breath in an effort to calm himself. He was fuming and he noticed the tremor of pent-up anger in his hand when he reached up to adjust his spectacles. He thought about what The Colonel had said. Was Grant being set up? Probably, he thought, but he knew that he could be next. As The Colonel had pointed out, he would be the prime suspect.

He needed to learn how deeply involved Grant was. Was the girl from the club's casino also involved in some way? He had to find out, he decided. He would speak to her before anyone else did, he decided. He didn't care if The Colonel thought that he was conceited.

He was sure that he would get to the bottom of things quicker than anyone else, especially if Major Green was going to be in charge of the investigation. He realised glumly that he was totally alone. He could trust no-one.

Taking as much comfort as he could from his self-belief and the knowledge that he would do whatever it took, he made his way towards the Casino. There was something about the way that The Colonel had said: "I will speak to the girl when she turns up for her shift," that was perplexing the little man.

Although he was not one for socialising, or for wasting money on inflated bar prices and gambling, Normanby had often found himself somewhat impressed by the club. Whilst the rest of the social world seemed Hell-bent on succumbing to the same forces of entropy that were decaying the rest of society, the club had managed to maintain order and had hung onto its traditions and dress codes like nowhere else.

Part of its attraction, he supposed, was that coming here was like stepping back in time. The club was like a fly that had been trapped in amber back in the days when those not wearing a tie were denied entry, when women wore ball gowns, or at least cocktail dresses and men would don a dinner jacket and bow tie to sit around tables of green baize and gamble.

Amid the polite busyness of the casino room, Normanby negotiated his way through the pockets of smart, moneyed people and finally came to a halt near the head of the roulette table.

"Place your bets please, Ladies and Gentlemen," said a stern looking woman of about fifty with jet black hair tied back in a severe bun. She glanced coldly at Normanby, and he realised that he had been staring at her. He doubted very much that this could be the woman that Grant had left with and taken back to his flat. She was, in all probability, old enough to be Grant's mother. Normanby made sure that his examination of her was not too intense. He concentrated his attention on the table and the game being played around it, choosing only to glance at the woman briefly and in passing.

She remained professionally cool, as the ball in the roulette wheel came to rest in the black number 26 slot, resulting in a large win for a cocky young man who treated the sharp intakes of breath from around the table as a round of applause for his prowess. He played to his audience by treating them to a smug smile and a falsely self-deprecating gesture.

The woman hid her disdain for the young man with a blandly happy smile and she expertly raked his winnings over to him. He scooped the chips greedily into the pockets of his jacket and ignored the look of coy challenge that she gave him in the hope of tempting him to bet again and give the house a chance to win back some of the money.

Normanby could see the game that she was playing, and he reflected sadly that a younger woman may well have succeeded where she had failed. She was not an unattractive woman by any means, but she was past the age where she could rely on flirting to part the young and impetuous men at the table from their money. The older men around the table, Normanby supposed, may well be attracted to her, but would generally be more cautious and less inclined to bet rashly just to impress a member of the opposite sex.

She was looking at him invitingly, he realised, and he gave a slight automatic smile which lasted about a second. When she realised that he was not interested in playing, either literally or figuratively, she turned her attention back to the players around the table. Normanby watched the game for a little longer and noticed that the woman was becoming increasingly impatient. The frequency with which she checked her watch had gradually increased, as had the number of times that she glanced back at the door marked 'staff only' at the back of the room.

The Colonel's words came back to Normanby. "I will speak to the girl when she turns up for her shift." Normanby knew The Colonel's speech patterns. He cursed himself the moment that he realised. The girl should have arrived by now, but she was late for some reason. Surely, if The Colonel had arrived before the girl was due to get here and he was simply waiting patiently for her start time, he would simply have said: "I will speak to her when she arrives…" Normanby felt sure that his deduction was correct. Even the subtlest changes in a person's speech pattern could speak volumes. He turned away from the roulette table and walked across to the bar that stretched almost the full length of the room on one side.

"Good evening sir. What can I get you?" asked an attentive young barman as Normanby hitched himself up onto a bar stool.

"Oh, nothing for me thanks," said Normanby. "I'm just waiting for a friend to finish." He indicated with a flick of the head in the direction of the roulette table and the young man's eyes followed the movement. "How come the other girl's not working the table," he continued conversationally, "young erm…"

"…Sophia," the bartender finished automatically. "I dunno. She hasn't turned up yet."

Normanby turned his attention back to the roulette table. He did not want to press the bartender for information and make him suspicious. The girl's first name would just have to be enough.

Looking warily around him, Normanby got up from the bar stool and walked out of the casino. Mercifully, the landing outside was empty. He walked across to an opening, through which a flight of stairs ascended to the top floor of the building. It was barred by a thick ornate rope which held a sign bearing the legend: 'STAFF ONLY BEYOND THIS POINT'. Normanby glanced furtively around him and then, swung his leg high and stepped over the rope.

He paused at the top of the staircase, listening. He could hear his own heartbeat thumping heavy and fast. In the darkness of the upper landing, he could make out the shape of three doors. The fact that there were no lights on up here gave him some small reassurance. He felt that this made it more likely that the floor was unoccupied. He tried the handle of the first door, praying that there would be nobody on the other side.

The door pulled open easily to reveal a broom cupboard containing various cleaning products, brushes, mops and buckets, and a vacuum cleaner. He pushed the door closed carefully and moved along.

The next door was slightly ajar. He pushed it open nonchalantly and peered into the darkness beyond, into a large cloakroom with tiled walls. In the dim light from a small, frosted window he could see coats hanging from a row of pegs along one wall. A long bench stretched along the centre of the room, and on the opposite wall were four lavatory cubicles, each with its own sink.

He was about to try the third door on the landing when he heard a sound. His pulse quickened as he realised that the noise was the ornate rope barrier at the bottom of the stairs being unfastened and then re-fastened.

He heard footsteps on the stairs behind him, and he slipped silently back inside the cloakroom. He was just in time. The landing light clicked on just as he moved behind the cloakroom door. He held his breath as he peered nervously through the crack in the door between the hinges.

Watkins walked purposefully along the landing and for a moment Normanby thought that he had been discovered. He clapped a hand to his mouth to stifle a sigh of relief as the other man carried on to the third door. He strained to listen, and he was rewarded by the sound of the door creaking open, and taking several steps on the polished boards. The office was not locked!

Normanby continued to listen carefully. There was the sound of a drawer being opened, and then a faint, dull metallic jingle. Next, there was some rattling and the sound of a metal filing cabinet sliding open. This was followed by a scraping noise and a small grunt from Watkins, then the sound of papers rustling. There was a long pause and Normanby crept to the open side of the door so that he could listen more closely. He heard the distinct and familiar sound of a rotary dial telephone being dialled. The call was to a local number, he noted absently, as only six digits had been dialled.

He stood in silence and listened as Watkins impatiently rapped out a military rhythm on a wooden surface with his fingernails before heaving an irritated sigh. The receiver was slammed down heavily, causing the bells in the telephone to ring slightly. The papers rustled again, and Watkins took two heavy footsteps.

There was the sound of the filing cabinet drawer being slammed shut and then locked, another quiet grunt, two steps, the clink of the keys being dropped onto a hard surface and the scraping sound of a drawer being roughly slammed shut.

Normanby retreated back into the cloakroom as he heard the click of the light switch. A moment later, Watkins stomped along the landing and back down the stairs.

As he heard the clattering of the rope barrier being unclipped and re-attached, Normanby poked his head out of the cloakroom door. He extended a finger and pushed his spectacles up to the bridge of his nose with a satisfied smile and then made his way to the room that the other man had just left.

It was highly likely, indeed almost certain, thought Normanby, that the girl who had gone home with Grant was now very late for work and had failed to ring in sick. He had little doubt that Watkins had been sent to call her in order to find out why she had not turned up for her shift. If he was right about this then she obviously lived somewhere reasonably close by, as the telephone number that had been dialled had only six digits and was therefore a local number with no area code needed.

He stepped into the office and clicked on the light. The room was very large and much more impressive than Normanby had expected, even taking into account the quality of the club's clientele. As he surveyed the space from the doorway, he let out an envious sigh.

The wall to his right was dominated by a huge open fireplace, similar to the one down in the reading room on the floor below. In the nearest fireside alcove, floor to ceiling shelves housed a neat array of leather-bound books, with one shelf reserved for bottles of rare and expensive single malt whiskies. On the centre of this shelf, between the bottles, was a rectangular silver tray holding six crystal whisky glasses. From above the fireplace, a massive stag's head surveyed the room with glassy eyes.

In the furthest alcove rested a large ornately carved oak desk. On the desk was a blotter, an old black Bakelite 300 series G.P.O. telephone, and an artillery shell that had been cut down for use as a pen holder.

Normanby could not help but be impressed by the stark neatness and simplicity of the desk's arrangement. There was no desktop computer to spoil the beautifully sparse display, though he guessed that there would at least be a laptop concealed in one of the two cupboards at each side of the desk's foot well. Just beneath the desks polished top were three shallow drawers, side by side.

On the wall above the desk was a shelf which held box files, and above this, a portrait in oil of an old army officer, staring down proudly from his gilt frame. In front of the desk was a captain's chair upholstered in old, but cared for, brown leather.

In the wall across from the door were two tall windows adorned with floor to ceiling curtains of red velvet. In between the two windows stood a large, dark green metal filing cabinet. Another, smaller portrait looked down from above it. In front of the left hand window was a high-backed leather chair with a beautifully polished side table beside it and in the centre of the room, facing the windows was a long leather chesterfield sofa, large enough to seat four.

The back wall of the room, to Normanby's left, was lined with dark wood shelving, again filled with an impressive collection of leather-bound volumes that reached almost to ceiling height. He peered around the door and saw another row of antique metal filing cabinets behind him.

He thought about the sounds that he had heard when he had listened to Watkins entering the room: There had been the sound of a wooden drawer being opened. The only such drawers in the room that Normanby could see were the three in the front of the desk. He opened the first drawer and saw nothing but a notebook and a desk diary. In the middle drawer, he found a bunch of keys. He picked them up and picked out four keys that were of the same make. It would be one of these four that he needed, he decided, as there were four filing cabinets in the room, all of the same design.

He had heard Watkins take two steps from the filing cabinet to the desk, which eliminated the three cabinets on the back wall. He took the two steps to the remaining cabinet in between the windows. He tried the keys in turn in the lock at the top right corner of the cabinet, and the third key turned with a satisfying click.

Because he had heard Watkins give a small grunt when removing and replacing paperwork from the filing cabinet, Normanby surmised that it had been stored in the bottom drawer. He crouched down and opened the drawer, then began flipping through the suspension files within.

He only knew that the girl's first name was Sophia, and the personnel files were stored in alphabetical order of surname, so he would still have to check each name individually, but he felt moderately pleased with himself that he had narrowed his search down to this one drawer simply by listening.

Within two minutes he had found two employees at the club with the forename of Sophia: The first, Sophia Ahmed, was one of the cleaning staff and was aged 54. The other was Sophia Costello, aged 29 and employed as a croupier.

Normanby gave a satisfied smile as he produced his notebook and pen. He noted her full name, date of birth, address and telephone number from the personnel file, and then quickly leafed through the pages to see what other potentially useful information it might contain.

He stopped, suddenly intrigued at the sight of the work references that she had obtained to secure her job at the club. The references had been provided by Major Michael Green and Andrew Burnett.

Normanby put away his notebook and took out his mobile phone, spending a moment to ensure that the references and the signatures at the bottom of the pages were in focus before photographing them. He returned the file to the drawer, closed and locked the cabinet and returned the keys. Before flicking off the light switch, he took one last look around the room to ensure that he had left no trace of his visit.

He would have to go and see the girl at her home, he decided, though there was a strong possibility that she was involved with the case and there may well be a sinister reason for her failure to attend work. He slipped a hand into the front of his jacket to feel the reassurance provided by the shape of the little Makarov pistol tucked into his waistband.

*

"She was bang tidy!" said Grant, for the umpteenth time as he fidgeted uncomfortably in the passenger seat of Major Green's car.

Green struggled to remain patient. "She wasn't all that Tom," he said as mildly as he could. He put his foot down on the accelerator and sped through an amber light just before it turned to red. He wanted to get back to the Empire Club and then get things over as quickly as possible.

Spiking Grant's food and drink with amphetamines had been a necessary part of the plan that was being played out, but the effect that it was having on his behaviour did make him annoying to be around, to say the least. It would be a relief to kill the stupid bastard, Green reflected coldly. He put the thought to the back of his mind and continued to play his role. "Anyway Tom," he said; "you'll be seeing your own bird in a few minutes, won't you? What's her name, the one from the casino?"

Grant looked across at him, a lascivious smile drawn across his face. "Sophia," he said with an eager nod. He remembered the smell of her perfume and the touch of her skin. "Oh yeah," he said. "She's a beauty, that one!" He rubbed his back against the seat like a bear scratching itself on a tree.

"You got an itch old son?" asked Green.

Grant gave an imbecilic giggle. "Not half," he said.

Green rolled his eyes and shook his head slightly at his companion's childish humour. "We're here now anyway Tom," he said, relieved as he swung the car into the car park of the club.

Grant had the door open before the car was properly parked. "Tom," Green barked sharply as he got out of the car. "Calm yourself down." He slammed the door shut and locked it with the electronic fob. Grant looked at him vacantly, swaying rhythmically in a barely perceptible, silent dance.

"Look mate," Green continued in a smoother tone. "You had a fair bit of Champagne in the last place and old Watkins, the concierge here is really strict on people being under the influence. Just try to act as sober and quiet as you can." He waited for Grant's acquiescent nod before continuing to the front door.

Watkins was not at his lectern when they stepped into the foyer of the club and for this Green was grateful. He quickly ushered Grant upstairs to the casino on the first floor, constantly wary in case anyone should try to engage them in conversation. This was always going to be the hardest part of the plan, Green reflected. Getting the girl to slip the initial doses of amphetamine into Grant's food and drink had been easy. She had been convinced that she was working for M.I.5., and that Grant was suspected of treason. It wasn't difficult to find plenty of publicly available references to the use of amphetamines as a truth drug, so she had believed what Green had told her.

He grinned coldly. Just as she had begun to outlive her usefulness in obtaining information from visitors to the club, she had become useful as a sacrificial lamb. Her death would be the perfect way to help shift the blame for Green's own criminal activities onto Tom Grant. It would also help to destroy The Colonel's department and allow Green to take over its operations.

Forming the alliance with Samuil Popov, and helping him get a foothold in the Russian Intelligence system had been a stroke of genius too. Green realised this without any hint of conceit. Popov had also played his part in game extremely well. Pretending to be Kurylenko had been a master stroke. The delusional and psychotic Gorszky had been convinced that he was working for the Russian G.R.U. under the orders of Kurylenko, and there was no reason that others would not believe the same.

It was a pity that Normanby had stumbled into the scheme and killed the madman, but it was not a major problem. Gorszky had, according to reports, told The Colonel's people that he was working for Kurylenko before he died. That testimony alone should be enough to have Kurylenko shipped back to Russia, and this would leave a vacancy for a trusted Russian agent in London.

Once Popov took the Russians their missing sniper rifle and Sarin nerve-agent, he would undoubtedly be offered the job. Between them, Popov and Green would have the power and influence to build a profitable criminal empire from their respective positions.

Life was sweet, Major Green decided, for those who had the strength to brush aside petty morals and grasp the prize with both hands.

"She's not at the table," whined Grant plaintively, causing Mike Green to start a little. "Bloody marvellous, that is!"

"Are you sure?" asked Green. "I'll get us a drink and ask the barman. He's bound to know where to find her. Take a seat, Tom, and remember what I said about acting sober."

Grant looked at him and flopped sulkily into one of the comfortable leather chairs that were dotted around the quieter edges of the casino's lounge area. Green hurried to the bar and ordered himself a gin and tonic. He thought for a moment and ordered the strong, lemon flavoured vodka martini variation for Grant. What had the idiot christened it? he thought. A 'Dame Judi'? He shook his head in contempt. At least it would give him a chance to spike the fool with more amphetamine before the endgame was played out.

When Green returned with the drinks, Grant was perched on the edge of his seat, leaning forward with his arms folded across his midriff. His head moved this way and that, watching the people passing by. His fidgety movements were both bizarre and inhuman, and they reminded Green of an old movie that he had seen in which a man gradually turned into a giant fly.

How easily a man can be transformed into something else, Green thought. The simple act of administering the right combination of narcotics could produce amazing results. How far, he wondered, would one be able to strip back a man's humanity by chemical means and turn them into something else?

It was an interesting thought, and one that he would have to pursue in depth at some point, he decided, when he could work out a way to profit financially from such an experiment.

Grant's head snapped around and his widely dilated pupils fixed on Major Green. "She's not here, is she?" he asked, his voice weak.

"Not at the moment mate," Green replied. "She's at home, but don't worry. Get this down you." He extended the cocktail glass.

"I don't feel too good," said Tom Grant in a pathetic whisper.

"Well," Green said firmly, "this'll make you feel better. Get it down you and I'll take you to see your young lady. I'm sure she'll nurse you back to health."

Grant took the drink with a shaking hand. "I don't know where she lives," he said despairingly.

"That's okay," Green reassured him, "I got the address from the bar staff. Drink up!"

Grant took a sip of the cocktail as instructed and gave a shiver. He looked around in confusion. "I'm really not feeling well Mike," he said.

"You'll be fine," lied Green, gently. "You just need to get cuddled up with that girl of yours." He smiled warmly at his victim. The massive amount of amphetamine in Grant's system had taken him past the state of energised euphoria that most recreational users of the drug sought. He was suffering from a premature 'burn out', where his body was rapidly running out of the energy that the drug had been forcing it to release.

"Come on mate," said Green. "Get it down in one swallow and we'll get off to your girlfriend's flat."

CHAPTER THIRTY THREE: SOPHIA

Sophia Costello's flat was located in a reasonably smart, white fronted Georgian town house a couple of streets away from Shepherd's Bush Market Tube Station. Normanby jogged up the five steps to the big, black-painted front door and was slightly surprised to see that it was open, and that the Yale latch was locked back in the 'open' position. Even on the quieter streets, he acknowledged, this was very unusual in modern London.

He pushed the front door open and stepped into the hallway, listening. Someone in the ground floor flat was listening to the soulless, mechanical rhythm of some kind of modern dance music. As he began to climb the stairs, he could hear the competing sound of a television with the volume turned up very high. He was fortunate, he reflected, that he, his landlady and the other two tenants in the house that he occupied all shared a love of peace and quiet.

At the top of the stairs, he realised that the sound of the television was coming from the flat on the very top floor. He began to feel rather sorry for Sophia, if the current noise levels in the house were the norm.

He was again surprised to see that the door to her flat was slightly ajar. Seeing it, he felt a sense of unease, and his hand once more strayed to the butt of the pistol in his waistband. He put his ear to the gap in the door and heard no sound from within the flat.

He took a deep breath and drew the pistol, clicking off the safety catch in a smooth movement as he did so.
He pushed the door wide open and carefully stepped forward into a short hallway. There was a door to his left, at the end of the hall, one closer on his left, another almost across from him, and lastly a partially open door to his immediate right. This door led to a lounge, illuminated by the low wattage bulb of a table lamp.

He stepped inside and scanned the tastefully furnished room. His eyes were drawn to the object on the wood effect laminate floor, barely visible in the dim light. He leaned closer and saw that it was a paring knife, lying in a small pool of blood that had dripped from the reddened blade.

He swallowed hard and looked warily over his shoulder. The bloodied weapon made him think of Gorszky and his unfortunate victims. He felt a shiver pass through his entire body at the thought of another such madman on the loose.

He thrust aside the feelings of guilt about killing the monster that were clawing at his mind and trying to cloud his judgement. He gave free rein to the anger that was growing deep within him, the hatred for people who thought that they could get away with the brutal murder of innocents. This was a more useful emotion, he reasoned.

He looked down at the gun in his hand and felt a cold sense of satisfaction that he was holding it steady. He would do whatever he had to in order to stop these people, he promised himself.

He turned and stepped out of the front room, carefully opening the door to his right, across from the front door of the flat. He held the little Makarov close to his chest and at the ready as he stepped forward into the bedroom. He fought to ignore the sight in front of him for long enough to throw a darting glance behind the door and reassure himself that the murderer was not still in the room.

When he looked back at the girl on the bed, he lowered the pistol and put a hand to his mouth. Although he had not known her, he felt himself touched by strong emotions.

He felt the strange, stark sense of loneliness that one feels in the presence of a body that life has abandoned, and the aching sadness of rekindled memories of his own loss.

He remembered being left alone in the room with the body of his wife, the crushing despair at realising that she would never awaken and return to him. For a moment he felt as though he was there again sitting patiently and waiting; stupidly wishing that the universe could be rewritten, and that Ruth could be with him again.

He gave a deliberate, angry sigh and turned his attention to the corpse on the bed. In life, Sophia Costello had been a beautiful woman. Her big brown eyes gazed sightlessly from a perfectly symmetrical face. Her golden-brown skin had a perfect and flawless complexion. Her body was athletic, slim, but with perfectly toned muscles. She lay now, sprawled awkwardly on her back in a thin silk shift, on the middle of the bed and the white sheets beneath her were stained red.

Normanby gave a sad sigh and tried to close his mind to the multitude of emotions that threatened to engulf him. He looked at the scene before him as dispassionately as he could, taking in each piece of evidence that came to him. He clicked on the safety catch of the pistol and slipped it back into his waistband before reaching into his pocket for his notebook, pen and mobile phone.

There was no sign of the frenzied multiple stab wounds that had been inflicted on Gorszky's victims. Whoever had killed Sophia Costello had done so coldly and professionally. Normanby suspected that if he were to turn the body over, which he had no intention of doing; he would probably find a single entry wound to one of her vital organs.

He wondered momentarily about the knife in the living room. The lack of blood trails indicated that it had been carefully carried and deposited there.

He glanced across the bed and his attention was drawn to a bedside table at the far side from him. He walked around and looked closer. The surface of the table was covered in white powder, some of which had been formed into thin lines a couple of inches long.

On the floor next to the table was some kind of credit card. He knelt down on the floor for a closer look and activated the torch on the mobile phone, which he used to read the printing on the card. It was an out-of-date discount card for a high end clothing store, and it had been issued to Thomas Grant. Along one edge of the card were traces of the fine white powder from the table. He got to his feet with a worried expression as he began to realise why the girl had been murdered, and why the knife had been so carefully deposited in the living room...

*

"Well, would you believe it?" said Major Green. "She doesn't live that far from you." He pulled the car smoothly into the resident's parking area marked by the broken white lines at the side of the narrow road.

Grant looked around him in confusion. With a very great effort, he focussed his eyes on Green. "Are we here?" he asked weakly.

"We are indeed old son," replied Green cheerfully. "Don't you worry. In a few minutes everything will be fine and you won't have a care in the world. Come on!" He got out of the car and waited patiently on the kerb for almost two minutes.

When it became apparent that Grant was not going to move without assistance, he walked around to the passenger side and opened the door. "Come on old son," he said gently, grabbing Grant by the arm and pulling him out of the car. He retained his hold on him and, after quietly closing the car door, steered him towards the town house.

At the top of the five steps from the pavement, he let go of Grant and was relieved to see that he could still stand unaided.

He pushed the front door open and gave a satisfied smile. Samuil had left the Yale latch open just as arranged. He took Grant's arm again and gently led him up the flight of stairs to Sophia's flat. He gently pushed Grant through the door of the flat and clicked on the light in the hallway.

Grant winced and put his hands up to his eyes to shield his dilated pupils from the sudden glare. He felt himself being gently guided by Green towards the door to the mercifully dimmer living room.

"Hello? What's that then?" asked Green, pointing to something on the floor. Grant blinked several times and tried to get his eyes to focus on the object. "Well don't just stand there, Tom," Green continued, with a touch of impatience. "See what it is!"

Grant stepped forward and felt dizzy as he bent to pick up the object. He managed to straighten up and then held the knife absurdly close to his eyes to examine it. It was wet and slippery with blood. "Oh my God," he said, a feeling of dread beginning to gnaw at his mind. He dropped the knife on the floor and rubbed his fingers together, feeling the oily blood as it smeared between them. "Sophia..." he said quietly, looking around with a growing sense of panic.

Mike Green turned on his heel and stepped into the hallway. "I'll check the bathroom," he said, walking straight to the end of the hall. "You look in the bedroom." He nodded towards a door to his right as he passed it, and Grant stumbled towards it, pushing it open and standing in the threshold of the room. His hand went to his mouth in shock and Green, watching from the bathroom, noted with satisfaction that a tiny spot of blood from his fingers had transferred to his cheek.

"What is it?" asked Green. He stepped up behind Grant and gave him a little shove in the back to propel him into the room. "My God!" he continued. "Check if she's alive Tom. Quick man, before it's too late!"

Grant shambled forward like a zombie. He flopped down bonelessly on the edge of the bed and reached out to check the pulse at her carotid artery. He pressed his bloodstained fingers to the cold flesh on her neck and felt no sign of life. His chin began to tremble in grief and despair. There was a faint metallic click from the doorway, and he turned his head in shock and bewilderment to see the pistol in Mike Green's hand. "What's going on Mike?" he asked, struggling to focus and make sense of the situation.

A cold, thin smile played on Mike Green's pale lips. "Beautiful," he said. "We've suspected that there was a traitor in the service for a while. Who'd have thought it would be someone from The Colonel's department? Off your head on drugs, your bloody fingerprints on the murder weapon and the girl. Good job I happened to drop by really, isn't it? 'Oh, I had to shoot him sir, he was a maniac!' It won't be hard to convince the Director General, not with all the evidence we have. I'll probably get another medal for it."

Green raised the pistol slowly. Grant closed his eyes and then covered them with his hands. There was nothing else that he could do.

Suddenly, Normanby's voice rang out, harsh and loud. "Drop the gun Major," he barked, stepping out from the broom closet into the hallway.

Green turned his head to look at the little man, his face a mask of contempt. His gun was still pointing at Grant inside the bedroom, and he realised that he would have to step back and drop his aim before swinging his gun around to aim at Normanby.

It wouldn't be a problem, he decided. The little fool was standing with his own pistol at his side, and Major Green doubted that the man had much experience of killing in cold blood. Green stepped back and began to swing his own gun around towards its new target, looking forward to seeing the little man suffer.

The Major's plan was flawed. Normanby's gun hand rose in a smooth, practiced motion and his finger squeezed the trigger as the barrel's aim swept across Green's abdomen.

Major Mike Green felt the crushing pain as the bullet punched its way through his skin and then smashed a section out of one of his ribs before spinning downwards inside his body. It ripped through soft tissue as it spun, and then finally came to rest deep within his colon.

He let out a ridiculous sounding whinny at the shock to his body, which added shame to the unbearable agony that he was suffering. He lost control of his hand, and his own pistol, a Browning 9mm, slipped from his grasp and thudded heavily in the floor. His arms drew in and his limp hands fell across the wound in his midriff before his knees buckled and he sank to the floor, letting out a long, low wail.

He rolled onto his side and his eyes met Normanby's. Even through the distorting lenses of the man's spectacles, Major Green could see now what he had failed to notice before: The clinical coldness, the lack of any warmth or feeling in the little man's eyes said everything Green needed to know about Normanby. He was capable of being totally ruthless. Deep down, Normanby was a killer.

"Mr. Grant?" shouted Normanby, keeping his gun pointed at Green. "Mr. Grant, are you alright?"

Normanby's attention shifted to the doorway of the bedroom and Green saw his chance. He willed his fingers to work, and he extended a hand towards the Browning. If he could just get a hand to it and get off one shot at the little bastard…

…There was another loud bang and Mike Green was jolted by a searing, agonising pain in his right knee. He screamed at the terrible agony and shock, and it took him seconds to realise through the pain that Normanby had shot him again, even before his hand had got near the Browning. His wild eyes were drawn to the gaping, bloody hole in his leg, little shards of white bone showing through the glistening red tissue. He heard a strange wailing sound and realised that it was his own voice as he lay on the floor, shaking convulsively.

"Keep still if you want to live," Normanby hissed venomously, before continuing in a louder, but gentler voice. "Mr Grant? Stay calm. Our people are already on their way, and no doubt, so are the police."

CHAPTER THIRTY FOUR: THE COMEDOWN

The Colonel was struggling to hide his sheer joy at the Director General's discomfort. He extended a finger suavely and used it to smooth down his already immaculately groomed moustache before continuing. "So, thanks to my man Normanby sir," he said, "we've managed to uncover evidence of Major Green's involvement in a great deal of criminal activity."

The Director General ground his teeth in annoyance. "I thought I'd told you to suspend Normanby pending an enquiry into Gorszky's death," he said.

"Oh, I did suspend him sir," The Colonel replied. "It's therefore very fortunate that the man was prepared to go the extra mile on his own time. If he hadn't done, a good man would have been murdered and Major Green's treachery may well have gone undiscovered, costing countless more innocent lives. I can't imagine how anyone could have passed someone like Green as fit to be an operative in this service," he added meaningfully.

The Colonel knew very well that the Director General's own trusted staff had brought in Major Green as part of his modernisation plan. He had hoped to drag The Colonel's department into the twenty first century, something which he had known the old man would resist. The D.G. held his temper and gave a patient sigh. "I take it that you've already begun going through the evidence, checking Green's files and started damage limitation procedures," he said.

The Colonel nodded slowly and gazed levelly at his superior. "I have sir," he said, "but with Normanby currently suspended on your orders and Grant still receiving medical treatment due to being drugged by Green and his co-conspirators, progress is going to be slow. I just hope that it won't be dangerously slow." He emphasised the last two words and kept his gaze firm and determined.

The Director General nodded and gave the barest hint of a cold smile. "You want me to lift Normanby's suspension?" he asked.

The Colonel gave a little shrug. "You must do what you think is best sir," he said with a smug expression; "though I'm sure that his contribution would be invaluable."

"Alright Colonel," the Director General said resignedly. "Just make sure that the little psychopath doesn't shoot anyone else for a day or two, will you?"

"I'll do my best," confirmed The Colonel, "and thank you sir." He stood and picked up his hat and umbrella from the vacant seat beside him, before turning to leave the room.

"Colonel," The Director General called, halting the old man before he reached the office door. "I want to be informed the moment Major Green regains consciousness," he said, "and when he does, *I* will decide who is to conduct his interrogation. Is that clear?"

The Colonel looked back over his shoulder from the doorway. "Perfectly clear sir," he acknowledged subserviently, before adding: "I don't think that the Major will tell us much under interrogation anyway. After we've done the decent thing and treated his wounds, it might be best to let him retire to his study with a glass of whisky and a loaded revolver."

He stepped though the doorway and out of the office before the Director General could formulate a reply, and stood smiling for a moment. He had heard speeches from The Director General in the past, claiming to have a fondness for those old military men that had run the service when he was just starting out. The Colonel doubted his sincerity, however. He felt that the D.G. considered him a dinosaur; a throwback to a brutal age that many would like to pretend had never existed, though it amused him to let people think that he wasn't aware of it.

The Colonel knew that he would not be able to do things his own way forever. He knew that men like himself and Normanby were becoming more and more scarce as the years went on, and he wondered sadly what would become of the world when the defence of the Realm was entirely in the hands of button pushing, entitled youths who had never even fought for anything in their lives, let alone their own survival.

He dismissed the gloomy thought from his mind. Whatever dark days the future may hold, this morning's meeting had been a victory. Normanby had managed to uncover Major Green's criminal activities, and that would certainly strengthen the position of The Colonel's department within the Service.

He strolled happily down the corridors of Thames House, the main Headquarters of M.I.5., tapping the ferrule of his umbrella on the ground in time with his own steps. He signed out of the building at the main reception area and took a deep, joyous breath of the morning air as he stood in the big archway at the entrance of the building.

He trotted happily down the flight of steps to the pavement and looked around for Normanby, who he knew would be waiting somewhere nearby.

He eventually found the little man standing on the corner of Thorney Street and Millbank, staring absently towards Millbank Pier and the Thames beyond. "Good morning Normanby," he said happily.

"Good morning sir," replied the little man, adjusting his spectacles. "How did the meeting go?"

"It went well," said The Colonel breezily. "I've convinced the D.G. that we need you on duty, so at least for now, your suspension has been lifted. Any investigations into the circumstances of Gorszky's death and Major Green's injuries should be a mere formality, as I suspect that I will be in charge of them."

Normanby was thoughtful and there was a long pause before he spoke. "Colonel; when you were at your club last night and Miss Costello had not arrived, did you suspect that she might have been murdered?" he asked.

The Colonel raised an eyebrow. "It was a distinct possibility," he acknowledged.

"And you knew that I would find out where she lived and go there, didn't you sir?" asked the little man.
"I was counting on it," The Colonel replied, a little uncomfortably. "I didn't have the authority to send anyone myself as the Director General had taken us off the case, but I knew that you wouldn't let go and I knew that you'd get to the bottom of things." With a flicker of self-loathing, he realised that he was feeling bad, not so much for using Normanby, but because the little man had realised it.

Normanby took in the words very solemnly and then used a finger to push his spectacles into position. "So, you don't actually think that I'm a conceited little bastard after all then sir?" he asked.

The Colonel's eyes widened, and he threw his head back and let out a sudden, bellowing laugh. "Come on Normanby," he said, chuckling happily. "I'll treat you to a breakfast before we go to work on Major Green's files."

*

Tom Grant felt sick and depressed. It was a new experience for him to feel this bad, he reflected, although the Doctor had told him that he would feel ill for a day or so. It was hard to focus on anything except the feeling of total emptiness that gripped him like a giant claw.

He stared blankly at the window across from him, watching the seemingly endless miles of ancient pipework that lined the tunnels of the London Underground whizzing by like wasted moments.

The view through the window had the reflection from inside the subway car superimposed upon it, showing the bored passengers silently rocking with the rhythm of the train. He caught his own reflection in the glass, and he hated it. For all of his ridiculous pride and self-importance at being a defender of the realm, he realised that he was no better than the other human livestock around him.

He wanted to get out; out of the subway car; out of London, and out of the terrible business that he was in. He fished around for some feeling of hope at the idea of escaping, and found none. There wouldn't be any point, he thought. There was no other job that he could do that he could imagine giving him any sense of fulfilment. Nothing interested him, and nobody cared.

'Why should they?' he reflected. The world was populated by people like Mike Green and his team; by others like Normanby and The Colonel, and none of them gave a damn about the people that they were supposed to be protecting.

The doors opened at Pimlico station and Grant stepped out onto the platform. He edged warily through the crowd of commuters there, hating every single one of them without needing a reason and then made his way up to the surface to face the dazzling sunlight and the cold air.

On the street outside the tube station, a bearded man in dirty and dishevelled clothes extended a paper cup towards the passers-by. He saw Grant shuffling along, gazing at the floor and decided that he would be a good target. "Got any spare change?" the man asked, with a hard stare intended to intimidate his mark into submission.

Grant looked up and saw the expression. His own face contorted with rage. "Fuck off, you parasite!" he spat venomously, slapping the paper cup out of the man's hand.

The few copper coins that had been in the bottom of the cup rolled out into the road, and the man took a step back in shock. His own expression turned to one of indignation, and then something like fear as he saw the fury displayed by Grant's bared teeth and the burning hatred in his eyes.

The beggar backed away and Grant walked on, scowling. A few moments later, he heard shouting and he realised that the beggar felt that there was now enough distance between them to make the issuing of threats a safe practice.

"You ever do that again and I'll rip you a new arsehole," he shouted. "You're the parasite, not me!"
Grant ignored the man's outburst and carried on. He was trying to concentrate on what he would say when he saw The Colonel. He would give the old bastard a piece of his mind and tell him what a filthy department he was running. Then, he decided, he would tell him that he was leaving. He would even write his own resignation letter in front of him, and then bang it down on the desk! It would make him feel good, he hoped. At least, it would make him feel *something*.

On reaching the headquarters building, Grant presented his credentials at the front desk and signed in, barely acknowledging the receptionist. He prowled the corridors silently on his way to The Colonel's office, ignoring the stares of colleagues who passed him.

He took a deep breath as he approached The Colonel's door, readying himself to barge in. He stopped dead and looked down at his shaking hand, inches from the door handle. A tidal wave of self-contempt washed over him as he pulled his hand away and then knocked timidly on the door.

"He's not in," said a cold female voice from somewhere to his right. He turned his head to see Betty, The Colonel's secretary, staring disapprovingly from the threshold of her own office next door. "He's up in Room 331," she continued, "and he's not happy with you. If I were you, I'd fasten your tie properly and all!" She disappeared back into her office and slammed the door shut before he could think of a riposte.

He stood for a moment, staring blankly at the closed door, and then reached up to feel the untidy knot of his loosened tie. He closed his eyes, exhausted and deflated. "For God's sake," he muttered bleakly.

The glass door of room 331 opened silently and Grant stepped inside. The Colonel, who was standing at the big table leafing through a scattered collection of buff card folders, looked up as Grant entered. He looked at his watch meaningfully. "Good morning Grant," he bellowed with a hint of sarcasm. "How are you feeling?"

"Like shit," Grant replied dejectedly.
The Colonel raised an eyebrow and glared. "Grant?" he said, simply.

"I'm sorry," replied the younger man. "I feel like shit *sir.*"

The Colonel nodded. "Good enough," he said. "Come and sit down. I have something to show you." He saw the other man's non-committal shrug and continued. "I understand that you're suffering the effects of what regular drug users refer to as a 'comedown'."

"Yes sir," Grant replied. "The Doctor thinks that I shouldn't be at work."

"No he doesn't," countered The Colonel in a matter-of-fact tone. "He thinks you should take it easy. There's a difference. After all, you're not a builder's labourer, are you?"

Grant clenched his teeth, and then stopped because it made his jaw ache. "You've spoken to him then?" he asked bitterly.

"Of course," The Colonel boomed. "The welfare of my operatives is very important to me. That's why I like to know when there's any friction between them. For instance, I would like to think that my people would bring their disagreements to me, rather than writing statements against each other." There was a long pause and Grant averted his eyes. He didn't quite know what to say.

"You seem to have a problem with Normanby's methods," the old man continued. He waited, staring at Grant in the pregnant silence. Seeing that no answer was likely, he continued. "I'm assuming that Major Green put you up to it," he said, "in order to throw *my* department into disrepute. No doubt you came in here and saw all *this*," he made a gesture that embraced the room around him, "and thought that you'd finally found your spiritual home! Major Green, the decorated hero with the swashbuckling, devil-may-care attitude must have seemed like the ideal colleague after a few weeks of working with Normanby. Am I right?"

Grant gave a snort. "Normanby," he said bitterly. "You must admit sir…"

"Shut up Grant and listen to me," The Colonel cut in harshly. "I'll tell you about Normanby. The man is a patriot and a hero. He's worth a hundred like Major Green. If it wasn't for that funny little man, you would not only be dead, you would also be remembered as a murderer and a traitor! Your friend Green fitted you up perfectly and you fell for it every step of the way."

"I know sir," Grant acknowledged continuing to stare at the ground in an effort to hide his shame, "but at the time…I mean, Normanby's not really…" he struggled to find a way of explaining his thoughts about the little man.

The Colonel gave the barest hint of a smile. "Yes, he's an annoying little bastard, isn't he?" he said.

Grant looked up quickly and for the first time that day he actually felt something positive. It was only the slightest flicker of relief that The Colonel's tone had lightened by a fraction, but Grant drank it in like a man who had been dying of thirst. "You must admit sir," he said quietly. "Normanby's not an easy man to understand."

"Oh, it's not so hard when you know the whole story," said The Colonel.

Grant silently seated himself at the huge table. "The whole story sir?" he asked hopefully.

The old man looked at him directly. "Oh yes," he said. "There's a lot more to Normanby than you could ever imagine."

"After the events of last night," said Grant flatly, "I can imagine quite a lot."

The Colonel gave a little nod, as if he had just made a decision. "Normanby was a soldier, and believe it or not, a very good one," he said. "He was the best shot in his regiment which, as you can imagine, led to him being given certain tasks that many men would refuse, even if they had the skills to carry them out." "He was a sniper?" asked Grant in surprise.

The Old Man nodded. "For a while, yes," he said. "When he left the Army, he decided to put all that behind him; to settle down with his wife and children."

The Colonel's gaze became vague, as if he was staring through the walls of the room and out into the distance. "I was his Company Commander at the time. I tried to convince him to stay; to sign on for another three years. After all, with the skill that he had, he was an extremely valuable asset." He paused, not sure if he should even be telling the story.

"So he left the Army, then what?" prompted Grant.

The Colonel took a deep breath and nodded again slowly, having decided that Grant should know it all. "He secured an administrative position in the security division of a large engineering firm operating in Saudi Arabia," he continued. "It was Normanby's job to analyze data, and to risk-assess projects for the company in the area; to make sure that their workers were not exposed to any more risk than was necessary. He'd done very well for himself for a humble gamekeeper's son. From what I gather, he was due for a promotion. He was preparing to start a new life in the United States, in a management position within the company."

"So how did he end up here?" asked Grant when The Colonel paused.

"There was an attack," The Old Man said slowly. "Terrorists struck the housing compound in which Normanby and his family were housed. His wife and daughter were killed, and Normanby blamed himself. He had convinced his wife that it would be safe. He'd researched the job and the culture of the area, but there was no way that he could have known that the attack was going to happen."

"But Normanby can't accept that, can he sir?" said Grant. "That's why everything that he does has to be perfect, neat, ordered. That's why he's…well, the way he is. Is that why he came to work here; to get back at the terrorists?"

The Colonel shook his head slowly, a sad smile in his face. "Oh no," he said. "Joining us was the last thing on his mind. There was an investigation of course. The American Intelligence Services very quickly worked out which group were responsible for the attack. They even assured the grief-stricken Normanby that they would bring these people to justice."

"And did they?" asked Grant, fascinated.

"They didn't get the chance," The Colonel replied with a cold, thin smile. "Arab politics can be very volatile. The faction who were believed to be responsible for the attack were due to meet another group with the intention of burying their old tribal differences and uniting in an alliance to strike at what they saw as Western invaders. There was still a good deal of suspicion and mistrust between the two factions, so when one of the tribal elders was shot dead at the meeting, all Hell broke loose. The two sides started slaughtering each other immediately. It was only some time afterwards that the U.S. Intelligence people were able to piece together what had happened."

"And what *had* happened sir?" Grant asked, already half guessing the answer.

"The tribal leader had been taken down by a skilled marksman hiding some distance away," said The Colonel. "The authorities traced the rifle back to the housing compound where Normanby had lived with his family. It was one that was normally issued to guards in a watchtower, so it was equipped with telescopic sights. It had been reported stolen after the attack. It didn't take the investigators long to work out that the only person from the compound that was unaccounted for at the time was also a former British Army marksman."

"My God," breathed Grant, staring at The Colonel with his mouth open and his eyebrows raised.

"Normanby had made his way back to London by the time the C.I.A. came looking for him," The Colonel continued. "I really didn't have much choice. I had to employ him myself and tell them that he was one of my people before they could get their hands on him."

Grant was still stunned. "The C.I.A.?" he asked. "Were they going to kill him, or take him back for trial?"

The Colonel's eyes suddenly focussed on Grant. "Good God man! They weren't going to waste that sort of asset," he said irritably. "They were going to hire him!"

"Oh," said Grant simply. "Then why did you need to intervene?"

The Old Man sighed. "Don't you think the man had suffered enough?" he asked. "If they had employed him, he would have been used for one purpose: To kill; again and again and again. Can you imagine what that does to a man; what it turns him into?" He breathed in and held it for long seconds before continuing. "When I first asked Normanby to stay in the Army, I had told him that fate has a way of ensuring that we end up using our gifts and talents. The Americans would have told him the same thing, and he would have believed them. You know, for all that he has done in the service of his country, I still can't help thinking of him as an innocent."

After a long, thoughtful pause, Grant spoke again: "Well maybe you were right," he said. "I've got reason to be thankful that fate intervened last night to lead Normanby to use his skills. Perhaps it *is* what he's meant to do."

The Colonel looked at him sadly. "Perhaps so," he said quietly. His expression changed quite suddenly. "It seems that your friend Major Green had been dipping his fingers into several pies," he continued loudly, before focussing his attention on the glass doors behind Grant.

Grant spun in his chair to see Normanby standing on the threshold of the room.

"Good morning, Mr. Grant," the little man said flatly. "Good morning Normanby," Grant replied feeling uncomfortable. He wondered how much of the conversation Normanby had heard. He wanted to say something, to try and explain why he had written the statement against him, but he knew that any excuse that he made would be pathetic.

He felt stupid at not being able to express either his guilt for betraying Normanby, or his gratitude for the fact that the little man had saved his life.

The Colonel broke the cold silence. "Any further developments Normanby?" he asked.

Normanby extended a finger and poked his spectacles up to the bridge of his nose. "There's still no word from Hughes, Goodman or Burnett," he said. "None of them are at their homes, although it has been easy enough to ascertain that their mobile telephones have all been left there. I think it entirely probable that they were not only aware of Major Green's activities, but that they were complicit in them. Would you agree Mr. Grant?"

Grant gave a start and then looked at Normanby. "Yes," he said. "I'm sure you're absolutely right."

Normanby nodded. "That being the case," he continued, "I think it safe to conclude that the Hussein gang have been left unwatched for a while. I feel that we should now follow Mr. Grant's original advice; raid Hussein's flat and bring them all in as soon as possible."

Grant followed Normanby's gaze and looked at The Colonel who nodded briskly. "I'll set the wheels in motion," he confirmed.

"Also, sir," Normanby added tentatively, "I feel that we should distribute photographs of Hughes, Goodman and Burnett to the Police."

"The Police?" echoed The Colonel with a hint of distaste at the idea. He would rather sort out Green's people without any help from the police, he thought. The service was in enough trouble without having to wash its dirty laundry on public. He paused, thoughtfully pulling at his moustache with his thumb and forefinger.

"Sir," said Normanby with a touch of urgency, "we have to. The very fact that Major Green was attempting to tie up loose ends by framing Mr. Grant means that his plan was coming to fruition. This means that he would not be able to continue taking a cut of Hussein's drug deals for much longer. This, in turn, means that Hussein's own plans were reaching the point of their own conclusion. We must use any means possible to find out exactly what is going on."

"What about Green?" asked Grant, hopefully. "Can't we beat anything out of him?"

Normanby shook his head. "Major Green is still in Intensive Care, unfortunately," he said, "and I doubt that we would be allowed to use the kind of force that would be required to get answers from him." He turned his attention back to The Colonel, having made it clear that there were no alternative courses of action.

"Alright," the old man answered with a sigh of resignation, "put their pictures out there."

Normanby and Grant nodded in unison and then waited in case The Colonel had any further instructions for them. He looked up from the files on the table in front of him and then scowled at each of them in turn. "Well go on then," he boomed. "Get cracking! You've got work to do! Get in touch with the Police."

He watched as the two men left the room and stepped purposefully, side by side, down the corridor towards the elevator. When they were out of sight, he gave a slight smile.

CHAPTER THIRTY FIVE: DEAD MEAT

Doug Taylor took a sip of the hot coffee and pulled the up the zip of his overcoat to protect him from the cold, damp air. He watched Grant and Normanby come marching towards him from the growing crowd that had gathered at the boundary of the crime scene. "Good morning gentlemen," he said as they neared him.

"Good morning, Detective Sergeant," said Normanby amiably. Grant simply gave a restrained nod. He didn't look well.

"Hangover Mr. Grant?" asked Taylor.

"Something like that," Grant replied weakly. "What have you got for us Doug?"
Taylor drained his coffee and crumpled the paper cup. "Triple homicide," he said, raising an eyebrow. He glanced around for somewhere suitable to dispose of the cup and, finding nowhere, he thrust the crumpled mess into his coat pocket. "I thought this might interest you though. It's the same people whose photo's you put out this morning. As soon as I heard that three white males had turned up dead, I had a feeling that it might be connected so I made sure nothing was touched until you got here."

"Thank you, Detective Taylor, that was most thoughtful of you," beamed Normanby happily.

"Looks like somebody's mad at you lot," said Taylor seriously, "to kill three of your agents at once."

"Operatives, Detective," Normanby corrected automatically. "Agents are something entirely different."

The Detective rolled his eyes. "Whatever they were, we'd better hurry up," he said. "Winston's eager to get 'em bagged and tagged, and he doesn't like standing about in the cold."

The three men fell into step and walked the remaining twenty yards to where Winston Lewis stood waiting impatiently with arms folded, shivering in his paper overalls. On the floor beside him were the bodies of the three victims, lying face down in a row.

"Mister Taylor," he said. "Can I get started on analysing this crime scene? I've got a lot of work to do and I…"

Taylor held up a hand for silence. "Patience, Winston," he said. "Just give these gentlemen a few minutes to have a quick look around and then it's all yours."

Winston glanced suspiciously at Normanby and Grant. He recognised the little man from the last crime scene that he had attended, and he wondered what was going on, and if the deaths were somehow connected. "Who the Hell are these guys?" he asked.

Taylor tapped a finger to his nose in the age-old signal for someone who has secret knowledge. "M.I.5." he said archly.

Winston gave a contemptuous snort. He didn't trust people like that, he thought. A modern, open society shouldn't have secret policemen running around without the accountability of public scrutiny. "So, you're letting M.I.5. agents tamper with a crime scene before the evidence can be properly examined?" he asked accusingly.

Taylor gave him a cold, withering stare. "*Operatives* Winston," he said pompously. "Agents are something quite different."

The two men turned their attention to Normanby and Grant who stood looking down at the three corpses on the floor. Grant felt sick and dizzy. He was still suffering from the after-effects of the previous night's ordeal, and the sight of the three bloody cadavers had caused him something of a relapse. He noticed that his hands were shaking, and he thrust them deep into his overcoat pockets.

Glancing across at Taylor and Winston, he wondered how he looked to them. Did they think that he was affected by the sight of the bodies, he wondered? His thoughts were racing erratically. An image of Sophia flashed into his mind, her empty, lifeless eyes staring accusingly. *Is that all it means to be dead?* she seemed to be asking. *Do we just become a freak-show to disturb the living?*

He brought up a trembling hand to wipe the cold sweat from his clammy forehead. He wanted to scream; to shout; to tell someone about the thoughts going around in his head.

"Mr. Grant!" said Normanby sharply.

Grant stared at him, suddenly pulled back into reality. The little man looked at him and seemed to give a barely perceptible nod. He took a deep breath and then let it out slowly, trying to relax.

"We shouldn't be too long here, Mr. Grant," Normanby said softly. He suddenly looked around him, surveying the landscape like a fearful animal on the lookout for predators. His brow furrowed in thought for a moment, and then relaxed. A thin smile slowly grew on his pale lips and his eyebrows raised and showed themselves above the rim of his spectacles.

The frightened animal was gone, thought Grant. It had been replaced by a cold efficient hunter. "Go on," Grant said with a wry smile. "You're itching to tell us whatever it is that you've just worked out, aren't you?"

"They weren't shot here," said Normanby, "but they *were* shot only a short distance away and then driven here and dumped." Taylor and Winston moved closer and stood beside Grant, each of the three men showing varying degrees of puzzlement and interest at Normanby's remark.

"What makes you say that?" asked Winston, unable to contain his curiosity.

Normanby smiled at him. "The entry wounds," he said. "They're all high up on the bodies and the larger exit wounds, as you can see on poor old Toby here, are lower down."

He indicated with a wave of the hand towards the corpses on the floor. "They've been ambushed and shot from above but not executed at close range, otherwise they would have all been hit in roughly the same place. They weren't all shot in the head or the back of the neck, which you would tend to expect from a close-range execution."

He glanced around and gave a sweeping gesture with one hand that embraced their surroundings before continuing: "There are no buildings or structures high enough in line of sight from this spot, so they weren't shot in the immediate vicinity. They haven't been moved very far though, as the volume of blood here indicates that at least one of them was still bleeding quite heavily. Judging by the wounds that they have received, I would guess that they were killed by a relatively skilled marksman, at a distance, with a silenced weapon."

"Silenced?" asked Grant.

Normanby pointed towards the bodies, jabbing the air emphatically with his outstretched finger as he spoke. "Two of them have been shot very cleanly from behind. The third has been shot twice: Once from the side and once from the front. These men were highly trained soldiers and yet it took at least two shots before the last man realised where the shots were coming from. Indeed, the second man to die probably did not even realise that the first had been shot until the same fate befell him."

"Amazing," said Winston Lewis, genuinely impressed by the little man's deductions.

"Smart arse," said Grant nonchalantly. "How do you know that they were driven here?"

Normanby habitually extended a finger and used it to poke the spectacles up to the bridge of his nose. He smiled broadly, playing to his audience.

"If they had been carried or dragged there would undoubtedly be a trail of blood," he said. "I would imagine that they would have been brought here together, along with their killer or killers, so perhaps we should be checking any local CCTV in the area for a large car or more probably a van, once we can ascertain a time of death."

"What time were the bodies discovered?" asked Grant.

"Two hours ago," Winston replied. "I've been here an hour and a half," he added with a touch of annoyance.

"Can we narrow it down any further?" asked Taylor.

Winston sucked in a deep breath and pulled a face. "I don't like guessing," he said. "I like to have all the evidence."

"Typical bloody scientist," said Grant with a grin. "Go on, nobody's going to pull you up if you're a little out."

"Well," Winston replied kneeling down for a closer look at the bodies. "I can tell you that the third man didn't actually stop bleeding until some time after the others. Most of the blood here seems to have come from his wounds. Judging by the rate at which it's congealing, I'd say probably any time in between midnight and four or five this morning. Don't hold me to it though until I've done proper tests, because I could be way out."

"Well, it narrows it down a bit. Thanks Winston," said Grant, "they're all yours."

He turned and looked around to see that Normanby had wandered off. "Normanby," he shouted. "Where are you going?"

The little man ignored him and took out his mobile phone, dialling a number from memory. "Normanby here," he said after standing patiently for two minutes with the device pressed to his ear. "I need details for any vehicles owned or used by Toby Hughes, Andrew Burnett and John 'Jacko' Goodman …yes…now…text them to this number as soon as you get them, please." He ended the call and then opened the 'Maps' application on the phone.

"You're onto something aren't you?" asked Grant, approaching the little man and looking down at the device in his hand.

"Possibly," replied Normanby, squinting as he pored over the map displayed on the little screen. "I believe that there may be suitably high structures *there*," he muttered thoughtfully.

"We're in London," mused Grant. "There are suitably high structures everywhere."

"We can narrow it down," replied Normanby, "to suitably high structures away from passing traffic or the public eye. Even at night many of these roads are busy…Hmm…somewhere close enough that our current location would seem the most convenient place to dump three bodies."

"Well, if they were somewhere quiet already, why dump the bodies here?" asked Grant with a puzzled expression.

"That's a fair question," conceded Normanby, looking intently at Grant and visibly giving the question some thought. "I would say that the most likely reason for transporting the bodies here is that there is something at the murder scene that we are not supposed to find."

"Well, none of Hussein's little gang live anywhere near here," Grant pointed out, "and they're your prime suspects."

"Undoubtedly," the little man replied absently. He was still fiddling with the map on his phone, expanding it every so often to check the detail, and then irritably reducing the image to scroll the map in increasingly wide circles from their current location. He muttered to himself as he searched: "…too far by road…too busy…housing…not likely…hmmm…interesting…"

"What about there?" asked Grant suddenly, pointing irritatingly over Normanby's shoulder at an area of parkland displayed on the screen. "The sniper could have been up a tree!" He smiled and nodded enthusiastically, sure that he was onto something.

Normanby gave him a short, withering look and then returned his attention to the screen. "Too muddy," he said dismissively. "It's wet and the victim's shoes are all clean. He paused and then expanded another area of the map. "Now this *does* look interesting," he said.

"What is it?" asked Grant, disappointed that his own suggestion had been so quickly disregarded.

"It appears to be an old railway depot," Normanby replied. He hastily flicked the on-screen button to switch the image from map to satellite view. "Yes," he said with quiet satisfaction. "It's an old railway depot or freight yard, full of large freight containers!"

Grant glanced over his shoulder to where Doug Taylor stood talking to Winston and a steady growing number of crime-scene personnel. "Doug," he shouted. "You're going to need some more crime-scene tape!"

Taylor's shoulders visibly sagged as heaved a sigh. "Where are you two off now?" he shouted wearily.

"We may have found the *actual* crime scene," Normanby announced. "It isn't far from here if my suspicions are correct."

Taylor gave Winston a nod and then set off walking hurriedly towards the two operatives. "Hang about," he said. "I'm coming with you. This is still my investigation as well; I don't care if you are shit-hot secret agents!"

"Operatives Detective," Normanby corrected brightly as Taylor jogged to catch up with them. "Agents are something quite different."

They set off walking towards the location of the goods yard with Normanby taking the lead. Taylor and Grant chatted amiably as they strolled along, whilst Normanby walked a few paces ahead, glancing frequently at the map displayed on his mobile phone.

As they turned a corner, the little man put away the phone and looked intently along the long line of cars parked at the roadside that ran through the industrial park. "If my suspicions are correct," he said, "we should find one of our people's cars parked nearby. The freight yard is just at the end of this road."

Grant had memorised the vehicle details that Normanby had received by text, and he was quite pleased with himself that he was the first to spot it. "Normanby," he called, stopping beside a shiny grey BMW, "I think this is Toby's car!"

Normanby wheeled around and walked back to the car. "Well done Mr. Grant," he said, double-checking the registration plate against the text on his phone. He stood beside the vehicle and looked down the road. "He parked where he had an unobstructed view of the freight yard entrance," he observed.

"Shall we pay them a visit?" asked Grant lightly.

"Perhaps we should wait for Detective Sergeant Taylor's colleagues to secure the situation," Normanby replied, nodding towards the detective with a worried expression.

Taylor shook his head sadly. "My people are more than overstretched already," he said. "We're already trying to run three crime scenes, all of which seem to be connected to your little mystery. It could be hours before we can get anything sorted out here."

Normanby unfastened the buttons of his mac and put a hand inside to feel the comforting grip of the pistol in his waistband. "I suppose that I had better go first," he said, "just in case the murderer is still in there."

Grant and Taylor exchanged worried glances. Neither of them had thought of that possibility until the little man had mentioned it. Grant opened his mouth to speak but Normanby had already turned and set off walking towards the gates. He had taken the Makarov from his belt and held it inside the front of his open raincoat, gripping it firmly with his finger on the trigger.

Taylor and Grant followed at a distance as Normanby marched determinedly through the gates, his eyes scanning the tops of the freight containers, his furtive glances darting this way and that to take in the gaps and darkened corners near the mouth of the freight yard.

Suddenly there was a shout that triggered him into lightning-fast movement. Before the echo from the single syllable shout of "Hey" had finished bouncing off the sides of the freight containers, Normanby had spun and dropped into a crouch like a low Karate stance, with the pistol levelled in a two-hand grip.

Grant and Taylor stopped dead as they heard the shout and saw Normanby's instantaneous response. Whilst Taylor was simply shocked by the sudden action, Grant found himself amazed. He had witnessed the little man use the gun twice before, but on each of those occasions it had been when Normanby had lain in wait and taken his targets by surprise. It has never occurred to him that the man could react so quickly and so professionally. He suddenly wondered what other kinds of training Normanby might have undergone in his army days.

A portly, middle-aged man in dirty, oil-stained overalls stood petrified by the cold and deadly stare from the 9mm black eye of the Makarov. "Don't move!" said Normanby without emotion. "Keep your hands where I can see them."

The man held his trembling hands outstretched in front of him. His wide, terrified eyes were transfixed on the gun. "Please," he said, "don't shoot me. You can take what you want."

Normanby's brow creased in thought. "Who are you?" he asked.

"Harry," the man stammered. "Harry Foreman."

Normanby straightened his legs and came fully upright, lowering the pistol a little but maintaining his grip, ready to spring back into action if necessary. "Are you the owner of this place?" he asked. Foreman nodded, still shaking.

"My colleagues would like to ask you some questions," said Normanby indicating with a quick glance towards Taylor and Grant.

Taylor stepped forward, feeling uncomfortable. In his many years on the force, he had learned a lot about reading people's reactions and he was convinced that Foreman was an innocent man who just happened to be in the wrong place at the wrong time. He saw the man flinch as he reached into his jacket, and then relax slightly as he drew out a little blue wallet containing his warrant card.

He deftly flipped the wallet open and extended it to display the card. "Detective Sergeant Taylor," he announced, "Homicide and Major Enquiries Team. You can lower your hands Mr. Foreman."

Foreman's wide eyes moved questioningly to the little man with the gun. Normanby gave a slight nod of confirmation and lowered the gun even further, before turning his attention back to the tops of the containers and the shadows between them.

"How long have you been here Mr. Foreman?" he called over his shoulder.

Foreman slowly lowered his hands. "A couple of years," he said. "I bought it off…"

"Today!" said Normanby with a hint of annoyance. "How long have you been here today?"

"Ah, I see." Harry Forman gave a little laugh that he cut short almost immediately for fear that he might become hysterical in his panicked state. "I got in at about nine this morning Officer," he said.

"Is there anybody else here with you Mr. Foreman?" asked Grant gently.

Foreman shook his head. "No," he said, "just me today. What's it about?"

Grant looked at Taylor and shrugged. It was up to the Police, he thought, to decide how much to tell the man.

"We think it entirely possible sir," said Taylor delicately, "that a serious crime may have been committed on or near your premises. Would you mind if we take a quick look around?"

Foreman took in a breath, shocked and surprised. "Well yeah of course. What sort of crime?" he asked.

"We can't disclose that at the moment sir," said the Detective in the matter-of-fact Policeman voice that he used for dealing with the public. "Would there have been anyone here last night Mr. Foreman, between midnight and your arrival this morning?"

"Yes," said Foreman, growing slightly more confident. "We have a Security guard on at night. Some of them are idle bleeders, but it was Mo's shift last night and he's alright. He'd have reported anything out of the ordinary."

"Mo?" asked Grant suddenly; "...as in 'Mohammed'? What's his surname?"

Foreman looked offended. "It's a proper firm," he said defensively. "They're all S.I.A. registered."

"I'm sure they are," said Grant before asking a little more sternly; "What's Mo's surname?"

"Iqbal," replied Foreman. "He's a good lad though. He's a hard worker. He's never been in trouble."

Grant and Normanby exchanged a long, meaningful look. "I'm sure that he's an excellent guard, Mr. Foreman," said Grant. "We just have to be very thorough and find out if he's seen anything at all on his patrols. Doug, do you want to get your people here? Normanby and I are going to have a look around."

Taylor nodded and gave a sigh. "No rest for the wicked," he said, and then turned to the bewildered owner of the yard. "Mr. Foreman," he asked, "do you have a cabin or somewhere where we can have a cuppa while we wait for my colleagues?"
"Yeah sure, Officer," replied Foreman, still watching Grant and Normanby as they walked off to search the yard.

"You reacted pretty fast back there, Normanby," said Grant.

"Thank you, Mr Grant," Normanby replied. He did not take his attention from the ground in front of him as he walked very slowly down the wide gap between the freight containers.

"So, what regiment were you in then," Grant asked casually, "S.A.S.; Paras; something like that?"

Normanby sighed and kept his attention focussed on the ground.

"You're not going to tell me, are you?" asked Grant.

"No Mr Grant," the little man confirmed, "I'm not."

Grant shrugged. He had already made up his mind that he would find out everything he could about Normanby's history, and the refusal simply made him more interested and more determined.

"I think we've found it," said Normanby suddenly. He stood very still for a moment with only his eyes moving, surveying every inch of the ground in front of him. He took one careful pace forward and then bent to examine the bloodstains more closely.
"This is where they died," he confirmed.

Grant felt a shudder as he looked down at the bloodstained floor. The sight seemed strangely as disturbing as seeing the corpses had been, knowing that this was the place where they had left the world of the living.

Normanby spent a moment looking at the shape and position of the bloodstains and then straightened and turned around. He used a hand to shield his eyes from the sun and looked at one of the rows of freight containers. "The sniper was on top of one of those two," he said pointing.

Grant stared down at the bloodstains. He knew that Normanby had made his deduction based on their examination, but he could not himself see the message that they had conveyed. "Go on," he said genuinely interested. "How do the stains tell you that they were shot from over there?"

Normanby looked happy to have been asked. "There seem to be three more or less distinct pools of blood, each over a metre apart," he said enthusiastically. "This indicates that the three men were walking in a row, spread out along this particular pathway. I believe that the first pool of blood, here on the right, represents where the first man fell."

"Why do you say that?" asked Grant, still puzzled.

Normanby smiled. "Because it's further back than the other two," he said. "This fits my theory about the use of a silenced weapon. The first man, on the right, has been shot and his companions have taken two full steps before the second man, in the middle, has also been shot. Now, if we look at the third stain on the left, we see that it is level with the one in the middle. Poor old Toby, the third victim, had stopped walking when the second of his colleagues fell. You will notice that this last bloodstain is less clearly defined than the others, and more spread out. This is because Toby was hit twice and did not immediately fall like the others. His reaction to his colleagues falling meant that the assassin did not have a clean shot. He staggered slightly and had to be shot a second time."

Grant scratched his chin in thought, trying to see if he could find an alternative explanation, whilst Normanby took out his mobile phone and used it to take photographs of the bloodstains.

"Can you be sure?" asked Grant. "How do you know which way they were going and how do you know that one or more of them weren't just knocked flying by the bullets?"

Normanby slipped the phone back into his pocket and took out his notebook. "The bloodstains fit very precisely with the theory that I formed from my observation of the bodies," he said. "As to the victims being 'knocked flying' as you put it; all three bodies appeared to have exit wounds. This means that the bullets went through them. When a bullet passes through a body, there is no force in action to push the body back. The idea of people being thrown back by the force of a bullet owes more to old Western films than to reality. A bullet will only knock you flying if it hasn't gone through."

"Really?" said Grant. He was surprised that he had never been told that fact during his training, but it made perfect sense when he thought about it. "Well, you learn something new every day," he said lightly.

"You do indeed," Normanby concurred, walking over to the container boxes that he had pointed out. He began scanning the floor near the bases of the boxes and Grant followed suit, feeling pleased that he knew exactly what to look for.

"Down here," said Grant, happily pointing to a brass shell casing on the floor between the two containers.

Normanby walked over to it and squatted to get as good a view of the cartridge as he could without touching it. "Well spotted Mr Grant," he said, squinting at the object. "It's a .308 calibre with Russian markings; definitely compatible with Mr Kurylenko's T-5000 sniper rifle. I think we need Detective Taylor's most diligent crime scene personnel here to gather the evidence."

He pulled a pen from the immaculate row in the breast pocket of his jacket and then glanced around, looking for some feature that would best help him describe the location of the discarded shell casing. His eyes rested for a moment on the serial number stencilled in white paint high on the back of the freight container. He glanced around at the other nearby containers to ascertain that the serial numbers were unique identifiers for each individual box…

CHAPTER THIRTY SIX: THE RAID

Grant peered carefully around the corner of the building and surveyed the front entrance of the seven-storey block of flats across the road. "I can't see any movement yet," he said, ducking back out of sight.

"Oh, I'm sure you won't have to wait long," said Normanby patiently.

A second later, an unmarked blue transit van pulled up to the kerb outside the flats. Four men in black coveralls, baseball caps and tactical vests disembarked from the vehicle. Each of the men carried a Heckler and Koch MP5 machine pistol and had Glock 9mm pistols holstered low on the hip. The men vanished into the entrance of the flats. Grant stepped out around the corner and watched the front of the block intently.

Suddenly, six uniformed police officers stormed out of a nearby alleyway and followed the black clad men into the entrance of the flats. "They're in!" said Grant excitedly. He could feel the surge of adrenaline in the pit of his stomach, and he relished the sensation.

Normanby nodded. "Then we had better join them before any evidence is ruined," he said, stepping out and walking nonchalantly across the road with Grant beside him.

Grant was out of breath and panting by the time that he reached the sixth floor. Once again, he had been surprised by Normanby who had jogged lightly up the stairs ahead of him and showed no signs of exertion.

One of the black clad Counter Terrorism Officers stepped out of the flat and onto the landing. He put the sling of his machine pistol casually over his shoulder. "They've already cleared out sir," he said to Normanby who was waiting expectantly at the top of the stairs. "It's been a complete waste of time and resources."

"Bloody marvelous!" said Grant bitterly between deep breaths. "I'd still like to take a look inside if you don't mind Officer," said Normanby.

The Policeman stood aside and gestured with a hand. "Be my guest," he said, "but you're wasting your time. They've left it as clean as a whistle."

Grant sighed heavily and watched with a sour expression as Normanby paused in the doorway of the flat. Before moving forward, he looked around. "Mr. Grant," he said. "We're needed."

Grant's look of bitterness was replaced by a slight, bemused smile as he followed the little man into the flat.

Inside the front door there were two more steps up to a hallway which ran nearly the full length of the flat. There were two doors on the left side of the hall, three doors on the right side, and one at the far end.

Normanby pushed open the first door on his left and then peered into the gloom of a windowless box room which housed the airing cupboard and little else except an old and worn single mattress and a pillow on the floor. He turned back and tried the first door on the right of the hall revealing the master bedroom furnished with a double bed, a dressing table, a two-door wardrobe and a large, leather swivel chair. The drawers of the dressing table had been left open and were all empty, as was the wardrobe.

The next room along was a smaller bedroom furnished with a single bed, a small wardrobe and a straight-backed chair. Once again, the bed had been stripped and the wardrobe was empty.

Normanby stepped across the hall to the second door on the left. He pushed it open to reveal the bathroom. He opened a tall cupboard and found that it connected to the airing cupboard in the box room next door. There was nothing of particular interest in the bathroom. It had been kept clean and in good order and the only items that had been left behind were two bars of soap, still in their cellophane wrappers, an empty plastic bottle on the floor next to the toilet, and two cardboard tubes from the inside of toilet rolls in the waste bin by the sink.

Normanby sighed and stepped back into the hall. There were two rooms left to check. He chose the door at the end of the hall. At the other side of the door, he found the kitchen. It was quite a large space with built in units on two walls, the cupboards and drawers left open and empty. In the third wall, above the kitchen sink, a window looked out over the spread of a housing estate. Here and there amongst the uniform expanse of neat rows of houses, occasional blocks of flats stood out like towering alien war machines standing sentry over the tiny homes of the masses.

The little man returned his attention to the interior of the room. Against the fourth wall was a blue, Formica-topped table with two cheap, PVC-upholstered dining chairs in the same colour. As Normanby stepped towards the table he felt something crunch under his foot. He squatted on his haunches and examined the floor around him, catching the glint of fine shards of broken glass here and there under the table. "Interesting," he said looking up at Grant who was standing in the doorway with his arms folded.

"What is?" asked Grant, still disappointed that Hussein and his people were not here when the flat was raided.

"There are tiny fragments of fine, broken glass here," Normanby said thoughtfully. "I wonder if it might be some kind of test tube. After all, our Russian friend was looking for some missing Sarin as well as the sniper rifle."

"Jesus," exclaimed Grant, suddenly very worried. "If they've been messing with that stuff and broken a test tube of it in here, we could be in big trouble!"

"Yes," replied Normanby seriously. His eyes fell on the wastepaper bin in the corner of the room and the exposed metal of the bayonette fitting from a broken lightbulb shoved in amongst the assorted waste. He heaved a huge sigh of relief and smiled slightly. "False alarm," he said. "It's just a broken light bulb."

"Thank God," said Grant. "I've had enough crap shoved into my system since this whole business began."

Normanby straightened and came smoothly up to his full height. "I suppose," he said, "that the remaining room must be the lounge. Let's see what we can find in there, shall we?"

Grant gave a non-committal shrug and followed Normanby to the lounge. The room was again spacious and well designed. Against two of the walls were long settees upholstered in cheap, colourful fabric. A low coffee table with a small TV set stood beside one of the settees. Against the third wall was a heavy, solid-looking dining table with two folding chairs tucked beneath, and a large leather upholstered swivel chair that matched the one in the master bedroom. The full length of the fourth wall was dominated by large windows which looked out over the neighbouring rooftops towards Marsh Road and the shopping complex.

Normanby stared out of the windows for several minutes. He could see the walled end of Trilby Street a quarter of a mile away amongst the labyrinth of ancient streets and the roof of the Shopping Centre just beyond, its glass canopy and the ornate domes of its floodlights inside, glinting with reflected sunlight.

"They haven't left much," said Grant from the doorway, not even trying to hide the disappointment from his voice. He stepped into the room and picked up a paperback copy of the Quran from beside one of the settees. He flicked through the pages and then tossed it dejectedly onto the table next to a two day old copy of the London Evening Standard.

Normanby looked down at the heavy pile of the carpet on the floor. There were four flattened areas in the middle of the room, each about two inches square. He glanced at the big table and realised that at some point it had stood there, in the centre of the room. Perhaps Hussein and his people had sat around it to make their plans, he thought. He looked back at the carpet with a puzzled expression. He could see no other flattened areas that would correspond to chairs placed around the table.

"Well, I'm not being funny Normanby," said Grant, "but if we'd brought them in when I first suggested it, we wouldn't be here like this."

Normanby glared at him, annoyed that his chain of thought had been broken. "If we had brought them in when you first suggested it," he said irritably, "we would be considerably worse off. At that time, we had no hard evidence against them. All we had was Shafiq Hussein's reports of drug deals and terrorist intent, with no proof whatsoever. They would have been released through lack of evidence and they would have been forewarned that we were onto them. We would also have remained unaware of Major Green's criminal operation, and he would be working on his next criminal endeavour!"

Grant drew in a sharp breath to reply and then realised that he did not have any suitable answers. Normanby was right, he acknowledged, not that it seemed to be doing them any good. "So, what do we do now?" he asked lamely.

"Now," the little man replied firmly, "we ensure that the Police preserve this flat as a crime scene and go over every inch of it in the search for clues."

"Are you kidding?" said Grant. "They don't even have the manpower to examine all the other crime scenes that this investigation's produced."

"Then it must be secured until they can get their best people on it," Normanby replied simply. He extracted the mobile phone from his pocket and dialled a number. "Ah, Detective Taylor," he said brightly, "you're probably not going to like this…"

CHAPTER THIRTY SEVEN: BOXES

Normanby did not like Room 331. The technology there did not impress him and the room's lack of windows to the outside world made him feel claustrophobic. There was a constant low hum in the room, just on the threshold of perceptibility and Normanby found it irritating. He glanced at Grant, seated beside him at the big, glass-topped table and saw no sign that the man was similarly affected. Indeed, Grant seemed to delight in the various toys and technological distractions that the room provided.

Normanby wished that the meeting had been convened in the comfort of Room 131 with real, cold air blowing in from open windows and the sounds of the London traffic, the people and the pigeons outside.

The Colonel cleared his throat loudly to ensure that he had the full attention of the two men across the table from him. Both men stared back at him expectantly and he gave a small nod. "Gentlemen," he said, "let's get down to business. For my part, I can tell you that since you exposed Major Green and his team as rogue operatives, I've had Lancer and Cole going through all of his team's files. It looks as though Green's been abusing his position for as long as he's been with the Service. He seems to have closed down each of his little criminal projects as they came to their natural conclusions. I dare say that the powers-that-be will want the details of these crimes sweeping under the carpet to avoid embarrassment, although I intend to ensure that other agencies will never again have the power to choose our operatives for us."

"If they do sweep it under the carpet," asked Grant, "what's going to happen to Green?"

The Colonel eyed grant steadily. "I imagine," he said seriously, "that that will depend on Major Green's level of co-operation, and it is no concern of yours."

Tom Grant made an effort to relax the muscles that were clenching his teeth tightly together. The thought of Green getting off lightly after all that he had done made him feel sick. He noticed that The Colonel was still watching him, and he let out a long, slow breath in an effort to show that he was relaxed and calm.

Satisfied, The Colonel gave another nod before turning his attention to the little man beside Grant. "Well, Normanby," he boomed jovially, "what have you got for us?"

Normanby adjusted his spectacles and opened the A4 card folder on the table in front of him. "Well," he said proudly, "I believe that we have found the route and the method that Hussein's people used to smuggle illicit drugs and weapons into the country. We can also narrow down the point of origin, and therefore the actual suppliers at the other end of the trail. This, in turn, can tell us which particular group or groups Hussein and his gang are affiliated to.

Grant turned his head and looked at the little man in surprise. "How on Earth have you learned all that?" he asked with an incredulous smile. He glanced across at The Colonel and saw the look of surprise and amusement on his face.

"Indeed Normanby," said the old man, "I must confess to sharing Mr. Grant's confusion. How have you obtained this information?"

Normanby extended a finger and used it to push up his spectacles. His thin lips widened in a proud smile. "I traced the freight containers from Foreman's yard," he said simply. "I noticed that each of the freight containers had a unique serial number, so I did a little reading. I found that the numbers on the container boxes, I.S.O. numbers as they're called, are issued by the International Organisation for Standardisation in Geneva. Each number is unique and contains an owner code, with an indicator for the type of container, followed by a registration number and a check digit."

He saw that his audience were beginning to look baffled. "To put it simply," he said, "you can trace the owner of a container and where it has been by following the paper-trail associated with the I.S.O. number."

"But surely," said The Colonel, "any smuggler would know this…"

"They would sir," Normanby conceded, "but it would be unlikely to bother them too much. There are over seventeen million of these containers in the world. At any given moment, there are around six million containers in transit. The actual chances of a container with all the right paperwork being really thoroughly checked are miniscule. Containers with all the right codes and paperwork routinely pass through several borders without even being opened, let alone checked. Some are examined in the countries at each end of their journey, but even these checks aren't always as thorough as they should be because everyone trusts everyone else in the supply chain. If you have a few contacts in the right places, it would appear that smuggling is not as difficult as most people would imagine."

"So, you checked all of the containers from the yard and found out where they'd all been?" asked Grant. "That must have taken you all night."

"It didn't take as long as you might think Mr. Grant," Normanby replied nonchalantly. "After all, I knew roughly where our container had come from, and I had a rough timescale for its arrival. It didn't take very long to narrow the search down to the one container that had travelled from the port of Gwadar in Pakistan, arriving in the U.K. within the last week. Bills of lading and other paperwork suggested that the main part of the cargo in the container should have been a consignment of plimsolls from a factory near Quetta. The manufacturer and associated paperwork checks out as authentic, but the location is interesting. I don't believe that the plimsolls were the only cargo in the container, and I have instructed the Forensics people to examine it thoroughly."

"And what makes you sure that they'll find anything useful to us Normanby?" asked The Colonel slowly.

"Because I traced the owner of the shipping container," the little man replied. "It belongs to a company owned by a Russian businessman called Samuil Popov."

"Samuil Popov," echoed The Colonel, deep in thought. "That is interesting!"

"What is even more interesting," Normanby continued, "is that, according to the paperwork at Foreman's yard, that same container box has been damaged on its way back from Pakistan four times in the last year and then brought to the yard for repairs."

Grant leaned forward and rested his elbows in the big table in front of him. "Well, I get that the supposedly damaged container comes back to the yard where one of our bad guys works as a security guard," he said. "It probably has a secret panel welded somewhere to hide stuff, and Hussein's boys come along at night and get their goods out of it. My question is: Who's this Samuil Popov character and what's he got to do with it all?"

The Colonel ran a hand under the tabletop in front of his seat. He found a switch and flicked it before slapping a hand down hard on the table to activate the built-in screen. The glass-topped expanse between the three men lit up and showed images of neatly arranged files.

"Samuil Popov," said The Colonel as if giving a lecture to a class, "was under investigation by Major Green just over a year ago. The Major's official conclusion, in his report submitted at that time, was that Popov posed no threat to the security of the United Kingdom and that he was an innocent Russian businessman." He awkwardly slid one of the virtual files to the centre of the table and then banged his palm down hard on the image several times to open the file.

Grant stared down at the photograph on the first page of the open file and felt sick. "Jesus Christ!" he exclaimed. "That's Sammy Parsons!"

"What?" asked The Colonel sharply.

"That's Sammy Parsons," Grant repeated. "He's the one that Green introduced me to at the club. He didn't sound Russian when I spoke to him."

The Colonel sat back down slowly. "Do we have enough to bring him in Normanby?" he asked.

The little man thought for a moment and gave a slight shake of the head. "Not unless we can find physical proof that his container has been used to smuggle illegal items," he said. "Even then, a good lawyer would get him off. After all, he may own the company that owns the container, but it would be hard to prove that he had any knowledge of it being used for smuggling, even if we can find him."

"He's the other member of Green's team," mumbled Grant.

"What?" barked The Colonel impatiently.

"Isn't it obvious?" Grant said coldly, looking straight at the old man. "Green was busy setting me up; Toby, Andy and Jacko were getting their brains blown out by Hussein's boys, and this bastard..." He jabbed an index finger at the picture on the desktop. "...This bastard was at Sophia's flat. He murdered her to set me up!"

"We don't know that for sure," said The Colonel.

"But it does make sense sir," said Normanby quietly. "I think that Mr. Grant is right."

Grant continued to stare at the picture on the desktop. His pointing finger shook with rage until he suddenly clenched his fists and thrust them into his pockets. "I don't want to hear about his *level of co-operation*, or what we can prove to the satisfaction of a court," he spat savagely. "I want to see that bastard dead!"

CHAPTER THIRTY EIGHT: SANDRA

PCSO Sandra Mercer pulled her arms back and stretched her aching muscles. She rocked backwards and forwards a few times on the balls of her feet to loosen her calf muscles, which has begun to seize up from standing in the same position for too long.

As the newest member of the Local Neighbourhood Policing Team, she had drawn the short straw for this shift. Whilst everyone else on the team would be working at the shopping centre today and getting to see the Royal couple, she had been assigned the unenviable task of guarding a crime scene. It wasn't as if it was even an interesting crime scene, she thought glumly.

From what she had been told, some local drug dealers had had their flat raided, only for the Police to find that they had already vacated the premises, taking their possessions with them. Apparently, nothing suspicious had been found at the flat, but it was still due to be examined once the Forensics Team had finished other, more important Crime Scene Investigations.

There was little or no chance of the tenants returning, the Detective Sergeant in charge of the investigation had said, but as the lock on the front door had been destroyed during the raid, somebody had to keep an eye on the place and ensure that no-one entered and destroyed what little evidence there may be in the flat.

She doubted that there would be any, and Detective Sergeant Taylor had agreed, but he had been given instructions by another agency that it should be checked. She had guessed that this 'other agency' he had spoken of would be the NCA (The National Crime Agency), which would indicate that the drug dealers had at least been running a serious operation.

She still had to admit that she felt somewhat bitter about being given such a dull task when everyone else had the excitement of a high security Royal visit to deal with.

She looked at her watch and sighed. It would be ages before Lou Fowler was due to come and relieve her on duty. It wasn't even as if there was anything interesting to look at out here on the landing.

She had not seen or heard any movement at either of the other two flats on this landing, and she had seen only the occasional resident from the floor above, passing by on their way downstairs. None of them had spoken to her as they passed, and she had a feeling that most of the residents in the block were immigrants, new to the area and with little trust of the Police.

Her head tilted to one side as she heard the sound of footsteps on the stairs from the floor below, and a strong Pakistani accent echoing in the stairwell. "Shopping should be woman's work," the man was saying jovially, "that's why you've got the bags and I don't have to carry anything." He gave a long chuckle, and Sandra sighed and rolled her eyes at his attitude.

The man came into view onto the landing. He looked quite young, maybe in his mid-twenties, though it was always hard to tell with those beards, and he wore traditional Asian dress with the long shirt, sandals and a prayer cap, all in black. A second later, what Sandra assumed to be the man's wife also emerged, struggling with the weight of two large canvas holdalls. She seemed quite heavily built and a little taller than her husband. Little else could be guessed about her as she was covered by a burka and some kind of long black dress that reached almost to the ground.

Sandra stepped back to let them pass so that they could get into whichever was their flat. She felt the strip of Crime Scene tape stretched across the doorway of the flat that she was guarding touch her arm.

As the couple drew level with her, the man was fumbling in his pocket for his keys. He stopped in front of Sandra and smiled. "Good morning Officer," he said.

"Good morning," Sandra replied without much feeling.

The man's head twitched to the left in some kind of nervous tic, and Sandra looked away, slightly embarrassed for him.

Suddenly, the figure in the burka dropped the bags and lunged at Sandra, clasping a big, strong hand over her mouth, and pushing her back against the doorframe.

Her eyes widened in shock as she realised that the figure beneath the black cloth was a man. She tried to struggle against him, to get a hand to her radio and call for help, but the other man moved in quickly to grab her wrists.

Amid the frantic struggle she felt a momentary spark of hope as she heard footsteps on the stairs. If someone saw what was happening, they would surely raise the alarm. All hope vanished and was replaced by total despair as a third man darted onto the landing and grabbed the front of her tactical vest.

Ali Hussein tightened the grip of his hand over the woman's mouth and then reached around with his free hand to switch off the radio on the front of her tactical vest. "Get her inside the flat," he ordered through gritted teeth.

They dragged her into the hallway of the flat and Iqbal kicked the door closed behind him. "Get her in the bedroom," he said. "Who's got the knife?"

At the mention of the knife, Sandra's eyes widened in blind panic. She tried to scream, but the strong hand over her mouth only allowed a faint, muffled sound to emerge. If only she could get him to take his hand away, she would be able to plead, to convince him that there was no need to kill her. Whatever they wanted, she would comply in order to save her life. There just wasn't any need for this.

"Get her hands," said Tariq. "Get her hands so I can get the knife!"

Sandra struggled desperately, twisting and writhing, trying to just get a hand free so that she could try to get the man's hand from her face. If she could do that much, she thought, she would be able to convince them, and she would survive.
"Stop struggling bitch and it'll be a lot easier for you," hissed Ali from beneath the burka.

She froze, her mind reeling. If he said that, she thought, at least they might not kill her, whatever terrible things they intended to do to her, at least she might live. Iqbal took a firm grasp of her wrists, and she did not struggle, accepting that her only chance of survival now lie in complying with her attackers. Her eyes widened again in terror, however, when Tariq fumbled under his clothing and brought out a knife. She tried in vain to produce a scream as he raised the weapon high above his head and glared at her.

"No Tariq," barked Ali, hoarsely, "You'll end up cutting us all up! Give me it here." He reached out with his free hand and took the knife from Tariq, who looked at him dejectedly.

Sandra felt her muscles go slack and her legs shook, her mind overloaded with waves of terror, hope and relief. With a feeling of shame and self-loathing, she realised that she had wet herself. She felt a sudden bolt of white-hot pain in the side of her neck and tried to scream. The pain grew worse and then she felt a terrifying shock as a huge spray of blood shot up the side of her face. Ali pushed the knife forward, slicing through the artery in her neck and then yanking it free.

Sandra's knees crumpled and Ali went to the ground with her, still holding her mouth. She saw the wall of the bedroom and the long spray of blood on the wall above her before the tears blurred her vision. She couldn't be dying, she thought. Surely God wouldn't let that happen. Who was going to tell the kids? Who was going to collect them from school this afternoon? What will happen to them? The kids… And then there was nothing.

Mohammed Iqbal put a hand to his mouth as he looked down into the woman's dead, still eyes. He began to tremble as the magnitude of what they were doing truly struck him for the first time. When he had seen Ali shoot the three gangsters, they had been armed; they had been the dangerous enemies, but this was different. "What the fuck have we done?" he whispered.

"*I've* done what we had to," replied Ali through gritted teeth. "We are fighting a war, and don't forget it for a second." He pushed the dead woman nonchalantly aside and stood up, dragging the burka from his head, and using it to wipe the blood from his hands and from the knife. He flipped the knife, caught it by the blade and handed it to Tariq before stripping off the long black dress and throwing it over the dead woman. "Get them bags off the landing," he said. "That rifle better not be damaged."

CHAPTER THIRTY NINE: PAWNS WERE MADE TO BE SACRIFICED

Tom Grant peered cautiously over the railing at the steadily growing crowds on the mall below. He glanced back at Detective Sergeant Doug Taylor and noticed that the policeman was staying carefully away from the edge of the rooftop. "What's the matter Doug?" asked Grant with a smile. "Don't you like heights?"

"Not particularly Tom," replied Taylor, edging forward and throwing a furtive glance over the precipice, "and to be honest, I don't think there's much reason for us to be up here."

"You could be right," Grant conceded. "I really can't see how anyone could get a shot at the Royal couple from anywhere but up here and the rooftop's crawling with armed coppers. What about the entrances to the shopping centre itself? Are they all covered?"

Taylor shrugged. "As far as I'm aware, but you'd probably be better asking the Counter Terrorism Unit," he said. "I'm only really here as an observer."

Grant sighed and leaned on the metal railing, trying to look relaxed as his eyes scanned the mall below him. "I can't see any gaps in the security that anyone could exploit," he said. "If the Royal car comes onto the mall as it should, there's nowhere that a sniper could get a shot. They've got security guards and armed police at all the entrances and everybody that comes in with so much as a handbag is going to get at least a basic search. On top of that, they've all got pictures of Hussein and his people."

He took a half step back and leaned against one of the short lamp posts that lined the edge of the roof, their lights pointing down so that they could illuminate the mall at night. "I'm beginning to think that this isn't the target, Doug," he said. "I reckon that Hussein and his little gang are long gone by now, probably on their way to Iraq or Syria to join I.S.I.S., or whatever they're calling themselves this week."

Taylor thrust his hands into his coat pockets and took a careful step forward to stand beside Grant. He glanced up at the light fitting inches above his head and then craned his neck to peer gingerly down to where it pointed on the mall. "I think you're right," he said. "I can't see how anybody could get to them with this level of security."

Grant gave a slight start as his mobile phone rang. He looked at the screen with a wry smile before answering. "Hello Normanby," he said. "Where are you and have you found any terrorists yet?"

"Not yet Mr. Grant," said Normanby coolly. "I'm at the Marsh Road entrance to the mall, near car park. Have you seen anything of note?"

"Not a thing," replied Grant looking down at the crowds. "It's starting to fill up a bit down there though. The local radio station have got a busy little stage down there with a roadshow event. Apparently, the whole thing's going to be broadcast live."

"Have the photographs of Hussein's group been distributed to all the police and security there?" Normanby asked, annoyed at Grant's flippant tone.

"Yes," replied Grant with tired patience, "they've all got the photos. To be honest Normanby, I think we're wasting our time. Hussein and his people have probably fled the country by now."

"Perhaps Mr. Grant," said Normanby, "but I would rather err on the side of caution. They have spent a long time planning their attack and I don't believe that they will be eager to abandon it."

Grant gave a shrug. "Okay Normanby," he said nonchalantly. "It's your call. We've got all the entrances sewn up here, and a dozen police snipers on the roof. Every inch of every floor of every shop has been swept for any sign of explosives in case Hussein left a device on his last shift. I can't see any possible way that anyone can get close enough to the V.I.P.'s to do anything. Even if we hadn't raided Hussein's flat, he wouldn't be able to get a shot at anyone down on the mall. The best he could have hoped for would be to get a couple of us up here on the roof, or a bit of wanton vandalism on the lights."

He looked around at the armed police officers who stood intently watching the crowds below. After a few seconds he realised that Normanby wasn't replying. "Normanby," he said, "are you still there?"

The little man was running down the pavement from the shopping centre towards the pelican crossing on Marsh Road. He stopped and jabbed the button at the crossing, frantically looking for a gap in the stream of traffic that poured down the carriageways of the busy road. Gasping from his exertion, he put the phone back to his ear. "Mr. Grant," he said urgently, "it's in the lights! The light bulbs! There were broken bulbs in the flat! That's why Hussein turned up for that last shift! All he has to do is shoot the lights."

Grant's gaze drifted upwards to the row of lamp posts lining the edges of the roof. "Jesus Christ!" he breathed.

"We need to stop them shooting the lights," panted Normanby as he pelted across the road, "but if they suspect you're putting anything in place they'll shoot anyway. Just don't let the Royals onto the mall!"

"Oh, Christ Almighty!" said Grant suddenly. "The cars are already here. They're turning onto the mall. There'll be no time to stop them!"

Normanby sprinted on, zigzagging up the path that led to Trilby Street. His leg muscles felt as though they were on fire, but he forced himself to go even faster, ignoring the pain. His chest was heaving, and his heart felt as though it might burst but he forced himself on.

They would be there, he was sure: Hussein and his gang would be back at the flat, the way that they had planned from the very beginning. He tried to stop thinking lest worry and panic slow him down, and he concentrated all of his energies into moving forward. He put a hand to his waistband to ensure that the pistol in his belt was not dislodged by his frantic sprinting.

*

Lou Fowler glanced down at the watch on her wrist without taking her hands out of the front of her yellow tactical vest. She made a quick count of people ahead of her in the queue in the little local branch of Greggs, and wondered if she would have enough time to get served and consume her bacon sandwich and cappuccino before she was due to take over guard duty on the crime scene.

She'd drawn the short straw with this shift, she decided. Everyone else would be at the shopping centre having fun whilst she was stuck watching a crime scene until the Forensics people got around to coming to it from more important jobs. She could have had a sick note for as long as she wanted after what had happened to her at that squat, she reflected. It still terrified her when she thought about it, and she still wasn't sure how she was going to react once she was left alone on guard. She shivered a little just thinking about it and she tried to clear her mind.

Inhaling slowly, she tensed every muscle in her body as hard as she could, and then tried to relax as she let the breath slowly back out. She was going to beat this, she told herself. She would not spend her life as a victim. She fought back against the tiny voice of panic that called distantly in the back of her mind.

Looking for comfort in the normality of everyday life, she looked about her at the people in the queue. Her glassy gaze drifted out of the shop window to the people strolling by. Suddenly she was jolted by a shock that made her skin come out in goosebumps and caused her to swear under her breath, as she saw the man outside dart past the window.

It was Mr. Normanby; she was sure of it. He had pelted down the pavement outside with an expression of panic and desperation on his face. He had been running with a hand clasped to his midriff. Had he been injured somehow, she wondered? After a moment of hesitation, she stepped towards the door and peered out onto the street. She glanced back over her shoulder and saw that her place in the queue had vanished as the other hungry shoppers had instantly stepped forward to close in on the counter. Each of them stared ahead blankly, careful not to catch her eye.

She tutted and stepped out onto the pavement and then used a hand to shield her eyes from the morning sun. She squinted into the glare, but could see no sign of Normanby. Ignoring the trembling that she felt in her knees, and the gnawing sense of unease and dread, she began walking in the direction that she had seen the little man run.

Normanby came to a halt in the entrance way of the block of flats. He slipped the Makarov from his belt and carefully slipped off the safety catch before setting off up the stairs. As he ascended the staircase, he tried to slow his breathing and steady his nerves. He took a breath in for two steps and then exhaled for the next two. He continued to do this all the way up to the sixth floor.

When he emerged onto the landing, holding the pistol in front of him in a two-hand grip, he was no longer gasping for breath. The measured breathing during his ascent had helped to calm him and had stopped him panicking, but he could still see that the hands holding the pistol were trembling.

He looked at the battered front door of Hussein's flat with a feeling of dread. The lock had been smashed off during the raid, and the door was simply pulled almost closed. There was no-one on guard on the landing, and the Police Crime Scene tape that had been stuck across the front door had been broken. The ends of the tape hung limply from each side of the door frame.

He edged closer to the door and listened. Somewhere inside the flat he could hear an excited voice of a radio presenter from the small speaker of a cheap transistor radio with the volume turned up too high. Alongside this, he could make out the occasional calmer voices on what sounded like a police or security radio.

Keeping the pistol clenched in his right hand, he let go with his left and silently cursed its uncontrollable shaking as he reached out to push the door wide open. He knew that he would have to act no matter how afraid he was, or what the odds were. There would be no time to call for back up; the moment was now...

Ali Hussein shifted his weight on the stool and rested his elbows on the big, heavy table in the centre of the room. He lifted the skeletal butt of the Orsis T-5000 sniper rifle and brought his shoulder up to it. The weapon's 6.5kg of weight was shared between Hussein's right hand on the pistol grip, and the bipod that rested on the table. He gently caressed the resin of the forward stock with his left hand until he found the most comfortable position and then he tightened his grip.

Taking a deep breath, he put his right eye to the rifle's scope and peered at the view through the wide-open window. He gently angled the weapon until the roofline of the shopping centre came into view through the scope. "There they are," he whispered quietly. "Who are these silly bastards wandering around on the roof?"

Tariq Malik was struggling to contain his excitement at what was about to be done. "We're gonna do it man, we're gonna do it!" he said shuffling his feet in something like a joyous little dance.

"Shut the fuck up Tariq," hissed Mohammed Iqbal, lowering the binoculars from his eyes. "Ali's got to concentrate, you fucking retard!"

Malik's head twitched a couple of times and his face reddened with anger, but he remained sulkily silent. He squinted at the distant outline of the shopping complex and stood with his arms folded, pouting like a petulant child.

Iqbal brought the binoculars back up to his eyes and focussed on the row of light domes that were visible just above the edge of the roof, under the glass canopy. He could see the figures of several of the police snipers as they watched the crowds down on the mall, and the two men in plain clothes who were annoyingly moving around and periodically blocking the view of the lights. "What the fuck are they doing?" he whispered. "They're getting in the way!"

"Don't worry brother," Hussein assured him with quiet patience. "I've got two five round magazines and plenty of time. As soon as their Royal Kuffar bastard Highnesses are out in the open, I'll drop anybody on the roof who's in the way and take the light bulbs out. They'll be in the middle of a military grade Sarin storm before they even know what's hit them."

The voice from the transistor radio blared out excitedly: "And here they come; The Royal couple will be stepping out to see the crowds any second."

All three men in the room held their breath until the radio scanner beside the little portable radio came to life: "All Sierra units please be aware," it said, "that our V.I.P.'s will be on stage in five seconds. Stay alert and stay in position."

Ali Hussein felt the thrill of adrenaline in the pit of his stomach as he centred his sights on the face of the man pacing about on the rooftop with the mobile phone pressed to his ear. He squeezed the trigger and saw the look of dumb shock appear on the man's face as the small hole appeared in the centre of his forehead and he fell down out of view.

Hussein gripped the fore-stock tightly with his left hand as he reached with his right for the bolt that would feed another round into the chamber, now that his view of the light domes was unobstructed.

There was a sudden noise from the hallway. The front door had been opened. Hussein's head snapped around to look behind him and a man with a gun appeared in the doorway. When Hussein saw Tariq Malik launch himself into action and draw a large hunting knife from inside his jacket, he calmly returned his attention to the rifle scope and the task in hand.

In that split second, Normanby saw that his choices were limited: He could defend himself against the man with the knife or he could shoot the sniper who was about to trigger a chemical attack, if he hadn't already done so. He knew that he would not have the time to do both effectively.

He instantly raised the Makarov and fired a single shot. Hussein's body jolted awkwardly as the bullet entered the back of his head, and carried a fine spray of blood, brain matter and tiny shards of bone out through his forehead and before going through the open window. A spread of matter adhered itself to the rifle in front of Hussein on the table.

In the same instant, Normanby cried out at the sickening agony as Malik's knife thrust deep into his abdomen. Malik growled in fury as he thrust forward, a murderous fire in his eyes. A fleck of spittle burst from between his bared, tightly clenched teeth and hung in his beard as he drove forward, shoving the broad blade deeply into the little man's gut, forcing him back against the wall. Normanby felt the strength being sapped from his body due to the shock, and then the searing pain increased and made him cry out again as the blade was pulled out of his body.

His knees began to buckle, and he started to slide slowly down the wall. He raised the pistol frantically, struggling to lift its weight, and he pulled the trigger. The sound of the gunshot made Iqbal jump, but he continued to stare in shock at the grotesque drama being played out before him. Malik gave an agonised, hateful grunt but he stayed on his feet. His face was a mask of savage rage as he hefted the knife to thrust again. Normanby screamed out as he fought to keep the gun levelled and he fired again into Malik's chest. This time, Malik stopped. He gave a look of bewilderment and then half-turned to look at the shocked and frozen Mohammed Iqbal.

"Finish him," gasped Malik. The knife fell from his lifeless fingers, and he fell straight back, making no attempt to break his fall.

Normanby's legs gave way and folded under him awkwardly. He brought up his shaking left hand to join his right in trying to hold the pistol level. He tried to speak, to issue a warning or a plea as Iqbal, his face blank, stepped forward and leaned down for the bloodied knife. The only sound that emerged from his lips was a strangled, gasping cough, and he tasted blood.

Iqbal straightened up and looked at the knife in his hand. He knew what he must do, but he had never killed anyone before. He took a deep breath, switched his grip on the blade so that it pointed downward, and then raised his hand.

Normanby fired again, his weakened hands shaking under the weight of the little gun, and Iqbal stumbled back against the doorframe. He pressed his left hand to the side of his stomach and an expression of panic grew on his face as he raised the hand and looked at the blood dripping from it. His mouth dropped open as he looked straight down the black eye of the pistol in Normanby's quivering hands. The little man gave a hateful, venomous snarl and squeezed the trigger again.

Iqbal flinched and cowered as the shot rang out. Splinters of wood stung his cheek as they were spat out by the impact of the bullet ploughing into the doorframe, inches from his head. He dived through the doorway, praying that he would be able to get out of the way before the little man could fire again. He gasped at the pain in his side as he stumbled forward and thrust the hand holding the knife inside his jacket.

Throughout the block of flats, front doors were being unlocked and cautiously opened a sliver so that worried, curious eyes could peer through the gaps. The Police would be on their way, Iqbal knew. He had to get away if he could. If he couldn't get away, he decided, he could take a hostage. He had to do something to stop this whole thing being a total waste, he decided as he stumbled down the stairs, leaving a smear of blood down the handrail as he used it to support his weight.

Normanby looked furiously at the pistol in his hands. The ejector slide had not returned to its original position, meaning that the gun was empty. The weapon fell from his fingers and dropped to the floor with a dull thud. He gave a growl of anger and frustration that Iqbal had got out of the room. After all they had attempted, after all they had *done*, he could not bear the thought that any of Hussein's gang might get away. He took a deep breath and pushed himself forward, struggling to move his legs from underneath himself so that he could at least crawl…

Lou Fowler cursed breathlessly as she brought the mobile phone down from her ear. She was beginning to worry. The phone had rung, and she had known straight away that it was Doug Taylor that was trying to contact her. He was the only person that had the number to the cheap little mobile phone. When she had answered the line had gone dead. She had tried ringing back three times and each time the call went straight to the voicemail service.

At first, she had not been too worried. Perhaps, she thought, something had just come up and he had felt the need to switch his phone off. She had begun to feel uneasy, however, when she started to hear the sound of sirens from the direction of Marsh Road. It sounded as though there was some kind of major incident happening, although she had heard no notifications on either her Police or her Town-link radios.

She quickened her pace, annoyed with herself for not keeping calm. Surely, she thought, if there was anything wrong, she would hear about it on her radios. Anyway, she concluded, seeing the direction in which Mr. Normanby had run down the road was an indication that if there was any trouble it was likely to be somewhere ahead of her.

Suddenly, in the distance, she heard a series of loud bangs. She wondered at first if they might be gunshots, but she tried to put the idea out of her mind. The sounds seemed to have come from the block of flats that she was heading towards. It must be something else, she thought; a car backfiring or something. Remembering the desperate look on Mr. Normanby's face when he had gone running by, she gave a quiet moan of worry and quickened her pace towards the flat. She was afraid and heading into the unknown, but she knew that she could not stand idly by. Whatever was happening, she had to play her part. Barely realising that she was doing so, Lou Fowler broke into a sprint.

She suddenly stopped running at the sight of the man who was running towards her, stumbling as he plunged forward, obviously in a great deal of pain and distress. When she saw that he had a hand inside the front of his jacket and saw the red stain growing beneath it, her hand automatically strayed up to the radio on the front of her tactical vest.

"Help me," he said. "There's been a murder. He's a madman!" He continued running awkwardly towards her, and as the distance closed between them, she saw the fear and desperation on his face. She put both hands out to catch him as he stumbled and fell against her. His legs buckled and he fell to his knees, his desperate grip on her arm pulling her down with him so that she had to go down into a crouch to avoid losing her balance completely.

She tried to sound reassuring when she spoke. "Alright, I'm going to get you some help," she said. "What's happened to you?" She saw a strange look on his face, almost as if there was a resigned smile trying to burst out from his look of despair.

He let go of her arm and suddenly grasped the front of her tactical vest, pulling her off balance. She rolled to one side to avoid landing on top of the injured man, trying to remain patient, despite his panicked behaviour. She tried to push herself up off the pavement, but his grip on her tactical vest was too tight. Then she felt a sudden confused dread when he used the pulling action against her to lever himself up, before throwing his leg over her like a man mounting a horse.

He came upright; straddling her on the pavement and his bloodied hand gripped her throat, the fingers digging painfully into the sides of her windpipe. She grabbed at his wrist with both hands trying to break the grip on her throat, but he was too strong.

She tried to scream for help, but the pressure of his grip would allow her no more than a pathetic gurgling sound. Her eyes darted around wildly. She knew that there were people on the street and cars driving by. Surely, she thought, somebody was bound to save her. She glimpsed people at the other side of the road, outside the flats. They were standing dumbstruck and frozen with fear and shock.

'Do something you fucking cowards,' she thought. As her vision began to blur, she realised that no-one was going to come to her aid in time. Her eyes widened in terror when her attacker's other hand emerged from his jacket holding the knife with its sharp blade pointing downwards towards her. He raised it high above his head and she saw the orgiastic, evil smile on his face and knew that she was helpless.

"I'm going to start with your eyes, bitch," he said.

Already blinded by her own tears, her chin quivered, and she sobbed. Her grip on his wrist slackened as the last of her strength was drained away along with all hope. She knew that there was nothing that she could do, and that she was going to die.

There was a slight popping sound and through the blurred curtain of tears, she saw his face suddenly change. A section of his cheek seemed to vanish and was replaced by a bloodied, cavernous black hole. His nose seemed to whip strangely to one side and then swing slowly back, held in place by a thin flap of skin that acted like a hinge.

His expression did not otherwise change except for a strange blankness that seemed to form in his eyes as they grew totally still. He fell forward on top of her, and she found herself frozen beneath the lifeless cadaver.

With a start, she burst into frantic movement, scrambling desperately to climb from beneath him. She automatically wiped her cheek where it felt wet, and her eyes widened when she saw the blood on her hand. She retched when she saw the little lump of grey matter in the blood and realised what it was. Shakily unzipping her tactical vest, she used it to wipe her face. She continued to scrub at her cheek, letting out a low, inhuman wail as she did so…

The Orsis T-5000 rifle slipped from the windowsill and fell back into the room with a clatter as Normanby's grip slackened. He groaned as the pain of supporting his own weight with his elbows on the window frame became too much for him. He slithered to the ground and rolled slowly onto his back, staring out of the open window at the sky. The clouds seemed oddly blurred and surreal. He tried to focus but he knew that it was pointless to do so. It was probably pointless to do anything now, he thought. The pain had gone from his stomach, but the weakness in his limbs had grown. He tried to lift a hand and found that he did not have the strength to do so.

So, this was what death felt like, he thought. It didn't hurt anymore: It didn't seem so terrifying really…just sad and a little lonely. He shrugged mentally; Normanby always felt sad and a little lonely. He had often wondered what it must have been like for those that he had killed, had spent many years wracked with guilt at having taken human lives. Now he felt that it had been foolish of him to do so. After all, he thought to himself; pawns were meant to be sacrificed…

CHAPTER FORTY: END GAME

Tom Grant unfastened the black armband and folded it carefully as he walked down the path towards the cemetery gates. He had insisted on going to the funeral, despite The Colonel's orders to the contrary. When Grant had told him, point blank, that he was going and that he did not care about the consequences, the Old Man had, quite remarkably, capitulated with no more than a wry smile.

He stopped at the cemetery gates and looked back at the crowd of people slowly making their way from the graveside. He saw Lou Fowler trampling through the piles of fallen leaves that lined the path. She seemed oblivious to the world. Her head was bowed, and her eyes were red and swollen from crying. She looked small and vulnerable as she walked along, ignoring the smartly dressed, older woman beside her.

"There's nothing you could have done Lou," the woman said tearfully. "He did what he had to do, just like he always did. He saved people." Her voice broke at the last word, and she sobbed before continuing. "He saved us a long time ago."

"I know Mum," Lou replied flatly. "If it wasn't for Doug, Dad would probably have killed us both when I was a toddler."

"That's right love," the woman continued, relieved that Lou had finally spoken after the hours of total silence. "He was so proud of you, you know. He always said, when you joined the Police, he'd do whatever he could to help your career…" She broke down again, fumbling frantically through her pockets for a tissue to wipe her eyes. "That's not all love," she gasped. She seemed to be fighting some huge battle in order to get the words out. "Terry Fowler wasn't your dad," she said. Her hand went up to her mouth as soon as the words had come out. She knew that she had picked the worst possible moment to break the news but, after all these years, she had simply been unable to contain herself any longer.

Lou's mouth fell open and she stared, aghast. "How do you mean he wasn't my dad?" she said in a dry whisper. Her mother sobbed again in anguish, and she shook her head, the tears rolling freely down her cheeks.

The realisation dawned on Lou, and she slowly turned her head to look back at the cemetery, towards Doug Taylor's grave.

"We couldn't risk telling anybody, love," her mother said quietly. "What with him being married, and the job he was in…" her voice trailed off.

Lou Fowler felt as though the world was spinning away from her, as if some kind of curtain was rolling down to seal her off from reality. She felt sick and dizzy, but more than that, she felt stupid. She should have known. She stood motionless, a blank expression on her face.

Grant looked on sadly. She had been broken by all that had happened to her, he thought. He doubted that she would ever be able to return to her duties with the police and he wondered if there was anything that could possibly rebuild her after the ordeals that she had been through.

He turned and tried to put her out of his mind as he stepped through the gate and onto the road. He must concentrate, he told himself. He had one last job to do for The Colonel's department and there would be no room for errors. Once that was done, it would be time leave this whole messy business behind him once and for all. He would be able to say goodbye to The Colonel and his dirty spy games and return to G- section at M.I.5. At least there the work was legal, he thought, and ethical. He stopped beside his car and gave a snort…and boring, he added finally.

*

Kurylenko wiped the sweat from his brow with a shaking hand and looked worriedly at Tom Grant, who eyed him coldly. Neither man had spoken since Kurylenko had been roughly manhandled out of the back of the van and the black hood had been pulled from his head, exposing his tired eyes to harsh daylight for the first time in days.

He rubbed his wrists, still sore from the handcuffs that had held him throughout the journey to the little park where he now sat. He pondered his chances of escape and realised that any attempt would be futile. This man, Grant would be armed. He had little doubt of that. Perhaps even the metal briefcase that he carried contained a weapon. Kurylenko had heard of much stranger things.

Grant looked at his watch. "It shouldn't be long now, Mr. Kurylenko," he said flatly. Kurylenko swallowed hard and looked at the wet leaves on the ground around the park bench on which he sat. He wondered if the British were going to kill him now that they had gotten the information that they wanted from him. If they didn't, he thought bleakly, his own people probably would. A diplomat who broke down under even the gentlest of interrogations and told foreign intelligence services about missing nerve agents and sniper rifles would be of little use to the Russian Government. Men had died for much less.

He looked up, startled, as Grant gave a satisfied grunt and then called out down the pathway through the trees. "Hello Sammy," he said cheerfully. "I bet you didn't expect to see me today."

Samuil Popov stopped mid-stride with a look of shock on his face. In an instant, the expression changed into a cocky smile, and he sauntered on, stopping fifteen feet away from Grant. "I thought that the text message didn't seem like Mike Green's style," he said nonchalantly, stuffing his hands into his trouser pockets. "I take it that you have his phone?"

"Yes," said Grant smoothly. "I have his phone, his department and his business interests. Mike Green underestimated me. He's out of the picture now and I'm running his operation. *All of his operations*," he added pointedly.

Popov looked at him, trying to figure out whether he was telling the truth. "And what about *him*?" he asked, nodding his head in Kurylenko's direction.

Grant gave a snort of contempt. "He got himself involved," he said. "He was hoping to take your prize for himself and go back to Russia a hero."
Popov threw his head back and let out a short bellowing laugh. "A hero," he said. "I like that!" He turned his gaze on the dishevelled and bewildered man on the bench. "There are no heroes, Kurylenko," he said, "and if there were, you would not be one. You are not smart enough. When I sent Gorszky to kill your little lover-boy, I convinced him that I was you! You will even get the blame for killing your own lover!" He gave a sneer of utter contempt as he watched the realisation dawn on Kurylenko's face, and then chuckled as he saw the tears in his eyes.

Grant glanced quickly through a gap in the trees at the row of neat Georgian houses at the other side of the park. "I've got my own plans for Kurylenko Sammy," he said ominously. "Besides, I've got something better for you, just to show that you're still welcome to be in on the deal like you were with Green." He held up the metal briefcase the way that the Chancellor of the Exchequer used to do on Budget Day. He took two careful steps forward and placed the case on the ground before stepping back and gesturing with open palms and a smile. "The case contains a sealed, secure container of missing Sarin nerve agent and an envelope with the location of the missing Orsis T-5000 sniper rifle. I'm sure that the G.R.U. will pay a very good reward for its return," he said.

Popov stepped forward towards the case, turning his head to sneer at the bedraggled figure of Kurylenko on the bench. "You want to fight me for it Kurylenko?" he chuckled. "I would enjoy killing you."

"I thought you preferred murdering women," muttered Grant, with a cold gleam in his eye.

Popov stopped; his arm still outstretched towards the case, a puzzled look on his face. He was not quite sure what Grant had just said. "What?" he asked.

Grant was sure that he heard a faint popping sound. He gazed at Samuil Popov. The man's expression did not change one iota. The only difference that Grant noticed in his face was the small black dot that had appeared in the centre of Popov's forehead. The dot turned from black to red and then a thick, slow stream of blood began to well from the hole and pour down the side of Popov's nose. He slowly leaned over to one side and then hit the floor like a felled tree.

Grant stared at the dead man for several long, satisfying seconds before turning his gaze slowly on the shocked Kurylenko.

"As I said; the sarin's in there along with the location of the rifle," said Grant. He pointed down at Popov. "As you can guess, that location isn't too far from here. I suggest that when you make arrangements to send them back to your people, you also arrange to return home yourself. I've no doubt that you'll be treated as a hero of the Motherland as long as you get out of Britain before the oncoming Diplomatic storm."

"But...I don't understand," said the Russian simply.

"Two Russian nationals have been killed in London recently Mr. Kurylenko," said Grant; "One was shot with a Russian Makarov pistol and the other with a Russian sniper rifle. There is a substantial amount of evidence linking you to the whole affair. Go back to Russia with your trophies and be a hero."

Kurylenko was still puzzled. "Why are you letting me go?" he asked.

"Because we know you'll be of use to us," Grant replied. "If the Russian establishment ever learned the truth about what you told us, and about your affair with Shafiq, your life wouldn't be worth living. Of course, we wouldn't tell them Mr. Kurylenko because we're friends."

The Russian closed his eyes and put a hand to his clammy forehead. The shock of Grants words had been like a punch in the gut, and he felt very sick. He was trapped and there was no way that he could manoeuvre his way out of it.

Grant leaned down; his lips close to Kurylenko's ear. "Check mate," he whispered.

Kurylenko watched Grant prowl steadily down the path out of the park before turning his attention to the briefcase. He got up slowly from the bench and picked up the case. There was nothing that he could do except make the best of the situation, he decided. He would try to enjoy the prestige and power that he would no doubt gain back home, and he would hope and pray that whatever the British had in store for him would not be too dangerous.

Grant took a couple of steps onto the pavement from the park gates and stopped when he saw the figure by his car. He let out a sigh as the man by the car turned his head to stare straight at him. A broad, triumphant smile beamed in the brown face as the man straightened up to reveal his Traffic Warden's uniform. "Haha! I got you this time mistah!" he shouted gleefully, slapping the fixed penalty notice onto Grant's windscreen, and then rubbing it to ensure that it adhered firmly to the glass. Grants lips widened in a wry smile. The smile grew and he chuckled. He carried on until the chuckle became a laugh, and he threw his head back overjoyed for the Traffic Warden and his little victory. He felt happy to be alive now that this whole dirty business was at an end.

The Colonel lowered the binoculars from his eyes and then squinted through the open window. "I think that Grant handled that rather well," he said. "In fact, I'm going to make his transfer permanent. I think that he might make an excellent operative for the department, don't you?"

The man beside him carefully lowered the stock of the Orsis T-5000 sniper rifle to the table top. He pressed a hand to his side and winced painfully as he straightened himself up to his full height. "I think he will, sir," he said, extending a thin forefinger and using it to push the spectacles up to the bridge of his nose. "I think he will."

THE END

APPENDIX I: THE CHESS GAME

The Chess game that Normanby sees Kurylenko playing out in the Westminster Reference Library was originally played between Anatoly Karpov and Gary Kasparov in Moscow on 15th October 1985. It was Round 16 of the tournament. Karpov played White and Kasparov, Black. Kasparov won the game on the 40th move.

The author would like to thank Mr Neil Hinchliffe for his invaluable help with the chess game featured in this book.

The complete original chess game was as follows:
1: e4/c5. 2: (kn)f3/e6. 3:d4/cxd4. 4: (kn)xd4/(kn)c6. 5: (kn)b5/d6. 6:c4/(kn)f6. 7: (kn)1c3/a6. 8: (kn)a3/d5. 9:cxd5/exd5. 10: exd5/(kn)b4. 11: (B)e2/(B)c5. 12: O-O/O-O. 13: (B)f3/(B)f5. 14: (B)g5/(R)e8. 15: (Q)d2/b5. 16: (R)ad1/(kn)d3. 17: (kn)ab1/h6. 18: (B)h4/b4. 19: (kn)a4/(B)d6. 20: (B)g3/(R)c8. 21: b3/g5.22: (B)xd6/(Q)d6. 23: g3/(kn)d7. 24: (B)g2/(Q)f6. 25: a3/a5. 26: axb4/axb4.27: (Q)a2/(B)g6. 28:d6/g4. 29: (Q)d2/(K)g7. 30: f3/(Q)xd6. 31:fxg4/(Q)d4+. 32: (K)h1/(kn)f6. 33: (R)f4/(kn)e4. 34: (Q)xd3/(kn)f2+. 35: (R)xf2/(B)xd3. 36: (R)fd2/(Q)e3. 37: (R)xd3/(R)c1. 38: (kn)b2/(Q)f2. 39: (kn)d2/(R)xd1. 40: (kn)xd1/(R)e1+. 0-1.
  Normanby changes the game on the 20th move of the game and wins from Karpov's position:
20: a3/(Q)b8. 21: axb4/(kn)g4. 22: h3/(B)h2+. 23: (K)h1/(B)e4. 24: (B)g3/(Q)b4. 25: (Q)xb4/(kn)xb4. 26: (B)xg4/(R)d8. 27: (B)xh2/(B)h5. 28: (B)f3/(kn)xd5. 29: (kn)c3/(kn)f6. 30: (kn)d2/(B)d3. 31: (R)e1/(B)h4. 32: (kn)e4/a5. 33: (kn)xf6/gxf6. 34: (R)e8+/(R)xe8. 35: (R)d1/a4. 36: (B)c6/(K)f8. 37: (B)d6+/(R)e7. 38: (B)xe7/(K)xe7. 39: (R)e1+/(K)f8. 40: (R)e8+/(K)g7. 41: (kn)f3/f5. 42: (kn)xh4/f4. 43: (R)e7/(K)h6. 44: (R)xf7/(K)h5. 45: (R)xf4/(K)g5.46: g3/(B)e2. 47: (kn)f5/(K)f6. 48: (kn)d4+/(K)e6. 49: (kn)xe2/(K)d6. 50: (kn)d4/(K)e5. 51: f3/(K)d6. 52: (B)xa4/…(only King remains; surrenders).

APPENDIX II: WEAPONS

THE MAKAROV PISTOL (PISTOLET MAKAROVA)

The Makarov pistol, inspired by the design of the Walther PP, was first selected by the Soviet authorities to replace the Tokarev as the standard handgun of the USSR in 1949. It was formally adopted and entered service in 1951. The pistol stood out from its competitors for its simplicity, reliability and robustness, and was subsequently adopted by many countries throughout the world.

The Makarov was officially replaced by the PYa pistol as the official Russian sidearm in 2003, but a great many still remain in service in the country and elsewhere. The popularity and effectiveness of the Makarov has ensured that it will continue to be produced in large numbers for some time to come.

PISTOLET MAKAROVA.

Calibre: 9mm or .380
Magazine capacity 8 rounds
Weight: 730g / 26oz
Muzzle velocity: 315m/s / 1,030fps
Range: 50m / 55yds.

THE ORSIS T-5000 SNIPER RIFLE.

The Orsis T-5000 was developed by Orsis and is produced at their Moscow factory. The weapon was first introduced in 2011 at the international exhibition of Russian weapons in the city of Nizhny Tagil.

In 2017 the newest variation of the weapon, the T-5000 Precision, was adopted by the FSB, and the FSO. The T-5000 is also used by the military of several other countries: China, Iraq, Saudi Arabia, Syria, Vietnam, The UAE Presidential Guard, Armenia, Belarussia, Uzbekistan, Nigeria and Thailand.

ORSIS T-5000

Bolt action. 5 Round detachable magazine
Weight: 6.5kg / 14.3lb
Length: 1180mm / 46.5 in
Barrel length: 660mm / 26in
Calibre: 7.62 x 51mm NATO (.308 Winchester), or
                  .300 Winchester magnum, or .338 Lapua
                  magnum.
Max Range: Over 2000metres

APPENDIX III: GROUPS AND ORGANISATIONS

TTP – Tehreek-E-Taliban Pakistan (The Taliban Movement of Pakistan). Founded in 2002, the TTP is an umbrella group for many militant factions and offers support to the Afghan Taliban.

TNSM – Tehreek-E-Nafaz-E-Shariat-E-Mohammadi (The Movement For The Enforcement Of Islamic Law): A hard-line religious group that promoted Islamic fundamentalism in Pakistan. Founded in 1992 and made illegal by President Pervez Musharraf on January 12th, 2002. (The TTP and the TNSM have been allies since 2007).

FSB – The Federal Security Service of the Russian Federation is the principal security agency of Russia and is the main successor to the USSR's KGB. The FSB was formed on 12th April 1995 and it operated from the old KGB Headquarters at Lubyanka Square in Moscow.

SVR – The Foreign Intelligence Service of the Russian Federation, founded in December 1991.

GRU – The Russian Military Intelligence Agency is, reportedly Russia's largest foreign intelligence agency. They have received global press coverage since 2018 due to their alleged involvement in the poisoning of Sergei and Yulia Skirpal in the UK.

MI5 – The Security Service. The Secret Service Bureau was established in the UK in 1909. The various departments were eventually split into separate organisations. MI5, also known as The Security Service is the UK's domestic intelligence service. Its motto is the Latin Phrase: *Regnum Defendae,* 'In Defence of the Realm'. MI5 is run by the Home Office and is under the authority of the Home Secretary. The Headquarters of MI5 is in Thames House, on Millbank, overlooking the river. The building also houses the Joint Terrorism Analysis Centre.

MI6 – The Secret Intelligence Service. Originally part of the Secret Service Bureau along with MI5, The Secret Intelligence Service, MI6, is the UK's Foreign Intelligence Agency. The Secret Intelligence Service is housed in its iconic headquarters building at Vauxhall Cross (as seen in many of the James Bond films), on the opposite bank of the Thames from MI5. The Secret Intelligence Service is a branch of the Foreign Office, under the control of the Foreign Secretary.

NCA – The National Crime Agency was established in 2013. It replaced the Serious Organised Crime Agency as the national law enforcement agency of the UK. Like its Predecessor, the NCA is often dubbed 'the British FBI' by the media. The NCA Headquarters is on Tinworth Street, London.

BRINDLE BOOKS

Brindle Books Ltd

We hope that you have enjoyed this book. To find out more about Brindle Books Ltd, including news of new releases, please visit our website:

http://www.brindlebooks.co.uk

There is a contact page on the website, should you have any queries, and you can let us know if you would like email updates of news and new releases. We promise that we won't spam you with lots of sales emails, and we will never sell or give your contact details to any third party.

If you purchased this book online, please consider leaving an honest review on the site from which you purchased it. Your feedback is important to us, and may influence future releases from our company.